THE BREATH OF GOD

by

PAUL W. FEENSTRA

Published by
Mellester Press

"Feenstra does an excellent job in bringing historical figures to vivid life."

"Highly recommended for fans of historical fiction."

"The Breath of God is an engaging, gripping tale that leaves the reader anticipating the next adventure in the series."

"Highly recommended for fans of historical fiction, particularly military fiction."

"Very satisfying read. Action, adventure, friendship, bravery, and just the right dash of romance."

Other historical fiction books
by
Paul W. Feenstra
Published by Mellester Press

Boundary

The Breath of God (Book 1 in Moana Rangitira series)

For Want of a Shilling (Book 2 in Moana Rangitira series)

Gunpowder Green

Into the Shade

Falls Ende short story eBooks
1. The Oath
2. Courser
3. The King

Falls Ende full length novels.
Falls Ende – Primus (eBooks 1,2 & 3)
Falls Ende – Secundus
Falls Ende – Tertium
Falls Ende – Quartus
Falls Ende – Quintus
Falls Ende – Sextus
Falls Ende – Outlaw

Leonard Hardy's
A Sinister Consequence
A Questionable Virtue

A Gentleman at Heart

The Breath of God
Fiction

Moana Rangitira Series
First published in 2016 by Lang Book Publishing, Ltd.
Published in 2018 by Mellester Press

Published in New Zealand
A catalogue record of this book is available from the National
Library of New Zealand.
Kei te *pātengi raraunga* o Te Puna Mātauranga o Aotearoa te
whakarārangi o tēnei pukapuka

Cover design by Chris Largent

www.PaulWFeenstra.net
ISBN 978-0-473-43626-1 Softcover
ISBN 978-0-473-43628-5 Hardcover
ISBN 978-0-473-43627-8 ePub
ISBN 978-0-473-43629-2 Kindle
ISBN 978-0-473-43630-8 iBook

Published by
Mellester Press

ACKNOWLEDGENTS

The Rev. Dr Scott Pedersen, Rector. All Saints Anglican Church, Long Beach, California; Staff Sergeant Regan Cherrington – Dismounted Operations Wing, Combat School, New Zealand Defence Force; Captain John Rowe and Chris Davies; Taranaki Library Plus – Waverley and Patea Branches; The wonderful people of Taranaki who gave me assistance and patiently answered my endless questions.

I am grateful to the expertise and brilliance of both, Jill Davis and Chris Largent; their hard-work and dedication is unsurpassed.

For

Rachel and Corey

THE BREATH OF GOD

A Novel of Faith, Fire,
and the New Zealand Frontier

PAUL W. FEENSTRA

"Guns and powder shall no longer be the protection of man. Our weapon is forbearance, patience, and non-resistance. God is our refuge and our strength."

Te Whiti o Rongomai,
1830-1907

PROLOGUE

S.S Lord Worsley, Sunday, August 31st, 1862

As far as ocean-going ships went, the *Lord Worsley* wasn't a big ship. At five hundred and fifty tons, the three-masted barque, with sails hoisted, was also propelled by a powerful two hundred and fifty-horsepower steam engine. She could carry a number of passengers, along with their luggage, and, of course, all the cargo required for her commission as an inter-colonial mail steamer.

Many of the sixty-six passengers aboard were in low spirits and displeased by the unplanned change of schedule on this particular voyage. Originally, *Lord Worsley* was to depart Nelson, at the top of New Zealand's southern island, and travel directly to Melbourne and then Sydney, Australia, but after a change of plans, the ship departed a day earlier and would first visit the New Zealand ports of New Plymouth and Manakau on the northern island before crossing the Tasman Sea.

The steamer departed Nelson at 1:00 pm with a moderate south-westerly breeze blowing from astern over her port quarter and immediately headed northward. Captain Bowden gave precise sailing instructions to the Officer-of-the-Watch and cautioned the helmsman to be mindful of their heading before retiring to his cabin. By all accounts, it should've been a routine sailing, and as everyone on board would soon come to learn, it wasn't to be.

After twelve and a half hours into their voyage, the *Lord Worsley* sailed approximately one hundred and twelve nautical miles north. The breeze stiffened, and the ship's bow yawed considerably in a following sea. The challenge for the inattentive helmsman was to interpret the radical swing of the compass needle and keep the *Lord Worsley* on her correct heading. In these conditions, it wasn't uncommon for the needle to fluctuate by ten degrees in either direction. Unknown to the helmsman, a small half-knot current was pulling the ship slightly off her charted course. Combined with compass errors, the *Lord Worsley* drifted approximately twenty-one miles to the east.

Bad weather closed in, reducing visibility, but after the deluge of a passing squall, a surprised lookout spotted breakers dead ahead, and he immediately issued a frantic warning. Captain Bowden, who'd just came on deck, urgently ordered the helm hard-a-starboard and reversed the engine to full astern. It made little difference. The ship's forward momentum in the heavy seas grounded *Lord Worsley* firmly on rocks, shearing her furiously spinning propeller with a loud clatter. She was held fast in five feet of water, fifty yards from shore in Te Namu Bay, Opunake, in the region of Taranaki. Fortunately, there were no injuries to passengers or crew.

As *Lord Worsley* was in no immediate danger of slipping beneath the waves, it was decided prudently that everyone should disembark in daylight. Meanwhile, tea and coffee were offered as refreshments to the inconvenienced passengers.

The following morning, as dawn approached, passengers and crew could clearly assess their situation. *Lord Worsley* had settled firmly aground at the entrance of a small, shallow bay, surrounded on three sides by sheer cliffs. Large rocks extended far out to sea at its edges, and three-foot-diameter boulders lay strewn beneath the moderate cliffs, which rose to almost forty feet. Passengers were amazed at their good fortune and praised their luck that the ship had managed to enter the bay without striking the large rocks that lay in wait at its entrance. However, that was as far as their luck would last. There was no welcoming sandy beach, and everyone would need to clamber awkwardly over slippery boulders to reach shore, then climb the cliffs to safety.

Conveniently or inconveniently, depending on one's point of view, *Lord Worsley* came to rest a short distance from Te Namu *pa*[1] in the magnificent shadow of Mount Egmont, or as *Māori*[2] named the towering volcano, *e Maunga o Taranaki* (The Mountain of Taranaki), or simply, Mount Taranaki, which lay directly ahead. This was considered very convenient for some Māori who lived in the nearby village, as they intended to loot and pillage the stricken ship and obediently enforce local Kingite law.

The war in Taranaki began over disputed land purchases between the government and *Māori* and escalated, finally ending the previous year with a ceasefire and no clear victor. However, *Māori* chief Wiremu Kingi Te Rangitake and his supporters, the Kingites, who fought the imperial forces, temporarily prevented the government from imposing sovereignty over them. For *Māori*, it was a victory of sorts.

In the aftermath, and in an effort to protect their lands, the Kingites imposed laws, one of which was quite clear. *Enemy trespassers should be punished by death.* Inconveniently for *Lord Worsley*'s passengers and crew, now scrambling ashore, *Māori* leaders on the cliff tops overlooking the calamity were actively debating that law. Standing to one side, listening intently to the animated arguments, was lay preacher Te Ua Horopāpera. Te Ua

---

[1] *Pa - Village*
[2] *Māori - Indigenous people native to New Zealand*

fought alongside Wiremu Kingi against the Government invaders and fully supported the Kingite movement, as did all the other men standing at the cliff top.

With the help of missionaries, Te Ua was taught to read and write from childhood and began to study the Bible conscientiously, ultimately becoming familiar with its tenets and parables. Supported by the Wesleyan missionaries, he'd become an influential lay preacher and held a strong belief in *his* interpretation of the Christian faith.

Te Ua was torn as he listened to the arguments for and against killing the stranded *Lord Worsley* survivors. Finally making up his mind, he stepped forward and interrupted the heated discussion. He spoke in *Te Reo*[3].

"They did not come here by choice - it was the result of an accident," he looked carefully from one man to the other. "Can we stand here arguing like old women when these people need our help?"

The men murmured in quiet agreement.

"We have a Christian duty to do what we can for these people, to help and protect them, and to ensure they are safely returned to their own kind." Heads nodded. Te Ua spoke wisely, "They are not soldiers and do not bring war on us. Let's go to them now and lend a welcoming hand," he pleaded.

Another man listened quietly. He stepped forward and commanded silence. "No good thing has ever been brought by force ... there is no reason why force should continue to have power over us," said Te Whiti o Rongomai, well known for his pacifist views. "Te Ua is right. We must feed these people and see to their safety."

---

[3] *Te Reo - Spoken language of Māori*

One or two protested, arguing that the stranded ship contained items of value that could benefit local *Māori*, but in the end everyone reluctantly agreed. Te Ua Horopāpera, Te Whiti o Rongomai and a local chief, Wiremu Kingi Matakatea, along with his people, finally came to the aid of the survivors *of* the *Lord Worsley*.

Brass fittings were destroyed; the ship's safe was broken into; the signal cannon and all guns were seized. Six kegs of gunpowder were found and thrown into the sea. Personal luggage was thoroughly examined, and money was taken. A blockade prevented any outside help from arriving, leaving the survivors entirely in the care and dependence of local *Māori*. As Te Ua was not a chief, he had no authority to make demands on his people, and despite his protestations, looting and pilfering continued, although one thousand ounces of gold which had been liberated from the ship was grudgingly returned to *Lord Worsley*'s officers.

To the relief of Te Ua, the local chief, Wiremu Kingi Matakatea, was largely supportive, ensuring the safety and protection of survivors and their possessions, but that support only went so far. He was also an opportunist. Graciously, Te Whiti arranged for a bullock to be slaughtered to feed passengers and crew, and for additional bullocks to be made available for transport. But when wagons and carts were assembled to transport the survivors to a settlement forty-five miles away, survivors were charged a levy before being permitted to leave and were relieved of what little money they had left. Despite the obstacles and dangers, everyone finally arrived safely and unharmed in New Plymouth, six days after departing from Nelson.

Te Ua was disappointed and embittered by how his people responded to the needs of *Lord Worsley*'s survivors. They showed little sympathy, choosing greed, theft and vandalism over Christian acts of compassion, kindness and goodwill. These were the same people who'd sat attentively and listened while he preached the gospel. He'd read them the scriptures and taught them the ways of Christianity. They'd accepted Jesus into their hearts, or so they'd told him, yet when faced with choices, his people so easily wavered from righteousness. Was their hatred for *Pākeha* [4]so overwhelming that they could forsake Christianity without remorse or guilt?

Missionaries were often involved in ambiguous land purchases, and many even sold weapons to fund their missions. Some spied on *Māori* and reported their actions to the Governor, their actions in sharp contrast to their religious vocation. This was where Te Ua took issue. He felt many missionaries' teachings were duplicitous. It made him pause and reflect, and he began to question the Christian beliefs he had been taught. How could he reconcile aggression and non-Christian actions when the Bible he knew and loved offered alternatives that spoke of non-violence, compassion and love? But Te Ua's conflict ran even deeper - he also loved his people and vehemently disapproved of Government actions against them. Could he accept his faith, be a good Christian, and support *Māori* causes at the same time?

Te Ua became ill, intellectually paralysed and unable to resolve the paradox that plagued him. Days passed; he didn't eat, sleep or leave his home. Whispers began to suggest that Te Ua had become irrational, perhaps even afflicted with a nervous disorder. At about the same time as *Lord Worsley's* survivors were nearing the safety of New Plymouth, Te Ua Horopāpera's prayers were answered.

---

[4] *Pākeha – A Māori term for New Zealanders of non-Māori, predominantly European, descent.*

"The archangel Gabriel came to me - it was a vision from God," he told anyone who'd listen. "God has chosen *me* as his prophet, and together we will cast off *Pākeha* oppression and return New Zealand to the righteous - to *Māori*."

Many believed he'd lost his mind. But that perception amongst *Māori* would change drastically in the coming weeks. It was rumoured that Te Ua had achieved supernatural powers, and this was never more evident than after a report claimed he deliberately mutilated the leg of a *Māori* boy. When a group of men came to investigate after the boy's mother complained, they found evidence of blood but no injury. Miraculously, Te Ua completely healed the boy's leg. He claimed Gabriel had gifted him these powers, and with his new status as a prophet, *Māori* began to listen.

In the vacuum created by the Taranaki War, Te Ua provided unity for fragmented Māori iwi[5] and offered them hope. He changed his name to Te Ua Haumene (Wind Man) and began preaching to an attentive, growing audience. Within three months, he'd created a new religion, called it *Pai Marire* (Goodness and Peace), and even written his own holy book, *Ua Rongopai.* It drew on selected elements of the Old Testament and blended Christianity with some traditional Māori religious beliefs. Te Ua wanted nothing more than a peaceful society where righteousness and justice triumphed.

"To achieve those goals," said Te Ua, "*Māori* must first rid itself of *Pākeha* domination."

Initially, Te Ua enlisted three enthusiastic disciples, Tohu Kakahi, Hatotoi Kahore and Paora Rakahuru, who immediately began travelling to *Māori pā* in the North Island, spreading Te Ua's message and the *Pai Marire* faith. He continued to recruit others, some of whom would distinguish themselves, and many would later

---

[5] *Iwi - In Māori culture, iwi is the largest kinship grouping, typically translated as 'tribe or 'nation'.*

achieve prophet status and become extremely influential among *Māori*. With growing support, many interpreted Te Ua's message as a call to action. Converts wanted to drive *Pākeha* from *Māori* land, and so a militant *Pai Marire* faction, led by Te Ua's disciples, was drawn into escalating conflicts and acts of horrific violence - they became known as *Hauhau*.

CHAPTER ONE

Papakura, 20 Miles South of Auckland, New Zealand. 1863.

The wagon rattled down the well-used track. Up front in the driver's seat, the old man was content to let the swayback mare plod along unhurriedly at a sedate, easy-going pace. He sat firmly on a well-worn pillow that protected his bony bottom from the hard wooden seat and the uneven, rutted surface they travelled over. The unlit pipe that protruded from the side of his mouth was clamped firmly between his gums and moved erratically up and down as he spoke - which was often. In fact, during the entire two-hour journey, he hadn't stopped jabbering over his shoulder to the two young men who sat uncomfortably in the wagon's rear.

The driver was presently informing his unappreciative audience about the best time to plant and harvest potatoes. With little interest in agriculture, neither man felt inclined to respond further and ignored the prattling driver. The only one mildly attentive to the old man's incessant chatter was the bay mare pulling the wagon, her ears twitching with curiosity as the farmer droned on.

In the wagon's rear, Rupert Potter felt the impact of another sizeable pothole and eased into a more comfortable position. Hoping for some respite, he repositioned his canvas holdall and, with a grunt, leaned back against it. He drew his knees up to his chest, wrapped his arms around them, and turned to face his companion.

As he'd been for a half hour or so, Moana Rangitira hadn't moved. His handsome, clean-shaven face remained impassive. If it were even possible in these conditions, and in the back of a bouncing wagon, Moana looked almost peaceful as he stared at a fixed point in the distance and seemed oblivious to all that was happening around him. Rupert knew better. He had known Moana for quite some time, since they were both teenagers, and understood that his best friend was more aware of their surroundings than he was. If asked, Moana told people he was meditating. Unfamiliar with such a peculiar disorder, many responded by shaking their heads in sympathy and enquired whether the condition was curable.

Rupert turned away from his friend and cast a keen, practiced eye over the countryside. The sun was beginning to sink in the west, casting long shadows across the low, rolling hills cleaved in two by a large, glistening river. In the distance, he could see dense bush draped across the valley's protective hills. Small farms dotted the landscape, mostly along the river, and, unusually, few people were in sight, preferring not to travel in these uncertain times. His stomach grumbled, a reminder that he was hungry.

"Yep, you've gotta be gentle with them spuds, 'specially when you're diggin' 'em up."

The horse's ears responded in agreement.

"No one wants bruised spuds, nope," the pipe jiggled.

Rupert felt Moana stir, then sit up on his knees and turn around to face the front. After a moment or two, he sat back down, faced Rupert, and silently mouthed 'smoke'. Rupert stuck his nose in the air and sniffed, but he couldn't smell anything.

"Gotta be careful with a shovel when harvesting. Spuds be like a woman, you treats 'em firm and gentle like, that-a-way, you ain't gonna bruise 'em when you dig 'em up."

"What's up ahead?" Moana interrupted the old man's dissertation.

"Oh, that'd be the Smith's place, lad. You'll get a room there more'n likely."

Moana looked questioningly at Rupert who nodded eagerly in affirmation.

"Keep 'em dry, you can't go baggin' wet spuds."

"Is it a farm?"

"Kinda, Ben Smith calls it the 'Travellers Rest'. S'pose you'd say it was more of an inn these days. Ben and his wife Martha run the place."

"We'll get off there, if it's no problem, Mr Sutherland," informed Moana politely.

"Righto! Is the worst thing you can do, yep, bag wet spuds," the old man cackled in response to something he thought amusing.

As the wagon slowly wound its way along the wide expanse of the valley floor, both young men eventually saw the source of the smoke Moana had detected. A significant cluster of stout, well-made buildings were proprietorially grouped together and appeared to be part of an organised, functioning farm. There was a general store, stables that could accommodate over fifty horses, outbuildings that looked suspiciously like barracks, sheds, a barn, and, not to forget, the large main building. As they drew near, they could see that the large structure had been fortified. Thick wooden boards were nailed over the windows, with loopholes that provided defensive firing positions. A few men, mostly in military uniform, wandered around or stood in small groups, talking. They paid little attention to the wagon as it approached and creaked to a halt.

"Thank you for your kindness, Mr Sutherland," said Moana once he was firmly on the ground. "I'll take your good advice on them spuds."

"No worries, and don't forget what I told you about that darn potato blight," the old man replied seriously, then looked at them quizzically. "Are you boys soldiers?" he finally asked.

"We were, but no longer. The Crimea," informed Moana, as if that explained everything.

The pipe bounced one or two times as the old man nodded, then doffed his hat and dipped his head in farewell. With an expert flick of the reins, the wagon rumbled off.

Potter stretched to his full six-foot-six-inch height, arched his back and rubbed where he felt discomfort. His shirt and jacket looked ready to be torn to shreds as he stretched and flexed. Moana was more concerned with restoring blood flow to his tender buttocks and was giving them a vigorous rub.

"I never knew that potato blight was such a serious problem, did you?" asked Moana, who then ducked as a well-muscled arm threatened to knock him senseless.

With a laugh, they picked up their canvas holdalls and headed towards the main building. Above the door, a sign proudly displayed 'Travellers Rest Hotel'.

CHAPTER TWO

Travellers Rest.

Potter pushed his plate away, leaned back in the protesting chair that threatened to collapse under his immense bulk, and let out a satisfying belch. He grinned at his friend, who was still finishing his meal, then swallowed the last of his beer, set his empty mug on the table, and surveyed the room.

It was dark and dismal inside the hotel. The boarded windows kept out natural light, and the few lanterns hanging from the ceiling were ineffectual, making it difficult to see clearly. Rupert counted eight other customers well on the way to intoxication. From their mannerisms and dress, he judged two of them to be young farmers' labourers; the others were, without question, soldiers.

Moana finished his beefsteak, pushed his plate aside, and smiled in appreciation. "That was the best dinner I've had in a while."

Rupert nodded in agreement.

With his appetite finally satiated and a few beers already under his belt, Moana was content to glance casually around the room. What caught his eye were the soldiers' unusual uniforms. "What unit do you reckon they belong to?"

Potter shrugged.

"And most of them are *Māori*. That's unusual."

"I overheard something a short while ago. I think they are part of a new volunteer force," Rupert replied.

Moana slid his chair back, slowly rose, and went to get more beer for them both. On his way back to the table with a full mug in each hand, he felt someone approaching from behind. A firm hand clutched his shoulder, jostling him. The beer sloshed over the sides of both mugs, spilling onto the wooden floor.

"You boys swaddies, eh?"

Moana ignored the question until he had both beers safely on the table. He sat down and appraised the *Māori* soldier warily as he wiped his wet hands on his trousers.

"Crimea," he replied.

The soldier flipped his head upwards in acknowledgement and then turned to look with curiosity at Potter. "Where you boys from?"

Potter remained typically quiet.

"We're both from Wellington," replied Moana casually, his voice not betraying his growing agitation.

The *Māori* soldier continued to stare at Rupert, not at all intimidated by his size. "Oh, that's too bad. I hate Wellington." He turned to his mates at the other table, all watching. "They're from Wellington!" he shouted.

In response, they hurled a few insults and jeers at the two newcomers, which only encouraged the soldier to continue. He shifted his attention back to Moana and placed his hand back on Moana's shoulder. "What *iwi*?"

"Ngati Ira."

The soldier began to laugh, doubling up in exaggerated mirth. When he had composed himself, he turned back to his companions. "Ngati Ira!" he yelled.

Moana made eye contact with Rupert, who remained unconcerned. He'd not spoken or moved, except to raise his mug to drink.

"Thought they were all dead," came a voice from one of the soldiers across the room. This prompted more laughter.

"What unit are you boys from? I don't recognise the uniform," asked Moana, wanting to change the subject.

The soldier leaned close to Moana's ear, his foul breath reeking of rum and onions. "Forest Rangers," he said slowly, with obvious pride. "I'm sure you've heard of us."

Moana hadn't, "Yep, sure have."

The soldier patted Moana's shoulder a couple of times, pleased with his response.

"And what's with the big knife?" continued Moana, who had noticed that only some of the soldiers carried the huge blades sheathed on their left hips.

"Hey Tane, wasn't it your people who destroyed the Ngati Ira?" shouted one of the drunken soldiers to a friend at Moana's side. "Well, you did a lousy job if there are still some who're alive."

The table erupted into fits of laughter again.

Moana looked up at the soldier and held his gaze. "Go and sit with your mates. Have a good time. We don't want any trouble with you boys."

Seeing that Moana was having a quiet word with his friend, one of the soldiers detached from the group and swaggered over.

"You gonna take care of the last of the Ira, Tane, or are you just gonna kiss him?"

Ben and Martha Smith, the Inn's proprietors, had an understanding. Ben would tend to the outside jobs, and Martha would administer the inside work, an arrangement that suited them both. Their six children were given suitable tasks, with some helping their mother and the others, more adept at hard physical work, assisting their father. If any of the hotel's patrons thought they could take advantage of a woman proprietor, they were in for an unpleasant surprise.

Tane was grabbed by the collar and hauled upright. His friend, who'd just arrived, had a stout piece of wood thrust into his chest. All clamour inside the peaceful establishment abruptly stopped. Martha Smith lowered the wood, released Tane, and placed both her hands on her expansive hips, one delicate hand still firmly grasping the piece of wood she wielded like a club.

"I warned you, boys. If I've told you once, I've told you a thousand times. Out, all of ya, out now! Major Jackson will hear of this, mark my words!"

Both soldiers resisted the urge to salute Martha and made a sensible tactical withdrawal. She turned, giving their six friends a scathing look that needed no explanation. They wisely decided to follow their mates and hurried out through the front door. The labourers also stood to leave, lest they offend the proprietor by staying, but a wave of her hand granted them a reprieve. Martha now turned her attention to Moana and Rupert.

"If I let you boys stay in here, those Rangers outside won't be happy 'bout that," she said, her thick American accent adding emphasis. "Oh yeah, and they'll be a'waitin' for ya when ya do leave. Now I figure either way you boys are gonna have to deal with 'em. It can be now, or later, your choice, fellas." Her foot tapped to some imaginary ditty as she waited for a response.

"May as well be now," said Moana with his best smile. "Then may we come back?"

"Give 'em hell. They deserve to be put in their place. Then you can come back," she replied with a smile and a wink, though she didn't expect to see them both standing again any time soon. With a nimble pirouette, she about-faced and marched back to the kitchen.

"I could love a woman like that," said Rupert, wistfully staring after her.

"Mister Smith may not take to that very kindly."

Rupert grunted.

Both men downed the last dregs of beer and wandered outside, where they were met by six very unhappy Forest Rangers. Two detached from the group and immediately headed towards them, their hostile intentions obvious.

Only two? wondered Moana. Disappointed, he sat on the hotel step to watch. Rupert would have been offended if he'd joined him to fight only two soldiers. He wished he'd taken a beer with him.

The Rangers were equally surprised to see one of the men they wanted to fight sit down. A few insults were hurled at Moana, accusing him of cowardice, but for the moment, he was content to let Rupert handle it and ignored the jibes. The two attackers turned their attention to their rather large opponent, who was blocking access to Moana. Rupert stood calmly, waiting, his arms hanging loosely at his sides.

In most situations, when two thugs or street brawlers attack a single man, they'll separate. Hoping to distract their victim, they'll approach from opposite directions, while one of them launches an attack. An experienced defender welcomes this tactic, as it enables him to focus on one opponent, deal with him quickly, then move on to the other. This was what Moana expected the soldiers to do.

Moana raised his eyebrows in surprise. The two soldiers approached Rupert shoulder to shoulder, close together. Their fists were raised to protect their faces, and their elbows were tucked in tight against their bodies. They didn't separate as expected; these boys weren't fools after all. Tane, the soldier who'd been causing trouble inside, was one of the men now facing Rupert. Moana guessed he must be one of their best fighters. Rupert would need to be careful, as the cocky young soldiers appeared to have had some formal training. He sat a little straighter and, in spite of the beer he'd consumed, paid closer attention. Regardless of their training, it shouldn't take Rupert too long to sort this lot out.

The other Rangers were shouting encouragement, egging on their two friends. Hearing the commotion, two more soldiers joined the party and watched. All were shouting enthusiastically. Potter remained motionless, one foot slightly in front of the other, and, for all outward appearances, seemed completely at ease.

Moana knew what was coming next, and true to form, Rupert raised both arms, extended them forward with his elbows slightly bent and his palms facing outwards. His chin was lowered and tucked casually into his shoulder. The move was designed to appear non-threatening. Moana knew the soldiers no longer had a head target, as Rupert's face and head were protected by his arms. The soldiers only had body shots available to them. That meant they would have to lower their hands when they punched, leaving their heads exposed.

"C'mon, boys, we don't need to do this. Let's go inside and have another beer," said Rupert in a friendly tone.

The soldiers watching jeered and shouted. Moana watched with interest. He appeared relaxed but was poised and ready to move at an instant.

Almost simultaneously, the two soldiers launched punches, both leading with their right hands. Rupert easily evaded them by stepping slightly to his right. Their fists slid past his ribs as he swayed. He stepped forward and threw almost simultaneous jabs with each hand. First the left, then, as he shifted his weight forward, the right. Both massive fists struck each soldier in the nose, and they collapsed backwards, falling onto the hard-packed earth in front of the hotel. The watching soldiers were stunned; they hadn't expected the giant to move so quickly, or for the fight to end so soon. The two Rangers on the ground were holding their noses as blood seeped through their fingers.

"Let's get 'em!" shouted one of the watching soldiers as he ran towards Rupert. The others followed, their confidence bolstered by their numbers.

Moana quickly leapt up and rushed to help his friend. Standing at his side, they waited for the first soldier to attack.

"Here we go again," said Moana with a grin.

If the soldiers thought the giant was unusually fast, Moana was even quicker. Before the first opponent could throw a punch, Moana opened with a coordinated flurry of blows and jabs. The soldier fell, landing heavily on the ground near his friends; he had the wind knocked out of him and was gasping for air, trying to regain his breath. The remaining soldiers came as a group; little good it did them, as one by one they dropped like flies. Potter received two unexpected blows to the head from a particularly skilful fighter and was now angered; he rushed the man, picked him up and hoisted him horizontally above his head, then tossed him to the ground with ease. The man lay prone on the ground, moaning; a sudden change of heart saw him unwilling to re-join the fight. Hearing the commotion, another couple of soldiers arrived and entered the fray; they were dealt with in a similar fashion – also ending up in the dirt. Moana was laughing as the last Ranger still standing realised he was alone. He looked unsure about continuing to fight and, with resignation, held up his hands in resignation as he backed away. Those on the ground who were able to move did – they crawled or just got up and ran.

It was over. Both men were breathing hard, and Rupert was rubbing his jaw where he'd been struck when a shout made them turn. A group of twenty Rangers was running towards them. Some carried lumps of wood, and one even had a hatchet. They were incensed that their comrades had been beaten so easily. It was time to salvage Company pride, and the approaching Forest Rangers sought revenge.

"I think we're unwelcome."

Potter grunted, and both men began laughing as they ran from the Travellers Rest Hotel and were swallowed by the night.

CHAPTER THREE

Training.

Captain Gustavus Von Tempsky had just finished his dinner in his office, which also served as his living quarters, as he wanted to update the training schedule for his newly formed Company. A timely knock on the door interrupted the unpleasant task he was about to begin.

"Yes?"

"Sir, do you have a moment?" asked Sergeant-Major Bowers once he'd stepped inside.

"What is it, Sergeant?"

"We have a problem, sir."

Von Tempsky turned to face the sergeant with a sigh.

"There's been a fight, actually more like a brawl, sir. About ten of our men were soundly beaten."

"Those bloody Irish! Have they been at it again, Sergeant?"

"No, sir, it wasn't the Irish, but..." Bowers paused. He knew the captain was especially proud of his company and their fighting abilities.

"What happened? Out with it, man."

"They were overcome by just two men."

Von Tempsky glared. "Two men! Was anyone hurt?"

"No, sir, not seriously."

The captain paused for a moment. "Well, if our best fighters had been there, it would have been different, I'm sure. What's that fellow's name, the good fighter?"

"Mahaia?"

"Yes, him. If he'd been there, perhaps a different outcome, eh?"

"Sir, Tane Mahaia and Moana Ngata both attempted to fight one of the men and were overcome in seconds. Both received only bloody noses. Then the second man joined in when a larger group of about eight more of our lads came to help; again, they were all soundly defeated."

"God damn it! Who are these men and where are they now?" the captain stood glaring at the sergeant.

"They were last heard laughing as they ran away, when the remainder of the company came in support, sir."

Captain Von Tempsky twirled his moustache as he thought things through, then returned to his seat. Sergeant-Major Bowers waited patiently.

"Have the Company assemble for an immediate training exercise, bloody noses and all - full kit. We will pursue these men and find out who they are. Understood, Sergeant?"

"Yes, sir."

"Good. We will put our unique skills to work; this is exactly what we train for, Bowers. Have the men ready in fifteen minutes. Oh yes, better have Lieutenant Small come and see me."

Sergeant-Major Bowers left to prepare the men, while Captain Gustavus Von Tempsky leaned back in his chair and rested his feet on the small writing desk in the corner. His hand went habitually to his moustache as an idea came to mind.

Under orders from General Cameron, head of New Zealand's armed forces, Major William Jackson recently formed the Forest

Rangers and commanded Company No. 1. Shortly after, he brought on Gustavus Von Tempsky, initially as a military adviser, then granted him an officer's commission and appointed him commander of Company No. 2.

The recruits were an eager assortment of ex-gold-diggers, sailors, and even farmers, men of adventure who welcomed the harshness of the bush and the rigorous training Von Tempsky and his officers put them through. They were paid more, had a larger rum allowance than regular troops, and were extensively trained in bushcraft and close-quarter fighting.

Of the two Companies, only Von Tempsky's was issued the large and impressive twelve-inch Bowie Knife. With considerable training and specialist experience in knife combat, Von Tempsky insisted that his Company be trained to use lethal knives competently. While regular forces still used the unpopular muzzle-loading Enfield rifle, the Rangers were issued with a mixture of the more modern breech-loading Calisher and Terry carbine, the Pattern Enfield .57 calibre musket, and a five-shot revolver.

When Captain Von Tempsky ordered Sergeant-Major Bowers to ensure his men were ready with their Full-Kit, he was referring to their weapons, a bottle of rum encased in leather for protection, and, for every four men, two blue blankets. When in the bush, the blankets were used as a tent, and the men were expected to sleep on a bed of ferns. It was standard operating procedure that the Company always be ready to move at a moment's notice. So tonight's orders were a real test of readiness for the fledgling, untested Company.

Unknown to Moana and Rupert, Captain Von Tempsky used the altercation as a pretext for a training exercise - to track, pursue and capture. The embarrassing defeat of his men in a simple brawl irked him, and they would now pay the consequences – first, for provoking a fight, and second, for losing. Officially, both Moana and Rupert were innocent of any wrongdoing, but the enterprising and opportunistic Von Tempsky was curious about the nature and skill of the men who could defeat his beloved Forest Rangers so easily, and he intended to find out under the guise of a training exercise.

Thirty rank-and-file soldiers, two officers and two sergeants, represented an understrength Company No. 2, standing impatiently at rest, ready to move out. Captain Von Tempsky appointed Lieutenant Small as commander, and ten men selected as scouts were given instructions and immediately jogged into the night. It was too dark to track effectively, and there were always other signs to look for. Although it was unusual for regular soldiers to operate at night in this way, Von Tempsky wanted his soldiers to be capable of operating effectively in total darkness. After a quiet word with his officers and a brief detailing of his orders, Forest Ranger Company No. 2 began marching in the direction Moana and Rupert were last seen heading. He watched them leave with a shake of his head – it was a futile exercise, but it was also punishment.

While the men of Forest Ranger Company No. 2 were taking the pursuit of the two strangers somewhat seriously, Moana and Rupert saw the fight as nothing more than a lark. Realising the odds weren't in their favour when about twenty angry Forest Rangers came after them, they quickly headed towards the bush half a mile away. When they realised they were no longer being chased, they collapsed on the ground in hysterics, tears streaming down their faces.

They'd not caused any serious injury to any of the Rangers, and a bloody nose in Moana's book was not considered an injury, merely a temporary inconvenience. Perhaps Ranger pride was the biggest casualty, howled Rupert between fits of laughter.

Moana and Rupert had no intention of spending a cold night in the bush when there was a comfortable bed with a horsehair mattress waiting for them at the hotel. They paid in advance for a room with two beds when they first arrived at the Travellers Rest, and they weren't going to waste their money. With that decision easily made, and in a more composed, subdued manner, they took a circular route and headed back to the hotel unnoticed. With relative ease, the two men were already back in their room, lying on their beds, when Von Tempsky's Company No. 2 marched out in search of them.

The sound of Rupert's snoring was interrupted by a knock on the door. Unable to sleep at such an early hour, Moana lay fully dressed on his bed, thinking about finding a beer when he heard the knock. He hadn't seen or heard from the Rangers since they'd returned to the hotel, so he doubted it was them. He rose from the bed, leaving Rupert asleep, and cautiously opened the door.

Standing in the hallway was a man, an officer. He carried an impressive cavalry sabre at his hip, two Colt Navy .36 pistols lay in shoulder belts across his tunic, and a huge knife was secured in a leather sheath at his hip, similar to those he had seen the Rangers wearing downstairs in the dining room. To complete the ensemble, he wore loose-fitting breeches tucked into cavalry boots polished to a dazzling sheen.

"Can I help you?" inquired Moana.

"Mr Rangitira?" asked the man.

Moana nodded, surprised the officer knew his name.

"My men are marching into the bush. They were sent there for a military training exercise - to apprehend *you* and your friend," the man said with a pleasant smile.

Moana detected a European accent but couldn't place where the man was from.

"How did you know we were here?"

The man laughed. "If I were in your position, the last thing I would do is spend a cold night in the bush when there is a warm bed waiting for me at the Inn."

Moana returned the smile.

"So, I would circle the hotel, approach from the opposite direction and then quietly slip into my room, and no one would know. Mrs Smith was kind enough to give me both your names."

Moana was impressed. This man may look like a dandy, but he was very astute. "I'm sorry, I don't believe we are unacquainted."

"Forgive me, yes. I am Captain Gustavus Von Tempsky, Commander of Forest Rangers Company No. 2." He held out his hand in greeting.

Moana took the proffered hand and noticed the captain's firm grip.

"Perhaps I could talk with you?" asked the captain.

"I was just going to have a drink in the dining room. You are welcome to join me," offered Moana.

The captain hesitated, looking past Moana's shoulder.

"He's asleep. I'd hate to disturb him as he gets rather grumpy when he's woken unexpectedly."

"Very well," said Von Tempsky.

Captain Von Tempsky nursed a rum, and Moana sipped a beer at the same table where he and Rupert had eaten earlier. They sat in a comfortable silence, appraising each other.

"Crimea?" asked the captain.

Moana nodded. "How did you know?"

"An educated guess. I understand you, and, ah … Mr Potter put on quite a show earlier this evening."

"Rupert was doing quite well with me just watching. It wasn't until your men decided a group effort was needed that I stepped in and lent a hand."

"From what I heard, your skills were almost, ah … supernatural, Mr Rangitira. You have acquired some form of special training, is this not so?"

"Perhaps, Captain, but we showed restraint. Your men were cocky, aggressive, and spoiling for a fight. We did nothing more than teach them a harmless lesson. No one was hurt, and what we did required no special skill."

"I see, and if needed, you could have killed a few of them?"

"A few? Captain, I could have killed them all," Moana said rather testily. "What did you want to talk to me about? If you're going to interrogate–"

"Are you familiar with the reason Major Jackson formed the Forest Rangers?" interrupted the captain.

"No, I'd never even heard of them until today."

"I see. I think you would agree that New Zealand and British regular forces are not suited for bush-fighting."

Moana inclined his head in agreement. He was also curious as to where this conversation was leading.

"Their training, the weapons … they are unsuitable for the conditions here. Increasingly, rebel *Māori* have taken to the bush to hide. They use the bush to launch attacks on innocent people, and no force has been able to stop them. Is this not so?"

"From what I've heard, I agree with you completely, Captain."

"Good, good. Yes, the Forest Rangers are an elite irregular force trained to fight rebels in their own backyard, in the bush. We do things a little differently from regular forces, Mr Rangitira. I demand and expect a higher level of ability in tracking, scouting, and fighting than you have ever seen from a small fighting force."

"Yes, I noticed. I even saw some of the men carrying large knives today..."

Captain Von Tempsky smiled and leaned back in his chair. This was his chance to impress the young man before him. Almost faster than the eye could see, his left hand shot up above the table, holding his huge knife. The blade faced backwards and lay along the length of his inside forearm. The captain's eyes grew wide, and his smile vanished. His left hand was held immobile in a vice-like grip by Moana's right hand above the table. Von Tempsky couldn't move the hand that held the knife.

"It's not a good idea to pull a knife on a soldier like that without warning … unless you intend to use it, Captain." To drive his point home, Moana stared intently at Von Tempsky, then released his grip.

Captain Von Tempsky swallowed hard. Never had he seen anyone anticipate a move with such speed as he had just witnessed. His smile quickly returned, along with his confidence. "I meant you no harm, Mr Rangitira. Perhaps a little demonstration was all. But I see you were the one to demonstrate remarkable ability." He placed the knife on the table slowly and deliberately so Moana could see it more clearly.

Easing the tension, Moana asked if he could hold the weapon and inspect it.

"This type of knife is known as the 'Bowie Knife'. Are you familiar with this name?"

Moana shook his head as he held the knife in the conventional manner, feeling its weight and balance. He thought of all its potential uses.

"The Bowie knife was originally designed by the Spanish and then altered and improved over time, mostly by an American called Rezin Bowie. His brother James used the knife with great success in Mississippi. You see, Mr Rangitira, there is a need for a knife for close-quarters fighting, almost like a short sword. Yes, as you can see, it's possible to slash, stab, and even use it as a cleaver. Of course, it is strong, very strong. A convenient and lethal tool *if* you know how to use it." The captain looked up at Moana. "Only Company No. 2 has the Bowie knife. That is why you saw some men with it. Major Jackson's men have not been issued this weapon."

Moana placed the knife back on the table.

"I suspect you were not rank and file in the Crimea, am I correct?"

"I made sergeant, Captain."

"Yes, that doesn't surprise me," Von Tempsky nodded. "And your friend Mr Potter?"

"Rupert preferred to remain a ranker."

"And no desire to improve his position?"

Moana shook his head and smiled.

The captain looked thoughtful. "Mr Rangitira, in addition to the Waikato area, the Taranaki region is beginning to experience considerable unrest again. I predict the situation there will worsen, and our small force will be very useful in providing support and quelling growing tensions in the region." Von Tempsky drained his rum, stood, reverently picked up his knife from the table, and returned it to its sheath. "That is where we are heading, and I'd like you to come with us - as sergeant, of course. You can find me here tomorrow; anyone will tell you where the Company office is. My Rangers will not bother you or your friend again. Good night, Mr Rangitira." Captain Von Tempsky dipped his head and strode off, leaving Moana surprised and alone to mull over the offer.

CHAPTER FOUR

Forest Rangers, Company No. 2

Sitting comfortably in the shade of a large Pohutukawa tree near the Travellers Rest barn, Rupert and Moana were quietly discussing Captain Von Tempsky's proposal. Company No. 2 returned from their futile evening exercise, and remarkably, no one said an unkind word or showed any animosity towards them. For the most part, they were simply ignored. Rupert urged his friend to accept the captain's offer, although he had no desire to enlist himself. It was always their intention to split up. Moana planned to go to the Taranaki region and work as a guide for surveyors, while Rupert would return to his home and family in Wellington.

The sound of approaching footsteps made them look up to see a man wearing a major's insignia walking towards them. His bearing and air of determination left no doubt about his intention. Out of habit and respect for rank, both men stood.

"I think he's come to see you. I'll be off," smiled Rupert, acknowledging the officer and walking away.

"Mr Rangitira, I am Major William Jackson, the Commanding Officer of the Forest Rangers." He held out his hand. "You've created quite a reputation for yourself in less than twenty-four hours." The major's statement did not require a response.

Like himself, the major was clean-shaven and looked remarkably fit and solid, as if he carried considerable muscle, like a man used to the rigours of physical labour. Moana shook the major's hand, feeling his calluses and quickly surmised that the man had once been a farmer.

"Perhaps we can go for a little stroll. It's a pleasant morning, a shame not to enjoy it, eh?"

Moana obediently fell into step with the major as they began to walk around the building's perimeter.

"According to the *Māori* calendar, they'll need to start planting their crops soon," advised the major as they passed a recently ploughed field.

"I'll be sure to remind them, sir," replied Moana with a grin.

"Something you find amusing, Mr Rangitira?"

Moana walked in silence for a few steps before speaking. "When we first met, I guessed you were a farmer."

"A farmer!" Major Jackson laughed. "More recently than you realise. And how I wish I still were, young man," he said wistfully, raising his eyes as if imagining his family and the simple life he missed.

Moana was struck by his sincerity.

"Far be it from me to discuss my officers' capabilities openly, but I think it is important, in this case, for you to understand a little about Captain Von Tempsky." The major walked on in silence for a few steps. "He has unique talents, you know. He's a gifted motivator, not afraid to rough it with the lads, and quite willing to get his hands dirty. He and I share the same vision, Mr Rangitira, and his ability to read others' intentions is quite uncanny. He's not just a tactical thinker but also has an extraordinary ability to think strategically." He looked to Moana, who nodded in understanding. "These are qualities I admire and want in my officers, even if their methods are a little unconventional."

Moana believed this was a time to listen. The major wanted to make a point, so he'd respect that and keep his mouth shut, lest he say something silly.

"Some see the captain as flashy, flamboyant and attention-seeking," continued Major Jackson. He turned to Moana, this time expecting an opinion.

"You forgot, Dandy, sir," Moana volunteered, immediately regretting it.

The major laughed again. "Yes, I suppose … The captain's a good man, a great officer, but he needs good men to support him, Mr Rangitira. For the Rangers to be effective and to do the job required of them, they need men like you."

Moana chose to remain silent for a moment, digesting the major's words. "Men like me, sir? With respect, Major, what do you know about men like me?"

Major Jackson looked thoughtful as he pondered his response. "You are a Crimean veteran, a survivor who achieved the rank of sergeant in a wicked, nasty war. Since arriving here, you've shown calm when provoked into a fight … and tried to defuse it, I may add. Then, when faced with trained soldiers in overwhelming numbers, you showed unbelievable, unusual fighting skills … and remain modest about it." The major turned to face him. "I'm also a good judge of people, and I'd bet my farm you are a moral man of sound character."

Moana remained quiet as the two men walked on.

"Why did you return to New Zealand after the Crimea?"

The question surprised Moana. "Ah, because New Zealand is home. It's where my family live, where my ancestors are buried. It's where I'm comfortable and familiar."

"Do you believe that rogue and lawless *Māori,* operating from the safety of the bush, threaten what you call home?"

"To be honest, sir, I hadn't considered that. But yes, I think some do."

"My family are threatened, Mr Rangitira. Even as we speak, the war in this region endangers them. This is why I am not farming, and why I am doing what I can to ensure everyone's safety, so they do not live in fear and can sleep at night knowing that men like us are doing our utmost to protect them." Major Jackson came to a halt and turned to face Moana. "Captain Von Tempsky is in the Company office over there," the major said, raising his arm to indicate a doorway only a few steps away. "Please visit him. Good day, Sergeant." The major strode off, hands clasped behind his back, head down, lost in thought.

"You look stupid wearing that hat!" laughed Rupert. "It won't keep water from running down your neck or shade your eyes from the sun."

Moana ripped the felt hat from his head and threw it at Rupert, who was stretched out on the bed in the inn. "Perhaps, but it won't be easily caught by branches and pulled off, and it will keep my head warm."

Moana adjusted his new Forest Ranger uniform and tried again to position the Bowie knife so he could reach it without accidentally grabbing the revolver. Potter lay on the bed, grinning as Moana fussed.

"When are you leaving?"

"There'll be a wagon leaving here tomorrow morning heading south. I'll catch a ride with them," Rupert replied. "When will the Company depart for Taranaki?"

"In about three or four days, I think. They're preparing supplies and equipment now. I also heard the captain wants to use the time for some extra training before we leave."

Potter nodded. "You'll need it."

CHAPTER FIVE

Bowie Knife

The sun had barely risen over the undulating hills, and the dark smudge of distant bush was already turning rich green as it devoured the nurturing morning light. A few puffy clouds drifted east, and the new day held promise for almost everyone. Rupert was again under the Pohutukawa tree, leaning against a protruding branch. His arms were folded, and he watched curiously as Captain Von Tempsky began instructing his Company in the use of the impressive knife. Rupert could see Moana listening carefully as the captain explained its history and how he had become familiar with it.

Moana was oblivious to the few hostile looks he received, and few, if any, made any attempt to make their newest sergeant feel welcome. Two men displayed severe bruising and swelling around their eyes and kept their distance, occasionally glancing at him, their looks speaking of the less-than-friendly feelings they still harboured.

The captain ensured that everyone, including the officers, took part in this morning's training. He cast an experienced, disapproving eye over the thirty-five men standing before him. His gaze halted as it fell on Moana. "Sergeant Rangitira! You are dressed incorrectly. See to it!"

A few men snickered, taking enjoyment from seeing their new sergeant singled out and admonished.

Puzzled, Moana was unsure what was wrong. He looked around and, as far as he could tell, he was dressed identically to the others. Sergeant-Major Bowers, standing to Moana's side, nudged him gently and nodded towards Moana's knife. Being right-handed, Moana automatically positioned the knife to his right. This was not what Von Tempsky wanted - the knife must be on the left. With a sigh, Moana undid his belt and repositioned the sheath.

"Moana, would you please tell the sergeant why the knife is on the left?"

Moana didn't know and was furiously trying to think of what to say. Before he could utter a word, another voice came.

"The right hand is for the revolver, the left hand for the knife, sir!" shouted the voice.

A few men began laughing, but were quickly silenced by Sergeant-Major Bowers, whose presence was as powerful as his voice.

"I don't believe Sergeant Rangitira will appreciate you calling him, sir, soldier!" Captain Von Tempsky tried his best to hide a smile and failed. It was an old joke and one that officers and non-commissioned officers, or NCOs, never tired of. Only officers were addressed as 'Sir'.

It was becoming increasingly clear to Moana that the Forest Rangers were less fastidious about military protocol than the regular army. He smiled, not at the captain's attempt at levity, but at the discovery that there was another Moana in the ranks.

All men were issued wooden replicas of the big knife, guaranteeing no one would be maimed or seriously hurt during training. They were about the same weight and size as the real knives, and before long the men were paired and practising basic defensive and offensive moves with repetitive monotony. Sergeant-Major Bowers carefully instructed Moana on how to hold the weapon. Known as the reverse grip, the blade lay alongside the forearm, just as Moana had seen the captain demonstrate in the hotel. With a flick of the wrist, the blade could be angled outward and used to stab in a downward thrust or slice in an upward or horizontal sweep. Feet position and balance were important, Bowers explained, but for Moana, who'd received careful instruction in fighting disciplines from an early age, that came naturally. Initially, he found it awkward to hold the knife in this manner, but soon discovered it also offered considerable protection and saved him from severe bruising along his arm. After an hour of training, he became more comfortable with the knife and began to appreciate the unusual fighting style. He understood there was much to learn, and he would do his best to become proficient.

Calling a rest, Von Tempsky ordered Tane Mahaia to step forward. "Let's hope you can see well enough with those swollen eyes, eh, soldier?" goaded the captain.

Immediately, both men went into a crouch, and with impressive speed, the captain slashed at the young soldier. Equally fast, Tane avoided the strike and launched a counterattack that the captain easily averted. Von Tempsky lured Tane in, closer he came, and before the young soldier could defend himself, the captain grabbed him, threw him to the ground, and had the wooden knife resting against his throat. The captain helped Tane to his feet.

"He was focused on the knife and not the free hand," said Von Tempsky, holding up his empty right hand. "It's not just about fighting with a knife and winning by using it in the engagement. Remember the objective, and that is to overcome your opponent by the fastest, and as in our case, the quietest means possible."

Moana was impressed. The captain spoke wisely and echoed his own fighting philosophy.

"Sergeant Walker, would you care to join me?"

The other sergeant, whom Moana hadn't formally met, stepped forward. He looked soft and, to an inexperienced eye, appeared an easy target. Moana noticed the way the man walked, his balance and body language. In Moana's opinion, Sergeant Walker could be formidable.

Again, the men crouched – Von Tempsky probed with a few thrusts, and the sergeant easily avoided being struck. The captain increased his speed, both arms swinging in opposing circles, the wooden knife moving quickly, almost too fast to see. Each time, the sergeant managed to stay one step ahead of the captain and defended well with both arms. Von Tempsky dropped his left arm; a feint, and Walker took the bait. He tried to second-guess the captain and attempted to slash him on his right wrist. The sergeant failed to see the danger. As he reached, he overextended his arm and placed all his weight on his front foot as he lunged forward. Unexpectedly, Von Tempsky dropped to the ground. With his right arm supporting his weight, he quickly pivoted, his leg sweeping around and catching the sergeant by surprise. Sergeant Walker's leg shot out from beneath him, and he fell to the ground with a grunt, holding a very sore calf.

"In addition to our hands, we also have two legs," the captain instructed, breathing hard as he dusted himself off. "With both men, I overcame them without inflicting a knife wound. But the knife was a real threat, and both opponents were focused on it, ignoring my other weapons, my right hand, and my legs." All the men listened carefully and took in every word the captain said. "We have time for one more. Any volunteers?" He waited, but no one was willing to be made a spectacle of. "Sergeant Rangitira, perhaps you'd enjoy testing your skills?"

It came as no surprise, as Moana had been expecting it. He stepped forward, holding the wooden practice knife, and crouched, just as he'd been instructed.

"Since Sergeant Rangitira has only had the one lesson, we'll go easy on him." A few soldiers laughed, but most hoped Moana would be humiliated.

Captain Von Tempsky's smile vanished as he focused on Moana. Both men faced each other, and Moana anticipated the first lightning-quick thrust aimed at his belly. He moved sideways with ease but forgot he had the knife. He was concentrating on avoiding the whooshing wooden blade the captain wielded with considerable skill. Each time the captain moved to slash or strike, Moana moved, and the knife hissed past. Realising he was supposed to be attacking the captain, he made some ungainly attempts, but the captain expertly blocked the awkward moves.

Moana moved easily; he was light on his feet, and the watching soldiers were reminded of seeing him fight. Moana avoided all Von Tempsky's attempts to strike him and could see the growing frustration in the captain's eyes.

Captain Von Tempsky feinted with a thrust. Instead of moving out of the way as he should have, Moana reached forward to block the move. To the immense satisfaction of the onlookers, the captain grabbed Moana's right arm and pulled him onto the wooden knife. Had it been a real fight, Moana would have found a knife embedded between his ribs. It hurt where the wooden knife struck, and he slipped, falling to his knees, clutching his chest where the knife had hit. The watching soldiers cheered.

Captain Von Tempsky straightened and looked down at Moana. His eyes narrowed slightly; he was puzzled. "We'll take a short break and then continue." He turned to a young lieutenant, "You may dismiss them, we'll continue in half an hour," and stalked off.

Rupert had his hold-all over his shoulder and walked to Moana, who was still massaging his ribs. "Why did you do that?"

"What was I expected to do, dance around all day avoiding his toy knife?"

Rupert grinned and shook his head.

"What do you think would have happened if I'd beaten the captain? Winning wasn't an option," whispered Moana. "From the look the captain gave me, I think he knew I'd deliberately lost." Moana rubbed his chest again. "Is your wagon leaving?"

"Yes, it's time to go. Behave yourself and don't get yourself killed by a wooden toy."

They shook hands, said their goodbyes, and Rupert turned and walked towards the waiting wagon. A few soldiers in his path scattered as the giant walked past. Moana felt a little sad to see his best friend leave and was unsure when he'd see him again.

The next couple of days were a blur. The Rangers finished their preparations for deployment, and Moana was readjusting to the rigours of military life. He'd not spoken directly to Captain Von Tempsky since their knife training exercise, and Sergeants Bowers and Walker kept him busy while he learned all about Company No. 2. The soldiers remained cool and distant, still avoiding any unnecessary contact with him.

Common to all armies, officers and NCOs took great delight in rousting soldiers from their slumber at an unreasonable and uncivilised hour. They gave little thought to the comfort of the men who did the hard graft and were closest to the enemy when fighting began, yet, as any soldier will tell you, those men were the ones who protected ungrateful officers from making silly mistakes and from harming themselves. The NCOs of the Forest Rangers, Company No. 2, were no different and turned a deaf ear to the unsavoury comments and accusations levelled against them when they roused the Company from their cots. It was still dark, and it was time to wake up.

After a quick breakfast, the men of Company No. 2 were still wiping sleep from their eyes as they began marching south towards New Plymouth. It would take them many days to reach their destination, and Moana was looking forward to the time on the road.

Again, the stark differences between the Rangers and the regular army became evident. The Rangers did not march in formation but in a long, strung-out line. The biggest difference was the pace. The Rangers marched quickly, at a faster rate than Moana had ever experienced, which explained the light kit they carried.

The day before the Rangers began their march, bullock carts carrying weapons, ammunition, food, bedding and other essentials departed. Normally, the slow pace of the bullocks meant the marching Rangers would easily leave the slow-moving wagons far behind. Captain Von Tempsky arranged for the wagons to leave well in advance and then make a forward camp at a pre-arranged location. When the Rangers arrived, hot food would be ready, tents would be erected, and even hot water would be available to wash dust and sweat from aching bodies.

Two hours into their march, Moana heard the first grumblings and complaints about sore feet. As in armies all over the world, the complaints were ignored.

CHAPTER SIX

Kaitake Assault

"When you're ready, please, Mr Martin," came the casual order from Colonel Warren.

Captain Martin nodded at his commanding officer, took a deep breath, and then yelled as loud as he could, "Fire!" He visibly tensed as he raised his hands to cover his ears.

Almost simultaneously, with a thunderous, explosive ripple, a battery of artillery belched a cloud of dark smoke, and four twelve-pound shells hurtled from rifled barrels towards the elevated and entrenched *Māori* positions of the Kaitake *pa,* one thousand and five hundred yards away.

As soon as the crew repositioned each gun against the wooden chocks, they immediately began reloading. The breech screw was loosened, the vent piece raised, and under the gunner's watchful eye the shell was inserted through the hollow breech screw and thrust home into the bore. After the powder cartridge was inserted and rammed home into the chamber, the vent piece was quickly lowered, and the breech screw was tightened with remarkable speed. Lastly, the lanyard was inserted into the hole on top of the vent piece, and the gun was ready to fire again.

An adjustment to the firing angle was ordered, and the gunner made the required one-degree change as instructed. The entire process was performed identically on three of the four Armstrong twelve-pounders, as most of the crews completed reloading at about the same time.

At the fourth gun, the loader tripped and dropped the shell he was carrying. He had to quickly retrieve another. Gun number four finished its reloading sequence about four seconds after the other three. The red-faced loader was studying his fingernails with unusual interest as he received a few discourteous comments about his parental lineage.

Although it was unnecessary, since Colonel Warren could see exactly where the shells landed through his telescope, the range spotter dutifully reported the fall of shot. The colonel gave no indication of whether he was pleased with the accuracy and outcome and ordered Captain Martin to commence a sustained barrage. With a crisp turn, the colonel headed off to his tent to discuss replenishing stores, while the barrage continued. A staff officer, protectively clutching a notebook, eagerly followed. The shells the Armstrongs fired at the rebel *Māori* stronghold cost a fortune, and eventually, the colonel knew, he'd have to answer to someone and justify the expenditure.

Just over two miles away, in the small community of Oakura, Captain Corbett and a group of officers from the Taranaki Bush Rangers, along with a few local militia, watched the shelling with interest. They'd been discussing the location and fortifications of the *pa* now under sustained fire and offered reluctant admiration and praise to Paora Rakahuru, a recent convert and *Pai Marire* disciple, the man who'd cleverly engineered the defensive positions of the Kaitake *pa*.

Situated on a high ridge overlooking the main road south from New Plymouth, the *pa* featured a front-facing stockade, two redoubts, one behind the other, and carefully positioned rifle pits, creating a strong, almost impregnable defensive position. Paora had even built parapets over the redoubts.

The men under Captain Corbett's command had no illusions that storming the Kaitake *pa* would be easy. The steep hills, fortifications, and inaccessibility would test their fortitude and skill. All the men with Corbett were locals, familiar with the terrain around the Kaitake *pa*, and it was to these locals that Corbett now turned.

Billy McFadden was a pig farmer; he'd purchased property not far from the Kaitake *pa*, on the lower, bush-cleared slopes of the Patua Ranges, and knew the area well. He hoisted a flabby arm and pointed a pudgy finger in frustration at a distant rocky outcrop below the *pa*.

"Damn it, Willy, you aren't listen'n to me. Th' only way round is ta go below th' spur, not above it," he shook his head in irritation, causing his jowls to jiggle.

Willy worked for Billy and handled most of the hard tasks on the pig farm. Billy liked to think that employers only gave instructions and never actually engaged in physical labour. Both Willy and Billy also served in the volunteer Taranaki Militia, and Captain Corbett wisely consulted Billy on how to approach the *pa* unnoticed.

Captain Corbett turned to Billy for confirmation. "You sure, Billy?"

Billy sighed. He wasn't a man gifted with patience. "'Member that quake we had last year? It created a rockslide and opened up a narrow track b'neath that spur. Above it is now a sheer face."

The captain turned to young Willy, hoping for his agreement.

"Yeah, you may be right, Mr McFadden," said Willy slowly, with less confidence than the captain would have preferred. Willy was not particularly quick of mind.

Billy McFadden raised his head, looked skywards for divine help and rolled his eyes; the movement unfolded layers of multiple chins resting on his chest.

There was no alternative, and Captain Corbett accepted Billy's recommendation. With a quiet sigh, he meticulously began outlining the exact route his eighty-strong militia would take to complete their portion of the mission.

The plan was straightforward yet very dangerous. Under the cover of darkness, Captain Corbett would covertly lead his Taranaki Militia along narrow tracks, up steep hills, and through dense bush, then conceal his force as close as possible to the *Māori* defensive rifle pits near the *pa*. At a prearranged time the next day, the shelling would stop, and Captain Corbett and his militia would surprise and attack the weakened *Māori* positions that were presently preventing Colonel Warren's troops from making a direct frontal assault.

The militia officers were gathered beneath a large awning, conveniently erected for their mission planning and briefing. The atmosphere was almost festive, which greatly concerned the captain. Men were using the gathering as an excuse to catch up on news or discuss family matters. It was even rumoured that a marriage was being arranged. Corbett tried desperately to impress on his volunteer force the seriousness of the mission, but with little success.

The weather remained agreeable, and, as anticipated, it shouldn't pose any problems. A cooling sea breeze kept everyone happy, except the corpulent Billy McFadden, who was sweating profusely and dabbing at his face with a well-worn, soiled handkerchief. The captain explained again that young Willy was only assigned as a guide for the first stage of their mission, and that when they reached thick bush, another man more adept in bushcraft would take over. It was a dangerous mission, not only because they would be attacking a cleverly engineered defensive position, but also because they would be traversing rugged country – a misstep in the dark could be fatal. The militia would be travelling in darkness over rugged terrain, ascending without the aid of lanterns, with the moon providing little illumination, if any. The distant boom of the Armstrong guns only underscored the importance of their undertaking.

Prior to Billy's arrival at the briefing, a junior lieutenant from the Taranaki Bush Rangers innocently asked how Billy would manage to carry his sizeable bulk to the dizzying heights near the *pa*. As the young lieutenant was sincere, Captain Corbett chose not to admonish the perplexed officer. Once the laughter subsided, the captain explained that Billy would not be going with them and had been assigned another equally important position. Billy McFadden's role would be purely supportive, more suited to his stature, Captain Corbett delicately explained. He quickly added that his expertise would be more valuable as a liaison between his militia and Colonel Warren's forces, a decision Billy wholeheartedly agreed with. The other officers silently concurred, understanding that Billy would be just a messenger. Earlier, it had been less tactfully suggested that if Billy went on the mission, his wheezing would alert not only the *Māori* defenders at the Kaitake *pa* to the impending assault but also the thousands of rebel *Māori* who were rumoured to be gathering about a hundred miles away at Waitotara. Captain Corbett was unable to hide his smile.

As the afternoon wore on, more of Corbett's volunteer force arrived, and the numbers swelled to just over eighty men. Under careful supervision, they began to address their clothes and tack in hopes of eliminating rattles and other unwanted noise. When darkness fell, he ordered all his men to rest and sleep if they could. Under orders, Billy McFadden rode off to visit Colonel Warren in case there were last-minute changes, and he would report back before the militia departed.

At midnight, the volunteer Taranaki militia were roused and fed. Billy returned with a message for Captain Corbett - 'Good luck and Godspeed'.

At 1:00 am, led by Willy, the eighty-strong militia force departed camp and slowly wound their way through open pasture and fields, then up into the Kaitake ranges. Miraculously, no one was seriously hurt, likely because Captain Corbett had insisted that stealth was more important than speed, although they'd become lost at one point and finally got back on track after an agonising hour's delay. Nine hours after leaving camp, all the militia were concealed within a stone's throw of the Kaitake *pa*'s defensive positions – and travelled only two and a half miles.

If Captain Corbett knew that the shelling was so devastatingly accurate and that most *Māori* had withdrawn, leaving their forward positions undefended, he might have felt considerably better. He lay in the shadows of a large fern, watching his hands shake uncontrollably from nerves and fear. At the prearranged time of 10:30 am, the shelling stopped – the moment they'd all waited for. Corbett issued his orders. The militia immediately rose from concealment and advanced on the *pa*. They met little resistance at the first rifle pits they encountered, and once secured, they used them in reverse to pour devastating fire into the rebel trenches behind the palisades.

Caught by surprise, *Māori* began to defend the *pa* valiantly, but when Colonel Warren's troops advanced up the steep hillside to support Corbett's militia, rebel *Māori* fled into the bush. The *pa* was captured with minimal casualties.

Troops immediately began to destroy *Māori* defensive earthworks and set about building their own redoubt on the uppermost levels of the *pa*. Bush surrounding the site was also cut down, and a road was created to allow easier access.

A token effort was made to pursue the rebels through the bush, but being ill-equipped and lacking specialist training in bushcraft, it proved fruitless. The weather closed in, and heavy rain washed away any tracks and signs of the retreating rebels.

Not all *Māori* fled. Four days after the assault, only one hundred and fifty yards from the redoubt, a single soldier was killed and another seriously wounded in an ambuscade.

CHAPTER SEVEN

Bonding

For three days, the unrelenting rain caused havoc. Dampening more than just spirits, it slowed the Forest Rangers' progress considerably as they headed towards New Plymouth. With their progress essentially stalled, all available Rangers were pushing wagons up slippery, muddy tracks as exhausted bullocks laboured, the powerful beasts unable to make headway in the torrid conditions. Eventually unharnessed, the bullocks were led to the summit and rested while men leaned a shoulder, a back, or pushed the heavy wagons upwards through the slush. Each treacherous step and each yard gained was another small victory during the incessant downpour. On reaching the summit, if the men cared enough to spare a glance, they'd probably see another hill to traverse, and perhaps another after that. Few cared, focusing only on the challenge of pushing or pulling the wagons to the top of the present hill.

Moana, like everyone else, was covered in mud, his clothes sodden. He was at the rear of the last wagon, along with three others, all pushing with their backs. Beside him, with rainwater streaming down his face, Tane Mahaia was grunting with effort. He didn't speak; no one did. All were too tired, and their thighs ached from exertion. Another fifteen or so men were positioned at the sides and the front. As everyone heaved together, the wagon slowly made headway, inching upwards through deep ruts and mud. If the wagon came to a halt, the wagon's brakes were applied, and men would place wooden blocks behind each wheel before they rested, preventing the wagon from rolling back down again.

Exhausted, the men called for a brief respite. Gratefully, blocks were placed behind the wheels, and the men straightened, easing tired backs and legs. The men at the front walked a little to restore circulation, while some swung their arms to loosen up. Moana stepped to the side of the track, away from the mud, and stretched. Tane walked a couple of paces away from the wagon and did the same, easing aching muscles as he looked back down the hill. The other two Rangers moved to the other side of the track, away from Moana, leaving him alone. Since the journey began, the men had kept their distance, isolating him and making it clear how they still felt. The two sergeants were friendly and seemed not to hold any grudge or hard feelings towards him, but no others made any real attempt to get close.

The fully loaded wagon creaked as one of the blocks chocking the rear wheel slid in the viscous mire. The other blocks, taking the full burden of the wagon's weight, began to slide and sink deeper into the mud. The brakes and chocks weren't holding. The heavy wagon began to roll slowly backwards.

"Look out!" came the cry. "Tane!"

Rangers rushed to the wagon to hold it in place but couldn't get a firm grip as their feet slid helplessly. Tane, directly in the wagon's path, heard the shouted warning and turned quickly. With legs still unsteady, he slipped, twisting his ankle in a deep rut, and fell into the sludge. In agony and rising panic, he struggled to find purchase on his only usable foot. He turned and grabbed at anything nearby. It wouldn't be enough – he had no time to move before the wagon struck. Gathering momentum, the wagon accelerated, and every attempt to stop or even slow it was useless. One Ranger picked up a wooden block and hurled it beneath a wheel, but the wagon rode over it, pressing the block deep into the mud.

Seeing Tane floundering in pain and fear, Moana took two quick steps, launched himself directly into the path of the moving wagon, and drove hard into him. They both slid towards the side of the track, but not enough to clear the wagon as it continued to build speed. Moving faster by the second, the massive steel-rimmed wheels bore down on Tane and Moana as both men lay across the deep rut that held the wagon on its downward course. It was unlikely the wagon would even slow as it dissected anything unfortunate enough to be in its way. There was no time to pick him up, and with a herculean effort, Moana grabbed Tane, rolled him over his own body, then rolled over Tane to the safety of the berm. Before he had even finished, the wagon bounced past, missing Tane by inches and spraying them with brown muddy water. Both men gasped for air as they watched the careening wagon hurtling down the track. It didn't make the turn at the bottom and fell onto its side, spilling its contents into the bush.

Moana wiped mud from his face as the rain continued its deluge.

Men rushed over to assist and tend to Tane while Moana stood to speak to Sergeant-Major Bowers, who'd been nearby. The wagon needed to be retrieved and repaired if they were to continue. Moana ordered men to attend to the damaged wagon as Captain Von Tempsky, arms wind-milling, slid clumsily down the track towards them.

"What happened, sergeant?" asked the captain, arriving ungracefully without mishap.

"The chocks didn't hold, captain, and the wagon took off. One of the men slipped and would have been crushed. He was lucky," replied Moana, still wiping mud from his face.

"Is he hurt?"

"He twisted an ankle, I think."

"Yes, he was very lucky."

"If there's nothing else, captain, I'll go and look at the wagon," Moana replied, then eased himself carefully down the berm to the men already trying to right the wagon.

Von Tempsky looked at the injured soldier and spoke to Sergeant-Major Bowers. "What did you see?"

"Was Rangitira, sir, saved Tane's life?" said Bowers.

Von Tempsky raised his eyebrows in surprise and watched the injured soldier as his ankle was wrapped.

"I'd better go and lend a hand, sir," Bowers said, following Moana's route down the berm.

To everyone's relief, the rain finally eased, and the nighttime bush seemed unnaturally quiet. The Rangers ate hot food, tried to clean themselves, and some changed into dry uniforms. Campfires blazed, and steaming clothes were creatively hung from branches to dry. Most were in good spirits and tomorrow promised an easier day as the mud began to dry.

The wayward wagon needed minor repairs, which were promptly addressed. Once loaded, everyone pitched in and hauled the unwilling wagon up the steep slope to the summit. It wasn't easy, but they managed. Once safely at the top, the captain admitted defeat and decided to call it a day. He ordered camp to be set up on the sheltered side of the hill, on a reasonably flat piece of cleared land previously used by other travellers for the same purpose.

Tonight, as he'd done every night when duty permitted, Moana walked into the bush near camp and repeated his knife drills. He spent a solitary hour practising everything he'd been taught. As promised, he was determined to become proficient with the knife.

In a crouch, he held the knife in his preferred reverse grip and kept it moving in circles or figure-eights. The right hand, especially in Moana's case, was also a very dangerous and serious offensive threat; he kept it in motion, mirroring the left. He practised blocks, thrusts, lunges, parries, and strikes. He practised again and again until he began to tire.

"Don't hold the knife so tightly– you'll choke it and limit your flexibility and speed," said Captain Von Tempsky as he stepped into the small clearing. He'd been standing and watching for some time. The orange glow of the campfire cast moving shadows across his face. "Here, let me show you."

The captain used his own knife and stood beside Moana where he crouched and went through identical drills.

He paused. "Now, do you feel the knife in my hand? Grab it. I'm not holding it very tightly until I need to."

Moana nodded; he understood. He chastised himself for not having realised it.

"Now you try."

Moana replicated the captain's moves, enjoying the difference.

"Yes, that's good, much better, Sergeant. I see some fluidity in your moves now."

Moana straightened, then returned the knife to its sheath. "Thank you, Captain."

Von Tempsky fell silent for a moment, looking at his sergeant. He decided not to mention the wagon incident with Tane. He didn't think it was in Moana's nature to accept praise for something any honourable man would have done, and any compliments would likely make him uncomfortable.

"Do you know the men have begun to call you 'Ira'?" Von Tempsky finally said, correctly pronouncing it 'Ear-Ruh'.

"Is that so?"

"Apparently, it's because of the other soldier called Moana – to save confusion," the captain smiled, although it was unlikely Moana saw. "Also, it's because of the *iwi* you are from, and I presume because 'Ira' is the last part of your surname. Although it is common practice to take the last part of a man's name as a pet name, I prefer not to be called 'Ski'."

Moana laughed. "I don't think 'Ira' or 'Ski' is derogatory."

"I think it also has something to do with what sparked the fight at the Travellers Rest. Those boys were mocking you because of your *iwi*," the captain added.

Moana remained silent, allowing the captain to talk.

"This is their way of accepting you. Do you understand this?" The captain squatted on his haunches and poked the soft dirt with the tip of his knife. "From observing you, I believe you are gifted with great power, though I have seen only flashes of it. Perhaps it is also a great responsibility and burden for you to bear. I'm only guessing, as you haven't talked about it, but I think you have had serious instruction in the art of unarmed combat."

Moana began to interrupt, "Captain …"

"No, please, allow me to finish. You had every right to defend your honour at the hotel, and you did so with remarkable ease. These men you march with have honour too. While they are young and often impetuous, you took their respect. The beating you administered to them hurt them in a way you can't possibly imagine. They are soldiers, special soldiers. Many have unique skills and qualities that make this fighting force special. This is why we are together. They believed in themselves and in their specialness, and then one day two men came into their lives and showed them total humiliation. Your impressive skills are unquestioned, Moana. You have the right to defend your honour, and you quite rightly did. However, the outcome has had lasting effects, and somehow, I will find a way to use that to make these boys work and train even harder." The captain again turned to Moana, who was listening carefully. "This is why these men," Von Tempsky waved his arm towards camp, "have been reluctant to warm to you. They don't need me to tell them they were wrong to provoke you; they know that. The pain they feel is not from lingering bruises but from damaged egos. Give them a reason to respect you, Moana, and they will accept you." The captain stood, sheathing his knife. "But do not shut yourself away from them as you have been doing; if you continue, they will grow to hate you. Do you understand this?"

Moana remained quiet for a moment as he contemplated his response. "Yes, sir, I do. Perhaps it will be better to just be myself?"

"Exactly, Moana, or can I call you 'Ira'?"

"I would welcome being called 'Ira' by my friends, sir."

Captain Von Tempsky held out his hand, a gesture of sincerity, respect, and friendship. Ira returned the gesture, accepting the invitation. The captain turned, ducked under a branch, and headed towards his command tent. "Good night, Sergeant," he said over his shoulder.

Moana was perplexed. Since they'd begun their journey to New Plymouth, Von Tempsky hardly acknowledged or spoke to him other than to issue an order or make a casual comment. Yet tonight he had spoken of things that he could not have known about. Someone kept the captain informed. His outward air of indifference towards him was intentional. Moana now knew that the captain's behaviour was deliberate. He'd wanted to leave him alone, watch him adjust, settle in, and see how the men accepted him, if they ever did.

Strolling casually back to the fire, Moana realised he had a newfound respect for Captain Gustavus Von Tempsky, the dandy, the officer, the gallant and skilled knife-fighter. He shook his head in amusement. If Rupert had witnessed all that had happened, he'd have something dry to say.

Every morning, Captain Von Tempsky held a briefing, and his two lieutenants and the three sergeants always attended. The meeting was usually held as the camp was being dismantled. Moana felt an air of nervous excitement as he entered the captain's command tent. Sergeant-Major Bowers, who was only a few steps behind him, also noticed.

"Something's going on, Ira."

Moana turned to Bowers, surprised at the use of the name.

"What? Didn't you know that is what we are calling you now?" said the sergeant with a big smile. "We think it suits you."

Moana didn't know what to say - he took no offence at being called Ira, as long as it came from a friend. Before he could respond, Captain Von Tempsky walked in.

"We received a dispatch this morning," said the captain without preamble. "Colonel Warren captured the Kaitake *pa* and sustained only minimal casualties." Heads nodded in approval of the good news.

Both lieutenants appeared slightly puzzled. "Sir?" interrupted Lieutenant Griggs, "Where is Kaitake?"

"Where is it?" asked the captain, "It's where we should be!"

The junior lieutenant looked down to study his notebook – he appeared to be fascinated by whatever it contained.

Von Tempsky continued. "Rebel *Māori* evaded capture and disappeared into the bush. Warren's forces were ill-suited to pursue. As a result, one man was killed and another wounded when the rebels crept back to waylay two soldiers. Our mission is to find the rebels and eliminate them. This is why the Forest Rangers exist; this is what we train for." The captain's face lit up, and his eyes danced around the tent, from face to face in excitement. "Any questions?"

"What are the estimated numbers of *Māori* rebels we'll be tracking, sir?" asked Sergeant Walker.

"Unknown at present. When the guns opened up and began shelling the fortifications, many fled. I believe we'll be up against superior numbers," offered the captain, turning to the other two sergeants, inviting them to ask questions, the lieutenants forgotten.

Moana could see the captain was enjoying this greatly. "Sir?"

"Yes, Sergeant?"

"Do we know who the rebel leader is?" asked Moana.

"Yes, we believe he is called Paora Rakahuru. Is anyone familiar with him?" Von Tempsky waited, but no one knew of him. "He designed and built the *pa* and its fortifications and did an admirable job, I'm told. He is also a fanatical member of the *Pai Marire* religion. But other than that, we know very little about him."

The captain reached across and lifted a document from the small camp table he used as a writing desk. "This brings me to the next detail. As we will be tracking and pursuing these rebels, we need to determine our effectiveness at scouting, more importantly, our ability to remain undetected in the bush. I understand most men have bush experience and remarkable skills." Von Tempsky consulted his document for details. Finding what he needed, the captain continued, "After we have had our evening meal, we will begin determining who has superior abilities. I want two groups of men formed. Group one will be men with little or no experience in bushcraft, and the other group will be those who are very adept and experienced. Everyone will participate in the test, including the three of you," the captain looked to the sergeants sternly. "Lieutenants Small and Griggs will command the exercise and determine a ranking. Failure by anyone to complete the test will result in punishment. Do I make myself understood?"

"Sir, if we do this after marching all day, the men may not perform at their best," volunteered Sergeant Walker.

Moana inwardly grimaced. He felt Bowers beside him tense.

Captain Von Tempsky looked intently at Walker. "We will leave this camp at dawn. See to it. Dismissed," he said, ignoring the comment.

More unseasonal rain threatened. Large, ominous clouds scurried across the evening sky, occasionally obscuring the full moon and any useful light. A moderate westerly breeze stirred leaves and grasses, creating noises that frustrated the two training officers. Lieutenant Small and Lieutenant Griggs stood on wooden crates, identifying the first group of less-experienced Rangers as they completed the training exercise to the best of their ability. One by one, each man in the small group was observed as he attempted to creep unseen towards the lieutenants. The distance each man travelled without being seen was diligently recorded in the small notebook held by Lieutenant Griggs.

Both officers held a pocketful of stones. If a Ranger was seen, they would throw a stone at the man and yell, ordering the man to stand and state his name. Markers were placed in the ground to help determine the distance each man travelled.

One man remained to be found, and Small believed he'd finally spotted him. He threw a stone, missed, then threw another that hit him, drawing a curse. The Ranger slowly stood, rubbing his hip where he'd been struck.

"In fifteen minutes, you've only managed to make about five yards!" yelled a very indignant Lieutenant Small. "You did not obey your orders!" Small had his hands on his hips and glowered at the man in the distance. "Come here!"

"I'm sorry, sir," the young Ranger apologised as he approached both officers.

"Explain yourself," Small asked, looking down at the Ranger.

The Ranger dropped his head. "I fell asleep, sir," he explained in a whisper.

"Speak up, I can't hear you, soldier."

"I fell asleep, sir!"

"Put him on punishment report," Small requested of Lieutenant Griggs, who scratched the details awkwardly into his notebook by the available moonlight.

As instructed, all Rangers not in the participating group were standing well away from the training exercise. On hearing the loud exchange, they were trying hard not to laugh.

The first inexperienced group performed as expected, and all were found within fifteen minutes. Both officers hoped for a better result from the second, more seasoned group, who were called over and given their final instructions.

Lieutenant Small explained, "This is a simple exercise. Get as close to Lieutenant Griggs or to me as you possibly can without being discovered." Small looked at the men before him—he was enjoying being in command and secretly imagined himself as a conquering general addressing his victorious troops.

In contrast, the Rangers were not warming or particularly receptive to his overbearing, pompous attitude.

"When a person has been spotted, he will immediately stand, identify himself, and leave the training course by retracing his steps. This way, he will not interfere with others who have yet to be discovered. Any questions?"

"Does the winner get a prize?" someone asked. Everyone laughed.

"War and death are not a frivolous matter; you will come to learn that," Small admonished. "You have exactly fifteen minutes to complete this exercise. Go to the starting point and wait for my command to begin."

A marker shrouded in total darkness marked the starting point. The two officers stood on wooden crates about thirty yards away, ten yards apart. Both lieutenants felt confident that if anyone were lucky enough to creep that close and remain unseen and unheard, they would certainly be identified within the fifteen-yard radius from where they stood.

Rather than release the men in one large group, the sergeants coordinated with the officers to let them begin in clusters. The sergeants were last to leave, lowering themselves into the bush amidst grumblings from both Bowers and Walker. Without a word, Moana, the last man to begin, lowered himself to the ground and promptly disappeared.

As predicted, this group demonstrated better skills and travelled further than the earlier, less-experienced men who had gone before them, and a few even showed patience and remarkable skill.

From an early age, grandfather Rangitira took a special interest in his grandson's education. He'd instinctively known that European colonists and settlers would not leave his country, and he was firm in his belief that turbulent times would follow. '*Pākeha*', as Europeans were called, also brought a written language and knowledge of the ways of the world. Grandfather Rangitira quickly came to understand that if his grandson was to thrive and prosper, he must learn about *Pākeha* from *Pākeha*.

"To read and write is not just a doorway into the minds of men; it is also a weapon," he frequently told his young grandson, and so Moana was sent to study at European schools to learn and understand European ways.

Moana's mother, Ata, was not content for her son to learn only from *Pākeha*. Conflict and fighting were commonplace, and she grew increasingly concerned for his safety. A local high priest recognised unusual qualities in Moana, and with his grandfather's and mother's blessing, the priest began to teach him the secretive and spiritual *Māori* martial art called 'Mau', a form of death-point striking that used mainly the hands in unarmed combat. Extensive training required Moana to study the human body and movement, specifically the ability to predict an opponent's movements. Through hours and hours of intensive training, he was instructed to observe a subject and react to their anticipated actions.

When an arm is raised to strike, the body balances differently. Muscles tense before the arm is raised and the fist is thrust forward. Moana was taught to recognise the subtle changes in balance and muscle tension that revealed an opponent's intention. He continued to learn and practise Mau through adolescence and diligently into adulthood.

Between regular schooling, his mother sent him to a *Whare Wānanga,* a special place of learning where he gained more knowledge of *Māori culture*, including bushcraft, a skill he became very proficient in. Moana learned to move through the bush like a ghost, to be invisible and become part of the living landscape. The training exercise the Rangers were required to perform tonight was something Moana enjoyed; this was where he felt at home and excelled.

As before, Lieutenants Small and Griggs began to identify each Ranger as they attempted to approach unseen. Many made it within the fifteen-yard radius, and on a few occasions, the officers were startled and impressed by how close some men came. Lieutenant Griggs recorded all the details he could in his notebook. After approximately thirty minutes, all the men were called together for a debriefing.

Lieutenant Small took the opportunity to address the men again, emphasising the importance of improving their skills and how it would save their lives. Bored and tired, the Rangers shuffled their feet. Some yawned, hoping to prompt the officers to release them to their tents and beds. With the aid of a lantern, Lieutenant Griggs was checking his notebook entries and discovered a discrepancy.

As the Rangers watched on in growing puzzlement, Lieutenant Griggs interrupted the more senior lieutenant and, in hushed tones, pointed and stabbed at his notebook. It was becoming increasingly clear to the Rangers that something displeased the officers.

Lieutenant Small cleared his throat, "Sergeant Rangitira, please step forward!"

As ordered and expected, Moana pushed through the men and stood in the small circle of light before the officers.

Hoping to make an example of the lazy sergeant, Lieutenant Small was relishing the chance to dress him down before the men. "Perhaps you would care to explain to us why you did not feel the need to participate in this evening's exercise, Sergeant? After all, everyone here gave it an honest attempt, and you didn't. Presumably, we weren't inconveniencing you in any way, were we?" said Lieutenant Small, his smile holding no warmth.

A general low murmur could be heard from the men standing and watching. The yawning stopped.

Moana looked up at the lieutenant, keeping his tone neutral. "I completed the exercise as ordered, sir!"

Sergeant-Major Bowers nudged Walker and whispered, "I saw him; he left after we did."

Lieutenant Small clasped his hands behind his back and rocked on his toes, as he had seen Major Jackson do. "Is that so? Could you explain to us why there is no entry for the distance you reached before you were seen?"

"Oh yes, sir, I can explain it very easily," replied Moana, enjoying the moment.

"I'm not here to play games with you, Sergeant. Why the hell didn't you complete the exercise as required?" Small yelled, losing patience.

Moana took stock of both officers and remained quiet for a heartbeat or two. "Because I was not seen, sir!" Moana said 'sir' as if he spat the word.

Both officers began to laugh. "That's not possible. If it were, how could you prove it?" asked Lieutenant Small.

"I crept unseen all the way to where you were standing, then went past and behind you, where I found a satchel lying in the grass," said Moana, pointing to the ground behind Lieutenant Small. "Then I slowly withdrew and joined the men to wait until the exercise was over, sir."

"Yes, that satchel belongs to me!"

"Well, sir, I was not aware it was yours, but now that I know who it belongs to, I can return this to its rightful owner," Moana pulled a notebook from his pocket and handed it to Lieutenant Small.

A few men snickered.

"This is mine. How dare you …" Small was incredulous. "You stole that notebook from me. This is theft! We do not tolerate thievery, Sergeant. You will be brought to account. What say you?"

"No, sir, I did not steal from you. Why would I admit to having your notebook and then offer to return it to you?" Moana replied carefully. "Oh yes, before I forget, if you'd care to look inside the satchel, sir, you'll find I left my Bowie knife there."

Immediately, Lieutenant Small reached down, retrieved the satchel, and opened it. Just as Rangitira had claimed, he found the sergeant's knife. He held it up to the light. It began as a quiet titter and grew into a full-blown laugh. Company No. 2 were hysterical. It was too dark to see Lieutenant Small's red face.

"Enough!" he bawled.

The lieutenant was astute enough to realise that the only way the sergeant could have exchanged the notebook for the knife was to have crept past them both unseen, make the exchange, then retreat safely and wait amongst the other men until the time limit had expired, just as he explained. This was unbelievable.

Moana held out his hand for the knife. Small held on to it.

"Wait here, all of you. I need to discuss this with Captain Von Tempsky," ordered Small, flustered. He quickly returned to the camp, a short distance away, while Lieutenant Griggs remained behind.

Captain Von Tempsky was in no mood for distractions this evening; he needed to write a complex report and wanted peace and quiet. The intrusion by his senior lieutenant didn't sit well with him.

Lieutenant Small stood confidently in front of his captain. He explained in detail what had transpired during training and the allegation of theft he intended to formally charge Sergeant Rangitira with. He waited for the captain's response.

Captain Von Tempsky was twirling his moustache as he contemplated the events reported to him by his lieutenant. His evening had just improved considerably. He was desperately trying not to laugh and to remain impassive in front of the agitated young officer. It was a sensitive situation, and the accusation of theft was a serious charge that needed careful handling. Secretly, Von Tempsky was thrilled. Ira had come through, as he knew he would. He'd challenged Ira to be himself, and Ira had done so with flying colours. If he was to believe Lieutenant Small, and there was no reason to doubt him, then Ira's incredible demonstration of skill was more astounding than he could have believed possible, but in doing so, it had ruffled the feathers of his two officers. As far as Von Tempsky believed, the real issue was with Lieutenant Small, not with Ira.

"Why did you leave your satchel unattended, and why were you not wearing it?" asked the captain casually.

"It was cumbersome and, in the way, sir," replied Lieutenant Small. "I placed it on the ground behind me while we conducted the exercise."

"So you just dropped it on the ground and forgot about it, is that right?"

"Well, yes sir."

"Perhaps it was a little careless and silly to leave the satchel on the ground unattended, don't you think?" asked Von Tempsky. "Surely you must have been concerned for the safety of all your valuables?"

"Oh no, sir, there was nothing of value in it, other than a notebook, but that has no real value, does it?" Lieutenant Small realised what he'd said. His cheeks flushed.

"Do you honestly believe Sergeant Rangitira's motive was theft? If the sergeant came across a satchel lying on the ground in the dark, which contained nothing of value but a notebook, and the man then admitted to you what he'd done …" Von Tempsky toyed with Moana's knife. "… does this seem like the actions of a thief?"

Small paused, giving the question some thought. "No, probably not, sir."

"Lieutenant, what provision did you make for the exercise in the event that a man was not seen or discovered?"

"Ah, none, sir, because we believed no one would complete the test and remain undetected."

Captain Von Tempsky remained silent for a dozen heartbeats. The silence emphasised his point.

"Do you think the sergeant used this exercise to demonstrate his capabilities to both of you and the entire Company?" he finally asked.

"I hadn't thought of it that way, sir," replied Small. "Are you suggesting that I not pursue a charge of theft?"

"I'm not suggesting anything of the kind, Lieutenant. It's your responsibility and your right to lodge an official complaint if you feel it is warranted. It would be inappropriate for me to influence your decision." Von Tempsky looked at Small. This was a crucial moment in the young Lieutenant's career. Whatever he said now would shape his future.

Lieutenant Small looked down at his feet, giving the matter due consideration. He looked up. "Perhaps my initial feelings were clouded by the fact that Sergeant Rangitira completed the test without being spotted. My pride was hurt." He took a deep breath. "I see no reason to pursue a charge of theft against Sergeant Rangitira, sir … uh, my complaint was a little petty, wasn't it?"

"Very well, Lieutenant," replied the captain, hoping his relief was not obvious. "Thank you for your honesty, but I doubt anyone could have detected the man, so don't take it personally." The captain offered a warm smile. "But Sergeant Rangitira still committed an offence, did he not?" Von Tempsky knew his officers needed to save face in front of the men. Ira must be found to have done something wrong. Such is the way of the military.

The lieutenant looked puzzled, not understanding where the captain was going.

"Lieutenant Small, I think Sergeant Rangitira needs to be punished for being out of uniform. The Bowie knife is part of our uniform, and he was without it. Is this not so?"

Small smiled, finally understanding what the captain was trying to do. "Yes, sir, most definitely, sir." His smile vanished, and he looked perplexed. "Sir, what should the punishment be for such an infringement? Nothing too severe?"

As if the idea had only just occurred to him, Captain Von Tempsky's eyes lit up. "I have it," he said, raising a finger. "As punishment, Sergeant Rangitira will be the new Company Bushcraft Training Instructor."

"Wonderful idea, sir. I'll pull him aside, apologise, and inform him of the, ah, penalty."

"Very well, see he is informed," the captain paused, mulling over a thought. "No, don't pull him aside. Do it in front of the entire Company, as soon as possible. I'd like to see the men eventually get to bed tonight, Lieutenant. Oh yes, and please return the knife to him."

Once the captain was alone, he creaked back on his campstool. His fingers automatically went back to his moustache as he considered his newest sergeant. Supported by Major Jackson, they both had a gut feeling about Moana Rangitira. As of today, Ira had surpassed their expectations, and an uncanny feeling led the captain to believe there was still more to learn about the mysterious man. If the Forest Rangers were to succeed as a specialised fighting force, they would need men like Ira. The captain smiled, the unpleasantness of the unfinished report forgotten.

Moana was standing before the two lieutenants again. The rest of the company, who'd been waiting in small groups chatting, all turned to watch and listen.

"Sergeant Rangitira, you've been found to be in violation of *The Volunteer Act Regulations* and the *New Zealand Dress Regulations*." The lieutenant paused for effect. "By not having your regulation-issued Bowie knife on your person, as required, you are therefore out of uniform," announced Lieutenant Small. "As punishment, the Commanding Officer, Company No. 2, Captain Von Tempsky, has ordered that you now assume the role of Company Bushcraft Training Instructor." The lieutenant returned Moana's knife. "After consideration, the accusation of theft has been dropped. Everyone is dismissed. Good night." In a quiet voice, the lieutenant apologised for the unfounded accusation. Moana nodded in acknowledgement, and both officers turned and walked off.

Moana stood transfixed; he knew that Von Tempsky had sneakily outmanoeuvred his lieutenants and had been behind his new role as instructor, but no matter what would have happened this evening, the captain would have ensured that position would have been his.

A soldier clapped Moana on the shoulder, "Nice job, Sergeant."

Another walked past, "We'd rather have you train us, Ira."

Tane walked towards him and self-consciously held out his hand, "Thank you."

Moana returned the gesture and stood in quiet amazement as the men, one by one, walked past and acknowledged him.

Finally, one more hand clapped him on the shoulder. Moana turned to see Sergeant-Major Bowers standing there, grinning. "I guess we live and learn, Ira. I've done variations on that exercise many times. Never have I seen a man do what you did tonight. Not only that, you put some humility into those young lieutenants' breeches. Let's hope they learn."

"I think they have learned something tonight," Moana said.

Bowers began to walk away, then stopped. "I think you can assume the men are beginning to accept you. Congratulations. Good night, Ira."

CHAPTER EIGHT

Friendship

Two *Māori* warriors stood apart from the others, looking over the mist-shrouded valley as soldiers obliterated their crops. Partially concealed in the shadow of a large tree, they watched as Colonel Warren's troops ripped potatoes from carefully cultivated fields. Maize, tobacco and other plants were shredded and destroyed, all part of Governor Grey's plan to drive them from their land.

Kaihoka Te Hua's fists were clenched in helpless rage as he watched; the destruction was total, the hatred festering and building. Beside him, Paora Rakahuru shook his head in overwhelming sadness as he saw the fields his people had so carefully tended reduced to nothing. *How will we feed ourselves,* he wondered?

Paora turned to his friend and newest disciple of Te Ua's *Pai Marire* faith, "We have made a grave mistake."

Tearing his gaze from the once fertile and productive fields, Kaihoka looked at Paora in question.

"I built a strong *pa* to defend our lands from the *Pākeha*," he pointed to a distant peak in the Kaitake hills where *Pākeha* soldiers, unseen, now clambered, strengthening fortifications and repairing damage inflicted by their own guns when they attacked. "And we failed. We cannot fight *Pākeha* this way; we will lose every battle if we do." Paora swallowed, keeping his emotions in check. "Te Ua says 'Israel will be restored to Canaan, as Māoridom will return here'."

"Then how can we defeat them?" asked Kaihoka, eager to enact revenge.

"We shall overcome. We must be mobile and not waste time building defensive structures," replied Paora distantly, his mind already calculating as he walked away to rejoin the others.

They sat in a small clearing deep within the folds of the Kaitake Ranges, safe from prying *Pākeha* eyes. A group of men, all faithful to *Pai Marire*, debated how to exact retribution and drive the soldiers from their lands. Hatotoi, another of Te Ua's chosen disciples, argued that they should lie in wait for the soldiers, who would surely begin destroying crops at another nearby *pa*.

"If we wait, they will come to us. God will deliver them to our hands," said Hatotoi.

"But we cannot fight their big guns, and we have fewer warriors and cannot defeat their army," pleaded another warrior.

Paora had been quiet since he returned from viewing the carnage inflicted by the *Pākeha* soldiers. He looked up at the men before him, "You are both correct. We must choose where we will fight and not let the *Pākeha* decide. If we are to win, then we must hide and wait for them to come to us."

"Hatotoi is right when he says the soldiers will pull crops at other *pa*," said Kaihoka. "I have an informer, a spy, who told me the *Pākeha* will next attack our crops at Te Ahuahu. We should go there and wait for them. Then, after we have killed them, we should disappear into the bush and strike again elsewhere and keep moving. If we do this, the *Pākeha* cannot bring his big guns - they move too slowly to be useful."

Paora looked concerned. "Are you sure of this?" he asked.

Kaihoka nodded. He turned his head slightly towards a warrior, a big man they called Big Pete Te Maha, who sometimes came with them, and gave an imperceptible smile. All the men murmured in agreement.

"*Pākeha* cannot fight in the bush– they cannot find us, or creep upon us while we sleep. They are noisy. But this information you speak of … this is what we want," concluded Paora, giving Kaihoka a pat on the shoulder. Big Pete smiled.

Paora was shrewd – the warriors all supported his reasoning.

"Are we sure they will go to Te Ahuahu? We may waste our time," a lone voice asked.

Kaihoka turned to the warrior, "Because I know they will come."

Tohu Kakahi, who'd remained silent, agreed with the consensus. He eased himself upright and stood, spreading his arms.

"Let the sword of Gabriel, who vanquished the unrighteous Philistines, smite the Syrian invaders."

"Amen," they said as one.

Te Ua Haumene preached to his warriors about visions and the powers granted to him by the archangel Gabriel. They'd listened to his passionate sermons and come to understand that *Māori* had the same holy pact with God as the persecuted Israelites, whose plight was prophesied and described in the Old Testament. In fact, much of the *Pai Marire* religion was founded on the writings of the Old Testament, and when Christian teachings conflicted with acts of violence and retribution, Te Ua used ancient *Māori* beliefs to justify his followers' actions. All the men here knew that Gabriel was represented through Te Ua, and the sword Tohu spoke of symbolised *Māori* warriors striking at *Pākeha* soldiers.

Lieutenant Roberts of the 57th Regiment pointed at a detailed map of an area south of New Plymouth, which included the small towns of Oakura and Te Ahuahu, as well as the Kaitake Ranges. Colonel Warren sat listening to the briefing but appeared distracted, if not bored. In contrast, Captain Von Tempsky sat slightly forward in his chair and listened attentively; his lieutenants, Small and Griggs, were diligently taking notes. Equally interested in the presentation by the well-informed intelligence officer were sergeants Bowers, Walker, and Rangitira.

Colonel Warren tried again to catch the eye of Lieutenant Roberts, who was presently fielding another question from Captain Von Tempsky. The colonel was eager to see the meeting end, and if the young officer was interested in furthering his career, it would be advisable to heed the colonel and conclude the meeting at his earliest convenience. Feeling a less-than-friendly eye on him, Lieutenant Roberts glanced at his commanding officer and was greeted with a raised eyebrow and a frown – not a good sign.

"Well, gentlemen, I wish you the best of luck. I'm sure you have more important things to attend to…" stated Roberts, taking the less-than-subtle hint.

"One more question, Lieutenant?" Von Tempsky asked.

The scraping of a chair prevented Captain Von Tempsky from finishing as Colonel Warren rose quickly. "Captain, I look forward to some positive results, eh. I'm sure you and your men are more than capable of accomplishing your mission with a high degree of success." He shook hands with Von Tempsky, ignored the others, and quickly left the room.

Lieutenant Roberts gathered his papers, offered an apologetic look, and followed the colonel out into the late-afternoon sun.

Captain Von Tempsky leaned back in his chair. His hand went to his moustache and began the compulsive twirl. The sergeants all stood and stretched their legs.

"So, Colonel Warren believes the rebels have retreated south and deep into the bush to avoid contact with the superior troop strength of the 57th Regiment. That surprises me a little," said the captain. "What do you think?" He looked to his sergeants.

Sergeant-Major Bowers, the most senior, spoke first. "Makes sense to me, Captain. They fled when the shelling began, and apart from the one attack near the redoubt, no one has seen hide nor hair of them. Why would they loiter and risk encountering an overwhelming force when they could regroup elsewhere and plan further attacks?"

Walker nodded in agreement. "It would be foolish to linger here. We should focus our efforts on heading them off where they are likely to regroup and pose a further threat."

Von Tempsky nodded.

Sergeant-Major Bowers turned to Moana, "Ira?"

"Lieutenant Roberts said that the 57th's scouts found no sign of the rebels. In fact, he said they had just disappeared," Moana said.

"Then we should try to determine where they will regroup and head them off, as Eric suggests," the captain affirmed, acknowledging Walker's recommendation.

Moana shook his head. "If you were retreating quickly, would you take the time and effort to hide all signs that you'd been there? That seems strange to me. If I were in the rebels' shoes and chose to stay close by and remain hidden, I would want to remove all signs of my men. Otherwise, it is meaningless, sir," Moana replied.

"Good point, Ira," said Von Tempsky, who turned to Small. "Lieutenant?

Surprised to be asked for his opinion, Lieutenant Small was briefly at a loss for words. "Ah, I ... Um, Sergeant Rangitira, how much effort would it take to mask all the tracks and signs of ..." Small checked his notes. "Um, Lieutenant Roberts estimates there were only about twenty rebels who remained behind to fight after the others withdrew, so would it require a lot of work to hide all tracks of, say, twenty rebels travelling through the bush?"

"Good question, Lieutenant," replied Moana. Small couldn't hide his smile. "Actually, twenty men travelling through the bush would leave a lot of signs. It would take a fair bit of work to remove all their tracks."

"Then I agree with Sergeant Rangitira, captain," replied Lieutenant Small.

"You'd go against the recommendation of Colonel Warren, Lieutenant Roberts, and Sergeants Bowers and Walker?" asked Von Tempsky, curious.

"Um, yes, sir."

"Very well. Lieutenant Griggs, your thoughts?"

"I think they have all left the area, sir," replied Griggs confidently.

Von Tempsky's hand returned to his moustache as he considered his options. After a few minutes of silence, he made a decision. "I think we should advise Colonel Warren that there is a high possibility that *Māori* rebels remain in the area and pose an immediate threat to the operations of the 57th. But we will focus our attention on locating the rebels' rally point, as we have been ordered to do. If any information becomes available that proves the rebels are still in the area, as Ira suggests, then we will act accordingly and begin scouting locally." The captain turned to look at the faces of the men in the room. "It's all we can do. Any questions?"

No one responded.

"Advise your men we will leave an hour before daybreak. Dismissed. The evening is yours, gentlemen. Ira, remain behind so we can speak to Colonel Warren and inform him."

Colonel Warren predictably wasn't available. Instead, Lieutenant Roberts met with the two Forest Rangers. Moana explained his reasoning for believing that rebel *Māori* remained in the area.

"You raise a good point, Sergeant," said Roberts. "Captain Boyd is scheduled to begin further operations on local *pa* and crops near Oakura and Te Ahuahu within a few days – we should advise him." Roberts looked over his shoulder towards a nearby building. "I just saw him a few moments ago. Please, come with me."

Roberts quickly led Captain Von Tempsky and Moana to the regimental office and introduced them to a large man with a ruddy complexion, wearing the uniform of a captain. The four men were alone in the office. Lieutenant Roberts asked Moana to repeat to Captain Boyd what he'd told him.

"Utter nonsense, sergeant. That's an absurd suggestion. Rebel *Māori* have retreated from this region and are now running for their lives. Even if they did remain, the superior skills of my men far outweigh the bush tactics of illiterate natives. We have absolutely nothing to fear," he said dismissively. "Now, if you will excuse me, I have more important matters to attend to. Good day," he nodded to Von Tempsky, indicating the meeting was over.

Captain Ewen Boyd wasn't having a spectacular day. He'd requested that his mission be delayed by twenty-four hours – and been refused. Mrs Boyd hadn't spent the night with her husband for about a week and was desperately missing him. Although he'd managed to find time during the day to quickly go home and visit her. She insisted that he ask Colonel Warren to postpone his mission so they could spend an evening together. The insensitive Colonel Warren, as Mrs Boyd described her husband's commanding officer, declined the request, which put Mrs Boyd in a rather disagreeable mood. Unable to appease his wife's volatile temperament, Captain Boyd's mood now matched that of his spouse.

"Captain, may I suggest you listen carefully to my sergeant's advice?" appealed Von Tempsky. "It may save countless lives."

Captain Boyd looked from Von Tempsky to Moana, then back to Von Tempsky, ignoring the lieutenant. "It appears to me, Captain, that your implausible story is nothing more than a gratuitous attempt to avoid real soldiering. And why, pray tell, would I believe the word of a native? For all you know, he is a rebel himself!" said Captain Boyd, pointing at Moana.

Before Moana could react, Captain Von Tempsky whipped his arm in front of him, preventing Moana from moving against the captain. He then stepped forward and placed himself directly between Moana and Boyd.

"Lieutenant Roberts, please escort Sergeant Rangitira outside and wait for me there!" ordered Von Tempsky in a clipped tone. The sound of his voice was enough for both Moana and the lieutenant to obey instantly.

Moana's eyes were slits. He paused and gave Captain Boyd a long hard look before he slowly turned and walked from the office. Lieutenant Roberts, in astonishment, followed closely.

Von Tempsky waited for both men to leave the room, keeping his gaze locked on the much larger Captain Boyd. "I just saved your life, Captain. You have no idea how close you came to death just now," spat Von Tempsky, leaning forward. Captain Boyd took an involuntary step back and hit the wall. "Next time you insult one of my men, I will regard it as a personal affront against me, and you will not be forgiven - regulations be damned! Consider that your final warning," Von Tempsky turned and walked to the door, eager to be gone from the detestable man.

Captain Boyd laughed. "It is true what they say about you, isn't it? You're nothing but a popinjay playing at soldiering."

Von Tempsky spun and dropped into a crouch, his left hand a blur. In a single underhand motion, he reached for the knife at his belt and threw it. The highly polished blade spun through the air, streaking towards Captain Boyd's face. With a loud whack, the knife embedded itself in the roughly hewn timber wall, only inches from the bewildered captain's head. The blade still vibrated as Von Tempsky quickly followed. He extracted the knife and placed it carefully back in its sheath on his hip. He strode from the room without saying another word. Captain Boyd's ruddy complexion turned a darker shade of red, more closely resembling scarlet. He was sweating profusely, and the realisation that he had come close to death twice in as many minutes was only just beginning to dawn on him.

"I'm sorry about that, Sergeant. I tried," Lieutenant Roberts apologised as Von Tempsky left the building and walked the few steps towards them.

Moana could see a vein on the captain's neck pulsing, his mouth a thin, compressed line.

"You're fairly certain the rebels haven't withdrawn and remain in this area, aren't you, Ira?" asked the captain, remaining tight-lipped about what had transpired inside the office.

"Based on the evidence from the lieutenant, yes, Captain."

Von Tempsky turned to Lieutenant Roberts and waited for his response.

"If what you suspect is true, sergeant, then God help the men of the 57th. The rebels who hide in this vicinity will be intent on revenge, while your Company pointlessly chases shadows in the south," stated Lieutenant Roberts, shaking his head.

The local Public Hotel was nearly full. Mr Conner, the harried publican, was pouring drinks as fast as he could, while his staff tried to deliver drinks and meals to satisfy the voracious thirst and appetites of his demanding customers. The room was mostly filled with soldiers, with only a few locals, and normal conversation was almost impossible. Groups of soldiers shouted over one another to be heard, while troops at adjacent tables tried even harder to be understood. Somehow, everyone managed to communicate, keeping the mood jolly.

Moana was tucked away in a far corner of the large room, safely out of harm's way, nursing another beer as he chatted amicably with an older *Māori*, a successful farmer he'd befriended. The old farmer, though friendly, was reluctant to talk much about his past and deftly avoided the inevitable topic of the land wars. With the late-afternoon incident with Captain Boyd largely forgotten, Moana was in a jovial mood. It was easier to chat in the nook, and Moana and the old man enjoyed each other's company. They talked of superficial things while they watched the antics of young soldiers enjoying a Saturday evening of well-earned liberty.

Moana noticed a young woman pushing her way through the rowdy patrons and walking towards him. She wasn't the only woman in the hotel; there were others. Many were either married or obviously attached, and the few single women of questionable virtue, looking for customers, held no immediate interest for him. This young woman didn't appear to be the type to solicit men and was unescorted. He watched her weave through the smoky haze with growing interest, and as she approached, he could see her more clearly.

She was beautiful in an elegant way and carried herself with poise and confidence, nor was she fearful or intimidated by the lustful stares of soldiers she passed. Without giving Moana a second look, she walked up to the old farmer, slid her arm through his, lowered her head, and spoke loudly into his ear. She stood almost directly in front of Moana, so close that he could smell her fragrance as she attempted to communicate with the older man.

The farmer shook his head – he didn't want to leave just yet. She raised her voice in frustration, believing, as women often do, that a raised voice is more likely to achieve results. Unswayed by the increased volume of her request, the farmer remained adamant and shook his head again. The young woman straightened, her displeasure and growing anger obvious to any sober person. Sadly, Moana and the farmer were far from sober. If Moana thought there was even a faint glimmer of hope that he and this lovely woman shared common interests and that a future of romance and passion awaited them, as he believed possible - he was horribly mistaken.

He leaned forward and shouted helpfully into her ear - the obvious. "He doesn't want to go!"

Unimpressed by his unsolicited observation, she looked him up and down as if he were a curious oddity, a cretin. With a dismissive flick of her hair, she turned back to the old man and bellowed into his ear again. The old man reached up and, with the feeble strength of a drunk, gently pushed her away, then tilted unsteadily towards Moana.

"Bloody woman, she won't listen!"

Moana readily agreed, having already arrived at the same conclusion. He turned towards the woman to speak to her again. "He wants to stay here!" he pleaded.

She didn't appear to have heard.

Moana shouted in the farmer's ear, "You want me to get rid of her, Tami?"

Tami Henare nodded enthusiastically and grinned.

Moana stood, swaying unsteadily, and gently put his arm around her shoulder to steer her away. "Take me instead," he offered, believing she would see his suggestion as an unselfish act of gallant chivalry.

She drove her shoe down firmly on his foot, sending a shooting pain up his leg. Satisfied with the result, she pushed her finger into his chest and spoke to him for the first time. Moana heard every word with perfect clarity, "Mind – your – business – Sergeant!"

Unable to form an appropriate response, Moana meekly returned to his stool.

The Field Exercise and Evolutions of Infantry manual, most frequently referred to as the 'Field Exercise book', contains many useful titbits of information. A good soldier may unexpectedly find himself in a difficult and awkward situation and require guidance that complies with army regulations. Buried in its voluminous pages, the manual offers solutions for a host of scenarios. However, the manual's learned authors were remiss in omitting a chapter on how to deal with a persistent, stubborn young lady intent on asserting her will.

Unsure what to do, Moana swallowed, and as the pain in his foot subsided, he turned to the farmer for direction. The old man was enjoying Moana's discomfort and was overcome with laughter. Inebriation impairs judgement, and Moana's judgement was severely diminished. Unwisely, he joined the old farmer in laughter.

With deliberation, the young *Māori* woman slowly turned her attention back to him, with the same fluidity of motion and purpose as a predatory animal about to deliver the coup de grâce to its prey. With a smile that didn't reach her eyes, she stepped closer to Moana, and again he inhaled her fragrance. He took a deep breath, nearly falling off his stool.

"What's your name?" she asked.

Proud of his recovery, Moana naively replied, "Moana Rangitira. My friends call me Ira." He flashed her his winning smile, normally reserved for special occasions.

She nodded slowly. "Who are you with?" she pointed to his uniform.

"Forest Rangers, Company No. 2," Moana figured his winning smile and charm had already worked wonders and saw no valid reason not to employ the same tactic again.

In preparation for the lethal strike, she extended a finger into the air, then curled it towards herself, an indication that she wanted him to come closer. Needing no further encouragement, Moana leaned precariously forward, like a lamb to slaughter, taking in her scent and admiring the curls of her seductive, long, coal-black hair as it swept over her shoulders and clung to the contours of her upper body.

She sprung the trap. "Now I know whom to avoid, Sergeant Rangitira. If you ever see me again, it will be in error!"

Unable to contain himself, the old man, overcome with laughter, wobbled and was in serious danger of falling from his stool. He wiped his teary eyes with one hand while the other clutched the table as he roared with delight.

Moana felt his cheeks flush, and his mouth hung open as she fixed him with a look that left no doubt about the seriousness of her intentions.

She turned back to Tami Henare and gave him the same look. His laughter stopped immediately.

"Papa, it's time to come home - now!"

Realising he could no longer forestall the inevitable, the farmer eased himself off his stool, teetered uncertainly for a moment, looked at Moana with a grin, and said, "Close your mouth, boy," before laughing uncontrollably again.

Obediently, Moana closed his mouth and leaned close to the old man. "What's her name?"

"That's Wiki. Isn't she something?" he said proudly with a laugh as his daughter linked arms with him and began to lead him towards the door. Wisely, the hotel's patrons made room.

Moana didn't move, transfixed, staring at the place where he had last seen her. His mouth fell into its familiar open position. Never had he been so captivated by a woman.

CHAPTER NINE

Captive

Moana plunged his head into the stream beneath the small waterfall, which cascaded freely over multicoloured moss and lichen-covered rocks. The water was cold, *bloody freezing,* he thought as he vigorously rubbed his scalp, hoping to shock his body into normality. It helped a little. The pounding in his head eased, and with a grimace, he carefully lowered his head back into the water to drink. Satiated, he slowly rose from the rocks where he lay and winced as he stood. He took a few deep breaths to steady himself. Still dripping, he turned to Taikaha with a resigned sigh, "Let's go."

Taikaha wisely kept his expression neutral, rose from the fallen tree he had sat on, and followed Moana as he headed deeper into the bowery of ferns and leafy trees. The sun, not long risen, failed to fully penetrate the canopy above them, but as it woke to its presence, the bush came alive with sound. Already, a fantail arrived to forage for insects amongst the dead leaves the two men had disturbed with their feet. Its dainty twittering was so different from the Tui that chattered and clacked high in the branches above them.

In addition to his new responsibilities as an instructor, Captain Von Tempsky appointed Moana chief scout. Moana immediately chose nine of the most capable Rangers and formed three scouting teams of two men each – all were *Māori.* Four men were held in reserve with the main group and kept on rotation. Each scouting team headed in a different direction, well ahead of Captain Von Tempsky and the remainder of the Company and attempted to locate any sign of rebel *Māori* who had passed through the area. They would meet the main group at a predetermined location in five hours, unless they found signs of the rebels. In that case, one of the two scouts would remain in contact and continue tracking them, while the other would immediately report back to the Company. That morning, Moana selected Taikaha as his partner. Perhaps the least experienced of the scouts, Taikaha struggled to maintain visual contact with Moana.

Even though the sun had partially risen, the bush was still very dark. Moana took advantage of the shadows and seemed to dissolve into them without a sound. Taikaha found it difficult to keep pace with his sergeant while remaining stealthy; his footsteps, by comparison, seemed loud. However, he would do his best and, hopefully, impress his sergeant.

Moana privately felt this mission was a waste of time and that his scouts would find no tracks. He believed that rebel *Māori* remained in the Kaitake or Oakura area to the north and intended to attack soldiers using hit-and-run tactics. Colonel Warren and Lieutenant Roberts were wrong to believe the rebels had retreated in this direction. However, orders were orders, and he would obey.

Moana and Taikaha crept up a steep ridge and now lay hidden beneath an umbrella of small ferns and low-growing bushes that grew in abundance near the wind-exposed summit. Moana suggested they wait a while and watch. This location afforded them a commanding view, and anyone nearby would see them easily from their elevated position. Taikaha immediately began sweeping his head from one side of the valley to the other. Moana nudged him and shook his head.

"Do not look at shadows and then at the bright light. Your eyes will not adjust to the changes between light and darkness; you will not see everything. Watch only the shadows, I will look at the bright open areas," he instructed.

Taikaha nodded in understanding as Moana explained the area that he should focus on. Moana slowly began searching in the area where the sun shone directly and where it was lighter. He began to think about the previous evening and the fool he made of himself to Wiki. He could kick himself for acting like an idiot– that woman was special. He allowed himself a smile, the throbbing in his head temporarily forgotten.

A brief flash of colour in his peripheral vision drew his gaze to the left. He nudged Taikaha and, without raising an arm, indicated with his head where Taikaha should look. Again, it appeared, moving slowly from left to right across their position, heading south. It was a man stumbling across the valley floor.

With impatience, Taikaha began to climb over the ridge to pursue. Moana placed an arm on his shoulder to restrain him.

"Wait and observe. Watch to see where he is going. If we are patient and clever, he will come to us," Moana whispered cautiously, in case the breeze carried her voice.

Both scouts watched from their secure shelter as the man shuffled through the bush. They saw him stumble and fall, only to pick himself up and press on. He made no effort to hide or keep quiet as he crashed through the undergrowth. After a few minutes, his route became clear.

"See, by waiting, we now know where he goes. He follows the stream. We passed that stream earlier, so we will return to that place and wait for him," Moana offered as he began to slide slowly backwards, dropping from sight.

Taikaha followed. Once clear of the ridge, he stood, brushing leaves and twigs from his clothes, as Moana stepped forward, placed an arm on his shoulder, and looked closely into his face.

"Are you ready?"

With seriousness, the young Ranger nodded, "Yes, Sergeant."

Without another word, Moana was gone, moving quickly down the hill with Taikaha in pursuit. Within seconds, they reached the valley floor and headed south, following a parallel path to that of their quarry. Taikaha pulled up – Moana had disappeared. Panic began to rise. Taikaha couldn't see his sergeant; he'd just vanished. A leaf moved, then again. A signal. Taikaha reached over and carefully pulled a fern frond, revealing Moana crouching out of sight amongst a shroud of ferns and expansive fronds. Moana turned to him with a wide grin, urging him to enter the natural hide.

They didn't have to wait long. The irregular sound of footsteps and ragged breathing alerted them long before they saw the warrior approach. He ran directly towards them, stumbling, exhausted and wounded. Just as it seemed the warrior would pass them, Moana stepped out from concealment, lunged forward, grabbed the injured man by the shoulders, and pulled him back to the ground. Remembering his role, Taikaha ran from behind the fern, drew his Bowie knife, and knelt near the head of the fallen man, the knife at the man's throat.

"He won't give us any trouble – he's badly wounded and has lost a lot of blood," said Moana.

The warrior weakly opened his eyes and blinked uncertainly, his fear evident. Moana stood over him as Taikaha kept the knife pressed against the wounded warrior's skin.

"I think Captain Von Tempsky will enjoy the pleasure of his company," said Moana.

As the days progressed, the scouting teams crept deeper into the hills. They crossed exposed ridges, slithered through cold streams, and crawled under rotting logs, finding nothing but abandoned *pa* sites and infrequently used paths. Far behind, Captain Von Tempsky and the remainder of the Company followed. They quietly journeyed further, deeper into remote areas. Morale was low, and the men had little faith in their orders to search this region; their progress was further slowed by the wounded rebel they carried on a makeshift litter. They believed, as Sergeant Rangitira, Ira, as everyone now called him, did, that he was right in his assessment that the rebels were lying in wait near the small community of Oakura.

Their prisoner was dying. He'd been gut-shot by a musket that damaged organs as it passed through his body. Sadly, there was nothing anyone could do for him. The festering wound oozed pus and was painfully swollen and inflamed. The rum they gave him proved ineffectual against the searing pain and infection. Wracked by fever, he grew weaker, and the captain was certain he would not survive another twenty-four hours.

Although reluctant at first, their captive eventually talked. He knew he was dying, and Von Tempsky skilfully encouraged him to speak without resorting to physical persuasion. As the prisoner explained, he'd fought alongside Paora at the Kaitake *pa* and had been shot as the last *Māori* retreated. Assuming he was dead, the rebels abandoned him. Eventually crawling to safety, he evaded capture by first climbing a tree, then taking a long, circuitous route, thereby avoiding patrols until he was captured by Ranger scouts. With a little further coaxing, the prisoner reluctantly provided more useful information to Captain Von Tempsky until he became incoherent and overcome by delirium. Unable to receive adequate medical care, he died during the night, just as the captain had predicted.

Everyone was constantly wet. Clothes and blankets were damp, and they had consumed the three days' worth of food they brought with them and were now eating from the land. At night, most slept on a bed of ferns, under sodden blankets suspended above them. Moana ordered the scouting teams to stay away from the camp and remain vigilant, just in case more rebels were in the area and travelling at night. Without exception, the entire Company was exhausted, dirty and frustrated. When the captain finally ordered the scouts to turn northwards, leading them back towards civilisation, the Company eagerly followed with renewed vigour.

CHAPTER TEN

The Surprise

One hundred and one men, comprising No. 1 Company, Grenadiers, of the 57th Regiment, and No. 9 Company of the Taranaki Military Settlers, under the command of Captain Ewen Boyd, marched with confidence towards Te Ahuahu, a small settlement near Oakura, from which the contingent had originally departed. Under orders from Colonel Warren, they were to destroy all rebel crops and force rebellious *Māori* from the area. Distinguishing dissident *Māori* from friendly *Māori* was purely interpretive, and Captain Boyd decided that any substantial crops he encountered tended by *Māori* must, therefore, be rebel crops. As ordered, he would destroy them with efficient ease.

Having recently arrived from England, Ewen Boyd intended to impress his superiors. After all, his superior training and background would expose the shortcomings of colonials and their unprofessional backwater ways. "They will remember me," he frequently reminded his wife – and he wouldn't be wrong.

As the track narrowed, a scout returned to inform Captain Boyd that the fields and crops he sought were only a short distance away. Ordering his force to split, he sent a platoon to circle the six-acre field they were approaching. Once everyone was in position, both forces would attack simultaneously from different sides. Early reconnaissance revealed a few rifle pits and trenches defending the nearby *pa*; his larger group would overrun those positions.

Not far from where Captain Boyd's men waited, a small cottage sat on a low hill overlooking the track. It had a well-tended small garden that grew mostly herbs and a few decorative flowers, and was surrounded by a rickety fence. Beside the cottage, enclosed by a hedge, a moderately-sized field grew a variety of vegetables that were sold at the local market or to locals who came to purchase directly from the farmer. Separated by dense bush, the field was not part of the *pa* and did not provide food to the rebels. Deemed inconsequential by the staff officers at headquarters, Captain Boyd decided to ignore the small farm.

As soldiers passed by the cottage, its occupants couldn't help but notice the unusual sight of a Company of soldiers preparing for battle. With some concern, the *Māori* farmer stepped from his doorway to watch from the veranda. His daughter arrived at his side a few moments later, and in the field, the farmer's three sons paused their work and raised their heads in growing alarm.

Captain Boyd took the opportunity to rest his men as he watched the platoon enter the thick bush surrounding the pa's fields. Although they'd only travelled a short distance, the corpulent captain never pushed his troops hard and wisely avoided over-exertion himself. Weapons were casually discarded as soldiers either sat on the grass or talked quietly amongst themselves. Some drank to quench their thirst.

Only yards away, expertly concealed, lay almost twenty of *Pai Marire*'s fanatical and militant rebels, whom Europeans called *Hauhau*. They waited patiently for a signal to attack.

Te Ua's favourite disciples, Hatotoi, Paora, Tohu and the newly converted Kaihoka Te Hua, observed Captain Boyd's detachment split and enter the bush. This was fortunate for the *Hauhau,* as it meant fewer soldiers to engage. Hatotoi waited until the platoon was as far from them as possible before giving the attack signal. The four disciples were surprised by the soldiers' lack of alertness and felt blessed as they watched them rest without weapons in hand. "T'was an omen from God," one later suggested.

Hatotoi turned to Kaihoka and whispered the reaffirmation Te Ua preached so often into his ear, "If we wait, they will come to us. God will deliver them into our hands."

Kaihoka nodded and smiled. Again, Te Ua made an accurate prediction, his powers an undeniable gift from God through the archangel Gabriel. Kaihoka turned to face the warriors behind him and gave a warning signal to prepare and stand ready. Silently, they moved into their rehearsed positions, flanking the resting soldiers. They were slightly elevated and would shoot down on the unsuspecting troops. In addition to a variety of well-used muskets, many of which were in poor condition, all the *Hauhau* carried knives, an assortment of clubs, small hatchets and revolvers. They were well-armed, motivated and ready. With infinite patience, Hatotoi delayed giving the signal; he waited, judging the moment carefully. If he gave the order too soon, the detachment could turn back and arrive quickly to offer support. If he delayed, the soldiers in front of him would begin to retrieve their weapons in preparation for their attack - timing was crucial.

Even though they rested, many of the grenadiers of the 57th Regiment were tense. Some of the veteran soldiers were uneasy, and a few stood, looking nervously around, sensing something was wrong. Captain Boyd showed no interest in the surroundings and was content to chew on some dried meat. A horse snickered and stamped a hoof. The ever-present birds fled, their tweeting and chirping conspicuous in their absence.

Hatotoi knew he could wait no longer. He raised his arm, making sure everyone could see. His warriors were ready. With a chopping motion, he dropped his hand. Immediately, the bush overlooking the resting soldiers was engulfed in smoke as the rebels discharged their weapons. Some misfired; others missed their targets completely, but many warriors were skilled enough to hit the unsuspecting troops. Soldiers fell. Some ran in disorganised panic, unsure where to go.

Captain Boyd reacted with surprising speed, diving into a shallow depression on the far side of the track. Men in agony screamed and bled. Unable to reach their weapons to return fire, many soldiers were helpless. Those who could run fled in all directions. Warriors leapt from the bush, brandishing knives and clubs, and immediately set upon those too slow to respond, silencing those who cried for their mothers or begged to be spared. A few of the severely wounded awaited their fate, numb and aware of the finality of the end.

Possessed by hatred and fuelled by the memory of his wife and children, so recently slaughtered by soldiers in the Waikato, Kaihoka plunged his knife between the ribs of a young soldier. He twisted the blade aggressively and pulled it out with a gush of blood. He stepped over the body as it twitched in the final throes of death and stalked towards Captain Boyd. Unable to offer any resistance to the enraged warrior, the captain lay in the depression and raised his hands in supplication. Intent on revenge, Kaihoka ignored his pleas, his eyes emotionless and dark as he appraised the cowering officer. With clinical precision, he swept aside the captain's hands, straddled him and plunged the still-dripping knife deep into Captain Boyd's chest. The captain's screams ended abruptly as blood welled up into his mouth and flowed down his chin to indelibly stain the immaculate uniform he wore so proudly. Driven by religious fanaticism, Kaihoka wasn't content to just kill the captain - he continued to defile him even in death. Repeating the names of his wife and children in an endless prayer, he began sawing at the neck, the sharp knife struggling to cut through tissue and grating against bone. Eventually, with the aid of a hatchet and a couple of quick blows, he severed the captain's head.

Seeing Kaihoka decapitate the officer, Paora decided he would follow suit and began sawing and hacking at the neck of the soldier he had just killed. Many bodies were stripped of clothing, and the heads of Captain Boyd and Private Granger were held in the air and displayed like trophies. Still caught up in the fury of revenge and fanaticism, Kaihoka raised his other hand, which still held the hatchet and licked the dripping blood from the weapon. Paora did the same. Warriors cheered.

The short battle was over; it had lasted mere minutes, and now it was time to leave before help arrived. The rebels could already hear the platoon returning, crashing through the bush, hurrying to offer support. Hatotoi yelled loudly, his cry of victory breaking the hypnotic, morbid spell that held his warriors in the evil grip of grotesque violence. Taking their grisly trophies, the *Hauhau* disappeared into the bush and vanished. Seven naked bodies lay on the track; two were headless, and twelve were wounded survivors. The remainder managed to escape unharmed.

Forest Ranger Company No. 2 emerged from the bush late the previous day and was immediately ordered by Colonel Warren to find and prosecute the *Pai Marire* rebels. He believed the last attack had gone awry for them, as their real intention was to ambuscade Governor Grey, who frequently passed through this area.

Lieutenant Roberts, Colonel Warren's intelligence officer, was investigating the ambush site and taking notes, while Captain Von

Tempsky and the rest of the Company were looking for tracks and scouting the area.

Moana jumped down from the bank where the rebels were concealed and walked to Captain Von Tempsky, who was discussing rebel tactics with Lieutenant Roberts.

"Ira?"

"The tracks have mostly been trampled, but I don't believe there were more than twenty rebels. They'd been hiding for quite some time, sir. I'd estimate at least a couple of days. The tracks lead eastward towards the Kaitake Ranges."

"Then it seems entirely possible that they were, in fact, waiting to waylay the Governor. If they were prepared to wait that long, they must have believed he was coming through here," said Lieutenant Roberts.

Moana made eye contact with Von Tempsky. The captain gave an imperceptible nod for Moana to continue.

"Lieutenant, if the rebels were lucky enough to learn that the Governor was passing through here, they would surely have known which day he would come. If they waited two whole days and risked detection, I believe they had no idea. Also, their force was too small to fight the Governor's experienced soldiers. No, sir, the rebels were opportunistic and here for other reasons– they were waiting for soldiers, just not the Governor's. It was a neatly executed and very successful ambuscade."

The Lieutenant looked carefully at Moana and slowly nodded as he digested Moana's assessment. "Your argument has merit. But … how did they know troops would pass through here?"

Moana shook his head, "Can't tell ya, Lieutenant. Maybe someone told them?"

Just then, one of Sergeant Walker's troops came running down the track. "Captain, sir. Sergeant Walker sends his compliments and begs your presence up there, sir." The Ranger pointed to the small cottage on the hill.

"What seems to be the problem?" asked Von Tempsky.

"The residents of that house aren't being helpful, sir, and are proving a mite difficult. It's getting a little unpleasant."

"Very well, I expect we should go and calm the locals, eh? Care to join me, Lieutenant Ira?"

The four men walked along the path towards the cottage on the low rise that partially overlooked the site of recent slaughter. As they approached, the sound of Sergeant Walker's raised voice could be clearly heard.

"Perhaps we should calm the sergeant?" Moana offered wryly.

Von Tempsky turned, giving Moana a look. Moana smiled and shrugged. The captain shook his head, trying to hide his grin.

Moana trailed the other men as he carefully assessed the surroundings. He could not see the occupants of the cottage but could easily hear the argument as they drew near. The house was well-maintained and attached to a field that produced healthy crops.

On reaching the cottage, Moana looked up. His heart skipped a beat. Standing directly in front of him was Wiki. Beside her stood her father, Tami, and both looked distressed. Wiki appeared as surprised to see Moana as he was to see her. Her father, obviously relieved to see Moana arrive, nodded in greeting, the look of concern and worry evident on them both.

"Ira," said Tami with relief.

"This is Mr Tami Henare and his daughter, Miss Wikitoria, sir," offered Walker.

Captain Von Tempsky shook hands with the farmer, nodded courteously to Wiki, and introduced Lieutenant Roberts. There was no need to introduce Moana.

"Now, what seems to be the problem, Sergeant?"

"Well, sir, I believe these people may be involved in the ambush," stated Sergeant Walker. "And they're not being helpful or answering my questions."

"Neither would I," replied the captain coldly. "What makes you suspect their involvement?"

"Ahh, well, sir, the house's location in relation to the Ahuahu *pa*, where the rebels hid, and the fact that they are *Māori*. They may have been providing the rebels with food and intelligence, sir."

"That's untrue!" said Wiki. She glared at Sergeant Walker.

Tami looked uncomfortable; he wasn't thrilled about being accused of aiding and abetting rebels.

Von Tempsky held up his hand to signal Wiki to wait. He turned back to Walker. "What possible intelligence could these people have provided the rebels?" he asked, raising an eyebrow.

The farmer and Wiki watched on in puzzlement. Moana watched Wiki from the corner of his eye. He felt his heart pounding. *Why does this woman affect me so much?*

Lieutenant Roberts awaited Walker's response. A small smile played across his face.

"Well, uh, you know sir, could be anything, couldn't it?"

"Hmmm, thank you, sergeant. Ira, I believe you are known to these people?"

Moana pointed towards the farmer, "I know Tami, sir," then inclined his head to Wiki, "I believe we have met, although today it must be in error."

Wiki's cheeks flushed, and she folded her arms tightly across her chest.

Captain Von Tempsky gave Moana another sidelong glance, then turned to the farmer. "Mr Henare, are you involved in any rebel activity?"

Wiki began to interrupt.

"Miss, please," cautioned Von Tempsky.

"No, captain, we don't support the rebel cause or their false religion," replied Tami quickly.

"Did you witness the battle?"

"We watched the soldiers waiting. When we heard musket fire, we all went inside for protection. We didn't know what was happening." Tami swallowed. "If I'd known what was going to happen, I'd have warned the soldiers." He shook his head, the recent memory of the brutality all too vivid.

"Did you recognise any rebels?" Moana asked.

"Yes, perhaps two of them, Kaihoka Te Hua and Big Pete. I did not know the others."

"Who is Big Pete?" asked Lieutenant Roberts.

"He is also known as Te Maha. I have seen him around here quite a bit," the farmer volunteered. "He's always snooping around, a bit of a troublemaker, that one."

Von Tempsky turned to Roberts, who shrugged, obviously unfamiliar with the name.

"Anything else we should know?" asked the captain.

"Just get the bastards," spat Tami.

"You've been very helpful, Mr Henare and Miss Wikitoria. Thank you," said Captain Von Tempsky, satisfied that the farmers and family were not involved in or abetting rebel *Māori*.

Von Tempsky turned to Sergeant Walker. "Sergeant, if this family had been providing rebels with food and intelligence, do you believe the rebels would have hidden in the bush for two days, waiting to ambuscade our troops, when they could have just waited here?"

"No, sir, probably not."

He raised his eyebrows in question. "And again, what kind of intelligence could this family have provided?"

"I can't think of any, sir," Walker said sullenly.

The relief was evident on Tami's face.

"This is why I don't believe they were involved. Perhaps you could ask Mr Henare for the names of his sons," smiled Von Tempsky.

Walker turned to Mr Henare with curiosity.

"My eldest son is called Charles, my middle son is called James, and Henry is my youngest," the old farmer said proudly.

Walker turned back to Von Tempsky. "Uh, they're all named after English kings, sir."

"Is the *Māori* father who names his children after English royalty likely to be a rebel?"

"No, sir, not likely at all, but how did you know?"

"Sergeant Walker, I make it my business to know," he replied with a smile.

Moana and Lieutenant Roberts looked at each other in surprise.

The old farmer and his daughter both visibly relaxed.

Von Tempsky apologised, thanked the family, and then departed. Moana lingered behind. He was unsure what to say and looked down at the ground near his feet for divine guidance.

"Good thing you turned up, Ira," said the farmer. "That sergeant wasn't the friendliest."

"Captain Von Tempsky and Lieutenant Roberts are good men. I'm pleased there are no problems," Moana replied.

The old man nodded. Sensing Moana wanted to be alone to talk to his daughter, he said, "Well, I've got things to do. See you again?"

"Yes, I hope so, but next time I'll drink less."

Tami Henare laughed as he walked inside the cottage leaving Moana and Wiki alone.

Feeling awkward Moana kicked a stone and risked a quick look at Wiki. She was watching him closely.

After a moment or two, she broke the silence. "You thought you were clever, didn't you?"

Moana looked up. Again, he was struck by her presence. Perhaps she was the most beautiful woman he'd ever seen. "What do you mean?" he asked quietly.

"We met in error?"

Moana felt his face redden. "I remember you stomping on my foot and telling me that the next time we met, it would be in error."

Captain Von Tempsky was walking down the path to the track. He turned and looked over his shoulder and could see Moana talking with the young lady. *He's smitten*, he thought. *Wonders never cease.*

Wiki appraised the handsome young man before her. He spoke well, was educated, and could probably even read and write the *Pākeha* language, she thought. She could see he felt self-conscious, and she accurately judged him to be intelligent and quick-witted. In front of the officers, he appeared comfortable and wasn't intimidated by them as many soldiers were, and it was also obvious the officers respected and liked him. She watched him kick a stone with his foot like a small boy.

"Perhaps the next time we meet, it won't be in error, Mr Rangitira."

"My friends call me Ira."

"We're not friends," she smiled, "Enjoy your day."

Moana watched her turn and walk inside. He marvelled at how she could make her skirts swish to and fro as she moved. She stopped in the doorway, turned her head and smiled. He wiped his sweaty hands on his breeches, then remembered to close his mouth.

Captain Von Tempsky ordered his exhausted men back into the bush. With less than twenty-four hours' rest, his men were again searching for renegade *Māori*. The *Hauhau* made only a token effort to hide their tracks, and the Rangers followed with ease but could not gain ground on the fresher warriors, who had almost a twenty-four-hour head start. While Moana's scouts could keep pace with the renegades, Company No. 2 was having difficulty. They were tired and hungry, and the distance continued to widen; it was futile to maintain the brutal pace, and the strain was beginning to tell.

After another torturously long day, the Rangers were no closer to their fleeing quarry. Disappointed, Moana and his scouting team rejoined the main group and studied a map with Captain Von Tempsky, hoping to find an easier, faster way to gain ground on the renegades.

"We believe the rebels are heading here, Captain," said Moana, pointing to the community of Waitotara, which lay about four days away.

"Why Waitotara?" asked the captain in puzzlement.

"If they keep heading in this direction, they'll end up there, and the prisoner mentioned Waitotara a couple of times. I thought nothing of it, but then I heard some locals say they believed followers of the *Pai Marire* religion were gathering there at the Wereroa *pa*, the home of their spiritual leader, Te Ua."

"The locals …" The captain looked distracted for a moment. "So you believe the rebels are linked to this new religion?"

Moana nodded. "Maybe. Remember, Mr Henare thought so. There are all sorts of crazy stories. Frankly, I don't know, but the mutilations aren't normal, sir. Could have something to do with that."

"Does anyone know how many warriors are gathering at the Wereroa *pa*?" the captain looked at each man.

"I'd heard they could be in the hundreds, sir," stated Tane.

"What do we know about this *Pai Marire* group? Should the Government be concerned?" Von Tempsky turned to his scouts. "These acts of despicable violence … was it an isolated incident or will it become normal?"

No one had an answer.

"The prisoner refused to answer these questions when I asked him. I want to learn more about this group, including what drives them, who their leader is, and why a religious group is engaging in extreme and irrational violence and involving itself in political issues?"

No one had answers.

Von Tempsky straightened and began twiddling his moustache. He began pacing while Moana and his scouts waited.

"As much as it pains me, we'll return to Oakura," said the captain with finality. "We've nothing to gain by chasing the rebels that far only to face a far superior force when we get there."

CHAPTER ELEVEN

Guidance

It was unusually hot and humid. Dark clouds blanketed the sky and lumbered eastward. Men stood in large groups, sweltering in the heat, hoping a cooling sea breeze would provide some relief. There was a general feeling of excitement throughout the *pa* as the warriors who had returned from Te Ahuahu during the night boasted of Hatotoi's foretold easy and bloody victory over the *Pākeha* soldiers.

Te Ua Haumene's devotees began to gather in increasing numbers at the Wereroa *pa* in Waitotara, waiting anxiously for him to speak. His sermons were more than the incoherent ranting of a madman, as some alleged. Instead, they believed passionately that he spoke the gospel truth and that his predictions, visions and promises came directly from Almighty God.

Standing on a small rise, relishing the hint of a cool breeze their position offered, Erepu Henare and his best friends, Riwha Titokowaru and Te Whiti o Rongomai, waited eagerly for Te Ua. Like his close friends, Erepu was taught by missionaries to read and write and was familiar with the scriptures and teachings of Christianity. Whenever possible, Erepu preached redemption to his people, expounding with conviction the virtues of Christianity and urging them to forsake traditional *Māori* deities and accept the love of a Christian God. As a lay preacher, Erepu was sincere, honest and genuine, although he wasn't a particularly gifted orator like his friend Te Whiti or a deep thinker like Riwha Titokowaru; however, his enthusiasm more than compensated for any shortcomings.

Erepu's friends supported the Kingite cause without question and opposed *Pākeha* aggression in taking *Māori* land. In the aftermath of the first Taranaki land wars in 1860, Te Ua drew fragmented *Māori* together, unified them around a single cause, and spoke of peace and non-violence that appealed to the Christian beliefs of many. This is what drew men like Erepu, Te Whiti and Riwha to Te Ua and the *Pai Marire* faith. These men, along with others, were inherently peaceful, although some accepted that a mild form of aggression was necessary to protect their land and culture, which were rightfully theirs.

Although not a warrior, Erepu fought at the Kaitake *pa*, armed with an old musket, and defended it to the best of his limited ability. When the shelling began, he and other defenders were told to seek shelter in the surrounding bush. Once it became clear that Paora would lose the *pa*, Erepu dutifully headed to Waitotara as instructed.

Meanwhile, Hatotoi, Kaihoka, Tohu, and Paora regrouped, retaining only their most fanatical and capable warriors, who went on to successfully defend Te Ahuahu against *Pākeha* soldiers in a swift and brutal ambush. Less pious and motivated by greed, Big Pete claimed he had matters to attend to in Oakura and departed. Having accomplished their mission beyond their wildest expectations, they returned to Waitotara as celebrated heroes.

The assembled warriors and followers stirred – someone spotted Te Ua, and all heads turned expectantly, hoping to catch sight of him. His four trusted disciples, Hatotoi, Kaihoka, Tohu and Paora, led Te Ua from a hut and walked solemnly through the crowd to a newly erected raised platform, where a tall wooden pole was now affixed. Spars were attached horizontally to the pole, with ropes dangling and flags hanging limply. All five men climbed the platform and stood so they could be seen and heard.

The murmuring slowly ceased as Kaihoka raised an arm. The crowd was shocked into silence. Suspended from his hand was the severed head of Captain Ewen Boyd. Emulating Kaihoka, Paora raised the hand holding Private Granger's head. Now everyone could clearly see the grisly trophies. Some, unsettled by the sight, began to whisper, while others voiced their concerns in raised voices. Caught up in the fervour, most yelled in support, raising their own hands above their heads and shouting with growing excitement. Unwilling to look upon the evil sight, Erepu looked at his feet and felt his eyes moisten. *How could Christian men commit such horrific acts*?

Seeing Erepu affected by the horror, Te Whiti, in agreement, turned to him and whispered gravely, "Though some, in darkness of heart, seeing their land ravaged, might wish to take arms and kill the aggressors … I say it must not be."

Erepu looked to his friends, his eyes glistening, and shuddered. "Then why do they do this?"

Neither Te Whiti nor Riwha could answer.

"We have come to worship here in the presence of God!" yelled Te Ua, his voice clear and strong, carried to all those gathered before him. "Here, above you, stands our *niu*, the pole, a gift from the *Lord Worsley* and our place of fellowship!" Te Ua preached with growing emotion.

He spread his arms wide, turned to face the mast that towered nineteen yards above them, and lowered his head in prayer. After a moment or two, he turned again to face his followers.

"To prove we have overcome the undeserving *Pākeha* and that righteousness lives within us, we have been blessed with two further gifts from God!"

Kaihoka and Paora firmly fixed the heads onto short poles stuck into the ground beside the *niu,* then stepped back.

"Through these heads Jehovah hears my voice!" Te Ua shouted.

His followers roared in frenzied support.

"Brothers and sisters!" Te Ua paused, raising his hands to quieten the enthusiastic crowd, skilfully heightening the drama of his oration. "Gabriel spoke to me. We must visit Te Morere. Our help is needed there, where we must continue to purge the unrighteous *Pākeha* from our lands."

Again, the warriors yelled in support of Te Ua. He let the noise swell and fade naturally as he smiled benevolently upon his flock. He began to chant, and others joined in. Many devotees slowly circled the *niu,* prostrating themselves after touching the trophy heads.

> *"Kill, one, two, three, four—Attention!*
> *River, big river, long river, stone, big stone—*
> *Attention!*
> *Road, big road, long road, bush, big bush—*
> *Attention!"*

Erepu was confounded and disgusted. This was wrong, nothing like the Christianity he'd been taught. He recalled the scripture he'd learned, *I am the way, and the truth, and the life. No one comes to the Father except through me.* He repeated it again and again, silently mouthing the words and revelling in the strength it gave him. With resolve, he turned his back on Te Ua and slowly walked away, eager to put some distance between himself and the evil incantations. Te Whiti nudged Riwha, and both men turned to watch their troubled friend. Tempted to follow and offer counsel, they chose to remain where they were, content to allow Erepu time alone to collect his thoughts.

Erepu covered his ears, the chant's nonsensical words eating away at his conscience and his beliefs. The words meant nothing. They were babble, yet his people, *Māori*, were mesmerised by the captivating Te Ua Haumene and his protestations. How could they support such sinful acts, venerate a ship's mast stolen from a shipwreck, and condone killing and mutilation in the name of God? This was not Christian; it was blasphemy, it was evil!

> *"Long bush, long stone, hill, big hill, long hill—*
> *Attention!*
> *Mountain, big mountain, long mountain, big staff,*
> *long staff—Attention!*
> *North, north-by-east, nor'-nor'-east, nor'-east-by-*
> *north, north-east, colony—Attention!*
> *Come to tea, all the men, round the niu—Attention!*
> *Shem, rule the wind, too much wind, come to tea—*
> *Attention."*

It was all too much for Erepu. Overcome, he began to run. The haunting echoes of the chant permeated his consciousness, reaching, clutching; they were tearing him apart. A hundred voices chased him, extending out with cold hands, trying to pull him back. All Erepu could see were severed heads, their unseeing eyes helplessly weeping tears of blood, their silent mouths open in tortured agony calling his name, and Te Ua, with wings spread, smiling deviously over them all. Erepu ran and offered his own prayers between laboured breaths, repeating them over and over like a healing mantra. He ran from his guilt, shouting, crying and asking forgiveness. He ran as a tormented man, seeking to outdistance the winds of shame, the breath of evil trying to consume him and inhale him back.

Using well-worn paths, Erepu ran blindly – he ran quickly over rolling hills and along cliff-tops that guarded black-sand beaches far below. He passed people, mostly women gathering crops and harvesting flax, and men tending to a variety of tasks. He ignored them all and ran.

Exhausted, he could go no further and stopped to rest. His sweat-soaked chest heaved as he gasped for air. A nearby stream offered water and a refreshing pool where he could sit and cleanse himself of the filth of Te Ua's nonsensical rantings. He let the purifying water flow over his body. It felt like a baptism, a reaffirmation of his Christian faith. It gave him strength and clarity; he felt safe and free from Te Ua's reach and the poison he preached.

Erepu felt better and was trying to decide what to do. He no longer felt any affinity for the *Pai Marire* religion and was appalled by all he had witnessed among Te Ua's extreme and violent devotees. Returning to Waitotara wasn't a wise choice. He needed to distance himself from Te Ua and his followers, make amends, tell someone, and warn them of Te Ua and the sickening deeds committed by his chosen disciples and their fanatical warriors.

Erepu knew of a missionary in Patea, and he would go to him to warn of the next planned attack at Te Morere. Perhaps by his actions, he could save lives and seek atonement for the misguided trust he'd placed in Te Ua.

Erepu's hasty departure did not go unnoticed, and many saw him leave. Seeing Erepu's distress and concerned for his friend, Te Whiti asked young Hape to discreetly follow Erepu and ensure he came to no harm. Hape enthusiastically agreed and set out immediately.

Erepu was fit, healthy and strong, capable of running tirelessly for hours at a time. Stopping frequently to drink from streams, he continued to ignore any *Māori* he encountered, not wishing to engage with them because he feared they might be *Pai Marire* supporters. He ran with determination along the well-travelled sandy paths that paralleled the dynamic coastline.

A short distance behind Erepu and out of sight, Hape ran. Lacking the muscular development and endurance of the slightly older man he pursued, Hape struggled to keep pace. Fearful of disappointing Te Whiti, he continued to follow with resolve and was quietly thankful for the brief respite whenever Erepu stopped to drink. The sun moved across the sky and shadows lengthened, signalling that the day was fast drawing to an end.

Named after Ruataranaki, the man who discovered the large volcano that dominated the plains and neighbouring foothills, Mount Taranaki and its majestic snow-capped peak were cast in a calming pink glow as the sun slowly began its descent. Erepu, totally unaware that Hape followed not far behind, continued at a blistering pace as he neared his destination.

The church and detached manse of the Wesleyan missionary, Reverend William Robertson, lay on the far side of the river, up the gentle slope among a jumble of small buildings in the community of Patea. A cluster of flowering geraniums grew on each side of the short path leading to the pastor's cottage, and a Kowhai tree, thoughtfully planted by a previous resident, provided a welcome canopy of shade during south Taranaki's hot summer days. The church's main door was closed. However, a faint orange glow from the cottage windows facing Patea's principal thoroughfare suggested that Reverend Robertson was in residence.

Erepu was lucky. A kindly gentleman ferried him across the river, and now safely on the far bank, he sought to improve his appearance before presenting himself to the Reverend Robertson.

He was exhausted, sweat-streaked and dusty, and if he hoped to make a favourable impression on the minister, he needed to attend to those details with some vigour. Again, he used the river to revitalise and clean himself. Once relatively dry, with dust shaken from his clothes and feeling more confident, he dressed quickly, approached the minister's home and nervously rapped on the door.

After an age, the door creaked open, and the Reverend William Robertson stepped forward, eyeing with suspicion the dishevelled young man standing before him.

Uncharacteristically, his white shirt was unbuttoned at the neck, and greying chest hair, liberated from the open collar, spilt freely outwards and mingled in a confused tangle with his large, untrimmed beard of a similar colour. His sleeves were rolled up high, past the elbows, and the shirt that stretched over his paunch was securely tucked into black breeches, miraculously held aloft by suspenders. His small eyes darted over Erepu's bare feet and clothes and finally settled on his face. His expression slowly changed, revealing a mix of mild annoyance and curiosity. He said nothing, cocked his head to one side, and waited.

"Grace to you and peace from God," said Erepu respectfully as he inclined his head in greeting. "I'm sorry for disturbing you, sir. We have met before. I uh, … I am Erepu Henare."

The Reverend Robertson's face immediately reverted to suspicion, and he remained silent.

"It is important that we speak, sir. I bring news, a warning."

The Reverend Robertson wiped his mouth with the back of his hand, dislodging crumbs from his beard, then clasped his hands around his ample belly and sighed disapprovingly. Unknown to Erepu, the good minister was enjoying his evening meal when Erepu knocked on his door, and he wasn't partial to having his pleasures interrupted.

"You *are* with Te Ua." It wasn't a question – it was an accusation. "I know of you, and you have nothing of importance to say to me," the Reverend Robertson shook his head in reproach and leaned forward. "You and your Galatian followers are all cursed by God!"

Erepu's mouth fell open.

"If anyone is preaching to you a gospel other than what you accepted," the Reverend Robertson unclasped his hands and pointed a finger accusingly at Erepu. "Let them be under God's curse!" he stated with vehemence, his finger stabbing in concert.

"But, sir…" pleaded Erepu.

"Do not darken my doorway again. Be gone with you, heathen!" The Reverend Robertson stepped back inside and slammed the door, reinforcing his need to continue his repast.

The news of the atrocities committed by Te Ua's disciples at Te Ahuahu spread quickly, the horrors not easily forgiven or forgotten. Erepu's support for Te Ua was well known among local missionaries, and they'd previously tried, unsuccessfully, to dissuade him from pursuing a cause that seemed most unchristian when Te Ua was gaining support and seeking followers. Erepu understood the minister's reticence to engage in dialogue; however, the hostile welcome was a surprise.

"The *Hauhau* will attack again. You must listen!" shouted Erepu at the unresponsive, heavy door, then banged on it in frustration. "They will attack the soldiers at Te Morere - you must warn them!" His pleas went unheeded.

Erepu felt lost and ashamed. No one trusted him, and he genuinely expected that every missionary he approached would give him the same response. Dejected, he wandered aimlessly from the Reverend William Robertson's cottage, deliberately not glancing at the darkened church as he passed by. With the rebuke still stinging his ears, he felt unworthy and disgraced, the humiliation unbearable.

Across the street, in the shadows of a stable and dripping wet from his swim across the river, Hape overheard the entire exchange. With his back to the wall, he slid to the ground, drew his knees up, rested his head in his hands, and wondered what he should do.

The same thoughts were also running through Erepu's mind. Te Morere was many days away, and even if he could reach there and warn the soldiers, would they listen to him? Perhaps he would be arrested, or worse, killed. Erepu's mother lived in Opunake, about forty-five miles away, but going to her would only prompt her to chastise him for his support of Te Ua. No, he decided, that wasn't an option.

As full darkness enveloped Erepu, a plan began to take shape. He would cut inland, skirt the western side of Mount Taranaki, and head towards Oakura, where his uncle and cousins lived on a small farm. They were respected within the community – he could explain what he knew to them, and they would talk to the soldiers and warn them of Te Ua. Feeling relieved to have a genuine strategy, Erepu changed his route and began to walk westward.

Equally exhausted, Hape watched as Erepu shifted from aimless wandering to walking in a new direction with purpose. *What to do?* he wondered. Follow or return to Waitotara and inform Te Whiti of Erepu's movements and the overheard conversation?

Already physically exhausted, Hape turned his back on Mount Taranaki and began his return to Waitotara to inform Te Whiti.

They discovered Hape the following day, exhausted and dehydrated, lying on the track not far from Waitotara. He'd run and walked throughout the night and collapsed mid-morning, his feet bruised and bloody. Realising the young man had a message of some importance, a handful of people, eager to learn more, squeezed into the *whare*[6] where he now rested, blocking the low doorway. A few gathered expectantly outside. Te Whiti was called and now attended to Hape. Kaihoka was also present and keen to hear what news the young man brought.

With agonising slowness, Hape told the listeners what he'd learned. Unable to stop Hape from revealing everything and implicating Erepu, Te Whiti realised, with a heavy heart, that he couldn't protect his friend. Kaihoka heard every word and even asked a question or two. In the dim light of the *whare*, Te Whiti saw Kaihoka's eyes blaze with ferocity. To Kaihoka, Erepu was nothing but a traitor. He was angry, and onlookers scattered as he stormed out of the *whare* in disgust. Te Whiti knew Erepu was in grave danger.

As he expected, Te Whiti was later summoned to appear before Hatotoi, Kaihoka and Paora. Their expressions were grim as he sat on a mat beside them.

"With your basket and my basket, the people will live," said Paora in a soft soothing voice.

Te Whiti understood the meaning– Paora sought cooperation. He nodded in reply and remained silent.

"Where has the dog run to?" yelled Kaihoka, unable to contain himself.

---

6 *Whare – Māori word for house or dwelling.*

Paora and Hatotoi both turned in annoyance to Kaihoka, who rose quickly from the mat, clenching his fists and glaring at Te Whiti, his loathing for Erepu more than evident.

"Erepu is troubled; he needs help," continued Paora. He turned from Kaihoka and looked to Te Whiti, clearly expecting a response.

"What will you do with him?" Te Whiti asked.

"Then they cried to the Lord in their trouble, and he saved them from distress," Paora quoted from scripture.

"Enough!" cried Kaihoka, weary of the cryptic conversation. He paced nervously behind the seated men. "When I catch him, he will suffer!" Kaihoka paused before Te Whiti and glared at him.

"Help us," requested Hatotoi in a friendly manner.

There was no alternative for Te Whiti, and he couldn't remain silent any longer. "I have no idea where he has gone, but I believe he probably travelled west to visit his uncle in Oakura," he offered, hoping that would be the last place Erepu would go.

"Not to his family?" asked Paora.

"No, his mother is disapproving of his belief in *Pai Marire*. Erepu wouldn't go there."

"Who is his uncle?" Kaihoka asked.

"He is called Tami Henare, a farmer," replied Te Whiti with some reluctance.

"Are you certain of this?" asked Paora, giving Te Whiti a careful look.

"How can I know the mind of a troubled man? No, I am not certain. You asked me what I thought, and I have told you," replied Te Whiti with some resentment.

"I know of Tami. He is a good man, but without faith," offered Hatotoi. "But no harm should come to him or his family."

A look of relief briefly washed over Te Whiti.

Hatotoi and Te Whiti exchanged a quick look.

"Is there anyone else he would go to?" asked Paora, ignoring Hatotoi.

Te Whiti shook his head and offered a silent prayer for Erepu and his uncle.

Kaihoka grunted in impatience and resumed pacing. "Send men to where his mother lives in Opunake, and we will go to Oakura. It's on the way to Te Morere." Kaihoka fixed Te Whiti with an icy stare. "I have people in Oakura who will help. We should fetch the *tipua* and leave now!"

Te Whiti sighed quietly. If they used horses, as Kaihoka suggested, he couldn't warn Tami Henare as he had hoped.

"Perhaps you can find Erepu before he reaches Oakura?" asked Te Whiti with some hope.

"The sooner the better," replied Paora.

The men remained quiet as they digested what needed to be done.

Te Whiti looked up at Kaihoka, "This is what the Lord Almighty said, 'Administer true justice, show mercy and compassion to one another.'"

"True Justice? Oh yes," Kaihoka laughed, "I will demonstrate justice."

CHAPTER TWELVE

The Farm

Sergeants Walker, Bowers, and Rangitira sat outside the local Public House, enjoying a beer and quiet conversation. Out of respect or fear, rankers were mindful and allowed them to discuss whatever sergeants talked about when not on duty, wisely keeping their distance. Less aware was the dog of conspicuous mixed heritage, which gave the three men a haughty look as it ambled past. It stopped briefly at the base of the tree that was providing them with shade, lowered its nose, sniffed once, then again to be absolutely certain. Ignoring the small audience who watched with satirical delight, it lifted its leg and, with practised ease, relieved itself. On completion of its toiletries, the dog scratched the ground with each of its rear legs, risked another quick sniff, then turned its attention to the sergeants and approached them cautiously. Unimpressed by a mysterious object that skipped close by, the motivated dog dodged the missile and wisely moved on in search of a more agreeable group of patrons willing to purchase friendship for food. With a chuckle, the sergeants watched the dog lope away.

"As I was sayin', I just hope you fellas will put me out of my misery with a quick shot to the head if I ever suffer a wound like that," Bowers said.

"Must have hurt like hell," offered Walker, shaking his head in sympathy.

"When you begin talking rubbish and sproutin' nonsense, then that's the time to do it," suggested Bowers with the authority of a man yet to be seriously wounded in battle.

"Why wait that long?" asked Moana, "I can do it now if you really want."

The sergeants laughed. In unrehearsed unison, they reached for their mugs and each took a healthy pull of beer.

"Do you think when you're, uh, del –"

"Delirious?" interjected Bowers.

"Yes, del-eree-ous. Do you think you really do talk rubbish or is it things actually in your head that you begin to talk about?" asked Walker.

"Why do you ask?"

"Cause the prisoner was going on about all sorts of things."

"And how do you know, you can't even understand *Māori*?" laughed Moana.

"I know when a *Māori* says, Waitotara, or Te Ahuahu or Te Morere."

"And he said those names?" asked Moana leaning forward.

"He sure did, and I recognised other names too, but they were people's names."

"Did the captain hear that?"

"No, he wasn't there."

"You should have told him," admonished Bowers.

"Why, he was talking rubbish and was del-eree-ous?"

Moana sat back in his chair and looked thoughtful.

"What are you thinking, Ira?" asked Bowers.

Moana paused before he replied, "Nothing really." He leaned forward again, "What were the other names you heard?"

"Oh, I can't remember them all," Walker looked up into the branches. "Paora, and definitely Kaihoka, that was an easy one to understand. I heard him say Te Ua many times, I know that. Can't think of others, though."

Moana leaned back and rubbed his chin. All the words seemed to make sense, except Te Morere. "Are you sure he said Te Morere, Eric?"

"Yes, plain as day."

"What's so special about Te Morere?" asked Bowers.

"Not much really, it's an outcrop of rocks on the banks of the Waiongona River, just a little way northeast of New Plymouth. *Māori* children use the rocks to leap into the river. It's an old *pa* site that is situated high enough to offer a good view of the neighbouring area. Or that's what it used to be. I haven't heard much about the place recently."

"Maybe that's where he is from," suggested Walker.

Moana shook his head, "He told the captain he was from the Ngati Maniapoto *iwi* and lived in Kawhia quite a few miles north of there. No, he didn't live in Te Morere."

"Must have meant something to him," added Bowers. "Otherwise why did he say it?"

"That's what I believe too," Moana replied.

All conversation ceased as Lieutenant Small approached. The sergeants all watched him suspiciously as they reluctantly stood to honour the rank.

"Sergeant Rangitira, Captain Von Tempsky requires the pleasure of your company."

As instructed, Moana strode purposefully towards the Company office, where he was told he'd find Captain Von Tempsky. It was late in the afternoon, and the offices were abandoned except for the captain, who always made a habit of staying late.

Moana knocked on the door and waited for the invitation to enter.

"Come!" came the muted voice.

Moana entered the office to find the captain stretched back in his chair, feet on the desk, his gleaming cavalry boots on the floor beside him. He held an empty glass as he acknowledged Moana.

"Nice of you to pay me a visit, Ira. Have a seat," said the captain, forgoing normal military protocol and waving to a chair. His moustache twitched, which was always an indication that the captain was trying to suppress a smile.

Moana eased himself into the uncomfortable chair and relaxed as he appraised his commander. *Some invitation*, thought Moana, *I was ordered here*.

Another glass magically appeared, and Von Tempsky, demonstrating remarkable dexterity, poured a healthy libation of Scotch Whiskey into each without changing position or spilling a drop. Moana was impressed and took the proffered glass and waited for the toast that was sure to come.

"What are ya waiting for? Drink up, man," said Von Tempsky, raising his glass and then downing its contents in a single swallow. He grimaced and shook his head.

Needing no encouragement, Moana did the same, completing the ritual with his own head-shake.

"That's better, eh?" the captain laughed.

Moana joined in, finding the unfamiliar informality refreshing.

"Now then, your um, uniform modification request has been approved, Ira. I received Major Peterson's response earlier today. That will make your boys happier."

Moana was surprised and pleased. The breeches the Forest Rangers wore were useless in the bush. Constant dampness made them prone to rot and tearing, and when wet, they were uncomfortable and difficult to dry. Moana casually suggested to the captain that the scouts adopt a traditional *Māori* skirt called a *rapaki* to replace their breeches when they entered the bush. Secured at the waist, the rapaki hung to the knees, and he assured him it would provide countless advantages to the Rangers. Woven from natural flax fibres, the rapaki shed water easily, dried rapidly, and was comfortable to wear. The adaptive Captain Von Tempsky readily agreed and, unknown to Moana, immediately filed a request.

"Uh, thank you, Captain."

Von Tempsky's moustache lifted in a smile. "Although, it won't be just the scouts who wear them; we all will." He began to laugh. "Oh yes, Ira, we'll be the laughingstock of New Zealand's military, but by god, they'll know we're the best." He leaned across, offering the bottle for a refill. "Cheers! To hardened men wearing skirts!" He drained the glass, repeating the first. Unwilling to be left out, Moana raised the glass to his lips, tilted his head back, and felt the liquid burn its way down.

Both men enjoyed a moment's silence as they savoured the distinctive taste.

Captain Von Tempsky swung his legs to the floor, placed his arms on the desk, and leaned on his elbows towards Moana. "What do you know about these *Hauhau*, Ira? Should we take them seriously, or are they nothing more than scoundrels looking for a fight?"

Moana collected his thoughts before answering, "I've been asking myself those same questions, sir. If we are to take them seriously, we must consider what we do know. Their weapons are standard, and their tactics appear somewhat structured, although I suspect luck has played a part in their success, but…" he paused.

"Go on," encouraged Von Tempsky, who was listening attentively as he always did.

"What bothers me is what drives them." Moana rose from the chair and began to pace the room. "If what we hear is true and the *Hauhau* are part of a religious militia, their behaviour becomes unpredictable. We won't know their reasoning, their motives, or how far they will go to achieve their goals."

"And we don't have any idea what their plans are," finished Von Tempsky. "Religious fanaticism has always been dangerous in that regard, Ira. Do you have any ideas?"

"Other than expelling all *Pākeha* from New Zealand, I have no idea. We could quietly ask around, sir. Not sure how willing *Māori* will be to talk, but you never know."

The captain nodded thoughtfully, and his hand rose to his moustache and began to compulsively fidget. Moana turned to a window and looked outside.

"What's their weakness, Ira?"

"Lack of training, the number of fighting warriors at their disposal…"

"No, no! You're thinking like one of those damned useless English officers, and that will get you killed, Ira, just like that poor fool, Captain Boyd. Think like a *Māori*!" expounded Von Tempsky, waving his arms in a frenzy of ideas.

Moana raised his eyebrows at the unexpected outburst. "I am *Māori*, just as the *Hauhau* are."

"And that's the answer, Ira," the captain banged his fist on the desk. "That's their weakness, which we will exploit. Don't you see?" Von Tempsky rose from behind his desk. His stockinged feet padded across the wooden floor as he walked to Moana. "You gave the answer earlier. I want you to select half a dozen scouts you think can best assimilate into the *Māori* community and conduct cultural reconnaissance. With patience, information about the *Hauhau* will come to you. A religious group needs followers, Ira. They will be recruiting, and to bolster their numbers, they will share information, brag about their successes and talk about their plans."

Moana understood the captain's unorthodox logic and nodded in agreement. "We probably shouldn't send the scouts very far away as this appears to be a regional conflict."

"For the moment, it's regional, but given the local support they're receiving, it wouldn't surprise me if they began expanding to other areas," added Von Tempsky sourly. "Let's think it over for a day or two, and we'll talk again."

"I think it's a good idea, sir, and makes sense to me."

"It should be, Ira, it was yours."

Moana left the captain's office and couldn't help but think he'd been cleverly outmanoeuvred – again.

The small market in Oakura offered a variety of products that Wikitoria couldn't grow or make herself. Twice a week, she would walk into town, visit the market, and spend time chatting and gossiping with other local women over tea and half a scone. Truth be told, her family could have survived on a single trip to the market, but she enjoyed the break from her father and brothers, and the second trip meant she carried less on her walk home. Wiki liked to think of herself as practical, and no one was prepared to argue with her about that.

She was not far from home, and as she rounded a bend in the track, she could see a wagon approaching. Wiki immediately tensed. The wagon belonged to a local dairy farmer who was fortunate to have a lucrative arrangement with the army to supply them with milk. Tami knew the farmer quite well, and in exchange for vegetables, he arranged for a reasonable quantity of milk to be delivered to his farm twice a week.

Wiki had an inherent dislike for the wagon driver, a young, scraggy man with an unhealthy complexion, called Pippi. He would leer at her whenever he came to the farm and never engaged in conversation, preferring to turn his head and look elsewhere if she approached him to talk. She preferred that he leave the milk urn on the porch and then leave.

As Pippi drew nearer, she could see the lecherous look on his face. With a polite nod and a quick step, Wiki said good morning and hurried past. The wagon never slowed, nor did Pippi acknowledge her greeting, but she felt his squinty eyes on her as he passed. She knew he'd be staring, as he habitually did, taking in all her feminine curves. Most troubling was that Pippi would turn up everywhere, delivering milk, and seldom a day would pass without encountering him. She risked a quick look over her shoulder and was relieved to see the wagon was a good distance down the track; she breathed easier.

As a treat, Wiki would buy apples when they were in season and, as she passed by on her way home, she'd toss them to her brothers, who worked tirelessly in their field. It was a game they had played for years. Wiki would throw apples or other seasonal fruit at them, and they pretended not to see her until the last moment, when they always turned and caught the fruit, snatching it from the air with ease. Her father couldn't eat a whole apple. Without front teeth, he found them difficult to bite into.

Today was like every other market day for Wiki; she walked towards home and approached the fields tended by her family.

As always, she began to walk stealthily, trying to stay quiet and out of sight as long as possible, hoping to surprise her brothers. She hugged the hedge and walked carefully to a small opening, where she risked a quick look to see where in the field they were working. The field was empty!

This was odd. Her brothers knew she was going to the market, and they always positioned themselves close to the hedge and within throwing range. Something must have called them away, she thought. Or worse, they were hiding to surprise her.

Wiki continued along the hedge that ran parallel to the track, keeping low, determined not to be seen. Another small opening let her look through the hedge into the field. She froze. On the other side, only yards away, two men with muskets sat on the ground, partly concealed by the hedge, eating carrots. She quickly withdrew her head.

In growing alarm, she realised the two *Māori* warriors were not in the field to buy food; they were lying in wait. *For whom? For her?* Quietly, she began to backtrack, keeping low and out of sight of the strangers. When she reached the end of the hedge, she skirted around and into the bush, not far from where the brutal fight had taken place a week earlier. Feeling secure, she stopped to think. How many men were there? Were her father and brothers in danger? What did they want? She needed to find out.

She placed her basket on the ground, lifted her skirts and bunched them tightly together, held them firmly with one hand to avoid catching on branches, and walked easily through the bush to a vantage point that would allow her to see the back of their cottage.

Stopping behind a large flax, she straightened and carefully moved the long leaves aside to see. Eight horses were tied to a rail. Another warrior stood with his back to her, hidden behind a tree at the rear of the cottage. Where were the others? Perhaps some were inside, where she hoped her brothers and father were. She needed help.

Wiki returned to her basket and considered her options.

An approaching noise alerted her to danger. She picked up the basket and quickly ran to the nearest shelter, a massive Rata tree large enough to hide behind. She waited with her back pressed against the trunk, her skirts held tightly, the basket on the ground at her feet. Her heart was pounding. If it were a warrior and she were caught, what would they do? She listened as the noise grew clearer. Footsteps crunched on dead leaves that littered the ground. Slow and steady, the steps grew louder. She couldn't risk a look, so she waited, holding her breath in terror. The footsteps stopped.

Wiki guessed someone had seen her. She imagined the warrior looking around, trying to work out where she had disappeared to, and it wouldn't take him long to look behind the tree. But she wasn't going to be taken without a fight. With quiet resolve, she slowly exhaled and focused on what to do.

Raised in a house full of brothers, she was inevitably exposed to the rough-and-tumble ways of boys. As the only girl, she was often picked on and, from an early age, learned to protect herself from them. She grew tough and resilient, learning not to be afraid. Living with extremely protective brothers as a teenager was a different experience, and they taught her to defend herself against bigger and stronger opponents. She may not have the strength of a man, but she had something else – brains, determination and some elementary skills taught to her by the sons of a farmer. For the first time in her life, those lessons would truly be put to the test.

Wiki closed her eyes and visualised the warrior who stalked her. She heard another slow step, the brittle crackle of dried leaves giving way under his weight as he crept closer. She turned her head slowly to the right, towards the direction he had come from, and estimated he was only about a yard away. Again, there it was, the slight snap of a small twig. She opened her eyes and could barely make out a shoulder. He moved again, quieter this time. It was difficult to hear, but she could see him. He stepped lightly backwards. She saw his back and a musket strapped over his left shoulder. His right shoulder remained out of view. He took another small step - he was so close - and began to turn to face her.

This was it. Wiki could delay no longer. Without turning her body, she stepped quickly to her right, placing herself almost directly behind him, and struck. Instinctively, he turned his head at the noise and at her unexpected appearance. Wiki kept her arms close to her sides, reached across her body with her right hand, clenched her fist tightly, and then swiftly pulled her arm back and upwards with as much force as she could manage. With considerable force, her elbow collided with the turning warrior and struck him on the head, between his ear and eye.

The elbow is much stronger than a fist and less likely to fracture than a hand when used as a weapon of force. If Wiki attempted to punch the warrior in the face, she would likely have broken bones in her hand and only slightly annoyed the man. Punching the tree she hid behind would have produced the same result.

The human skull is remarkably resilient to frontal impact, but less so to side impacts. When Wiki used her elbow, she couldn't have chosen a better weapon against him. The quickly turning head added velocity to the blow. He immediately collapsed, unconscious to the ground. She stood over him, breathing hard, rubbing her elbow and surprised by the result.

She looked more closely and could see the man was alive and breathing, though she was unsure how long he'd remain stunned. She feared he would come to and take her. Leaving her basket, she ran.

Reaching the open stretch of the track, Wiki headed back towards Oakura, only a short distance away, where there was help.

At first, she ran until she was tired, then slowed to a brisk walk. Looking behind her, she saw no one following.

Rounding a bend, she saw a figure leaning against a bank. As she drew nearer, she saw it was a man. He was dirty and unkempt, and his clothes were torn. She veered away, uncertain.

"Wiki!" the weak voice yelled. "Wiki!"

She stopped and looked more closely, recognising the voice. "Erepu, is that you?" Wiki ran over. "What has happened to you, and what in God's name is going on around here?" she asked, glancing back over her shoulder.

"Wiki, you must warn them, you must, or more soldiers will die," Erepu pleaded.

Wiki looked at him, not comprehending what he was saying. "First, we need to get to safety. What happened to you? Can you walk?" She saw his shredded, bloodstained feet for the first time and gasped.

"Safety, why?" asked Erepu in confusion.

"There are warriors at the house, eight of them…" She was struck by the coincidence of the warriors' presence and Erepu's sudden appearance. "They've come for you, haven't they, Erepu? What have you done?" she yelled.

The threat of warriors charging down the track on horseback was very real. "I have to hide you, Erepu, then I will get help." Wiki paused. "Were you seen here? What about the milk wagon that passed here a while ago?"

"Yes, I waved to him to stop and help me, but he carried on."

"I just hope he doesn't tell anyone he saw you."

With difficulty, Wiki helped Erepu up the small bank, then limped him into the low bush that covered the side of the track and propped him against a large rock. As long as he stayed quiet, no one would see him.

With her hands on her hips, Wiki looked down at him and shook her head slowly from side to side. "Erepu Henare, you've done something horrible, and we're all suffering because of it. There'd better be a good reason for this, or you'll have more than sore feet when I'm finished with you. Do you understand?" She gave him a withering stare.

He nodded despondently.

She turned and began to walk away, "I'll be back soon with help."

Wiki returned to the path and continued walking towards Oakura. She rounded a corner and walked straight into six rebel warriors who were waiting for her.

Erepu was tired and hungry. His feet hurt to walk on, and to add to his woes, he had upset his cousin Wikitoria. He dozed for a short time while he waited for her to return, but she never did.

She'd talked of warriors— had Te Ua's disciples sent warriors after him? Through the fog of exhaustion, he remembered her fear and what she had said, *'There are eight warriors at the house'*. He realised he must move— if she'd been captured, then she would eventually tell them where he was.

He eased himself off the rock he had been leaning against, slid down the bank and stood unsteadily. He found a dead branch and used it for support as he tentatively took a painful step. The first few steps sent shooting pains through his feet and up his legs. On reaching the track, he thought it best to go back to Oakura and tell the soldiers there about Wiki's capture. They must listen to him now and take his warning of an attack at Te Morere seriously. The pain was unbearable, but after a minute or two it settled, and he could walk slowly without fear of falling.

CHAPTER THIRTEEN

Hauhau

The moon shone with brilliant intensity; it hung suspended in the inky blackness, set against a backdrop of twinkling lights. Te Ua thought the moon was the eye of God, the all-seeing, unblinking eye that peered into the dark recesses of a man's mind. Nothing could be hidden; everything would be revealed, and the true believers would triumph while the unfaithful and unrepentant would perish.

There was no wind to speak of, but there was a hint of a gentle breeze. It was the breath of God, leaving a slight chill, a casual reminder that God watched over them all. Te Ua repositioned his cloak– it was a special cloak called a *parawai*, a thoughtful gift he used to keep warm when he wandered alone at night seeking spiritual guidance.

It was during these late evening walks that God spoke to him, and tonight was no different. Te Ua quietly made his way to the *niu*, knelt before it, and gave thanks in prayer. God was generous, and Te Ua was grateful. In the morning, he would share his latest revelations and visions with his prophets.

Mats were laid in front of the *niu*, and *Pai Marire*'s prophets, disciples and trusted lieutenants sat and listened to Te Ua. Hatotoi and Tohu Kakahi occupied positions of honour on either side of Te Ua, facing outwards. Two key men were absent; the vengeful Kaihoka was now in Poverty Bay on the east coast with Captain

Boyd's head, and Paora, with Private Granger's head, was dispatched by a different route to the same location. Once they both arrived, they were to present the heads to Hirini Te Kani, a Poverty Bay chief. It was a peaceful mission, and the objective was to obtain support from all the tribes of the lands they passed through.

"I have seen a vision on my bed, as if a great cloud had arisen, darkening the sun and its light. I heard a voice crying out in space. Alas, my people are like stars falling from the heavens, never to return to their place. That which I chose has been judged," Te Ua paused for a heartbeat, letting his words sink in.

"We *will* drive *Pākeha* from our lands," he continued. "We *will* succeed. As God's chosen people, we will ensure victory for the faithful and deliver us salvation." He cast his gaze over the eager, attentive faces before him. "Hatotoi Kahore will lead the purge at Te Morere and drive the *Pākeha* soldiers back into the sea."

His men cheered in support.

Hatotoi sat impassively and raised his hand for quiet. "We are waiting for news of the rescue of our brother, Erepu Henare," Hatotoi risked a subtle glance at Te Whiti, who sat facing him at the front of the group. "He is unwell, and we will care for him and pray for his recovery. When Erepu is again amongst us, then in God's name we will seek vengeance on *Pākeha* and return Te Morere to the chosen ones."

Te Ua stood. He turned to face Te Whiti. "My brother Te Whiti o Rongomai, you and Riwha Titokowaru will go to Te Morere in support of Hatotoi. But fear not, God will watch over and protect us all. *Pākeha* muskets will not harm the righteous; their bullets will fall short." The men began to murmur, surprised by Te Ua's words. "We will create a *niu* at the Manutahi *pa,* very near Te Morere, where we will assemble and prepare. Gather your warriors!"

As one, everyone stood and cheered. They waved their arms high and shouted in support of Te Ua. Their voices echoed through the early-morning air at the Wereroa *pa* in Waitotara, drawing young and old to the *niu* where Te Ua stood, their numbers swelling to almost two thousand fervent devotees.

Perplexed, Te Whiti scratched his chin. As a pacifist, he was about to witness the death of more *Pākeha* at Te Morere, a paradox he was trying to reconcile. As instructed, he would go to Te Morere, but he would not raise a hand to harm others. He would stand in support of Hatotoi, but he would not kill.

He thought of his friend Erepu's sudden departure just over a week ago. Were Erepu's misgivings merely a matter of simple doubt? Te Whiti raised his head and looked through the throng of followers towards Te Ua's glowing face. Unbidden, a quote from the scriptures came to mind, *The cunning and craftiness of men in their deceitful scheming.* Te Whiti shook the thought from his head and joined the others in shouting with joyful elation.

"I don't believe the man to be of sound mind and character, Captain. Certainly, we will look into the absurd claim that warriors abducted a local woman, and I will send a man to the property in the morning to ascertain the validity of his assertion," Colonel Warren laughed. "As for the preposterous notion that rebels will attack Sentry Hill, or Te Morere, as locals like to call the place, such an attack would be foolhardy. You may not be aware, but the well-defended redoubt is commanded by the very capable Captain Shortt. I sincerely doubt there is any credence to the claim. The poor chap is suffering and obviously somewhat mistaken," the colonel ended with a patronising smile.

"Perhaps you are correct, sir. However–"

"Perhaps, Captain," interrupted Colonel Warren. "Do you doubt the analysis and intelligence reports of our fine officers?"

"Of course not, sir." Von Tempsky offered his own practised smile. "I am sure your officers have more important things to do than waste time pondering a ridiculous claim from a vagrant."

"Indeed."

"The Rangers could assume that responsibility and ease the burden from your overworked staff," offered Captain Von Tempsky.

Colonel Warren leaned forward in his chair and looked at Von Tempsky. He didn't approve of Von Tempsky's garish clothes. He found the length of Von Tempsky's hair unacceptable and had little faith in the Forest Rangers as an irregular force. "Captain, may I remind you that the Forest Rangers are best suited to traipsing through swamps and over hills, not frolicking in grass skirts on the roads of Oakura and frightening locals. Stay away from Mr Henare, Captain. It's plain to see that his ridiculous claim has you distracted. This incident is outside the scope of your responsibilities." He leaned back in his chair and smiled at Von Tempsky. "You may have an independent command, but I insist that your entire Company not involve itself in these matters. Do I make myself clear, sir?"

Lieutenant Roberts shifted uncomfortably in his chair.

"Do you have something to say, Lieutenant?"

"No, sir."

"Very well." The colonel turned back to Von Tempsky, "Captain?"

"I understand completely, sir. I will not have my entire Company involve itself in these matters."

Lieutenant Roberts studied the face of Captain Von Tempsky carefully.

"Now gentlemen, I have other matters to attend to, if you'll excuse me."

It was late afternoon, and Captain Von Tempsky was back in the Company office. He dismissed Lieutenants Small and Griggs and now sat in solitary pleasure, his feet comfortably on his desk and his cavalry boots at his side. He toyed with his knife, spinning it expertly in his hands.

Since Erepu Henare's arrival a couple of hours ago and the surprising news he brought, the Rangers were chafing at the bit to deploy and effect an immediate rescue of the Henare family. Erepu was now under a doctor's care and receiving treatment for his foot injuries. In barely concealed frustration, Captain Von Tempsky was not permitted to interview Erepu, despite having many questions to ask him. It was unlikely that Colonel Warren would extend that courtesy to him, given his position within the Forest Rangers and the informant's emotional distress. Captain Von Tempsky sent word to his NCOs, who were training nearby with the Company, that he wished to see them.

As expected, a measured knock on the door announced the arrival of Sergeants Walker, Bowers and Rangitira. Once seated, the captain provided an update.

"Colonel Warren has expressly forbidden the entire Ranger Company from involving itself in this matter–"

"But, sir!" protested Moana.

"That's enough, Sergeant!" rebuked the captain.

Moana was seething – his fists were clenched and his knuckles white. Blood congealed on his hand from a minor training injury earlier in the afternoon; it began to bleed again. He ignored it and, as ordered, kept quiet.

"The colonel believes the informant to be unreliable and irrational. However, he can't completely ignore the young man, so he will send someone to investigate the claim in the morning."

"He can't be serious," Bowers interrupted.

Sergeant Walker shook his head.

Moana looked at the floor.

"Surely there is something we can do, Captain, we have an independent command?" suggested Bowers.

"Technically, we do, but we remain here in Oakura to support the 57th Regiment at Colonel Warren's pleasure. If I directly disobey his orders, our principal role here may be in jeopardy." Von Tempsky looked at each man in turn. "Do you understand?"

Moana looked up sullenly, "Yes, sir."

"Yes, sir," replied Walker and Bowers in unison.

Captain Von Tempsky rose from his chair, padded in his stockinged feet to the window, and stood with his hands clasped behind his back, looking out. A milk wagon passed by. The office was deathly quiet as he formulated his thoughts.

"According to Lieutenant Roberts, Mr Henare is recovering under the doctor's care. I understand he is quite lucid," the captain said, turning to face his men. He looked at Moana's bloodstained knuckle as if noticing it for the first time.

"Ira, I think you need to have your injury attended to."

"It's minor, sir, and not a problem."

"Ira, you will go to the doctor to have your wound cared for," repeated the captain slowly with emphasis.

Bowers and Walker looked on in puzzlement.

Moana looked up at Von Tempsky's face and saw his twitching moustache. With realisation, Moana replied enthusiastically, "Yes, sir, I'd hate for sepsis to set in."

Sergeant Walker turned to Moana, looking perplexed.

Von Tempsky turned his attentions on Sergeant-Major Bowers who was only just grasping the situation, "How is the back injury of that chap, uh …?"

Sergeant-Major Bowers paused briefly. "Murphy, sir. He hurt his back again during training this afternoon," offered Bowers quickly with mock seriousness.

"It must be difficult for him to move, surely?" asked the captain.

"Yes, I believe he is in his cot and totally immobile, sir. I was going to request that the doctor pay him a visit after this meeting is over," answered Bowers.

Von Tempsky nodded in agreement. The bait was offered and now he waited; after a moment or two came the response he'd hoped for.

Moana gave Walker a nudge and whispered in his ear.

"Captain, I'd like your permission to take the Company on a training exercise this evening," suggested Walker innocently.

"Yes, perhaps. Although Ira may want to work on some scouting issues separately with his men. They need some special training," smiled the captain. "Sergeant Walker, you may want to consider heading south, and Ira can go north– that way you won't interfere with each other." The captain studied the faces of his sergeants carefully. "Make sure your training request is in writing, and I will approve and sign the document immediately."

Walker was only just beginning to understand what was happening.

"I suggest that your training exercise is realistic, Sergeant Walker. Please make sure your men are fully armed."

"Yes, sir," smiled Walker.

"Ensure the armoury is unlocked," the captain told Bowers, then paused briefly before changing the subject. "What time do we normally receive our milk deliveries?"

"Ah, I'm sorry, sir, what was that?"

"Our milk, what time is the milk usually delivered?"

Moana and Bowers exchanged glances.

"Normally, before mid-morning, sir. Ah, did you want some milk?" Bowers asked.

"No, no. I'm sorry, just curious," replied the captain. "That is all." Von Tempsky returned to the window.

Why would the captain question the milk delivery, thought Moana.

Moana entered the small infirmary and immediately saw a man of his own age lying in a cot. His feet were bandaged, and the doctor sat at a small bureau, completing his notes. The doctor looked up at Moana in question. "How can I be of assistance, Sergeant?"

"I scraped my knuckle earlier this afternoon. It isn't a problem at present, but later I discovered that I'd crawled through shi … some manure from the bullocks. I'm worried it may begin to fester, sir." Moana held up his hand, which had begun to bleed a little.

The doctor reached for a few items to address the minor abrasion when a Ranger came running to the infirmary in a mild panic, and clearly out of breath. "Doctor, doctor, quick, we need help. Private Murphy has come to grief, he hurt his back, sir, can't move," the soldier hopped up and down with urgency.

The doctor turned to his bedridden patient, then to Moana, and appeared flustered, "I, uh … I really shouldn't leave the patient. Colonel's orders."

"Doctor, please, Murphy's in a bad way, sir."

Moana generously offered a solution, "Doctor, I'll stay here with the patient until you return. You'd better go."

"Somewhat appeased, the young doctor grabbed his bag of instruments and headed out the door. "Hopefully, I won't be long, Sergeant. Lead the way, Trooper.'"

Moana immediately went to Erepu and introduced himself. "I don't have long before the doctor returns. Please tell me everything you know about the abduction."

About a hundred yards away, Sergeant-Major Bowers was leaning over Trooper Murphy. "I swear on the Holy Father, Patrick Murphy, that you'd better convince that doctor you're dying, or so help me, the next time a doctor visits you, it'll be to sign your death certificate!"

Murphy lay in a cot and was genuinely frightened. Under his sergeant's verbal attack, he began to sweat and his face flushed.

Just then, the doctor arrived. Sergeant-Major Bowers stepped back and pointed to Murphy. "Seems the poor lad has hurt himself, doc." Bowers assumed the expression of a caring, concerned father.

The doctor began his preliminary diagnosis. "This man is in some discomfort and quite distressed. How long have you been like this?"

"Since training this afternoon, Doctor," offered Bowers.

"I think the patient can speak for himself, sergeant."

"As the sergeant says, Doctor. I hurt me back when I jumped. Right here," Murphy pointed to the area on his back he deemed appropriate for such a painful injury.

Moana extracted what little information Erepu knew about the warriors and a possible kidnapping. Puzzled by the reason, Moana pressed Erepu to share more about his condition and what he had done to have warriors track him to Oakura. Erepu, reluctant to be open, resisted at first, but as Moana persisted, he loosened up and told all he knew. Moana believed the answer lay with the Reverend Robertson in Patea. Either the reverend had told someone, or Erepu may have been followed. Perhaps both.

The doctor returned after a short time and was relieved to find Moana sitting amicably chatting with his patient.

"How was Murphy, Doctor?"

"The man's a malingerer, and shame on the sergeant, whatever his name, for falling for it. Oldest damn trick in the book," muttered the doctor as he began to clean and bandage Moana's scrape.

"Bowers, Sergeant-Major Bowers, sir," offered Moana, hiding a grin.

"And you, Sergeant, are no better. This injury is hardly worth my attention. I'm sure you have duties to attend to. Be off with you."

Moana winked at Erepu, who was hiding his own smile behind his hand. "Thank you, Doctor."

"It was simple," Moana explained to Bowers and Walker. "We don't know for certain whether the eight warriors are at the Henare farm or whether they have taken any of the family. From what I gather, it's Erepu they want. If they took Wikitoria, they did so because she must have seen them, and they did not want her to warn Erepu."

"Then we don't know if the rebels know if Wikitoria told Erepu they were at the farm waiting?" asked Bowers.

"That's right," said Moana glumly. "All we can do is approach the farm and capture any warriors we find. Hopefully, all family members will be in the cottage."

"Why must I take the remainder of the company south?" asked Walker.

"Because you will make sure the town knows the Rangers are on a training exercise by making lots of noise and heading away from the Henare farm in the opposite direction. That way, if things go wrong and questions are asked, we can say we were all together and nowhere near their farm."

Walker nodded.

"What about me, Ira?" asked Bowers.

"You, my friend, will come with us and be our reserve and look-out. And make sure you are well-armed."

"When did you want to leave?"

"In about two hours. Slowly make your way up the track to the bush line on the other side of the stream and wait there. Others will join us."

"When should the Company leave?"

"About the same time. Any more questions?"

A few men had already arrived at the rally point, and Moana impatiently waited for the rest. None of his scouts took the direct path– all emerged from the bush, grinning from ear to ear. The only one to walk up the main track was Sergeant-Major Bowers. He was the last to arrive.

"How many have we got, Ira?" asked Bowers.

"Including you, there are eleven of us."

Moana had sent two scouts ahead a few minutes earlier and was now ready to follow. "Let's go."

"Wait one moment!" came a voice from the dark.

Moana whipped his head around– from out of the darkness stepped Captain Von Tempsky. "Captain?"

"Do you think I would sit by and allow you all to go off and leave me behind? I think not. Lead the way, Ira."

Moana shook his head; he should've expected this.

Bowers was stunned. He couldn't believe it.

Sticking to the side of the road, with five men on each side and two scouts ahead, the group cautiously made their way north. The full moon provided more light than Moana preferred, but that worked both ways. The moonlight made them easier to see, but it also made the warriors easier to see. They were making good progress when one of the scouts came running down the track.

Surprised to see Captain Von Tempsky with the group, the scout was unsure whom to report to. The captain inclined his head towards Moana.

"There is a soldier waiting off the track around the next bend. He hasn't seen or heard us, Sergeant. What should we do?" reported Tane.

"We'll go around him, but let me look first," Moana offered.

He ran with Tane up the track, then disappeared into the bush to reappear a few minutes later. He returned to the group and approached Von Tempsky.

"It's Lieutenant Roberts, sir. He's waiting in the bushes, and I think he's waiting for us. Did he know we were doing this?" asked Moana.

"No, certainly not, Ira. I haven't told anyone because this exercise isn't even happening."

Moana instructed the scout to return with the lieutenant.

They waited nervously until two figures emerged from the darkness and approached.

"Taking an evening stroll, Lieutenant?" asked Von Tempsky.

"Uh, actually, I was, sir. It looked like a pleasant night to be out."

The captain looked at Roberts for a moment, sizing him up. Deciding, he turned to Moana. "Can you use a man going for an evening stroll?"

Moana grinned, "Is the 57th camped around the corner, Lieutenant?"

"Just me," laughed Roberts.

"With respect, sirs," said Moana, "I have only Sergeant-Major Bowers as a reserve. I could use extra men in case they make a break for the track. When we reach the farm, I'll send one scout with the sergeant to protect the north side of the track. If both of you could remain on this side, it would give us better coverage."

"As you wish, Ira."

The group continued to where the scouts waited near the farm's boundary. Moana briefed his men, then sent two men out to check the perimeter. After a quick reconnaissance, they returned and reported eight horses hobbled behind the cottage, four disinterested rebels in various locations, and a single lit lantern in the cottage, with no visible people inside.

Silently, each man slipped into the bush and disappeared. Only four men remained standing on the track, two on the north side and two on the south. Not a sound was heard, nothing to indicate anything was amiss.

Captain Von Tempsky glowed with pride. He watched his sergeant lead the unauthorised exercise with confidence. Everyone listened and obeyed eagerly; even the veteran Sergeant-Major Bowers didn't question Ira. In fact, Von Tempsky found himself readily succumbing to Ira's instructions. Seeing his men vanish into the night without a sound and begin to track suspected rebels made him proud– this is what they trained for; this is where the Forest Rangers shone.

Von Tempsky turned to Roberts and whispered, "Why are you here, Lieutenant? You risk your career?"

"I agreed with your assessment at this afternoon's briefing and believe the informant is credible. Waiting, as Colonel Warren suggested, and then sending one man in the morning isn't prudent, in my opinion. When I saw your face, I knew what you were planning, sir. There are innocent civilians' lives at stake, Captain. I can't sit by and do nothing."

"I didn't plan anything, Lieutenant. I'm asleep in my bed while Company No. 2 is out on the south side of Oakura, carrying out a planned training exercise. If you were in your bed, you'd no doubt have heard the noise they made."

Moana crept quietly through the bush and cautiously approached the cottage. He lay concealed in the hedge and waited. It didn't take long to identify four rebels positioned around the perimeter of the cottage. Three of the rebels were easy targets, situated near suitable cover; the fourth man was in a more open area, and reaching him would prove more challenging. Moana assigned himself to that man.

He also posted two of his men to cover the only possible escape route. On the track were his four reserves. He'd hoped they wouldn't be needed. Now he waited for his Ranger scouts to do their job before he could attempt his. Once each rebel warrior was disabled, a scout would signal by briefly waving a white cloth. Each two-man scout team would perform their task in a predetermined order. Normally, they might use birdcalls to signal, but against *Māori* warriors, such calls would be easily identified as fake. Moana stressed that the priority was to take prisoners, not to kill them. Questioning the prisoners, he'd hoped, would yield useful intelligence.

Lying under the hedge was uncomfortable. Branches dug into his side and legs and grazed his face. He could feel small creatures crawling over his body. Still, he didn't move and resisted the temptation to scratch or reposition. Moana thought about Wiki as he waited– he hoped she was unhurt.

One of the six hobbled horses lifted its head and twitched its ears. Moana held his breath, hoping it wouldn't snicker. It didn't, and he let out a sigh of relief. The guard nearest him didn't notice. A moment later, he saw a flash of white. One down, three more to go. Ever so slowly, Moana repositioned to see from a new angle, from where another rebel waited.

Time seemed to stop. The waiting was endless, but he could visualise his scout creeping towards the unsuspecting warrior, drawing nearer, ever closer. He thought again of Wiki and remembered her swishing skirts as she walked away from him. The defiant look she gave him, the proud way she carried herself. He allowed himself a smile. It disappeared quickly at the muted sound of a grunt. Moana tensed and readied himself to spring from the hedge and leap towards the nearby warrior if he reacted to the noise.

The warrior turned unhurriedly and yelled a question.

The reply came back, "A piss!"

Quietness again enveloped the area around the cottage. The warrior near Moana took a few steps, turned, and walked back. Oblivious to what was happening around him, he leaned his musket against the tree and began some stretching exercises. Moana knew how he felt. There it was, another quick flash of white. Two down, and two to go. The stretching stopped, followed by a yawn. He retrieved his musket, faced the track, and waited. Moana relaxed a little– the odds were changing rapidly.

The third warrior stood on the far side, almost out of his line of sight. The full moon was helping tonight, after all. Turning his attention to the cottage, Moana could see a lamp burning, but, unusually, no movement. Once the warriors outside were removed, four more remained. Getting inside may prove difficult. He allowed his eyes to slowly readjust to the darkness.

Something puzzled Moana; it gnawed at him, but he couldn't put his finger on it. It bothered him, yet so far everything was going to plan. Nothing was wrong; in fact, it was easy – too easy? Using the available light, he slowly turned his head and surveyed the surroundings. Everything seemed as it should. The fourth rebel yawned again, and then it struck Moana. It was wrong - this was a set-up!

Almost immediately, Moana saw the white flash of cloth, and the third man was down. Without waiting, and forgoing stealth, Moana sprang up and took four steps to the surprised fourth warrior. Without breaking stride, Moana reached out and grabbed the warrior by the neck. The man collapsed to the ground, unconscious.

"To me!" he yelled. "To me!"

With puzzled looks, the Rangers, with their captives securely held, ran from the darkness and surrounded Moana. Von Tempsky and Roberts joined them moments later, followed soon after by Bowers and a scout. No one questioned Moana about why he had yelled, which risked alerting the warriors in the cottage. They trusted his judgement and anxiously waited for his explanation.

Moana turned to the captain. "This is a setup, sir." He instructed Tane to look in the cottage. "He won't find anyone. The place will be empty. We need to get back to Oakura. Erepu is in danger if we are not too late. This was a ruse, and I fell for it."

"The cottage is empty!" reported Tane.

"Then where are the Henare family?" asked Von Tempsky, turning to a rebel.

"Probably up in the hills, sir. That's the only place they could have taken them, and they've probably left them there. While we came here wasting our time, the rebels went to Oakura. These four men will tell us nothing. They are inexperienced, young, and they've actually done nothing wrong, so we'll probably have to let them go."

One of the rebels laughed, mocking the Rangers. He accidentally received a kick in the kidneys from an unapologetic Sergeant-Major Bowers. The laughing stopped.

"Then we need to return to Oakura immediately," said Von Tempsky, taking charge and issuing a string of commands. "Lieutenant, I'll leave these four men in your care to do with as you please. Sergeant-Major Bowers, please assign two men to assist the Lieutenant, then send your best man on one of those horses to find Sergeant Walker and recall the Company – they won't be far away. Ira, take Tane and go find the Henare family. Let's hope we're not too late. Time to move, Rangers!"

Men began to move quickly, and Moana and Tane went to the cottage and retrieved the lantern. Without delay, they began searching for tracks as Von Tempsky and the remainder returned to Oakura with haste. Lieutenant Roberts had a few questions he wanted answered of the young rebels.

Doctor Winthorp was in the infirmary, looking a little pale. He was applying a dressing to a wound on his head when Von Tempsky, accompanied by Sergeant-Major Bowers, flung open the door and entered. He quickly glanced around the room and expertly assessed the situation.

"How long ago did they come for him, doctor?"

"I'm not sure, Captain, perhaps fifteen minutes ago, maybe longer."

"By any chance, did you see which direction they went?"

"No, I'd been struck on the head and rendered unconscious."

Von Tempsky's hand automatically went to his moustache as he thought.

"How many warriors were there?" he asked after a brief pause.

"Only three came in here, but there were more outside."

"I see … Are you in need of further attention?"

"No, I will be fine. Nothing some medicinal alcohol won't cure."

"You were very lucky, Doctor."

The doctor remained silent as he dabbed at his scalp with a cloth.

Von Tempsky left the doctor to self-medicate and strode to the Company office.

"Notify me once the Company has returned, and see they are fed and rested. Tomorrow will be a long day, Sergeant."

"Very well, sir."

Moana and Tane scoured the ground for signs. The hard-packed earth made it difficult to find anything useful, especially at night. They searched in a zigzag pattern, leaving the cottage behind them and slowly working their way towards the foothills of the Kaitake Ranges. There were no clues, no indication that a group of people had passed this way only hours before, and no tracks they could see. It was time-consuming as they crossed and re-crossed the path that led into the hills.

They stopped to reassess their progress and consider alternatives.

"Wait, did you hear that?" questioned Moana, lifting his head and slowly turning his body to identify the direction from which the sound came.

"I didn't hear anything– "

"Shhhh … Yes, there it is again."

Both men shut their eyes and listened. Simultaneously, they pointed in the same direction and began to run cautiously towards the noise.

As they approached a fenceline bordered by large trees, they saw a small barn emerge from the darkness, the yellow light from the lantern making the building's weathered, unpainted timber appear white. Moana led the way, and Tane kept close to the edge of the lantern's pool of light. The yelling grew louder as they approached. Then a woman's voice could be clearly heard telling the shouting men to stop. Moana heard her muted words quite clearly; it was definitely Wiki, and, as ordered, the voices stopped.

"Thank you. Now I have a headache," came the muffled voice of Wiki.

A quiet returned to the night as Moana and Tane arrived at the barn door.

Moana smiled. *At least, Wiki seemed unhurt.*

A solid wooden bar lay across the doorway, preventing anyone from swinging it open and leaving. Placing the lantern on the ground, both men heaved the bar away. Moana swung open the large door and looked inside. Blinking in the light, with hands raised to shield their eyes, stood all five members of the Henare family.

"Good evening!" said Moana cheerfully.

"Ira?" questioned Tami Henare. "Thank goodness you found us– we thought we'd be here all night."

"If we hadn't heard the yelling, you would've been," replied Moana as the family moved outside. "Uh, hello Wikitoria, are you hurt?"

She stopped and looked up at him. "We've been locked up in here for hours, and the first words out of your mouth are 'Good evening' … I do wonder about men!" she said, then walked off quickly.

Tane winced.

"She has to go pee," volunteered her youngest brother, which earned him a clip across the ear from the old man.

"Have you found Erepu?" she asked over her shoulder as she disappeared into the night.

"I'll explain back at your home," yelled Ira.

"I think she likes you," cackled the farmer, his annoyance forgotten. "Ira, these are my boys, Charles, James and the youngest, Henry, whom you've just met."

For the first time, Ira met Wiki's brothers. They each introduced themselves, shook Moana's hand, and politely thanked him and Tane for rescuing them. Charles explained that they had tried to break out of the barn, but the darkness made it difficult in the confined space. Staying in the barn all night wasn't something any of them were looking forward to, and they were relieved to finally be free. Moana and Tane accompanied the Henares back to the cottage. Moana was keen to learn as much as he could about the rebels.

"Cup of tea, Ira?" asked Wiki, once the stove was lit.

Ira was again struck by her poise. Even after her abduction and hours locked up, she remained self-assured and beautiful. He smiled at her use of his nickname.

"What of Erepu?" asked Tami.

Moana reluctantly turned away from Wiki and explained that Erepu was under a doctor's care in the infirmary and that she had spoken to him earlier. "But now, I don't know … we don't have any idea at this time."

"He should be safe, shouldn't he?" Wiki asked.

"I can't answer that, Wiki, but the rebels drew us here. While we were trying to rescue you, they may have returned to Oakura and taken him. We won't know until we return or Captain Von Tempsky sends us word."

"How would they know where to find him?" asked Wiki over her shoulder as she stood in the small kitchen.

Moana shrugged, "I've been wondering exactly the same thing."

"And where would they take him?" she continued.

"If they do have him, I'd say they'll take him back to Waitotara," reasoned the farmer.

"Why's that?" asked Moana.

"That's where they've told all the *Pai Marire* people to go. The Wereroa *pa*, at Waitotara, is where their leader, Te Ua Haumene, lives," Tami said.

"I heard they pray before a big pole and dance around, going crazy and shouting rubbish," suggested Charles. "I'd say they've all lost their minds, the lot of 'em."

"If Erepu has been taken as you think, will you go after them and bring him back?" asked Wiki.

"It isn't my decision to make, but if I know Captain Von Tempsky, he will send men after the rebels."

"Will it be you?"

"I can't say," replied Moana.

The sound of her voice suggested some concern, but with Wiki it was hard to tell, he thought.

"Did you know the *Hauhau* believe that *Pākeha* bullets can't harm them?" volunteered Henry, the youngest.

Everyone turned to him in surprise. "Where did you hear that?" asked his father.

Tane turned to Moana with concern.

"From Tai, who brings us the fertiliser. He said his cousin lives in Opunake and that his neighbour joined the *Pai Marire*. He's been at Waitotara and has heard Te Ua speak," answered Henry.

"What exactly is a *Hauhau*?" Moana asked.

"Oh, they're the *Pai Marire* crazy men. Many of them are warriors like Paora, Hatotoi, and Kaihoka. Kaihoka and Paora were the ones who chopped the *Pākeha* soldiers' heads off."

"That's enough Henry!" cautioned Wiki.

Tami was quiet and looked thoughtful.

Moana looked to Tane, "I think we need to go and report back to the captain. He'll be wondering where we are."

Moana and Tane again received heartfelt thanks from everyone. Tane received a hug from Wiki, but Moana did not.

Wiki waited at the door until her father and brothers returned indoors. Tane discreetly continued down the path and waited.

"Thank you, Ira. I apologise for being cross with you. It wasn't you I was angry at," she said, looking up at him as their eyes met. She leaned forward and quickly pecked him on the cheek. "Be careful, Ira." She turned with a rustle of skirts and disappeared inside, leaving him giddy.

Under the lantern's dim yellow light on the veranda, Tane saw the kiss. He couldn't wait to return to the barracks to tell the boys.

CHAPTER FOURTEEN

Pursuit

Colonel Warren's fingers drummed on the desk with impatience. The tempo of his manicured nails striking the polished oak surface was a clear indication of his volatile mood. Mixed with anger and a little frustration, and lacking proficiency in percussive rhythms, the colonel's incessant tapping was erratic, annoying and rude, especially whilst an officer was delivering a report of some consequence that had occurred during the previous evening.

As Captain Von Tempsky finished his account, the colonel managed to bring his disagreeable cadence to an end. Lieutenant Roberts, who sat in uncomfortable silence, stole a furtive glance at the captain. The sound of a wagoner hurling abuse at his lazy bullocks filled the colonel's office as he passed the building. The drumming began again, but only for a second, then stopped, much to the relief of the colonel's guests as he arrived at a conclusion.

"And your men just happened to be out on an evening exercise, Captain?" quizzed the colonel, raising an eyebrow.

"Yes, sir. To maintain a high level of readiness, the Rangers train constantly, in all weather, at any time of day or evening," offered Von Tempsky, keeping his voice neutral, lest he offend.

Colonel Warren turned his massive head towards his intelligence officer, Lieutenant Roberts. "Where were you when this incident occurred?"

"Asleep, sir. Or rather, I was until the Company marched past, waking me."

The colonel sucked noisily at some newly discovered debris left over from breakfast, which he found between his teeth, as he thought the matter through. The room remained quiet, save for the disagreeable sound of the colonel's exploratory tongue. He looked down at the many small paintings that neatly adorned his desk. He selected one framed in pewter and stared at it wistfully as he stroked the metal frame. Von Tempsky kept his eyes firmly on the colonel's face. The oppressive silence was broken by laughter as two soldiers walked by the window.

"And what is the current Ranger status, Captain?"

"We are ready to deploy soon as our scouts return."

"I see," the colonel tenderly replaced the picture and wiped a fleck of dust from the glass. "Inform me, Lieutenant, what you have gleaned from this unfortunate incident. Are we likely to be attacked by marauding rebels while we lie comfortably asleep in our beds?"

Roberts shifted in his seat. "Colonel, we believe the rebels are part of a larger force currently camped in the Waitotara region. Information that's come to light suggests the abduction was intended to prevent Mr Henare from disclosing details of the next *Hauhau* attack at Te Morere or Sentry Hill. I doubt the rebels' intention is to attack here, sir."

Colonel Warren laughed as he rose from his chair. He leaned forward, resting both hands on his desk. "As an intelligence officer, you will understand the enemy's desire to spread misinformation. Mr Henare's claim is preposterous, and I will not be part of it!" He turned to address both men. "As officers, both of you should know better than to fall for unfounded speculation spread by a confessed member of a ragtag religious cult!"

Unfazed, Von Tempsky held his gaze.

"Can I apprise you of more useful information?" Warren asked sarcastically.

"Sir? One question I am unable to answer. How did the rebels know that Mr Henare was being held here?"

The colonel shook his head, wondering how on earth he'd been saddled with an idiot of an intelligence officer. "Because the man was injured! An infirmary is where we take the injured, is it not?"

"Yes, but sir–"

"I'm not going to argue this with you, Roberts. I have more important things to deal with. Both of you are dismissed," the colonel returned to his chair with a sigh.

Captain Von Tempsky and Lieutenant Roberts walked to the door, eager to be gone.

"Oh, Captain?"

Von Tempsky paused and slowly turned to face the colonel.

"Perhaps the Forest Rangers could make better use of their time, eh?"

"Will that be all, sir?" asked the captain in an even, respectful voice.

Colonel Warren stared at the door long after Captain Von Tempsky had left his office. *The man frightened him.*

At about the same time that Captain Von Tempsky and Lieutenant Roberts were being dismissed from Colonel Warren's office, two Ranger scouts on horseback were rapidly closing on the small band of *Hauhau* rebels who'd abducted Erepu Henare. Surprisingly, the tracks headed northeast, in the opposite direction to Waitotara, where everyone believed they were heading.

It wasn't until a cloud of blue smoke and the sound of a single musket discharge alerted them to how close they were to the rear-guard rebels. The ambitious long-range shot taken by an enthusiastic sharpshooter fell short, and the two scouts, Tane and Moana Ngata, reined in to observe from a safe distance.

Their role wasn't to engage the rebels but to pursue, identify, and determine the route they had taken. Moana immediately returned to Oakura to report their find, and Tane continued to follow them.

The rebels left two men behind to harass and persuade the lone Ranger scout to abandon his pursuit. Every now and then, a rebel would pop up, fire his weapon, remount his horse and disappear at speed. This continued for some time until the rebels finally entered the bush, abandoning their horses.

Tane cautiously entered the bush and searched for tracks. The rebels made some effort to hide their trail, but within a short time, the scout had found signs and continued to pursue. The rebels were swinging east around the northern side of Mount Taranaki. Wisely, Tane decided to stop and return to Oakura to report back.

Ira studied the map thoroughly. With him were the two scouts, Lieutenants Griggs and Small, and Captain Von Tempsky. Tane indicated the route the rebels used, then pointed to where they disappeared into the bush and left their horses.

"Where are the devils going?" wondered Von Tempsky out loud.

"Not to Waitotara, that's for sure," replied Ira.

Remembering Erepu's warning, Moana quickly found Te Morere on the map and stabbed. "There! That's where they're going!"

The captain leaned over and looked carefully. "Then why enter the bush and continue on foot when they didn't need to?" He answered his own question, "Perhaps they feared we would catch them and decided they stood a better chance of evading us in the bush?"

"Seems very likely to me. Remember, they don't know we know where they're heading," replied the sergeant. He drew a line on the map parallel to the rebels' expected route. "We can easily catch them here. Their progress will be slower, and we can make up time easily."

The captain straightened and returned to his desk, his fingers entwined in his moustache. "So be it. Well done, Ira. I will pay Lieutenant Roberts a brief visit and inform him of our intentions. I think we can safely assign ourselves two tasks: recover the prisoner, then proceed to Te Morere and inform the commander of an impending attack. Gentlemen, prepare your men. We march in thirty minutes."

Company No. 2 was strung out in a long, untidy line, marching double time. For the Rangers, that was almost jogging. At the rear of the long column, Sergeant Walker barked, hurling insults at stragglers, threatening punishments, and, on occasion, even using his right foot. Thus motivated, the Rangers ate up the miles, marching across rolling hills and through pastures, although the captain insisted they not destroy crops, and at times, travelling along well-used tracks. Ahead, scouts were assessing the easiest route and leaving visible markers.

Captain Von Tempsky's Company No. 2 travelled light– no support wagons were used. Each man carried food for three days, a leather-clad bottle of rum, and his weapons. Additionally, for every two men, they carried a single blanket. With luck, the Rangers would find some foliage to lie on at night, as they were expected to sleep on the ground. While the Rangers often boasted they were paid more than regular troops, the facts were simple. They endured severe conditions that no regular troops ever did. The Forest Rangers were a proud group of men who relished the harshness and challenges unique to their specialised service.

Ira was marching at the centre of the column. He'd found his rhythm and used his arms to drive his body forward as he strode purposefully onward. He didn't talk to anyone and stayed quiet and focused, often staring at a fixed point in the distance as if in a trance. Apart from the stragglers at the rear being harried by Sergeant Walker, all the Rangers wore a grim look of determination.

When they stopped to rest for a few minutes for refreshments and to attend to toiletries, they were not allowed to sit or lie on the ground; Captain Von Tempsky insisted his men remain standing. Once muscles were allowed to rest, they would tighten, making it difficult to resume the pace and rhythm, he wisely informed them. Company No. 2 was fit, healthy and well-practised, yet for the most part they followed the captain's orders, not out of fear but out of respect. The captain marched alongside his men, forded the same streams, slept on the ground and ate the same food, just as the rankers did. When they marched, he'd walk alongside his men, offering support and encouragement, and often shared a joke or a laugh. Company No. 2 was tight, their commander popular, and they were a highly skilled and lethal fighting force, and they knew it.

Using the light of a campfire, Captain Von Tempsky was assessing their progress with his officers and sergeants. He was studying a map and informed everyone that they'd now passed the point where the rebels entered the bush and had travelled a good deal further.

He thrust a finger at a spot on the map with enthusiasm. "Tomorrow, sometime in the early afternoon, we will reach the valley, enter the bush, and follow the river west. I believe they will follow the same river east, so our goal for tomorrow is to find a suitable spot to prepare our positions for an ambuscade." He looked at his men in turn, searching for doubt on their faces. Seeing none, he continued, "When the scouts report the rebels approaching our position, we will engage them, with the understanding that our priority is to liberate the captive." He carefully folded his map and turned to Moana. "Ira, I want you as the forward scout, along with one other. I want to minimise the chance they will detect us. The fewer scouts we have up front, the less likely that will happen. I also want you to take the Enfield with you."

Moana groaned inwardly. The single-shot Pattern Enfield musket was a long, fifty-five-inch weapon, cumbersome for a scout to carry. It frequently caught in branches, was heavy, and slow to reload. A newer Terry and Calisher rifled breech-loading carbine was introduced and used successfully by the Rangers. However, the .57-calibre Pattern Enfield was still preferred by marksmen.

"Once you've established the rebels are approaching," continued the captain, "I want you to pull back to a forward flanking position and cover any defensive positions they hold. You'll be a cut-off group and, hopefully, help prevent their retreat. You'll have five men in your team and will operate as we've trained. A sharpshooter, that's you, Ira; a lookout; and the other three will provide protection."

"Do you want us to take two Enfields?" asked Moana.

"No, just the one. While you are one of our most accurate marksmen, I want another five-man team to cover the other flank and provide interlocking coverage with you, but further back. I want to ensure you have a clear field of fire. You will cover the rebels' rearmost positions and be our most forward point. The remainder of the Enfields will be used with our two main kill-group platoons and the other five-man sniping team. Any questions?"

"No, sir."

The captain turned to Lieutenant Griggs. "I want ten men held in reserve as a rear-protection platoon. You will command them and be prepared to cover any position as needed at a moment's notice. Sergeant-Major Bowers will be with you as second-in-command. You must be alert to any offensive or flanking manoeuvres the rebels attempt." Von Tempsky raised an eyebrow. "Or lend support in the unlikely event that our positions are in danger of being overrun, including the rear. Understood, Lieutenant?"

"Yes, sir,"

"The main force will be split into two platoons, each with fifteen men. Lieutenant Small, you will command the left 'kill' side, with Sergeant Walker as your second-in-command. I will command the right 'kill' side." The captain paused and took a deep breath. "Very well then. We will go over more details tomorrow, once we've chosen our site and can refine the plan. Oh yes, Ira? Remember, when we first enter the bush tomorrow, I only want you and one other scout with you. All other scouts will remain with us."

Moana nodded.

"Good. Now you have time to think about your responsibilities and inform your men. I suggest you have an early night. We have a big day tomorrow."

Even before the sun rose, the serenity of another early Taranaki morning was broken by the creative epithets hurled at disinclined Rangers who were less willing than others to enjoy an early dawn stroll. Arguably, Sergeant Walker's definition of a stroll was purely interpretive and subject to surly debate amongst the troops at the very rear of the Forest Rangers' elongated marching column. Selective in his hearing, the sergeant chose to ignore certain portions of the carping directed at him, the Forest Rangers, and the military in general. However, in some cases his response was to position himself near the source of the bellicose comments. This had a remarkable effect on subsequent vocal assertions, which unsurprisingly shifted to a more moderate and flattering tone. To appease the disgruntled, Sergeant Walker invited all complainants to correspond in writing to the Forest Rangers 'Office of Grievances, of which he, Sergeant Eric Walker, was solely in charge. No one bothered to ask him for the postal address.

Sergeant Walker's needling distracted his men from their troubles, and while they vented their anger and frustrations on him, they forgot about the quick pace and their tiredness. Within an hour or two, they had covered considerable miles. Captain Von Tempsky was pleased; he estimated they were slightly ahead of his schedule.

It was late morning, and the sun had yet to reach its zenith when the Ranger Company approached their destination and were met by scouts lounging in wait beneath the shade of a tree. This was the place where the Rangers would enter the dense bush on either side of the narrow river valley. With some compassion, the captain granted permission for his Rangers to stand down and rest. Gratefully, some men took the opportunity to soak their aching feet or cleanse themselves in the river while others just dozed. Standing orders required all men to retain their weapons, and scouts were dispatched to guard their perimeter.

All three sergeants, both lieutenants, and the captain were sitting on large rocks in the middle of the river, their feet dangling in the cool water.

"Let's hope Mr Henare's injured feet have slowed the rebels' progress, eh?" said the captain.

"I wonder how far behind us they are?" asked Sergeant-Major Bowers.

A response wasn't forthcoming – no one knew.

Moana was in good spirits. He enjoyed the exertions of a march, the weather was perfect, and he was focused on the mission ahead. His toes played with small pebbles underfoot as the cool, clear water gurgled around them.

"I recently read a journal article," he said to the surprise of all.

Heads turned to him.

"A learned gentleman of some academic and scientific distinction discovered an unusual aquatic specimen in the waterways surrounding Mount Taranaki. Apparently quite a fearsome and savage creature." He paused as if that were the end.

"Yes, and…?" asked Bowers with curiosity.

Moana kept his gaze on the gentle flowing water and fought to keep a straight face. "He called it 'The Great Taranaki Toe-Biter'."

"What!" cried Lieutenant Griggs and immediately jerked his feet out of the river.

Everyone burst out laughing. Sergeant Walker sat upright and laughed so hard he slipped backwards off the rock and tumbled into the river which made them laugh even harder. Sergeant-Major Bowers was wiping tears from his face, and Captain Von Tempsky, unable to contain himself, looked as if he would urinate into his breeches.

The rest of the Company turned with puzzlement towards the sound and activity, convinced the sun had done irreversible damage to their sergeants and officers. Whilst the reason for the merriment was unknown, the officers' infectious hysteria caused many Rangers to smile, and some began to chuckle. As Sergeant Walker picked himself up from the stream, still laughing and dripping water, most of Forest Ranger Company No. 2 joined in, especially those who'd been marching at the column's rear.

He sat in solitude, a man in the privacy of prayer. Te Ua spoke to God and solemnly offered his faith and devotion. He reaffirmed his love and sought forgiveness for his sins and shortcomings - his failings.

Was he not a man born into sin, so his sins should be forgiven? Te Ua had sinned; men died and continued to die – from his hand? He didn't want another man's death on his conscience and then be judged unfairly by God. But death was inevitable, he reasoned; certainly everyone must die. Could he justify death in the holy struggle for redemption and righteousness? Those who perished in the name of God did so of their own free will. Even heathens had a choice, he admitted. He offered a short prayer for the dead, that their souls would find everlasting peace.

His thoughts returned to the persecuted Israelites and their continued struggle. Te Ua looked at the mountain that rose high above the plains before him, Taranaki, and thought back to his earliest recollections of Bible study. Something happened on a mountain called Sinai that the people were never allowed to forget. This marked them off from the world as God's own people – the Jews. God gave them rules for government; above all, he gave them religion. And he, Te Ua Haumene, was the voice of God, and he gave them *Pai Marire*, faith, and hope. As an instrument of God, as a messenger and a minister, he would bring about peace. As Christians are called to live holy, pleasing lives, we will please God and return to Him what is rightfully His.

Te Ua adjusted his position to a more comfortable one and smiled. He thanked God for his wisdom and love, feeling secure in the knowledge that his actions were those of a believer, a true Christian.

How could he not be? It was signified by the Spirit to his angel that salvation might be disclosed to this generation, as it was to John when it was revealed to him by the Spirit on the Isle of Patmos. He also uttered the name of Christ and spoke of all the things he saw, including the salvation of his people. *Let the name of the Lord be praised throughout the world, for it is He who guides me with clouds from His breath.*

Te Ua rose and stretched his cramped legs. He looked up at the *niu*, the brilliant blue sky highlighting the tall mast in splendid glory, the darkness of its shadow receding in the early-morning light. He offered blessings to those who would be spared from death, while his disciples justly drove the *Pākeha* from the lands of his people. Are not *Pākeha* the same as the Assyrians, the oppressors who drove the Ten Lost Tribes of Israel from Samaria? Yes, he reflected, the Island of Two Halves is our Samaria, and we will not be lost to the ages. *Pākeha* will be driven into the ocean.

Appeased, Te Ua walked from the *niu* and stepped down from the raised platform, ready to begin his day. It was time to meet his people. They needed him and asked for guidance, and with God's help, he would save and love them. They continued to show support in ever-growing numbers. Even as he prayed at the *niu*, the Taranaki *iwi*, Ati Awa, were gathering to reclaim Te Morere. He sent men to assist, and his faithful Hatotoi Kahore would lead them to triumph.

Te Ua had educated him well, and now it was Hatotoi's turn to teach *Pai Marire* devotees how to fight *Pākeha* soldiers. They gathered at the Manutahi *pa*, near Te Morere, and stood in rapt attention as Hatotoi preached.

"Hapa, hapa, hapa! Hau, hau, hau! Pai-marire, rire, rire — hau!" cried Hatotoi.

As shown, the followers raised their right hands level with their heads, palm forward, and shouted in chorus, "Hapa, hapa, hapa! Hau, hau, hau! Pai-marire, rire, rire — hau!"

He raised his own right hand, and again, with passion he yelled, "Hapa, hapa, hapa! Hau, hau, hau! Pai-marire, rire, rire — hau!"

They answered in zeal, "Hapa, hapa, hapa! Hau, hau, hau! Pai-marire, rire, rire — hau!"

And they repeated the chant again and again until they were familiar with its sound, its meaning and significance.

"This is how God loves us and will protect us! And Te Ua has shown us how we will overcome the *Pākeha*!" Hatotoi repeated. "His bullets *will* pass overhead or fall short, and we *will* be protected. As true believers, we *will not* be harmed! Hapa, hapa, hapa! Hau, hau, hau! Pai-marire, rire, rire — hau!"

As one, the assembled warriors raised their right hands and repeated the incantation. The cry of 'Hau' grew ever more like the barking of dogs. Some were reticent, unsure whether the chant would ward off *Pākeha* bullets. Hatotoi knew that uncertainty would persist amongst his warriors. Carefully, he scanned the faces for doubters.

"We must believe and have faith!" he walked among his men, stopping in front of those he'd identified. "Do you believe?" he questioned. "Do you have faith?"

In affirmation, they replied, their confidence growing. When he was convinced, he'd move on to another and repeat the questions. Little did Hatotoi know that his own faith would soon be called into question.

Deep in the shadows beneath the low, leafy green canopy of fern, Moana and Tane lay in absolute stillness. All traces of their tracks were expertly removed - they were invisible. The absence of any breeze meant they exercised extreme caution; a moving branch or leaf would signal their presence to an experienced eye. Both men smeared mud over their faces and blended into the surroundings as though they were part of it.

Moana chose their position wisely. It offered them a high, unobstructed view of the gully and a quick, safe retreat when the rebels came. Even the skittish birds returned, and the natural order of bush life was restored as the two intruders were accepted and ignored. All was as it should be.

Earlier, both Rangers slithered over the ridgeline, using low-growing foliage as cover, then moved down a few yards to their present position, where the undergrowth was thicker. With the Company approximately one mile behind them, this was as far forward as Moana dared go. Once the rebels were detected, they would attempt to determine their strength. Then both men would quietly slither back over the ridge, drop down the far side, quickly withdraw, and report to Captain Von Tempsky.

With practised ease, both Rangers lay motionless in absolute silence; they waited patiently. Time meant nothing - it was irrelevant. The pounding of blood that had filled their ears and coursed through their bodies earlier slowed to a measured, controlled rhythm. The pebble that pressed uncomfortably into Moana's thigh was ignored, as was the branch that poked into Tane's ribs. It was too late to adjust and move; they had to endure the discomfort or risk detection. They waited.

Time passed, one hour became two; Moana lost count. It mattered not; he was patient and invisible.

He sensed a change in the bush atmosphere, an imperceptible shift, a sixth sense alerting him to impending danger. Without a word, he pressed his elbow into Tane's side, a subtle warning. Tane didn't acknowledge it; he understood. His own senses were heightened.

Midway up the gully, a branch of a low bush, approximately thirty yards away, swayed. The dappled light filtering onto its glossy, thick green leaves flickered as the leaves moved, drawing Moana's attention. There was no apparent reason for the sudden movement. It was unnatural, and as he knew, manmade. A scout. Moana immediately began to scan the opposite side of the gully, hoping to detect another rebel scout, but nothing stirred. Again, his attention returned to where the branch moved and was rewarded with the movement of a shadow. It was a lone rebel warrior. The scout's attention was fixed on the valley floor; he wasn't looking up and couldn't see Moana and Tane. No one could.

With patience that suggested some skill, the rebel scout concealed himself to observe the gully below. Like the two Rangers who watched him, the scout sat unmoving, his outline merging into the greens and darkness of the bush that enveloped him.

Ignoring the tiny stone pressing uncomfortably into his thigh, Moana went through the next steps in his mind and visualised the events he predicted would occur.

A stick snapped, bringing him back to the present, the sound in sharp contrast to the familiar, comforting sounds around them. Responding to the sharp intrusion of noise, a protesting bird flew away in fright, drawing attention to the unwelcome presence of another man, an intruder. Resisting the temptation to turn their heads, Moana and Tane shifted only their eyes towards the source of the sound. As expected, a face slowly appeared, cautiously rising behind a fallen tree. With his head now easily visible, the inexperienced warrior peered cautiously above the trunk and scanned the small banks on either side of the stream as it meandered and twisted through the narrow valley. Now there were two rebel scouts.

A Tui, a native New Zealand bird, flew with remarkable agility and speed through the tangle of branches across the narrow gully, then landed high on a limb almost directly above the two Ranger scouts. Its untimely arrival caused the small branch to move, dislodging a large leaf that drifted in graceful arcs until it came to rest just in front of the fern canopy beneath which Moana and Tane lay. Both men tensed – the leaf's path pointed directly to where they lay concealed.

Neither rebel scout responded, remaining still, preferring to search for threats amongst the rocks and trees lining either side of the stream. They spared only casual glances upwards, focusing mostly on the easiest and quickest path the rebel group could use. Moana and Tane were careful and never ventured down into the gully; there were no tracks to be found.

Feeling assured no danger lurked, and forgoing stealth, both rebels rose from their hiding places and slid down the steep sides of the gully, meeting at the bottom and immediately continuing their search for signs. From their high vantage point, Moana and Tane watched. They were waiting for the main group of rebels, and it wouldn't be far behind.

Exposed, the two rebel scouts talked quietly for a moment or two, then walked slowly along the stream for a short distance before disappearing from sight. Moana knew they would eventually climb back up into the gully and resume their scouting from the safety of the bush. With some relief, he eased into a more comfortable position, removing the pebble that had been causing discomfort. Tane also adjusted his position slightly.

The birds gave the first warning of the approaching rebel group. With their foraging disrupted by more intruders, the birds took flight, and moments later, the first rebels rounded the distant bend at the far end of the gully. They walked in a long, strung-out line and followed the path alongside the stream, where the going was easiest. At the very rear of the small column, Moana finally saw Erepu. In obvious pain and assisted by a warrior who held his arm, Erepu limped on bandaged feet, aided by a sturdy stick. Every now and then, the warrior tugged impatiently, encouraging Erepu to move more quickly. The progress of the warriors was dictated by the speed of their injured captive, and it was plainly obvious they weren't happy with their slow pace.

Including the two scouts, Moana counted thirteen men and Erepu. Rather than leave now, he waited to see whether any warriors were guarding the rear. After a reasonable time, he judged that there was no rear guard and signalled for Tane to retreat slowly. Backing out of their position, Tane crawled up the gully's side, over the summit, and disappeared.

Just then, two more rebels appeared, tailing the main group by a considerable distance. Alert, they swivelled their heads from side to side, frequently checking their rear. They shared a joke and laughed. Moana froze. These two men increased the rebel force to a total of fifteen, posing a real challenge to Erepu's rescue, thought Moana. The rebel force was strung out over such a long distance that while the Forest Rangers could engage the main group, the two rebels at the rear were effectively out of range. At the first sign of trouble, they could kill Erepu.

Moana gave one last check, then slithered out and crawled up and over the ridgeline to where Tane waited. With a steep hill separating them from the war band, they were now completely out of sight of the warriors and could move quickly through the bush without fear of discovery.

Without delay, the two Rangers set off. Moana jogged cautiously back towards the Company; every foot placement was carefully judged. He dodged fallen trees and leapt over moss-covered boulders scattered over the valley floor. When he encountered obstacles, he skirted around them, always searching for the easiest path. Tane followed closely behind, and neither man spoke.

Having determined he was far enough ahead of the rebels, Moana stopped to drink from a stream.

"There are two more of them. Rear guard."

Tane was on his knees, drinking. He stood and looked up in surprise. "They're a long way back."

Moana grunted.

After a dozen heartbeats, he continued, "We have to remove them. If the captain proceeds as planned, those two at the rear could kill the prisoner."

Tane understood the dilemma and remained quiet, deferring the decision-making to his sergeant.

"We can cross back over the ridge here and wait for the advance scouts. Once they've passed us, we'll move closer and then wait for the main group of rebels. When they've moved on, we'll go to our final position and wait for the two at the back. The hard part will be getting into that position once the group has passed, so we must move quickly."

"They might miss the two at the rear," stated Tane.

"No one in the main group was looking behind them, so it's unlikely they'll be missed. The two at the rear were looking everywhere except where they were walking, so I think we can do this easily." Moana looked into Tane's face for confirmation. "Can you do it?"

Without a moment's pause, Tane nodded confidently.

"Good, we should go."

Moana flicked his eyes down at the large spider crawling down his wrist and onto the back of his right hand. Resisting the urge to fling it away, he kept his composure and let the large, hairy creature go about its business. He felt its legs as it walked unhurriedly through and over the hairs on his wrist, and he could clearly see its fangs. His head was only inches from the eight-legged monster. He wanted to scratch where it tickled, to hurl his arm out and shake the spider free. Instead, he took a slow, deep breath, exhaled slowly, and forced the spider from his mind as he refocused on the two approaching warriors who guarded the rear of the rebel group. Tane lay about four yards away, hidden behind a tree on top of a six-foot bank beside the stream. It was a perfect place to lie in wait.

Moana lay prone between two trees on a slightly elevated bank, separated from Tane by the stream and directly opposite him. Leafy bushes provided cover and wouldn't hinder his movements when he attacked. The warriors were only steps away and would pass between the two Rangers in the natural bottleneck.

As the two rear-guard rebels walked past, Tane moved first. From behind, he leapt from the bank, his right arm outstretched, encircling the warrior's face. As he'd been instructed during endless hours of training, he clamped his hand firmly over the rebel's mouth and pinched his nostrils shut. Quickly raising his elbow to avoid stabbing himself in his arm, he placed the knife against the side of the neck and, in a single fluid motion, pulled across. The sharp blade bit deeply, and the struggling warrior was helpless to prevent the Bowie knife from cleanly severing the carotid artery. In a gush of crimson blood, both men fell heavily to the ground, the rebel's body cushioning the hard landing into the stream and rocks. The rebel stood no chance, his lifeblood draining freely, tinting the water red. Tane maintained his hold until he was sure the rebel was dead. The warrior hadn't made a sound.

The other rebel caught movement in his peripheral vision and instinctively turned towards the threat and crouched. Moana's timing was perfect. Seeing the rebel's exposed back, he lunged forward, giving the surprised warrior no time to bring any weapons to bear or defend himself. The startled spider fell amongst the leaves and quickly scuttled away to freedom. But for the remaining warrior, it was too late. The realisation that he was being attacked from behind dawned on him when Moana drove hard into his back, expelling the air from his lungs. Moana's hand covered the warrior's mouth and nose, preventing any sound from escaping, but his other hand was empty; he didn't use a knife. Using his skill in the secretive and little-known *Māori* martial art of *Mau*, Moana quickly stabbed a precise point in the warrior's neck with only a finger. Both men fell heavily onto the rocks beside the stream. The warrior felt no pain from his awkward fall; he was dead long before he hit the ground.

Still feeling the effects of the adrenaline rush, Tane rose, his chest heaving as he stared at the corpse before him. His heart pounded. This was his first close-combat kill.

Moana stood, rubbing his shoulder where it had struck a rock when he fell. He looked at Tane with concern. Tearing his gaze from the lifeless body he'd just slain, Tane met Moana's gaze. He said nothing.

"Let's move the bodies from the stream and head back to the Company," Moana said softly.

Preferring to remain silent, Tane just nodded.

Both men quickly dragged the rebels away from the stream, hid them behind a bush, and Tane threw leaves over the spilt blood. After a quick check to make sure no warriors were double-backing, they climbed back over the ridge and began their run back to the Company. They didn't have much time, and Moana was thankful that the rebels' pace was slow.

Mahi's stomach was the source of his grief, and he knew the cause of his discomfort and cramps was the fish he'd eaten. The intense pain came in waves, began slowly, and then rose in strength, causing him to double over. It was impossible to keep up with even the warriors' slow pace as they led their captive through the bush towards the Manutahi *pa*. The distress Mahi felt grew worse, and each successive wave of pain made his eyes water. He knew he had to empty his stomach and bowels as soon as possible. Finally spotting a suitable spot, Mahi informed the group's leader of his problem and fell back into the privacy and shadow of a large bush that *Māori* affectionately called Pukapuka and also known as the 'bushman's friend'. The large leaves had a white, furry underside that conveniently made them useful for wiping the *nono* clean. Mahi placed his musket within easy reach, squatted in relief, and without a moment's delay voided his bowels as the main group walked on, leaving him behind. The rear guard wisely kept their distance and offered some desultory ribald comments as they passed him by. The sound of their laughter disappeared, and Mahi was left alone to endure the slow, painful, and undignified motion.

After a satisfactory result and the Pukapuka tree picked clean of its leaves, Mahi began to gingerly catch up to his brother warriors, his own pace limited by the rawness he felt between his buttocks.

Mahi may have been suffering from eating tainted fish, but he was still observant and vigilant. He easily saw the blood beside the stream and nervously searched for its source. Within a short time, he discovered the bodies of his two friends. He scanned the area around him and listened; he saw and heard nothing. One warrior had his throat cut, but the other, strangely, had no visible marks – Mahi was puzzled. He wondered who had killed them. Then it dawned on him. He felt a chill unrelated to his ailment and realised they were walking into a trap. He must warn the others. Ignoring the rawness of his *nono*, Mahi began to run.

CHAPTER FIFTEEN

Ambuscade

Captain Gustavus Von Tempsky wasn't particularly thrilled when Moana reported that he and Tane had engaged two rebels. Failure could have jeopardised their mission, but like any experienced commander, he knew that, despite meticulous planning and foresight, the ambiguities of the unforeseen and unexpected often meant the best-laid plans went awry. As it turned out, the outcome, thankfully, was acceptable, and if he were in the same position as Ira, he probably would have taken a similar course of action.

From behind the trunk of a large tree, the captain watched Ira hurry to his forward marksman's position, where four other Rangers waited about thirty yards away on the left side of the steep-sided gully.

He shifted position and peered from the right side of the tree towards where he knew the second forward marksman team, comprising another four men and Tane, were located about twenty yards away. The captain called these two marksmen teams the cut-off groups. As hard as he looked, they couldn't be seen, as expected.

Heavy foliage, suspended by thick branches, spread across the immediate area and mingled with smaller trees, casting dark shadows. Within the darkness, men hid, camouflaged by leaves, rocks and ferns. Behind larger boulders, men crouched or lay. Some hid behind fallen trees or in crevices that dissected the gully's sides. Only when almost upon them could the unnatural straight lines of musket barrels be seen protruding like a nest of thorns.

Sergeant-Major Bowers stood beside the captain, both men safely obscured by the large tree on the right bank of the stream. The captain turned his attention to the platoon of thirteen Rangers hidden near him; this was the right kill-group, and these men were scattered in various positions beside the stream and a little way up the gully's side. On the other side of the stream, also expertly concealed, were twelve men under the command of Lieutenant Small and Sergeant Walker; this was the left kill-group.

Turning to face behind him, Von Tempsky again failed to see his reserve force of ten men, commanded by Lieutenants Griggs and Sergeant-Major Bowers. He knew they were about twelve yards away, protected where the narrow valley turned. The gully's sheer sides provided complete shelter.

"Nuttin' more we can do, sir," commented Bowers, whose experienced eyes constantly searched for flaws in their positions.

"They'll be here soon. Better get back to your position, Sergeant," Von Tempsky said quietly.

Sergeant Bowers nodded, bent low, and kept the large tree between him and the direction from which the rebels would come as he clambered over the rocks in the stream and returned to his rear protection group.

Captain Von Tempsky was wound as tight as a drum. His mouth was dry, and he was frightened. His fear gave him the motivation to survive and to ensure his ambush was successful. Again, he reviewed his men's positions and looked for flaws in his strategy. Their interlocking fields of fire were perfect, and his best men were in positions perfectly suited to their abilities and the terrain. His

Company even met the correct ratio of Rangers to rebels, at a close 3:1. It was the unexpected that bothered him, and he wondered in what form it would manifest.

Completely hidden from view by anyone approaching from the south, the entire Company remained deathly silent. However, the rude invasion by fifty men upset the balance of bush life, and the skittish birds that inhabited New Zealand in abundance kept their distance, preferring to observe from the safety of their perches on the periphery, high in the canopy above. To any experienced bushman, the absence of bird sounds was a dire warning, and little could be done to restore their confidence and entice them to return. All the men of Forest Ranger Company No. 2 were aware of this, and most prayed the approaching rebels wouldn't notice until it was too late.

Company No. 2 waited.

Moana heard them first; the two scouts he'd observed earlier in the day were now walking and talking quietly, side by side, along the stream. Their voices gave them away. He tightened his grip on the Enfield rifle and, when they came into view, he habitually sighted on the first target of opportunity; in this situation, it was the rebel on the left. He knew Tane would soon target the rebel on the right. But they wouldn't fire or initiate the skirmish; they'd both wait until the rebel scouts led the main group of rebel warriors into the area of engagement, directly in front of the captain's right kill group and the lieutenant's left kill group. Moana's job was to shoot and kill the rebel guarding the prisoner and then try to protect him.

The two scouts walked past Moana's position and kept talking, though their heads kept swivelling as they surveyed the area around them. The absence of birds could be due to the noise they made, or so Moana hoped they thought. Both rebels paused and listened intently. One turned around to look, but there was nothing to see. Sensing something wasn't as it should be, with muskets raised and ready, both rebels began to move cautiously again. This time they didn't speak, and as they approached the hidden Ranger kill groups, they nervously stopped.

Not far behind them, the main rebel group was catching up and slowly began to concertina as the strung-out line began to congregate. The rebel scouts were gesticulating and pointing ahead to the bend in the stream where the gully turned; this was also where the Ranger reserves were hidden. The rebel scouts felt uneasy and were reluctant to move further without support.

As one, all heads quickly turned behind them as Mahi ran awkwardly, crashing through the bush towards them, waving his arms and shouting. A few men snickered as they remembered his earlier predicament and discomfort. As he approached the rebel leader, the expression on his face told a different story. Looks of amusement were replaced by apprehension.

Moana waited impatiently for the last of the rebels to come within effective musket range. As yet, the rebel guarding the Erepu was too far away to risk firing. He could see him and could risk a long-range shot, as he was well within the range of the Enfield, but he preferred they came closer. Wisely, Captain Von Tempsky resisted giving the order to engage.

Mahi began explaining to the rebel leader that he'd discovered two bodies and pointed behind. Immediately, the rebel commander began issuing orders for his men to fall into defensive positions as they began a slow retreat.

Seeing the rebels raise their weapons and react to the unseen threat, Captain Von Tempsky had no option but to give the command. Instantly, the small gully was enveloped in a cloud of blue smoke. The staggered musket fire galvanised the nervous rebels into immediate action. For some, it was too late; the first volley was lethal. The two scouts were the first to die; others who began raising their muskets fell, their bodies indelibly marked with spreading crimson stains.

The fifty-five-inch-long Pattern Enfield musket was lined up perfectly on the rebel guarding Erepu. The rear sight was flipped up, and Moana estimated the distance at a staggering five hundred yards. An extremely difficult, but certainly not an impossible shot. Before the sound of the Rangers' first fusillade had dissipated, the rebel guard was already pulling Erepu back and away from danger. Moana's carefully chosen elevated position offered him a clear, unobstructed six-hundred-yard view down the length of the gully. While the stream zigzagged across the valley floor, the gully itself was reasonably straight. Suddenly, his view of the rebel guard was obstructed. Another rebel had come to his aid, and now there were two warriors pulling the reluctant prisoner away to safety. He needed to act quickly, or the opportunity would be lost.

Moana blocked out the sound of musket fire, the horrific screams, yelling and mayhem that pervaded the air around him, and concentrated on the difficult shot he needed to take. Without conscious thought, he determined that there was no wind or humidity affecting his accuracy. He calculated the arc of the shot as it travelled the enormous distance to the target and made a minute adjustment to his aim. He lay prone, and his heart rate slowed to that of a man at rest. The Pattern Enfield was held firmly but not tightly and rested securely on a fallen branch; his legs were splayed, and, through habit, he kept a slight bend in his body.

All movement around him slowed, and time seemed to stall. His heart thumped loudly and slowly; the adrenaline rush heightened his senses. The four Rangers with him remained hidden and quiet. His finger slipped through the trigger guard, and he made another slight correction, elevating the barrel a whisker. From his position, the rebels were heading directly away from him and not veering sideways, which made it easier. With calm, precise judgement and hoping for luck, he squeezed the trigger between heartbeats.

Propelled by expanding gases, the .57-calibre slug left the barrel at enormous velocity and travelled upwards towards its target. To Moana, fighting to see through the haze of gun smoke, the wait seemed an eternity. The slug, rapidly expending its energy, began to slow and descend. It could have travelled considerably further, but its flight was interrupted by a human form. The thirty-four-gram slug entered the rebel's chest, slightly right of centre, and drove the body to the ground. He would die within seconds as his lifeblood flowed freely from his body.

The remaining rebel paused for a single heartbeat, then, with renewed vigour, began frantically dragging Erepu away even faster.

Moana rolled onto his back and began reloading. Now that he'd given away his position, a few shots began heading his way. The other four Rangers with him opened fire on the quickly retreating survivors.

Nine seconds later, with his Enfield reloaded, Moana rolled back onto his stomach and began to sight his next target. He estimated the range had increased by about thirty yards as the lone rebel pulled Erepu away to safety. Following the same routine as before, Moana held the nine-and-a-half-pound musket with the barrel resting on the stout branch he'd placed there earlier and sighted on his new target. Bits of dirt and rock chips flew near his face as bullets and musket shot were sporadically directed towards him. One stone chip struck his cheek and drew blood. At this point, he didn't even notice. Again, he squeezed the trigger. The Pattern Enfield musket kicked into his shoulder, and the slug rotated in the rifled barrel, accelerating to a speed of one thousand four hundred feet per second.

Just over a second later, the rebel guard jerked and spun, falling heavily to the ground after the slug's powerful impact on the shoulder. This time, Moana handed the Enfield to a Ranger with a terse order to reload quickly, while he kept his eyes firmly on the tiny shapes far in the distance.

A few retreating rebels came to the wounded guard's assistance; another quickly picked up Erepu, threw him over his shoulder, and began to stagger away. Moana couldn't chance another shot.

With a quick glance over his shoulder, Moana saw the Rangers leave their positions and begin a structured advance and pursuit. They were spread out on either side of the gully, mopping up any survivors. He turned back to the fleeing warriors and made a quick decision.

"You and you!" he shouted. His ears were still ringing from the sound of musket fire. "Come with me. And you two report to Sergeant-Major Bowers and inform him we're in pursuit and will recover the prisoner!"

Leaving the Enfield to the care of a trooper, he rose and began climbing up towards the ridgeline as fast as he could; two surprised Rangers with muskets followed. Moana was familiar with the terrain on the other side of the gully, having spent most of the earlier part of the day there, and felt he could gain ground on the few rebels who fled.

Once over the summit, he quickly explained to the two Rangers that their responsibility was to provide protection and ensure that no rebels could counter-attack while he attempted to rescue the prisoner. Receiving confirmation, the three Rangers slid down into the gully and began running a parallel route to the rebels.

Moana maintained a fast pace. The two Rangers, Arthur Fieldsman and Taikaha Juergens, were fit and in good physical condition, keeping pace easily as they followed a few steps behind their sergeant.

They ran hard and navigated fallen trees and boulders with ease. As they leapt over a small stream, Arthur misjudged his footing and splashed heavily through the water only to see Taikaha trip on a root and fall a few seconds later. The valley floor was uneven and strewn with lichen-covered boulders and tree roots. It was tiring, and all three men were breathing hard when Moana finally paused to rest.

"This is where we will climb over," Moana pointed to a lower part of the hill that separated the two gullies. His hands rested on his thighs as he sucked in lungfuls of air.

Both Arthur and Taikaha were red-faced and out of breath.

They ascended and quickly descended the other side, careful to remain as quiet as possible. Moana instructed both Rangers to conceal themselves and stay vigilant for any rebels while he checked for tracks on the valley floor. After a quick search, he decided no rebel warriors had passed this way; they were still coming.

Just then, he heard a noise and quickly searched for the nearest place to hide. It was too late to climb back up the gully's side. His only option was a nearby low-growing fern, its bright green fronds hanging down like a large fan, creating deep shadows. Without delay, he dove through the fronds. It wouldn't stand up to close scrutiny, and hopefully any rebels who'd managed to evade the pursuing Rangers were in too much of a hurry to notice.

He was just out of sight when the first rebel passed. As he peeked out from beneath the fern, he saw the rebel shot in the thigh and bleeding. Without pause, he hobbled past Moana, sparing no thought for his surroundings other than to outdistance the Rangers before he bled to death. Not far behind, two others followed, one bleeding profusely from a wounded arm while the other appeared to be uninjured.

More footsteps and laboured breathing alerted them to two more warriors. One was unharmed; the other was the rebel he had wounded in the shoulder. Both jogged at a measured pace and ran past Moana, who was only a few feet away. Moana was growing increasingly concerned. There was no sign of the prisoner or the rebel warrior guard. While he waited, he scooped handfuls of dead leaves and threw them over his legs and back for added camouflage.

He was growing impatient and thinking of moving when he heard voices and shuffling feet. He slowly turned his head and saw two men approaching. The warrior half-supported, half-tugged Erepu. Too heavy to carry any distance, Erepu was forced to run. His feet were bloody and raw, and the unsympathetic guard pulled, cursing him to move faster. Every few seconds, the guard looked over his shoulder, expecting to see the Rangers bearing down on him. Erepu's face was a grim mask of pain.

Moana needed to silence the guard without alerting any other rebels, but as the prisoner was between them, he'd need to wait until they passed by before he could leap out.

He judged the moment carefully and launched himself upwards through the fronds. Erepu and the guard caught the movement in their peripheral vision, and in panic, the guard began to yell. Unable to use *Mau*, Moana held the Bowie knife firmly in his left hand, while his right hand batted away the pistol the guard tried to raise. The knife plunged deep between the rebel's ribs as his right hand came up and clamped firmly over the rebel's mouth and nose– the yell ended abruptly. Both men crashed to the ground in a tangle of limbs and spreading blood.

In unbearable pain, Erepu sank to the ground, relieved to be off his feet. Moana separated himself from the dead rebel and slowly rose. A sixth sense alerted him to danger, and he glanced around uncertainly. Something was wrong; he could feel it.

Arthur and Taikaha rose from their positions and intended to descend to the valley floor to assist with Erepu, but Moana waved them back. He took two quick steps towards Erepu, intending to drag him to safety. As he bent down, a musket cracked, and a slug bit deep into the ground beside him, scattering leaves and dirt.

Seeing the danger, Taikaha responded immediately. Only forty yards away, a rebel began to reload when Taikaha's accurate return shot struck his head, killing him instantly. Another rebel warrior was hidden from both Rangers' view, but he stepped forward from behind the tree, revealing himself to Arthur, his musket already levelled and aimed at Erepu. Arthur's musket was fully cocked and sighted on the new threat as Moana hurried to protect Erepu. He needed to hurry, or their prisoner would be hit. Certain of the shot, Arthur squeezed the trigger.

The hammer struck the percussion cap, immediately sending flame down the nipple and into the barrel to ignite the powder. Nothing happened; the black powder failed to ignite - it was wet. Arthur reacted instinctively. In disgust, he discarded the musket, rose from his hiding place, and charged down the gully, scattering leaves and stones in a gallant effort to save Erepu. Taikaha followed. The second rebel, unaware of how close he'd just come to death, fired in terror. The slug travelled quickly over the short distance towards the rebel prisoner. Seeing the danger, Moana knocked Erepu aside. The .57-calibre ball struck Moana in the side, just above the hip and below the ribcage. In fear for his life, the rebel panicked and ran. The entire exchange lasted less than five seconds.

Moana was hurled to the ground, the impact knocking the breath from his body. He lay gasping for air as searing pain began to overwhelm him in waves of increasing intensity. Taikaha and Arthur arrived at Moana's side, Arthur to attend to his wounded sergeant, and Taikaha, who'd managed to reload his musket, took a defensive position. All surviving rebel warriors fled. Erepu was on his knees, trying to stem the bleeding from Moana's wound.

Torn abdominal muscles prevented Moana from sitting up to inspect the wound. He felt the sticky mess and raised a bloodstained hand to his face.

"Arthur, run back down and report to the captain," Moana rasped. Even breathing hurt. "Taikaha, you need some height. Climb back up the gully and…" He couldn't finish as another wave of pain threatened to pull him into unconsciousness. Both Rangers responded, and he heard the sound of running as Arthur departed. Taikaha also vanished. He waited a moment to collect his strength, then turned his head to Erepu. "We need to stop the bleeding. Find some moss by the stream."

The blackness provided sanctuary.

Captain Von Tempsky was visibly upset. He crouched over his sergeant, watching as Lieutenant Small, their closest thing to a doctor, tended to Moana. Lieutenant Griggs and Sergeant-Major Bowers took half the company in pursuit of the surviving rebels, while the remainder buried the bodies and, unsuccessfully, tried to interrogate two injured survivors they'd captured. The prisoners were fatally wounded, and it was unlikely either would last the day. There was little the captain could do for them, and seeing his best Ranger fighting for life was distressing. He mulled over his options.

"Sir? Sergeant Rangitira needs expert medical care. I can't tell whether any cloth has been driven into the wound. I have no equipment or training to perform that procedure here in the bush," stated the lieutenant. "The longer we wait, the greater the chance the wound will fester. We must take him back."

The captain nodded, "Thank you, Lieutenant."

Lieutenant Small carried a small amount of laudanum, which he'd administered to Moana when Moana regained consciousness. Derived from opium and taken orally as a solution, the tincture offered some pain relief, but its effects wouldn't last long.

Small was deeply worried about Sergeant Rangitira's condition – he had done all he could for him, but Moana needed a doctor, and soon. Once he'd taken care of him, he'd tended to the torn and bloodied feet of Erepu. The young man was resilient and uncomplaining, even though his feet were a painful fleshy mess. He'd not offered him any laudanum, preferring to save it for the severely wounded sergeant.

The engagement had been brief and bloody. For Captain Von Tempsky, it was a success. In addition to Ira, at least six Rangers sustained minor musket wounds, one sprained ankle, and a few deep cuts. Including the two mortally wounded prisoners, the rebels were virtually decimated, though perhaps four escaped. The captain hoped Sergeant-Major Bowers would quickly capture all survivors and return. The Rangers needed to leave the area as quickly as possible.

On completing his medical duties, Lieutenant Small approached Captain Von Tempsky, who was talking with Erepu. Erepu was recounting all he'd heard about Te Ua's plans for Sentry Hill.

"Captain? Will we return to Oakura with Sergeant Rangitira?" Small wiped the blood from his hands on a small rag.

"The problem, Lieutenant, is that Colonel Warren has moved his forces south, heading towards Opunake, which leaves us without proper medical care. Taking Ira all the way to the Manutahi *pa* isn't possible. It's too far and will slow us down."

Lieutenant Small looked thoughtful.

"May I offer a suggestion?" asked Erepu.

The captain turned to him and nodded.

"Perhaps you could take Sergeant Rangitira to Oakura. My cousin, Miss Henare, can look after him until you find a better place. She is known for her medical skills."

Captain Von Tempsky's hand went to his moustache as he weighed up the options.

"Sir, perhaps we could send a runner to the Henare farm to inform them of what has happened. They could bring a wagon or carriage to transport the sergeant and Mr Henare. Meanwhile, we can carry both of them out on litters. As Mr Henare is unable to walk, it makes sense that he will seek care from his family, who live close by," volunteered the lieutenant.

Erepu nodded eagerly in support

The captain looked to his young, largely inexperienced lieutenant with some surprise. "Your suggestion is a good one, Lieutenant." The captain remembered the captivating young woman Ira was infatuated with. She may be exactly what he needs. He made a decision. "Very well. Find your two fastest runners, Lieutenant, and dispatch them with haste. In the interim, I suggest you oversee the construction of two sturdy litters. We will depart from here as soon as Lieutenant Griggs and Sergeant-Major Bowers return.

CHAPTER SIXTEEN

The Letter

Emma stood at the window of their modest cottage in Opotiki, Bay of Plenty, and impatiently waited for her husband, the Reverend Karl Menshen, to return home. She held a letter from New Zealand's Governor, Sir George Grey, delivered to their home a short time earlier. The eagerly anticipated reply did not bode well for Emma, and with the certainty borne of a woman's intuition, she hoped her husband would act with prudence and restraint. She knew the letter would fire his passions, and his response would probably rile local *Māori* and possibly put them both in danger.

Again, she moved the white lacy curtain aside and peered anxiously out of the small window, hoping to catch sight of him. Even though she knew it was five o'clock, she instinctively turned her head at the chime of the clock as it marked the hour, then resumed her observation. This time she was rewarded with the sight of Karl as he slowly ambled towards home. With habitual fastidiousness bordering on obsession, the Reverend approached the cottage precisely on time. Deep in thought, he hooked both thumbs into his jacket over the top button, his elbows hung suspended over his stomach, and his chin rested on his chest. Emma tut-tutted, knowing the buttons would again become loose and require the attention of needle and thread.

She walked from the window towards the door and paused briefly at the hallway mirror to reposition some wayward strands of hair. She re-pinned her conservative coiffure, gave it a pat, and adjusted her shawl to reflect her modesty. Imminently pleased with the result, she opened the door and, with a warm smile, greeted her husband.

Once inside, the door closed, and they were safe from prying eyes. Karl gently grasped his wife's shoulders, leaned forward, and offered her a diffident kiss on the cheek before retiring to the sitting room, with Emma trailing deferentially behind. He'd seen the letter she clutched possessively and, appropriately, allowed her to present it to him, as proper decorum dictated.

As the Reverend kicked off his shoes, he upset the cat that lay on the carpet, basking in the warmth of the day's last rays of sunshine. Emma politely asked him about his day. With a weary sigh, he settled into his favourite chair and told her about the afternoon's mundane events, complaining about the ambivalence and lack of commitment to God among a member of his congregation.

"Was that Mr Chadwick?" asked Emma.

The Reverend did not reply immediately and hooked his thumbs through the top button of his jacket.

"The man is troubled, and yet I found his death-bed admission disquieting."

"What was it he said that distressed you so?" questioned Emma with some concern.

Karl inhaled through his nose and let out a long, drawn-out sigh. "He said, 'I have lived long enough to know that at one time I did not believe – that no society can be upheld in happiness and honour without the sentiments of religion.'"

Emma frowned and looked puzzled, "I don't understand. Why is that troubling?"

Reverend Menshen removed his hands from his jacket and looked up at his devoted wife. "Because there is no evidence to suggest that even then, with his final days drawing near, he perceived clearly the verities of theology or esteemed them otherwise than as useful measures or obscure ideas. Mr Chadwick's mind is in a constant state of unquiet itching and troubled flux."

From the mahogany and pine cabinet set against the far wall, a precious gift from Karl's uncle Horst, Emma poured a moderate amount of sherry into two small glasses, then sat down in her chair and adjusted her skirts. She took a healthy sip of the sherry after her husband, then briefly commiserated on the state of Mr Chadwick's addled mind. Only then did she inform Karl of the missive he'd received from the Governor, handing the envelope to his outstretched, waiting hand.

Turning to Emma, who was leaning curiously towards him, he gave her a pleasant smile and asked how her Bible study group had fared today. She straightened into a prim, upright position and explained that all had gone well. One woman had been poorly and had chosen not to attend, and that today's topic on Pantheism, as suggested by Karl, had been well received. He nodded appreciatively and extracted his spectacles and a handkerchief from his pocket. He held them to his mouth, breathed on each lens, then gave them a vigorous buffing before returning the handkerchief to its pocket and placing the spectacles at the end of his nose. Now able to see the fine handwritten scrawl with ease, he read the front of the envelope carefully, then turned it over and perused the back, just in case there were words written that were worthy of attention. Emma handed him a letter opener, which he used to slit the envelope, then returned it to her. She in turn placed it precisely back where it belonged on the small table that separated them. He slid the letter from the envelope and unfolded it carefully. Temptation proving too much to resist, Emma leaned slightly towards her husband, hoping for a better view.

The ticking clock broke the silence.

Government House,

Office of the Governor,

Auckland.

April 1863

My Dear Reverend Menshen,

It is my honour to acknowledge the receipt of your missive and the valuable information you provided. You do your country and Church a great service.

With some misgivings I bring tidings of continued unrest and tribulation. Uprisings and rebellion, led by false prophets strewing mendacious religious doctrine to the gullible native populace, destabilise our nation and continue to threaten not only the church and our faith, but also our very existence.

With trepidation and urgency, I call on you and your learned colleague, the Reverend Thomas Grace, to attend to this immediate need and, with dispatch, arrive at my office forthwith to provide the benefit of your acumen and counsel both General Cameron and me.

In consequence of your participation, and if I am to conduct these affairs to a conclusion, General Cameron

will bring about a satisfactory solution to the disturbed
state of affairs that prevails here.

Thank you for your continued cooperation.

I have, &c.,
G. Grey, K.C.B.
His Excellency, The Governor of New Zealand.

The Governor's cleverly worded letter was designed to provoke a strong response from the Reverend, and he'd succeeded. Karl Menshen, a member of the Church Missionary Society (CMS), was furious. Seeing the danger, he advocated and demanded immediate retribution for the atrocities committed by members of the *Pai Marire* faith. As a matter of conscience and duty, Menshen provided useful intelligence to the Governor, especially when Kaihoka Te Hua, in a sign of spiritual victory, brought the smoke-dried head of Captain Boyd to the Bay of Plenty and sought to recruit new members to their organisation. The CMS, administered by the Anglican and Protestant churches, was not anti-*Māori,* but it abhorred the repugnant behaviour of individuals who distorted Christian values with violence, under the guise of Christian doctrine, to serve their own agenda.

Karl handed the letter to Emma and sat in silence, seething.

"The clever manoeuvres of Machiavellian prophets…" said Karl, thinking aloud, leaving the sentence unfinished.

After quickly reading it, Emma folded the letter and returned it to her husband. She knew no good would come of the Governor's request. Wisely, she chose not to provoke her husband's anger and held her tongue.

"We need to offer a prayer, Emma, for the salvation of lost souls and their redemption," Karl nodded as if agreeing with himself. "And for those who have suffered as innocent lambs under the violence inflicted upon them."

He removed his spectacles, reached across the narrow table, and held her hand. "O God, we ask that you intervene in this abominable persecution against your people and our faith. Father, may the *Pai Marire* cease syncretism, the fusion of false doctrine with orthodox Christian sentiments. May these false teachings end by Your grace and help. We pray that these people may cease violence and return to you and to right belief. In Thy name, Amen."

Emma continued to hold Karl's hand. "Your trip … your visit to the Governor," she urged.

"Ah, yes. May you protect me on my journey to see the Governor," Karl added.

"Amen," responded Emma, releasing his hand. She sat thoughtfully as Karl replaced his spectacles and reread the Governor's letter.

"Why does the Governor wish to see Reverend Grace?" she asked.

Reverend Menshen patiently removed his spectacles and fiddled with them for a moment as he contemplated his reply. "Thomas is a liberal thinker, Emma. He is earnest in his belief that the natives have been unjustly treated and supports their desire for greater religious autonomy and economic independence."

Emma nodded.

"While I disagree with his less-than-orthodox beliefs, he is, none the less, a good clergyman. The Governor places high value on Thomas's understanding of native cultural affairs and his sympathies."

"Isn't that what you provide?"

"Yes, dear. Whereas my perspective is not adversely tainted by neo-liberal potencies."

"I see," replied Emma.

With its dignity somewhat restored, the cat rose, walked a few steps, arched its back, and began to rub itself against the stockinged foot of the Reverend.

Later that evening, in the yellow glow of an oil lamp, Karl Menshen composed a letter to his esteemed colleague, the Reverend Thomas Grace. Thomas now lived in Auckland with his wife, Sarah, and a brood of twelve children, having recently relocated from the Mission at Pukawa at the southern end of Lake Taupo. Without his own parish, Thomas Grace travelled frequently and at great peril into the interior to visit and minister to *Māori*.

Karl provided details of their forthcoming meeting and urged his friend to respond urgently. Once his correspondence was sealed and addressed, the Reverend began to prepare for his long journey.

CHAPTER SEVENTEEN

The Fight

It hadn't rained for a while, and she wished it would. Wiki lifted her head skywards and searched for clouds that would bring much-needed precipitation. Crops needed water and sunlight for nourishment, and without either, their growth would be severely affected. What rain clouds she saw were in the far north and swept across the sky in an easterly direction, and it seemed unlikely they would offer any relief today. Fed by the nearby ranges, a stream meandered through the countryside and ran through the lower regions of the Henares' modest property. While water from the stream was available to irrigate crops, it was still hard, tiring work to carry it uphill. With the aid of her brothers, her father toiled obsessively to dig a well and, after many failures, eventually succeeded. It saved them hours of hard work, and the investment in time and effort was worth it. The Henares purchased the property five years earlier, and the improvements they'd made in that short time were a testament to hard work and dedication.

From the well, Wikitoria carried two buckets of water, suspended from hooks attached to a pole that rested across her shoulders. By taking short, quick steps, she managed to carry the heavy load to her own garden, which she tended with loving care.

She grew a variety of herbs and vegetables that her father did not cultivate in the fields, and an assortment of decorative flowers in colourful borders that fronted the cottage. Ensuring no water was needlessly spilt or wasted, she carefully dispensed the precious liquid to her plot and returned to the well on the lower side of the cottage for another load. Her shoulders ached, she was hot and tired, but she was also a strong and determined young woman and, much to her family's annoyance, sought no assistance from them with this task.

Both buckets were full, and she was about to hoist the pole to her shoulders again when she saw two Forest Rangers approaching the cottage at a run. Wiki moved into the shade on her veranda, dabbed her brow with her apron, and waited with curiosity as the Rangers walked the last few steps up the path. They greeted her breathlessly and, with some urgency, asked to speak to Mr Henare. No amount of prompting would loosen their tongues, and they weren't about to share the nature of their visit with her. Wiki wasn't amused. She reached up and rang the bell that hung from the veranda. Alerted by the warning peal of the clanging bell, her brothers and father hurried to the cottage, anxious about the reason for their summons. She could see that both Rangers were exhausted and dirty, and while she waited for her father and brothers to arrive, she quickly fetched two tin mugs and offered them a refreshing, cool drink from one of her buckets.

Unable to contain herself, "Are you here about Erepu?" she asked with growing impatience.

Arthur and Taikaha looked at each other uncomfortably and chose to remain quiet.

If the two Rangers were wiser in the ways of the world and women, they would have responded with some fervour and answered her question eagerly. Choosing to remain silent was asking for trouble. Sadly, they missed the warning signs as her eyes turned to slits. Wiki took a step forward, placed both her hands on her hips and asked again, her voice barely above a whisper.

"Is – this – about – Erepu?"

The clomp of heavy boots on the veranda saved them. "Afternoon, boys, how can I help yer?"

"Mr Henare, I'm Private Arthur Fieldsman, and this is Private Taikaha Juergens–"

"Call me Tami," interrupted Mr Henare. "You boys want to take a seat, and get outa the sun?"

"Father, let them finish, they have something to say," rebuked Wiki.

"Go ahead, fellas," encouraged Mr Henare.

"Uh, Tami, I've been, uh, we've been sent here to request your assistance, sir. Captain Von Tempsky extends his greetings and wishes to inform you that we got Erepu Henare back from the rebels."

"Oh, that's wonderful news," Wiki responded happily.

"Yes, Miss, but he has injured feet and can't walk. We need a wagon to carry him."

More footsteps clomped on the veranda, and Wiki's three brothers arrived.

"And you can take those boots off. I'm not going to clean up after you again. I have better things to do," warned Wiki.

Her brothers quickly stepped off the veranda, as did her father, leaving clods of earth behind.

"But we also have another problem," said Arthur, ignoring Wiki's outburst. "One of our sergeants has been severely wounded and needs medical care."

Unable to restrain herself, Wiki's hands unconsciously flew to her mouth.

"Who is it, lad? Is it Ira?" asked Tami Henare.

"Yes, sir, it is."

"Oh my God!" cried Wiki. "What's wrong with him?"

"He was hit by musket fire, got 'em here," Arthur pointed to his side.

"Where is he now, and when did this happen?" she asked.

"The Company is bringing Ira, I mean Sergeant Rangitira and Erepu, out of the bush now, and the captain was hoping, Miss Henare, that you might be able to tend to their well-being, as there is nowhere else we can take them. It happened yesterday afternoon, Miss. We're supposed to take you there."

Wiki took immediate control and began issuing instructions. "What are you boys still standing around for? Get Punga harnessed to the wagon." She turned to the two Rangers, who thought she was addressing them. "Father, show these two where they can wash up and give them some bread and cheese while I get ready."

The Henare farm became a hive of activity as everyone set to their duties. Wiki found clean bandages, some laudanum, and blankets. She packed food and other essentials, and within the hour, Punga was pulling the creaky wagon up the trail towards the distant hills, with Arthur leading the way on one of the Henares' horses. Taikaha sat in the wagon with Wiki and two brothers, Charles and James. Wiki thought it best that her father remain at home with the youngest, who was to advise Doctor Will and arrange for him to arrive at the cottage later the following morning.

"Is it far?" Wiki asked.

"We should be able to continue in the dark, with Arthur leading the way, Miss, but I reckon three hours or so," informed Taikaha.

Wiki peppered Taikaha with questions about the details of how Ira was wounded during Erepu's rescue. She was deeply worried and knew enough about treating wounds and illness to recognise the seriousness of the injury described to her. Left untreated, such a wound would succumb to sepsis, and in many cases the infection would ultimately prove fatal. She again urged everyone to hurry.

The late-afternoon sun melted into inky blackness, and the small group eventually caught sight of the orange glow of a campfire in the distance. Ordering the wagon to stop and wait, Arthur cautiously left his position and rode quietly away to investigate. Everyone hoped it was the detachment of Rangers they expected, not a war band of rebels. Within minutes, he returned with confirmation and guided the wagon safely to the small Ranger camp.

Erepu was sitting up and talking. The injuries he'd sustained to his feet were not life-threatening or serious, and, according to Wiki, he needed to rest his feet and avoid walking to give them a fair chance to heal. Ira, on the other hand, was a different matter.

When she finally arrived at camp, Ira was conscious and had a mild fever. She removed the dirty bandage Lieutenant Small had used to stem the bleeding and extracted the moss Erepu had compressed into a tight ball and placed in the entrance and exit wounds. A casual inspection showed that the musket slug had passed cleanly through his body. Whether it had struck bone or vital organs was unclear – he needed the expertise of a doctor as soon as possible. The wound on Ira's back was considerably larger and jagged, as the slug had exited at an acute angle.

Moana was surprised to open his eyes and find Wiki leaning over him. Her hair was tied back, but a few errant strands fell forward, brushing his cheek. He thought it was a dream and, despite his discomfort, closed his eyes and smiled. With firelight and the assistance of Charlie, who held a lantern, she cleaned both wounds with water and lye soap and administered a small amount of laudanum. Once the opiate took effect and the wounds were wrapped in clean bandages, Ira felt more comfortable and quickly drifted into a restless sleep.

While he slept, she washed him as much as was decently possible, cleaned the small cut on his cheek, and to ease the effects of his fever, she placed a wet cloth on his forehead. It was all she could do. If anyone approached or inquired after him, she shooed them away and insisted everyone remain quiet. No one argued. Wiki was in charge. Of that there was no doubt.

Assured that he was asleep, she went to Erepu and insisted he recount exactly what had happened to him since the day he ran from Waitotara, and then the circumstances surrounding how Ira was wounded.

Erepu spared no praise. "If he hadn't acted as he did, the rebel would have shot me. Ira saved my life, and God spared me. I'm very grateful."

"And what of the musket that misfired?" she asked,

"That was of concern to Captain Von Tempsky," Erepu paused, leaned in close to Wiki, and spoke quietly. "It was Arthur Fieldsman. It was his musket that misfired. When they were trying to rescue me, Arthur splashed through the water, and somehow water entered the musket barrel and wet the powder cartridge."

Wiki grimaced. A costly mistake, she understood. She turned to face the fire and watched the Rangers on the other side as they relaxed in preparation for their departure in the morning. The Ranger she knew as Arthur sat alone, knees drawn to his chin, staring at the dancing flames. She could see he was thinking and knew he blamed himself for the misfire. Wiki left Erepu, walked to him, and sat down. She said nothing.

"How is he, Miss?" Arthur finally asked.

"It's hard to tell. At the moment, he's sleeping, but he has a mild fever, and I think there's some debris or cloth in the wound, which is causing it."

"Can't you find it?" he asked.

"Not until we get him home and in a good position where the doctor can begin a search."

Arthur nodded.

"You know it was my fault he was shot," he quickly added.

"I didn't know it was your fault," replied Wiki, with some concern creeping into her voice.

"My musket misfired after water got in the barrel."

"Oh my, that's horrible," Wiki declared.

Arthur turned to look at her, surprised at her comment.

"Did you do it on purpose?" she asked, meeting his look. Orange flames created flickering patterns on his face.

"Of course not!" he spat, becoming angry. The other Rangers all stopped what they were doing and looked towards them.

"Did the slug that hit Ira come from your musket?"

"No!"

"Then why was it your fault?"

Arthur let out a long, drawn-out sigh. "Because I was carrying my musket incorrectly and water got into the barrel, Miss Henare."

Wiki nodded. "Then you are guilty only of carrying your musket incorrectly. And perhaps, if you had been able to fire at the rebel, you might have missed him, and Ira could still be lying here. But you will never know this for sure, will you? Forget the guilt, it wasn't your fault."

Arthur remained silent and stared morosely into the fire. Wiki went back to Ira who'd woken and was in some distress.

Even before the sun rose, the Henare family said farewell to the Rangers, who were heading off to catch up with Captain Von Tempsky and the rest of the Company. With her brother up front driving, they began the slow journey towards home. Wiki dispensed a larger-than-normal quantity of laudanum to Moana to ease the pain caused by the bouncing wagon, and with the light of a new day she could see his condition worsen.

She didn't sleep during the night, and although exhausted, she refused to rest. Without incident, they returned home late in the morning, and Moana was carefully moved into her bedroom, the only room in the cottage that offered quiet and privacy. Erepu was made comfortable and lay on a cot in the rear bedroom he would share with his cousins. Her father and brothers were dismissed, and she ordered them back into the fields.

"You'll only be in the way," she told them.

While she waited for the doctor to arrive, she prepared more bandages and boiled water to clean the soiled ones.

Young Henry came bounding inside and yelled that the doctor was walking towards the cottage. With relief, Wiki waited on the veranda as Doctor Will arrived.

Wilbur Cok walked spritely along the path towards Miss Wikitoria Henare, who stood on the veranda, waiting anxiously for him. As he approached, he could see she looked tired and a little dishevelled, but in his opinion she was still as beautiful as ever. His smile faded as the realisation struck him again that she would never show him any interest as a suitor. *Why would she,* he thought?

Approaching his mid-thirties and reed thin, Wilbur or Doctor Will, as the locals incorrectly called him, was not a doctor at all. An

Australian by birth, he attended medical school at the Sydney Infirmary with aspirations to become a noted surgeon, until some wayward behaviour led to his physical removal and expulsion from the institution.

Wilbur studied diligently and demonstrated extraordinary promise, but towards the end of the syllabus, he discovered more than a casual fondness for the remedies and concoctions dispensed by the infirmary's apothecary. Unable to control his cravings, he liberated sufficient quantities of his favourite potions and consumed them with a gusto only an addict could appreciate. Unfortunately, the evidence against him was overwhelming. He was found on the floor inside the apothecary, incoherent, with numerous empty vessels and containers scattered about him. Unable to offer any excuse for his abhorrent behaviour, the incensed director of the medical school ordered Wilbur tossed onto Macquarie Street, where he remained incapacitated and ignored for quite some time.

In disgrace, with his dreams shattered, Wilbur Cok borrowed money from friends and departed Australia, bound for New Zealand, where the romance of finding gold and riches seemed a healthy alternative. Sadly for Wilbur, his dreams of wealth and fortune were short-lived. He showed no aptitude for his new occupation as a gold miner. Instead, he found himself constantly coming to the aid of those in need of medical attention. He was a natural and would often treat patients in remote areas with no doctors.

Through dogged determination and sheer willpower, Wilbur learned to control his cravings, but the effects of the constant abuse his body had suffered were lasting. He was thin and looked emaciated; many of his teeth were rotting, and some were even missing, far removed from the handsome and buoyant young man who had first entered medical school some years earlier. His ragged appearance was now overshadowed by his abilities and understanding of applied medicine. Wilbur Cok became highly proficient in caring for the afflicted and injured, and his knowledge and capabilities were adroit.

After a few years of aimless wandering around New Zealand, he settled into a quiet, modest life in Oakura and took on duties normally associated with those of a doctor. He dispensed his own medicinal potions and remedies to those in need and never misrepresented himself as a Doctor of Medicine. Wilbur read voraciously– he obtained journals of recent medical discoveries and advancements and experimented with surprisingly positive results. If judged fairly, Wilbur Cok was more than competent at doctoring; he was exceptional. However, despite all his protestations about not being called 'doctor', the locals, out of respect and some deference, still preferred to address him as Doctor Will.

Wilbur politely lifted his hat, revealing a shock of coal-black hair that fell over his eyes as he greeted Wiki. He quickly tucked his hair back behind his ears and bowed slightly at the waist as he appraised the young woman standing above him on the veranda.

"Doctor Will, I'm so pleased you came," greeted Wiki tensely.

"Miss Wiki, as always, you are like an angel, a gift from God to the unworthy like me," gushed Wilbur. His droopy moustache, strategically wrapped around his gaunt face, hid decaying teeth.

"Enough of that, Doctor," warned Wiki with a tired smile. "You're not here to flatter me but to attend to the two patients in dire need of your fine skills."

"Very well, then I shan't be proposing a blissful marriage to you today … perhaps another day, eh?" Wilbur theatrically climbed the steps onto the veranda. "Take me to the stricken. Lead the way, m'dear."

Wiki rolled her eyes and led Wilbur inside, first to Erepu, who received a quick examination, then to Ira, who was asleep.

Wilbur Cok's demeanour changed instantly. The smile vanished, replaced by a grim, serious expression. Gone was the flirtatious bravura of a Lothario. Now the man who stood over Ira cast an experienced, practised eye over the patient with the confident self-assurance of a professional.

"Do you have hot water?" asked Wilbur.

"Yes, to clean bandages."

"I need to clean my hands. Lye soap?"

"This way, Doctor," replied Wiki, puzzled by the unusual request. She looked at his hands, which appeared clean, and showed him the water and soap he had requested.

Placing his oversized medical bag on the floor, Wilbur followed.

"I recently came across the writings of a delightful and dedicated young woman, a nurse, actually," Wilbur said as he scrubbed his hands vigorously. "A Miss Florence Nightingale; she's made some astounding claims." Wilbur turned to Wiki to make sure she was listening and continued, "It is often thought that medicine is the curative process. It is no such thing ... nature alone cures ... and what nursing has to do is to put the patient in the best condition for nature to act upon him. Not only must the patient be in a clean environment, but we who administer must also practise cleanliness."

"Why?" asked Wiki, handing him a clean cloth to dry his hands.

"There are some who believe that infection can be transmitted and promoted by uncleanliness."

Wiki gave Wilbur's assertion some thought. "I agree. It seems sensible to me."

"So do I," replied Wilbur over his shoulder as he returned to Ira. "I suggest you always cleanse your hands before touching the patient, and again afterwards," he said, beginning to unwrap Ira's bandage.

Ira woke with a grunt and grimace– his wounds were painful and swollen.

"Ira, this is Doctor Will. He's the man I told you about."

Ira nodded in acknowledgement but said nothing.

Once the bandages were removed, Wilbur bent down and carefully examined the entrance wound. As he expected, the edges were inflamed and red. He inhaled through his nose, sniffing for infection.

"I need a clean, wet cloth, Wiki. Use hot water."

Wiki immediately fetched a cloth, and Wilbur gently wiped away the seepage and pus. Beads of sweat gathered on Ira's forehead, the pain excruciating.

"I'm going to need to move you onto your side. It's going to hurt, Moana. Wiki, help me!"

Ira cried out as he was partially turned, then fell silent as he fainted. The exit wound was similar. The torn jagged edges of flesh were red, inflamed and the wound seeped. Wilbur cleaned and inspected the damaged area as thoroughly as he could. "Has he been vomiting?" asked Wilbur.

"No, he hasn't."

"Good."

"Why is that good?" Wiki questioned.

"I don't believe any internal organs have been ruptured, although I do believe fragments of cloth may still be present, causing the infection. I have to explore the wound and look for any foreign matter."

This is what Wiki feared.

"I need to see the clothes he was wearing," said Wilbur, straightening up and wiping his hands.

Wiki handed Wilbur Ira's shirt. He laid the garment flat on the bed, smoothed the fabric, and inspected the area around a dark red bloodstain. A small hole, clearly showing that a piece of fabric was missing, was easily visible where the slug had passed through the cloth.

Wilbur poked at the shirt with his finger. "See, there is cloth missing, only a little piece, but nonetheless enough to kill him."

He looked around the room. "I can't operate here in the bedroom; the bed is too low. We will need to do this on the kitchen table, where it's brighter, so I can see better."

Wiki was staring at Ira and didn't appear to be paying attention.

"Wiki, we need to do this as soon as possible!"

She looked up at Wilbur, her eyes moist. "Of course," she said, her expression hardening. "Let me call my brothers– they can help move him."

"That's good. You need to clean the table thoroughly, then lay clean sheets over it, and continue boiling water. We'll need it."

Everyone was called to the cottage to help, and Ira was lifted onto the kitchen table using a sheet. The table was then carefully dragged into position near a window, where sunshine streamed through. Wiki again insisted that everyone leave, including Charles, who wanted to watch. Charles hurriedly left the kitchen, rubbing his ear.

Wilbur removed his jacket and rolled the sleeves of his white shirt high above his elbows. He then handed an assortment of surgical instruments to Wiki, including scalpels, tweezers, a tool resembling a miniature speculum, a head mirror, needles, and some small forceps. He insisted that she use a clean cloth and hot water to wipe away old skin tissue and dried blood from previous patients that had accumulated on his tools. She placed them on a tray and went to her stove, where water was boiling. With a cloth and hot water, she cleaned the instruments as best she could and returned them to the wooden tray. Once completed, she picked up the tray and turned quickly. The abrupt motion caused the forceps to slide from the tray and fall into the boiling water with a splash that made her flinch. Her reaction to droplets of scalding water landing on her wrist caused the edge of the tray to dip. Except for the head mirror, the remaining surgical tools ended up in the pot of boiling water, followed by a most unladylike epithet.

Wiki turned apologetically to Wilbur, who was tending to Ira. He looked up in surprise at the clatter and profanity.

"I'm sorry. They all fell into the water."

"They're precision instruments, Wiki. Please treat them with care," scolded Wilbur, then returned to cleaning the exit wound.

Wiki fussed over how to remove the tools from the water without emptying the pot.

"Just leave them, they won't go anywhere. I need your help to turn him."

Once they'd repositioned him and Wiki had removed and dried the instruments from the boiling water, Wilbur was ready to begin.

"I must be honest with you, Wiki, the prognosis doesn't look good," said Wilbur, straightening and stretching his back. "Infection has set in, and I'm concerned about necrosis. I may be able to retrieve the foreign matter, but the procedure is invasive and often results in sepsis and death."

Wiki stared back at Wilbur Cok and nodded slowly.

Wilbur sighed. "I've experimented with treating infection. Sometimes I've met with remarkable success … other times … I've failed miserably. Modern medicine has come a long way in recent years, and its advances have saved many lives." Wilbur leaned forward and looked into Wiki's eyes. He placed a hand on her shoulder. "But we will do all we can, eh?"

Wiki wiped the tears from her eyes and smiled bravely as the doctor tied an apron around his waist.

Ira was given a strong dose of laudanum. After a minute or two, Wilbur checked Ira's heart with a wooden monoscope and was satisfied that all was well. The dosage was sufficient. Normally, surgeons used their fingers to explore for bullets or other matter inside the body, but Wilbur used a probe and special tweezers he had made. With care, he extracted a tool resembling a speculum, inserted it into the entrance wound, and, by adjusting the handles, slowly stretched the opening. Ira groaned. With a cool, damp cloth, Wiki dabbed at Ira's forehead and talked soothingly, offering assurances and tenderness that surprised her.

As anticipated, it was difficult to see inside the wound, a battle Wilbur always fought, but because he'd positioned Ira so that sunshine shone directly onto the area, his exploration was easier. He placed the head-mirror on his head, moved the mirror over his left eye, and peered into the wound through the aperture. The light reflected brilliantly from the mirror into the wound. Every now and then, Ira groaned or cried out, the opiate unable to mask the extreme pain he felt. Wilbur again reached into his bag and extracted a rolled-up piece of leather. To Wiki, he said, "Put that in his mouth, please."

He used a probe and explored deeper into the cavity, and Ira reacted instinctively by twisting and turning, trying to escape the pain that racked his body. He bit hard into the leather.

Blood flowed freely onto the table and floor. Wiki tried to clean, but she kept getting in Wilbur's way. He was totally focused and shifted his position frequently. She gave up cleaning and concentrated on Ira, keeping him calm. She leaned over him, her arms lying over his chest as she used her weight to keep him still, her face inches from his. Occasionally, their eyes met; his were unfocused and red, his pupils dilated. Hers were wet; tears ran freely down her face and onto his bare chest. She talked and whispered to him, speaking from her heart, of private things, anything to distract him from the agony.

Wilbur searched deep into the wound, and Ira thrashed in excruciating pain, cursing as he quickly withdrew the probe. Ira settled down, and Wiki could feel his heart racing.

"I can't find it," Wilbur said in despair. He removed the head-mirror, shook his head slowly, then reached for Ira's shirt, which hung on a nearby chair. He studied the cloth again and closed his eyes, imagining the slug tearing through it, puncturing Ira's skin and dragging a torn fragment of the shirt with it as it entered his body. He pictured the small piece of fabric being pushed aside as the slug continued through … it was blue in colour and nestled against organs … he could see it in his mind, he could visualise it.

"Keep him still, Wiki!"

This time, Wilbur used a long pair of tweezers. Ira cried out and tried to heave Wiki away, but he was weak; the effort proved too much, and he fainted. The tweezers probed deeper, further into the cavity the .57-calibre slug had created as it cleaved its way through his body. Wilbur closed his eyes. There wasn't much to see, the tweezers were in too far. He could feel resistance as he encountered organs. He carefully pushed them aside and slowly withdrew the tweezers hoping to scoop something, anything with the blunt and enlarged ends of the tool. When he opened his eyes, the tweezers were empty, they dripped blood and a little pus, but no shirt fragment.

Wilbur looked down at the floor in hopelessness. "I'm sorry, Wiki … I can't find it … there's nothing more I can do except cut him up, and he'll be sure to die then. His body won't take the stress in this state."

Ira groaned and tried to speak – a mumble. Wiki turned to him, removed the leather and moved her head close to his mouth. His bloodshot eyes flickered open, and through dry lips she heard, "Again."

"He wants you to try again!" cried Wiki, "He said, again!"

Wilbur sighed and looked at Ira's face. "Keep him still, Wiki."

Wiki nodded and turned back to Moana. She gently stroked his face, "I'm sorry."

"Hold him, Wiki!"

With renewed effort, Wilbur repositioned himself and knelt on the floor amongst the blood. He now had a different angle from which to probe. With his right hand, he adjusted the miniature speculum and opened the wound a little more. Ira felt Wiki tense and bite down on the leather, his jaw clenched tightly, the muscles on his face rigid. Again, the tweezers entered his body from a different angle. Wilbur began exploring, searching for matter that shouldn't be there. Just as before, Wilbur scooped the tweezers back. They caught on something, and Ira cried. His hips bucked uncontrollably and he weakly tried to throw Wilbur off, but she lay completely across his chest. His feeble attempt was futile.

With infinite patience, Wilbur retracted the tweezers; held tentatively by a single thread hung a small piece of fabric.

"Got it!" yelled Wilbur.

He rose from the floor and grabbed Ira's shirt and laid it across his chest. He placed the small piece of cloth across the small hole in the fabric– it was a perfect match.

"It appears, my beautiful Wikitoria, that there are no other bits of fabric embedded in Moana's body. This is it!"

Wiki slid down from Ira and turned to face Wilbur. Ignoring the blood on his apron, she embraced him, "Thank you, thank you, thank you, Doctor."

"I'm not a doctor, Wiki," said Wilbur with a grin. "But poor Moana is not out of the woods yet. I don't know how he's going to do it, but he needs to fight this infection."

Wilbur cleaned the infected areas and sewed both the entrance and exit wounds closed, leaving a small portion unsutured. "I believe the wounds need to drain," he explained. "This goes against conventional medical practice, but I believe this will assist the healing process."

After cleaning his hands, he went to his large medical bag and, to Wiki's surprise, extracted a jar of honey.

"Are you hungry?" she asked.

Wilbur laughed, "This, my lovely creature, is the secret ingredient that may save him."

Wiki was taken back.

"Bee's Honey from the Manuka tree has unique properties and has been used for centuries by ancient cultures to treat infections. If it's good enough for the Egyptians, it's good enough for Moana."

Wilbur spread a thick layer of honey over both wounds, then bound Ira loosely in a clean bandage that Wiki provided.

"I don't want him to eat anything. Give him liquids and a little more laudanum. Not too much, though. Opiates are dangerous, Wiki."

Will reached into the pocket of his jacket and extracted a small jar and handed it to Wiki.

"Mix a small portion of this with water and administer it daily. It contains quinine and will help reduce fever. I will return tomorrow morning to attend to the dressings."

"Shall I spread the honey on Erepu's feet?" Wiki asked.

"But of course, then bandage them loosely."

With the help of her brothers and father, Wiki moved Ira back to her bedroom. Once alone, she looked at him carefully. His face was red, his breathing shallow, and he had a raging fever.

With Moana in Wiki's care, Will departed the Henare farm and walked slowly down the path– he was exhausted. Privately, he had little hope his patient would recover and most likely would succumb and die. He prepared Wiki for the inevitable and told her that few survived such wounds. With the onset of contagion, and within days, the condition frequently worsened and eventually proved fatal.

He'd experimented with varying degrees of success and read as much as he could to broaden his knowledge. When the opportunity arose, he consulted doctors and surgeons and presented his theories that cleanliness and hygiene were contributing factors to recovery and good health. He sought their advice and wisdom; more often than not, his ideas were scoffed at as nothing more than quackery, and he was shown the door. He took the failures personally and endeavoured to do everything humanly possible to reduce the mortality rate among his patients. He didn't expect to be called back to the Henare farm to treat Moana, and it made him feel sad.

CHAPTER EIGHTEEN

Mantra

"Poached eggs are best eaten hot," suggested Captain William Shortt, commander of the garrison at Sentry Hill, "unless of course you have no liking for eggs?" he added with some hope.

He received no response.

"Captain?" inquired William Shortt.

Captain Von Tempsky looked apologetically towards his host, "I'm sorry, William. Forgive me, I'm a little preoccupied this morning."

"If you don't want those eggs, then I'll take them from you," Captain Shortt waved his fork over Von Tempsky's breakfast plate. "Hate to see those fine eggs go to waste, eh?"

"Can you hear them? They're up to something," observed Von Tempsky, with his head cocked to one side, listening intently.

"Those fools have been fussing like that for days," replied Shortt. "Like a troop of Piccadilly whores at a baby christening," he laughed at his joke, but received no reaction from his guest.

"It's different this morning; something has them wound up."

A quick look of concern flashed across Shortt's face. "You think so?"

Von Tempsky nodded, "Yes, I do."

Everyone inside the Sentry Hill redoubt could clearly hear the chanting and yelling of the *Hauhau* across the river at the Manutahi *pa*. According to Von Tempsky's scouts, their numbers swelled dramatically and grew to over two hundred, far outnumbering the small force of seventy-five soldiers inside the secure earthen walls of the redoubt.

"I have a suggestion, William."

Captain Shortt paused in his breakfast and looked expectantly towards Von Tempsky.

"The *Hauhau* don't know the Rangers are here. Let's keep it that way, shall we? Perhaps if we keep my men hidden, the garrison can maintain an appearance of normalcy for all outward appearances."

Captain Shortt chewed his food thoughtfully and nodded in agreement. Egg dripped from his fork, held midway between his plate and his mouth. "Yes, indeed, perhaps adopting some tactical chicanery will work in our favour, eh?"

"If you'll excuse me, William," Von Tempsky slid his chair back and stood. He placed his napkin on the table. "I will ensure my men remain concealed and in a state of readiness … uh, it may be prudent for me to deploy them in defensive positions in lieu of an attack … perhaps if…"

"Ah, yes, let me finish my breakfast, and I shall join you and my men promptly," said Captain Shortt.

"Thank you for your hospitality, Captain," offered Von Tempsky, and dipped his head. He turned and quickly headed towards the door, taking his hat along the way.

"Ah, Gustav?"

Von Tempsky stopped and turned.

"Will you be returning to finish your breakfast?"

"No, unlikely," smiled Von Tempsky.

"Very well, I'd rather not see your poached eggs go to waste," said Shortt, reaching across the table.

It was just after 6:30 am, and Company No. 2 had performed their usual pre-breakfast exercise routine as ordered and were now enjoying their well-earned meal alongside the garrison, a small detachment of the 57th Regiment under Captain Shortt's command – although, unlike their commander, they weren't enjoying poached eggs.

To Captain Shortt's surprise and pleasure, the Rangers arrived two days earlier, and Von Tempsky quickly reported that he believed the redoubt would come under attack by a rebel force of fanatical *Pai Marire* warriors, whom the colonists called *Hauhau*.

Sergeant-Major Bowers was waiting nervously for Captain Von Tempsky. Relief was evident as his commander approached. "They're gonna attack this morn'n, Captain. I can feel it."

"You're not the only one, Sergeant."

The Sentry Hill Redoubt was fairly new, having only recently been constructed by Captain Messenger on Ati Awa *iwi* lands. Using earthworks, the redoubt created a secure, fully enclosed area where a small number of men could defend against a superior force. In military terms, 'redoubt' means a place of retreat, although, for General Cameron's army, redoubts were temporary forts built to garrison troops in relative safety.

While they waited for Captain Shortt, Bowers and Von Tempsky walked around the inside perimeter of the redoubt, and the captain outlined the strategy for surprising the *Hauhau* and where he wanted his men positioned. Unsettled by the chanting and incantations, Bowers had already taken steps to prepare the Rangers, and they were ready and eager.

Captain Shortt arrived with a lieutenant and sergeant following close behind. "Looks like it will be another beautiful day, eh, Captain?"

"The weather may be pleasant, Captain, but for men who will die today, I doubt it will be beautiful," offered Von Tempsky reflectively.

Captain Shortt swallowed, "You're convinced they will attack us today, aren't you?"

"Listen to the noise. It's not fully daylight yet, and they are in full voice already."

Filling the still morning air, the voices of scores of *Hauhau* warriors chanting drifted across the river; the disconcerting sound made the troops nervous.

"Sir?" questioned Lieutenant Chandler, waiting for orders.

Captain Shortt turned to his officer. "Yes, Lieutenant, prepare the men. Have them fall into defensive positions. See they have water and everything else they need – it may be a long day. Make sure not to change the sentry roster rotation. We want everything to appear as normal."

Von Tempsky let out a sigh of relief. From the corner of his eye, Sergeant-Major Bowers noticed his captain's exhalation and unease.

"Gentlemen, if you'll excuse me," stated Captain Shortt, who strode off in the general direction of the latrines. His sergeant immediately began barking out commands under the watchful eye of Lieutenant Chandler.

"Sir, if I may, what's troubling you?" asked Bowers. "Are you worried about the *Hauhau*?"

Captain Von Tempsky slowly turned in a three-hundred-and-sixty-degree circle and surveyed the interior of the redoubt. When he returned to Bowers, he stopped. "I have confidence we can hold off any attackers, Travis, but that's not what is on my mind."

The astute Sergeant-Major nodded thoughtfully, "May I suggest sending someone to check on Ira later today, Captain?"

"Let's see how the day plays out first, shall we?"

"Very well, sir."

The combined troops of the 57th Regiment and Forest Ranger, Company No. 2, were all in position. Sentries patrolled the inner wall along an elevated earthen bank reinforced with fascines. Made from bundles of branches tied together with dirt piled on top, the fascines strengthened the earthworks and prevented erosion. As Captain Von Tempsky intended, the *Hauhau* were unaware that the Forest Rangers now supported the garrison, and they must have believed that, with superior numbers, a short, decisive battle was merely a formality.

Today was the day; Hatotoi knew in his heart that they were ready. He looked out over the mass of warriors gathered at the Manutahi *pa* with a grim smile. Fuelled by religious fervour and passion, he'd delivered Te Ua's gospel to them, taught his people chants and incantations, and shown them how to attain immortality. Each day their numbers grew, strengthening their force, and each new morning renewed their thirst for justice. The *Pākeha*, the white man, came and took their land, their dignity, and even their culture. Today would be the day, he affirmed; he wouldn't hold his people back. They would reclaim what was theirs.

On the other side of the river, dawn revealed the ominous gloom of the earthen walls the *Pākeha* soldiers had built at Te Morere. When the sun fully rose from its slumber, he knew the soldiers would be patrolling arrogantly back and forth behind the safety of their fortifications, as they always did.

His warriors were ready; they'd already been chanting and yelling for some time and now stood in tribal groups, waiting restlessly. Hatotoi took a big breath and shouted.

"*Porini hoia, teihana!*"

The call for his warriors to pay attention had an immediate effect. Hatotoi looked up at the *niu* standing in the centre of the *pa*, and with his arms he indicated that his men should gather around the pole. Warriors of all ages responded, some mere boys as young as twelve carrying guns; most carried the usual assortment of old muskets, clubs and spears. Tribal leaders encouraged their men, firing their passion with personal words of encouragement or quotes from Te Ua.

Unbidden and of its own accord, the chanting began again, "Hapa, hapa, hapa! Hau, hau, hau! Pai-marire, rire, rire — hau!"

In the growing light, Hatotoi could see the pacifist Te Whiti o Rongomai standing to one side. Although he carried no weapons, only a wooden staff, he too was chanting. Other leaders, caught up in the emotion of the pre-dawn ritual, watched and chanted. Wiremu Kingi Te Rangitaake and Tohu Kakahi were in full voice, urging their men and driving them into a frenzy.

The first rays of sunshine struck the top of the elevated redoubt, and, as he expected, the sentries patrolled, unconcerned, paying no attention to the gathered *Māori*.

Calling for silence, Hatotoi briefed his warriors.

"We will walk proudly and without fear. *Pākeha* bullets will not strike the faithful!" he yelled. More than two hundred warriors roared their support.

"With our right hands raised, we will cast aside the bullets and drive the soldiers from these lands – we will reclaim what is rightfully ours!"

Again, his men cheered.

"We do this with God's blessing—we are the chosen people!"

Two hundred and fifty ardent followers of Te Ua's *Pai Marire* faith responded as one. The sound drifted across the river, enveloping the earthen walls of the redoubt and the seventy-five men inside.

Captain Von Tempsky appeared outwardly calm as he walked along the inside perimeter of the Sentry Hill redoubt. He joked with soldiers of the 57th, spoke with his own men, and exuded confidence and capability. At his side, Captain Shortt did his best to appear relaxed, but to those who knew him, he was nervous and fidgeting.

Sentries continued their patrol from the fascines, and a few anxious soldiers peered through the firing loopholes, but the remainder of the 57th Regiment and the Forest Rangers remained hidden from view.

Captain Shortt reached for his fob-watch, flicked it open, and checked the time. It was only eight o'clock. He felt as if they had been waiting for hours.

"Here they come, sir!" cried a sentry in warning.

All soldiers stirred. Those sitting rose, while others who were already standing unshouldered their weapons and looked anxiously towards their officers. Captain Shortt conferred in hushed tones with Von Tempsky, then nodded to his Sergeant-Major. A string of orders was issued, and men immediately went to their pre-arranged positions. Only a few weapons poked through the loopholes. Von Tempsky was counting on the element of surprise to secure a decisive victory.

He moved to the wall and peered through a firing slit. Outnumbered by over three-to-one, the rebel warriors marched slowly and deliberately towards the redoubt. Still well outside firing range, the odds were still reasonably in their favour, thought the captain, unless the rebels had a plan he had no contingency for.

"What are they doing?" questioned Captain Shortt who was also peering through a firing slit. "They march as if they're on a damned parade."

Von Tempsky also noticed. Normally, the rebels would have sent skirmishers ahead and tried to hide their movements, but not today. Now the rebels walked, no, they were actually marching, if that was even possible. *A distraction perhaps?*

Von Tempsky spoke quickly to Sergeant-Major Bowers, who was nearby. "Double-check our rear and flanks. Make sure they aren't creeping up on us."

Bowers ran off and Von Tempsky and Shortt watched the approaching rebels cross the ford at the Waiongana River in growing puzzlement.

The grass was still wet with dew. Hatotoi was quietly grateful they weren't rushing towards the redoubt in an uncontrolled charge and risking a slip. It was funny, he mused, that he should be thinking these things while marching towards the *Pākeha*-defended redoubt, with death close at hand. Either side of him, warriors marched bravely, their voices rising in a crescendo as others joined, the ominous mantra so familiar to them all.

"Hapa, hapa, hapa! Hau, hau, hau! Pai-marire, rire, rire — hau!" Hatotoi shouted as loudly as he could, his voice lost in the chorus of hundreds of other warriors, their feet stamping in time with the vocal cadence.

He raised his right hand, palm facing forward, and held it steady beside his face. Like him, others followed suit. Of their own accord, his mouth opened; again he repeated the incantation, over and over. He shouted at the top of his voice; spittle flew from his mouth as he screamed. The warriors' syncopated advance was a challenge, daring the *Pākeha* soldiers to fire their weapons, but still the soldiers did not respond. He could see the sentries watching him with curiosity, but as far as he could tell, there was no sign of frenzied activity or of the soldiers rushing out from the safety of their walls to fight them. *With so few defenders in the redoubt, he thought, this battle would be won with ease.*

On Captain Von Tempsky's urging, Captain Shortt dispatched a rider north to Mahoetahi to enlist the support of Major Butler and his detachment from the 57th. Both men hoped the messenger arrived safely and that the Major was on his way south with reinforcements. At present, there had been no acknowledgement of the request.

The redoubt lay about eight hundred yards west of the Waiongana River, which the *Hauhau had* only just crossed. They were still a considerable distance away and continued to march with purpose.

"Hold your fire," trumpeted Sergeant-Major Bowers. "Wait for the order."

Captain Shortt was nervously licking his lips. "What are they yelling? They sound like barking dogs."

Von Tempsky called Tane to them, "What is it they are saying, what does it mean?"

"It doesn't make much sense, sir." Tane looked at both officers and shrugged.

Von Tempsky gave Tane a questioning look.

"The best I could guess is they are yelling, 'Pass over like breath, the good and the peaceful, amen, sir.'"

"That's it, that's all it means?" laughed Captain Shortt. "Pure gibberish."

"What do you think they are referring too?" asked Von Tempsky.

"The idiots have their religions confused," Captain Shortt continued, still laughing. "I thought these fellows were Christians. Passover is a Jewish holiday."

Tane looked with uncertainty at Captain Von Tempsky.

"Thank you, Tane. Return to your position."

Von Tempsky peered through the loopholes and watched the approaching *Hauhau*; the sound of their feet stamping in perfect synchronisation with their chant reverberated inside the redoubt.

Captain Shortt was sharing his joke with Sergeant-Major Bowers.

Von Tempsky continued to observe the warriors for a few moments; he saw their right hands raised while their left hands held a weapon. They're marching to their death, he realised. They need two hands to fire their muskets, and as long as one hand is raised, they can't do so. He stepped back and straightened. His hand went to his moustache and tweaked it … *Passover, pass-over, pass...*

"Pass over!" exclaimed Von Tempsky.

Captain Shortt and Bowers turned to Von Tempsky in puzzlement.

"It's not the Jewish holiday, Passover, it's 'Pass Over'. They don't believe the bullets will hit them. Pass over is referring to the bullets. It must be."

"I think you've been in the sun a little too long," suggested Shortt.

"We should delay firing until they are very close, perhaps one hundred and fifty yards. They will not fire until we do," urged Captain Von Tempsky. "We can overcome them easily if we hit as many targets as possible in our first volley."

Bowers was peeking through a firing slit. He stood and returned to his captain's side. "I agree, sir. They'd be acting very peculiar. Don't think they can use their muskets one-handed."

"Five-hundred yards!" yelled a sentry.

Captain Short ordered all sentries to drop down behind the walls.

"We should give the order to fire at four hundred yards," suggested Shortt.

Captain Von Tempsky turned quickly, bent his head and whispered into Shortt's ear, "If you give the command to fire at that distance, we will likely miss our targets, and the rebels will scatter and continue their attack from concealment and from multiple directions. Need I remind you that they outnumber us by more than three to one? We'll be fighting for our lives, mark my words." Von Tempsky grabbed Captain Shortt's arm. "We should hold off until they are close, very close, nothing beyond one hundred and fifty yards." He realised he was still holding Shortt's arm and released it.

The *Hauhau* chant grew even louder as they drew near.

Captain Shortt swallowed and glanced around him. Many soldiers were nervous, staring at the two commanders and waiting anxiously for the order to fire. He took a deep breath and swallowed, and turned to Von Tempsky, "Very well, one hundred and fifty yards."

Immediately, orders were given to hold fire and wait.

"Two-hundred-and-fifty yards!" came a report.

The seventy-five soldiers of the 57th regiment and Forest Ranger Company No. 2 were all in their final positions and, as ordered, remained out of sight.

As they slowly approached, Hatotoi studied the fortifications. He could make out the outlines of a few faces behind musket barrels that poked out, but nothing that posed a serious threat. Moments earlier, the sentries had disappeared, another sign that *Pākeha* feared them, and as foretold, victory was assured. He paused his chanting and allowed himself a brief smile.

Already, he felt elation– the bond between God and himself was strong. This was what it was like to feel immortal, to have divine guidance and protection. Te Ua was right; *we are the chosen people, and we will overcome*. Hatotoi felt invincible, emboldened by the courageous men of faith who marched beside him. There were no doubts, no questions, and no uncertainties; the powers given to him would be rewarded tenfold.

God smiled down on him, as did Gabriel, who hovered at his shoulder. Their calming, loving voices urged him forward, onward to battle, victory and glory. It was almost euphoric; the heightened sense of righteousness, spirituality and strength in faith gave him power, and as he knew, eternal life.

Then it went black.

Te Ua felt a chill; the prevailing winds from the west blew over snow-capped Mount Taranaki, which towered above the plains and low-lying hills like a sentinel, then swept eastward to the Wereroa *pa* and beyond. He shivered as the fingers of evil reached out and touched him, and he knew in his heart that death came to his people. The joy he had felt was gone, replaced by a cold, austere emptiness. He rose from his seat beneath the *niu* where he'd been preaching and stretched. Faces gazed expectantly, waiting for answers to his abrupt shift in mood.

He took a slow step towards them and looked lovingly at his congregation, his people, his brothers and sisters, young and old. "For the wages of sin is death, but the free gift of God is eternal life."

"Amen," they responded but did not understand.

Te Ua nodded, his expression forbidding. "It has come to pass that a great tragedy has befallen us." He paused to look at the faces of those seated before him. "I spoke of faith, and what good is it, my brothers, if someone says he has belief but lacks faith? Can that belief save him?"

A few people muttered quietly, others yelled in unison, "No!"

"Then hear me!" Te Ua spoke loudly so all could understand him. "Many of our brothers perished this morning. They went to Te Morere to do God's work, yet their belief did not save them. Do you know why?" He shrugged the *parawai* from his shoulders. The ornate cloak fell to the ground behind him in an untidy heap. He raised his arms skyward and paused for emphasis. "Because our brothers said they had faith - but they did not! The righteous survived the *Pākeha* bullets, just as I said. Just as Gabriel told me!" Te Ua paused and made eye contact with those before him. "And just as it is appointed for man to die once – some died this morning. Then, before God comes, their judgement. And they will be judged!"

Some women and children began to weep, their mournful cries drawing attention to the sadness and sense of loss.

"May they find themselves in your presence, O God!"

An elderly man rose unsteadily, removed his hat, and held it under his arm while he waited patiently to be recognised.

Te Ua saw the man and nodded for him to speak.

"I came here to Wereroa to hear your words, Te Ua. If what you say is true, your words have brought death and suffering to many people here. You sent brave men to fight the *Pākeha* in a battle that could not be won … of this I want no part."

Without waiting for a response, the old man donned his hat, stepped carefully around people, and began a slow, arthritic shuffle away. A few others murmured in assent but were quickly silenced.

"Give heed. Let the people who do not have faith, or understand, be angry with me," Te Ua waved an accusing finger at those before him and ended by pointing at the departing elder's back. "The reason is that such behaviour will turn on them. Man does not see my form. You may say it is the form of a man. I am a spirit, everything, a host borne of mankind!"

Te Ua's face was red; he was angry.

"Who has died, Te Ua? Tell us, please!" appealed an unknown female voice.

"God wants us to prepare ourselves. Go to your homes, your families, and wait. News will come later," he said sadly, his anger dissipating, dissolving into sadness.

Sensing death, a lone Kārearea, or, as Europeans called it, a Bush Hawk, patrolled ominously from high above, watching the carnage with caution. Bodies lay where they fell, and orders were given not to move them until they could be identified. Captain Von Tempsky sent a messenger to the surviving rebels to inform them that they could take their dead, but the messenger returned to report that the *Hauhau* mistrusted the *Pākeha* soldiers and would not return.

Drawn by the coppery odour of blood pooled beneath each body, flies appeared en masse and began feasting on the freshly slain corpses. The incessant buzzing was unsettling, and the soldiers of the 57th who tended to the wounded rebels constantly swatted at the insects and cursed in revulsion. The scene was horrific; a few wounded groaned, and another screamed as a soldier tried to ease him into a more comfortable position. One rebel hurled a string of epithets at a soldier who came to his aid.

The first warriors to succumb to the lethal fusillade fell almost one hundred and fifty yards from the redoubt. Up to that point, they hadn't fired a shot. They lay in almost a perfect line, just as they had when they marched. After the first volley, the surviving warriors, unsure what to do, paused momentarily, then continued. The second volley ripped through their ranks, and more men died; many were spared, but they still bravely marched towards the earthen walls of the redoubt that protected the soldiers. Confusion set in; the chanting stopped, and where the faces of brave warriors, only seconds ago, had shown defiance, they now displayed doubt, uncertainty and fear. Sporadic and accurate musket fire continued to find targets. At first, a few turned and ran; then panic set in, and the surviving *Hauhau* warriors quickly fled to safety.

Captain Von Tempsky, Lieutenant Small, Sergeant-Major Bowers and Tane were slowly walking along the first line of dead *Hauhau*. No-one spoke; words didn't seem appropriate. Tane turned the bodies, hoping to recognise someone. They moved from one body to the next; most of the dead's faces were frozen in an expression of disbelief.

He stopped and pointed. His mouth was dry. "I know this one, sir," Tane pulled the coat worn by the warrior and respectfully draped it over his face. "This is Hatotoi Kahore, a leader. Some say he is a *Pai Marire* apostle."

Lieutenant Small scratched the name in his notebook, the list of names growing longer.

Von Tempsky knew of Hatotoi; he'd been briefed by Lieutenant Roberts on who the rebel leaders were. The group moved on. Around them, the few wounded were being tended to, and the deceased were being identified by other groups of soldiers. The body count was staggering. Captain Shortt was informed that during the brief exchange, nearly thirty-six warriors were killed. Many of the wounded rebels would eventually die, bringing the total death toll to almost fifty. Another sixty wounded would survive. One brave soul even managed to reach the deep ditch in front of the redoubt before he was struck down in a hail of lead.

Only one soldier from the 57th Regiment died. Against orders, the young and inexperienced trooper raised himself up in full view of the rebels to have a look. A single musket shot entered his head, killing him instantly.

Holding a handkerchief to his nose, Captain Shortt walked up, his expression grim. "I don't think this is something I'll ever get used to."

Von Tempsky nodded and turned away. He took a cleansing breath, refocused, and said, "We'll be leaving here tomorrow morning and returning to Oakura."

Both men remained silent as they surveyed the carnage. A messenger came running from the redoubt.

"Sir, Major Butler is arriving with a small contingent; they're about a mile away."

"Better late than never, eh?" replied Shortt to Von Tempsky as he strode back to the redoubt.

CHAPTER NINETEEN

Sacrifice

A very large pot sat boiling on the stove. Left unattended, the fire needed stoking, and sensing its need, Wiki rushed back into the kitchen, grabbed a cloth, safely opened the hot door, and deftly tossed three logs into the burner from a neatly stacked pile. Using her foot, she closed the burner and turned the handle, securing the door in position. She then carefully lifted the lid from the pot and began stirring the liquid with a well-used, very worn wooden spoon. A frantic cry from the bedroom caused her to abandon the pot and rush back to her patient.

Moana was soaking wet, delirious and consumed by a raging fever. She dabbed at his face, neck and chest with a wet cloth and spoke soothingly.

Nothing worked. She tried everything to reduce his fever, but it made little difference, and he showed no noticeable signs of improvement.

As Doctor Will instructed, she'd changed his dressings twice a day, and, modesty be damned, cleaned him thoroughly with soap and hot water. His condition continued to deteriorate, and she was deeply worried. Unable to sleep, she sat in the chair her father had placed in the room, near total exhaustion.

Moana's face was red; he was burning up. His eyes were bloodshot, his cheeks sunken, and he'd lost weight. Wiki didn't know what to do. Not for the first time, she sobbed. It began with a small sigh, then another, and escalated into a tearful episode of futility, frustration and fear. She leaned forward and rested her head on his shoulder, weeping. It wasn't just tiredness; it was something else– a sensation she had never experienced before that left her feeling emotional and vulnerable. Wiki was no stranger to hardship and affliction, nor to nursing the ill, but with Ira, it was different. She felt all his pain and suffering, as if she were infected with the poison that wracked his body. Her back heaved with the upwelling of emotion; tears spilt down her face and ran freely onto his shoulder, where the fever's heat dried them in moments. In delirium, Moana was unaware of the emotional outpouring.

Tami stood unseen in the open doorway and watched his daughter's anguish with sadness. He frowned, took a quiet step back and returned to the kitchen to greet Doctor Will, who had just arrived.

"Give her some time, Will, she's had a rough couple of days."

Tami went to the unattended stove, lifted the lid, and began to stir the boiling liquid with a spoon.

"Is she making soap?" asked Will, recognising the distinctive smell of wood ash wafting from the pot.

"Yep, used up nearly all we had on Ira. I'm certain that boy be cleaner than a whistle."

"Good, that's good. I told her to keep him clean. And where is Erepu?"

"Oh, we put him in a barrow and wheeled him to the shed. He's keeping Henry and Charles company. Keep him out of harm's way, eh," said Tami with a wink. "He's healing fast and will be walking normally in a day or so."

Doctor Will was surprised and pleased that Moana was still alive. He didn't expect to be back.

"I thought I heard voices," said Wiki, her eyes puffy and red.

"Miss Wikitoria, as always, it's a delight to behold your astonishing beauty again. You're like a ray of sunshine in a desolate, drab world," Wilbur Cok did his best to offer a gentlemanly bow with a theatrical sweep of his hand, but the gesture was met with scorn when he knocked the broom to the floor with a clatter.

Tami winced.

Wiki wasn't impressed.

"Perhaps another day, eh?" offered Will sheepishly.

Tami laughed, replaced the pot lid, and decided to return to the fields where it was safe.

Moana was turned on his side, and the dressings were carefully removed. Will inspected both wounds and looked with some surprise at the nasty wound where the slug had entered. The skin was neither inflamed nor red and no longer appeared infected.

Will scratched the back of his head, "Well I never…"

Wiki turned expectantly to Will, seeking an answer.

"I'm astounded. There is no sign of infection," volunteered Will.

The exit wound was a different matter; pus seeped, and it was still inflamed, swollen and red. It looked painful and, according to Will, was the cause of Moana's distress.

"This is what concerns me," said Will as he carefully cleaned the area and applied fresh bandages. "This infection will kill him; we need to prevent it from worsening and promote healing."

Will washed his hands and looked thoughtfully around the room. Wiki sat in the chair and looked hopefully at him, waiting for a solution.

Seeing her questioning look, he responded, "We've done everything we can, Wiki. There is nothing more we can do. I'm sorry, it's now a matter of waiting."

"Could we not try bloodletting?"

"I don't think bloodletting is an effective treatment for corruption, Wikitoria, in spite of what physicians and barbers still advocate." Will leaned against the wall, his hand cupped under his chin as he considered options. "The patient is at great risk when the temperature of the blood and internal organs rises above one hundred and six degrees. If Moana's temperature reaches that, I suggest a cold bath."

"A bath? For him or me?" Wiki raised her eyebrows in question.

Will cleared his throat. "Ahhh, yes, for him. As long as his body is immersed in water that is colder than his blood. It's a simple cooling effect." Will shifted position. "The cooler water will help keep his internal body temperature at safe levels."

"Very well, I will do that."

"And indulge his need to drink. Provide him with as much water as he can consume, Wiki."

Wiki nodded and looked pensive.

"Why was the entrance wound not infected?" she asked.

Will shook his head. "I don't know… There should be no difference between the entrance and exit wounds. In fact, the entrance seems more likely to be infected because of the additional trauma the area suffered when I removed the foreign matter. I've seldom seen a wound like this begin to heal without infection setting in."

"You must know, surely? What was different this time to other times?" Wiki asked with some desperation.

"Perhaps you are the difference, Wiki."

"I did nothing more other than attend to him as you told me."

Will gave the matter some thought as Moana groaned.

"No, you didn't do exactly as I asked."

Wiki's mouth fell open.

"You began cleaning the instruments, and then you accidentally dropped them into the boiling water…"

"It was an accident. I hope that wasn't the cause."

"No … No! No, it can't be the cause because the entrance wound was where I began … and it never became infected."

"Well, something happened to the instruments between the time you spent on the entrance wound and the exit wound. What was the difference?"

Will shrugged.

Allowing Moana some quiet, Wilbur Cok and Wiki returned to the kitchen.

"Look, Wiki, there has been much discussion about infection and its causes. What I can tell you is that the air is filled with the spores of cryptogamous plants, which distribute fungus and all varieties of mould. So the air is filled with floating particles of disease, gathered not only from swamps and sick beds but also from sloughs of confessedly and notoriously unclean matter."

Wiki was scooping the accumulated lye from boiling wood ash and water into a bucket as Will spoke.

"Learned men of medicine tell us that the spores of cholera, diphtheria, measles, and kindred diseases are so small that twenty thousand of them, laid end-to-end, would not reach the length of an inch. Yet each spore could cause its own disease in a human frame and settle on some tissue that is irritated by cold, inflamed, weakened, or even healthy."

Wiki looked up in astonishment. "But my bedroom, where Ira now lays…"

Will nodded and smiled, "Yes, m'dear. I think we need to ensure our patient is in a clean environment. Shut-up rooms and dirt will breed pestilence."

"Are you saying my home is filthy and full of pestilence?" Wiki wielded the ladle like a weapon.

"Of course not, Miss Wikitoria," said Will with both hands raised as he backed away. "I was passing on relevant information … is all," he smiled, hoping to appease her. "Fresh air and sunshine– that will work miracles."

"Fresh air and miracles? Then that's what he'll get."

"If Erepu requires no attention, then I must depart to visit my next patient. For now, Wiki, I suggest you feed Moana liquids. Give him plenty of water and something like mutton broth, or chicken soup, and when he shows signs of stability, try feeding him broiled fowl."

Wiki nodded.

Will bent down and looked at Wiki closely, "And further … put a poultice on both wounds– no point in tempting fate and then have the other wound become infected, eh? But you need rest. You'll not help Moana if you are exhausted or succumb to illness yourself."

Wiki took Will's advice and, with the help of her brothers, moved Moana and the bed from the stuffy bedroom to the veranda, where the cooler breeze offered some relief. Still feverish, Moana's condition did not improve. Tami insisted on sitting with him for a few hours each day while Wiki slept; even Erepu helped out. Moana was then moved back into the bedroom in the late afternoon.

Doctor Will's words haunted her; they were frightening. She thought of what he'd said about infection, and as a result she applied a bread poultice to both wounds, cleaned them more frequently, changed the sheets on the bed daily, and even insisted that everyone washed their hands before touching him. Rugs and unnecessary furniture were removed from the bedroom, and then she scrubbed the floors and walls until her fingers bled.

When Ira was struck by a raging fever, her brothers carried her to a large tub she had filled with water, just as Doctor Will had suggested. She couldn't have managed without everyone's help. Unable to prepare meals, friends and neighbours brought food, cloth for bandages, and anything else they could to help the Henare family.

It was early afternoon. Wiki and Moana were on the veranda, where she was spoon-feeding him chicken soup. He was virtually unresponsive. Tired and concentrating entirely on feeding him, she failed to hear the approaching footsteps. She spoke quietly to him as she carefully spooned another nutritious mouthful of broth into his mouth. Much of it ran down his chin onto a cloth she held. With infinite patience, she persisted until he'd consumed enough. She turned to put the bowl on the small table and was shocked to find Captain Von Tempsky and Sergeant-Major Bowers standing a short distance away, watching.

"Oh my, you startled me, Captain!" said Wiki, putting her hand to her mouth.

Unable to speak, Von Tempsky said nothing. Bowers shifted his feet uncomfortably and dropped his head to look at the ground. Overwhelmed at the pitiful sight of Moana, neither man could utter a word.

Captain Von Tempsky swallowed and blinked a couple of times. "Please forgive the intrusion, Miss Henare. We've come to … to see how Ira is faring under your care." He cleared his throat. "I can see … we can see he is poorly."

"He's not doing well, Captain. We are doing all we can for him, but he's still not showing any signs of improvement."

"Has the doctor been? Is there anything you need?" asked the captain. "What can we do?"

Wiki looked at the two dirty, travel-weary men standing about four yards away. She turned her gaze past them and down the hill, where she saw the entire Forest Ranger company waiting on the path. They stood in small groups, quietly talking, and most were looking up at her with interest. She couldn't believe she hadn't heard them coming.

She turned her attention back to Von Tempsky. "For the moment, I need nothing but clean bandages and more laudanum."

"Very well, Miss–" said the captain, who was about to step forward.

"But if you take one more step closer to Ira, I'll wrestle you to the ground, Captain."

Von Tempsky immediately stopped with a look of total surprise. Sergeant-Major Bowers took an involuntary step back and managed a grin.

"When you freshen up and have on clean clothes, you may visit with him, but I will not risk infection while you are filthy. Do you hear me?"

Admonished for their thoughtlessness, both men nodded meekly.

"You can visit him early this evening," invited Wiki in a softer voice. She smiled briefly, showing them a touch of warmth.

"Thank you, Miss Henare. I will return with the items you need," said the captain, returning the smile. "Good day." Both men gave Ira another look, then turned and walked down the path. Their faces were bleak.

As instructed, Captain Von Tempsky returned later that day, freshly scrubbed, and, as promised, brought bandages and a bottle of laudanum. Under the watchful eye of Wiki, he sat in her chair and, with delicate care, gave Moana water.

"I will sit with him, Miss Henare. I'm sure you have other things to attend to. Please allow me to help in this way."

Gustavus Von Tempsky sat with Ira for hours. Like Wiki, he spoke calmly to him about the latest adventures the Rangers had been involved in. He talked about life on the road, their excursions into the bush looking for rebels, and how he and the rest of the company missed their favourite sergeant and looked forward to his imminent return. Tired beyond comprehension, Wiki slept while her brothers and father took care of themselves and Erepu and kept the house clean.

What no one knew was the personal sacrifice the captain was making. Having not seen his wife, Emelia, and his two sons and daughter for some months, he arranged for his family to relocate, and they finally arrived safely in Oakura during his expedition to Sentry Hill. Instead of a long, joyous reunion with his family, Gustav spent only a short time with them before excusing himself and returning to the Henare farm to see Ira. Emelia was an understanding woman and knew her husband well. He'd written constantly about Ira in his letters, and she knew the responsibility he felt for his wounded friend's well-being. Although disappointed, she respected his decision and allowed him to leave them without fuss, knowing he would return later that evening.

Captain Von Tempsky granted the Rangers a few days' rest. They needed time to see their families and loved ones, recover from the rigours of marching, and enjoy some healthy food. Rather than remain only with his family, the captain divided his time between nursing Ira and being with his wife and children. It was an unselfish act, and the entire Henare and Von Tempsky families understood the sacrifice he was making.

Von Tempsky was again at Ira's side. It was mid-morning, and he'd arrived in a wagon carrying food for the Henares, more bandages, and an easel, canvas, paint and brushes.

Ira was asleep, and the captain fully intended to use the time productively to paint. He sat in front of the canvas and roughly sketched basic outlines with a small piece of charcoal. Every now and then he'd turn to look at Ira, then raise his head and gaze into the distance, then resume. The hours passed quickly. Wiki brought some food for the captain and then sat at Ira's side. Seeing that he was asleep, she decided to wait before feeding him and watched the captain enjoying his favourite pastime. He was skilful, creative, and showed remarkable talent.

Provided he wore shoes, Erepu's feet healed enough to allow him to walk without pain. With the aid of a staff, he'd hobble to the fields and help his uncle and cousins however he could. It was something he enjoyed doing and also a distraction from the turmoil of *Pai Marire* and the *Hau Hau*. He felt guilty for deserting his friends at the Wereroa *pa* and was deeply worried about the militant direction some of the *Pai Marire* disciples were taking.

It was a beautiful morning. The sun shone, a light, pleasant breeze kept the temperature moderate, and everyone was in reasonable spirits, although tired.

"Who are the people in the painting?" asked Wiki with curiosity.

The charcoal outline represented three men; one was lying prone on his back.

"That's Ira," pointed the captain to the man on his back, "The other two who are standing are Arthur Fieldsman and Taikaha Juergens. See how they are protecting Ira after he was shot?"

The painting was unfinished, and Wiki couldn't see the likeness yet; she nodded as if she did.

"Water," croaked Moana.

Wiki and Von Tempsky turned quickly, surprised to hear him speak.

"Ira!" She reached out, held his head forward, and carefully allowed him a small sip. He wanted another.

"How are you feeling?" she asked once he'd had his fill.

He grunted and closed his eyes, his breathing irregular; he was asleep again.

Wiki turned to Von Tempsky, "That's an improvement!" and to the immense surprise of the captain, she burst into tears.

From concealment, rebel warriors watched the Henare farm. They were heavily armed with the usual assortment of worn muskets, pistols, and traditional clubs and spears. For about two hours, they'd expertly reconnoitred around the farm's perimeter, moving unseen along the boundaries and establishing who was there and whether they posed a threat. They'd been watching from the shadows for some time. What they didn't expect to see was the *Pākeha* soldier who arrived in a wagon earlier in the day. The rebels were still alive because they were vigilant, and they exercised extreme caution and patience as they observed the farm. Unbeknownst to the Henares, the entire property was surrounded.

Feeling secure that they were in no immediate danger, their leader broke cover and, with his head held high, walked slowly and confidently up the path to the Henare home. He carried no weapons, only a staff which he used as a walking aid, although he didn't require it.

As he carefully made his way towards the house, he could see two people on the veranda and a third on a bed.

He stopped a short distance from the cottage and waited to be acknowledged. His eyes took in the scene before him, and with the assurance of his warriors close by, he felt secure, confident he was in no immediate danger.

Captain Von Tempsky was watching Wiki, who was attending to Ira. A sixth sense warned him of a threat, and the hair on the back of his neck rose. Without making it obvious, he placed the piece of charcoal he'd been using on the lip of the easel and, on reflex, casually dropped his hand to the knife at his hip. He slowly turned his head and saw the imposing figure of a man watching them.

"Miss Henare, I think you have a visitor," said the captain. He was annoyed with himself for not seeing the man approach. With a practiced eye, he casually looked around for others and easily spotted two more heavily armed warriors who made no attempt to hide. He suspected there were others nearby, a sure indication that he could be in peril. His eyes returned to the man and reassessed him; other than a staff, he saw the man was unarmed.

"Wiki!"

She'd been fussing over Ira and had not heard her name called. This time, she reacted, and with a sigh she straightened to address the captain when she saw the warrior.

Recovering from her surprise and showing no fear, she stood straight, her hands clasped in front, and looked confidently at the warrior. She spoke respectfully to him in *Te Reo*, the spoken language of her people. "You have come to the farm and home of the Henare family. How may I help you?" This man was a stranger, and she had never seen him before.

Even the captain, who understood only a few words of *Māori*, could hear the tension in her voice.

The warrior's face remained impassive as he glanced inquisitively from Wiki to Von Tempsky and then to the bed where

Moana lay. He stood nearly six feet tall, and bright, intelligent eyes took in the scene before him; he saw everything and missed nothing. A full grey beard framed a handsome face that showed no hostility. Von Tempsky was ready to move, his body coiled and poised to spring to the safety of Wiki and Moana.

"Would you like some water?" Wiki asked when she received no reply.

After half a dozen heartbeats, the warrior inclined his head slightly and smiled warmly, easing the tension. Wiki poured some water into a mug and began to move towards the warrior when he took an unexpected step forward to look at Moana.

"Come no closer!" she warned him. Her eyes blazed.

Immediately the warrior stopped; his eyes briefly flashed a look of surprise.

"I have a patient who is severely injured," she said, pointing to Moana. "With the dirt you carry, you risk infecting him," she added, then walked to the warrior and offered him the mug of water.

Von Tempsky, unable to understand the words she spoke, knew her tone of voice all too well. He couldn't help but smile and believed she probably threatened the warrior in some way. Whatever she said to him worked; he hadn't moved since. The captain's moustache twitched.

The warrior and Wiki exchanged a few words while Von Tempsky listened, hoping to glean some knowledge about the mysterious visitor and his presence here. His voice was clear, authoritative, and articulate, a voice familiar with communicating to others, Von Tempsky guessed. Again, the captain surveyed the area surrounding the cottage. Warriors stood deep in the shadows, many with their backs to him, looking out. These men were anxious, concerned for the safety of the man before him, guessed the captain. Who was he?

Wiki turned back towards the veranda and gave the captain a genuine look of concern. She reached for the bell.

CHAPTER TWENTY

"I'm partial to a well-cooked lamb," said New Zealand's Governor, Sir George Grey, as he attacked another healthy portion of meat with his knife and fork. "I must say, however, that South African lamb is far inferior—not by a long chalk." Having successfully severed a mouth-sized morsel from the larger portion on his plate, he held the piece of meat with his fork halfway to his mouth and inspected it with some anticipation. "I recall that when I lived in South Africa, I'd often have to enquire of our cook whether the meat we were served was in fact lamb or some half-starved bush creature." He gave a short laugh, impatiently thrust the meat into his mouth, and began chewing, savouring the flavour.

The head of New Zealand's armed forces, General Duncan Cameron, who sat directly opposite the Governor, was more pragmatic about eating. Having spent most of his life in the military, he adhered to the fundamental military principle of eating as much as you can, when you can. As any soldier will tell you, you don't know when you'll eat next. The newly promoted general preferred to eat quietly and quickly, saving conversation until after he had devoured his meal. He regarded the Governor with a subtle look as he methodically worked his way through his food.

As the Governor was about to spear another portion of lamb, he noticed that the meat on the Reverend Thomas Grace's plate was largely untouched. He pointed his knife at the juicy cuts pushed to one side. "Not to your liking, Reverend?"

Seated to the right of the governor, the reverend looked up. "I'm not convinced that animal flesh is good for the constitution. It certainly has an adverse effect on me."

"Then you have not eaten good meat when it is cooked to perfection, Thomas. Mrs Menshen can cook meat so tender and succulent you'll be asking her for more," suggested the Reverend Karl Menshen, who sat opposite Thomas Grace and beside the general.

Governor Grey nodded in heartfelt agreement, while the general chose to remain silent.

"That may be so, Karl, but I still prefer vegetables," added Thomas.

"If you can get them," General Cameron finally decided to contribute to the conversation.

"Ahhh, herein lies the problem, Duncan," said the governor, turning his attention to the General. "Why is it that you constantly cite a lack of food as an excuse for your army's inability to move forward and prosecute *Māori*?" The governor smiled, gratuitously.

Governor Grey invited his three guests to dinner at his official residence this evening to hear a range of views on the ongoing problems with *Māori* in the central North Island. Frustrated with the army for its lack of progress and its continued random violence against them, he sought answers and constructive advice. The informal meal, he hoped, would promote candid discussion and free-flowing dialogue, and hopefully generate some ideas.

General Cameron placed his knife and fork diagonally across his empty plate, then pushed it away. With a napkin, he dabbed at the corners of his mouth, then neatly folded it and placed it back on his lap. He rested his elbows on the table, leaned forward slightly, and looked directly across at the governor. "With respect, sir, I have under my command over fourteen thousand men. They are scattered across the North Island in various capacities. Some are building redoubts, others are garrisoning existing ones. We have detachments hunting down rebels, destroying their crops, and forcing them from lands they are contesting – as you ordered."

"Yes, Duncan, we are familiar with the mundane routines of army life," said Governor Grey dismissively. "But then you should use the food you capture."

General Cameron held up his hand. "Please, let me finish." He waited for silence before continuing. "The success of any armed military force depends on maintaining reliable and efficient supply lines. What will soldiers do when they run out of ammunition, food or water? We must be able to support them when we send them into hostile territory." He cast a quick glance around the table. "The vegetables we confiscate will last only days."

"Then why haven't those supply lines been created?" responded the governor.

"They are, and it takes time. But the supply lines and redoubts we have now aren't enough. We need more, and we are building them as we speak." The general sat back in his chair, quietly frustrated at having to explain basic military strategy to a civilian, even if the man was New Zealand's Governor, an argument he'd had before with him.

"I believe we need to take a firmer hand with all lawbreakers and anyone who offers resistance to our well-trained imperial forces," said Reverend Karl Menshen. He looked to each of the other dinner guests in turn to drive home his point. "Far too many *Māori* are resisting and are influenced by unscrupulous men who claim divine guidance. Even in the Bay of Plenty, that repugnant heathen, Kaihoka, brought heads, human heads, to my parish. They come seeking to convert my good people to the sinful ways of religious fanaticism. It has to stop!" Reverend Menshen turned from General Cameron to Governor Grey. "I don't care if the supply lines are inadequate. I need to know that God's people, my congregation, and others like them, are safe from rebels and zealots."

Governor Grey nodded and wiped his mouth with a napkin. "The Reverend Menshen sent me a missive explaining that *Māori* were planning to attack Auckland. They believe it is lightly defended. Do you recall this letter, Duncan?"

"Yes, I remember. You came by this information from Wiremu Kingi?"

Karl nodded.

"I have taken steps– "

"Yes, General, we are well aware of your response, but this is exactly my point. Do you see the problem?"

"If I may?" asked Reverend Thomas Grace, interrupting. All heads swivelled to face him. "Rather than destroy *Māori*, incur their wrath, and propagate hatred, perhaps we should allow them independence and let them retain their culture and lands. From my experience, this is what they want, and if they achieve that, lives on both sides will be spared. They honestly believe they have moral and legal justification to resist imperial domination."

"In my book, that's a declaration of hostilities; it's paramount to war," offered Governor Grey.

"And Reverend Grace, do you know what men say about war?" asked General Cameron.

Thomas looked to the general over the top of the brightly coloured dahlia flower arrangement, which sat as the table's centrepiece, and shook his head.

"In war, both sides believe they are right."

A servant entered the dining room and began clearing away the dishes.

"And what of those responsible for the decapitations? Are you any closer to apprehending them?" queried Governor Grey.

"I'm sure that if you look in Opotiki, you'll find those responsible," Karl interjected quickly.

"We are taking every conceivable step and committing considerable resources to bring them to justice. Her Majesty's government are quite motivated to make an example of them," offered Cameron.

"Let's hope we don't have any more acts of barbarism. The colonists aren't amused, and, needless to say, they're quite frightened," said the governor.

"It won't stop," suggested Reverend Thomas Grace.

"Nonsense, Thomas," Karl retorted. "Treat them like children. They are nothing more than uneducated savages who require only a little discipline and punishment. Once they have accepted Jesus into their hearts and live piously, they'll no longer be a threat." The reverend nodded to General Cameron. "And the good general is our saviour, a God-fearing man who wields the sword of righteousness. I pray for his success and for an end, once and for all, to the evil that pervades our lands."

"You might have faith, Karl, but I'm not convinced that praying will save your head from parting from your neck," said Thomas.

"Gentlemen, please," interrupted their host. "Save this for another day."

"Don't you see, sir, that government policy is folly," appealed Thomas Grace to the Governor.

The reverend's comment struck a nerve, and a vein in Governor Grey's neck began to pulse.

General Duncan Cameron took the opportunity to weigh in.

"Governor, this … uh, scorched-earth policy and land confiscations you support go against my better judgment. It's nothing more than plunder. As an alternative, may I suggest withdrawing our troops and working with *Māori* rather than challenging them?" the general bravely suggested.

Reverend Thomas Grace nodded in agreement.

All conversation paused as Governor Grey considered his response. Reverend Karl Menshen was finishing the last of his meal, the clink of cutlery on his plate the only sound in the room.

"I have an obligation to the crown, as you do," Grey snapped, pointing his finger at Cameron. "I will not admit defeat or allow the reprehensible actions of a few radicals to influence policy and further unsettle colonists. You have your orders, General, and you will support me, the New Zealand and imperial Governments, and fulfil your duties with obedience and loyalty!" Governor Grey could no longer contain himself, his anger now palpable. "Your presence here this evening was to offer insights so we can successfully administer government policies and consider viable alternative strategies, not to challenge them with your petty personal beliefs and liberal views." The governor's eyes blazed in anger. "How dare you! It is not your job to create policy but to enforce it with the tools the government provides you. You don't have to like them, General, just obey and do your damn job!" Governor Grey's hand shook slightly as he reached for a glass of water. He took a mouthful. "If you are unable to fulfil your duties to the level expected of you, then I'm sure Her Majesty's government will accept your resignation." The governor ended his tirade by slamming the glass back onto the table with a resounding smack. The water sloshed and spilt over the table and nearby dinnerware.

As a soldier, General Cameron was used to being shouted at. Unfazed by the outburst, he appraised the governor carefully. With controlled politeness, he considered his riposte as the governor wiped his hands on a napkin. "I am a servant of the crown, Governor, and will obey my orders. Now, if you'll excuse me, I have pressing matters to attend to," Cameron rose from the table and placed his serviette on the chair. "Thank you for a wonderful meal, Governor." Cameron respectfully dipped his head to Grey and turned to each of the two clergymen, who sat in surprised silence. "Reverends, it was a pleasure to meet you both." The general dipped his head again, politely, and calmly exited the dining room.

"Well then, that was sudden," said Karl, breaking the silence and continuing as if nothing had happened. "As I was saying … I fail to see what the problem is. If the natives misbehave, then punish them severely. They'll soon get the message."

The Governor was livid. He needed a few moments to compose himself.

"And what will that achieve? Peace? Come now, Karl, you and I both know better than that. We need to focus on teaching *Māori* about repentance and turning from sin," Thomas replied.

"And practice *Sole Fide*?" [7] mocked Reverend Karl Menshen.

"Of course, by faith alone God's pardon is asserted for guilty sinners," replied Thomas, warming to their debate. "Belief in biblical inerrancy isn't the answer, Karl, and you know it. The Bible isn't without error or fault in its teachings, and we must embrace the belief that God will forgive our sins through our faith and commitment to Him. Think about compassion rather than the literal biblical context."

----

[7] *Sole Fide. Latin: By faith alone*

Governor Grey sat back in his chair, folded his arms, and listened as the two reverends expounded on their theological discourse.

"We've discussed this before, Thomas, and as I keep reminding you, your permissive views of biblical infallibility are incorrect."

"If you ventured out from the comforts of your cosy parish and into the community more often, then you'd see things in a different light. Times have changed from when the Bible was written. We, above all men, must adapt," suggested Thomas with a smile.

"And if I can interrupt?" stated Governor Grey, unfolding his arms and leaning forward. "How does the *Pai Marire* faith and those addlepated *Hauhau* fit into this? Is there a religious solution?"

"Not to the irrational mind of Te Ua. The man is manipulating his devotees through radical and incorrect interpretations of scripture," said Karl, shrugging. "The man's no Christian."

Governor Grey turned to Reverend Thomas Grace and waited for his response.

"On the first point, I agree with Karl. However, I believe that if I can talk with Te Ua and reaffirm Christian tenets, he may come to understand the error of his ways."

Karl laughed, "You can't be serious, Thomas. Why would he even listen to you?"

"Because I truly believe that, first and foremost, Te Ua is a genuine man of faith who's been led astray."

The Reverend Karl Menshen shook his head.

"And you're prepared to make contact with him? You're placing yourself in great peril," said the governor.

Thomas nodded in affirmation.

"What they need is a firm hand, not negotiation," said Karl under his breath.

"What they need is compassion," muttered Thomas, hoping for the last word.

"What we need, Reverends, are results."

The servant reappeared with dessert, bringing the conversation to a temporary halt.

CHAPTER TWENTY-ONE

Captain Von Tempsky slowly rose from his chair; his hand firmly grasped the knife that still lay sheathed on his hip.

"Please remain seated, Captain," ordered the warrior leader in perfectly clear English.

Two warriors stepped forward to shield him. They were poised to strike at the first sign of aggression. Seeing the futility of the situation, Von Tempsky sat back on his chair, and with his foot slid the easel away to allow room to move.

"Can I enquire to your name?" asked Von Tempsky, once again seated.

The leader was watching Von Tempsky with interest. He saw his hand on the hilt of the knife, and then raised his gaze to look at the captain's face. After a beat or two, he answered, "I am Te Whiti o Rongomai. You must be the renowned Captain Gustavus Von Tempsky."

"Yes, I am," answered the captain, quietly pleased at the recognition. "Were you not at Sentry Hill?"

A look of sadness crossed over Te Whiti's face, and he dropped his gaze to the ground as if offering a word or two of prayer for the loss of so many lives. He took a big breath, lifted his head and replied, his words almost inaudible, "I was."

"Yet you escaped?"

"No, I didn't escape, I just wasn't shot," Te Whiti replied artfully. He turned from Von Tempsky and looked to the bed. "Who is your patient?"

Wiki protectively positioned herself between Te Whiti and the bed. "He is Moana Rangitira."

Te Whiti nodded, "I know of him; he is a brave soldier. Why is he here?"

Unsure what to say, Wiki turned to Von Tempsky for help.

"He is recovering from a wound," he said.

"From Te Morere?" asked Te Whiti, raising an eyebrow.

Captain Von Tempsky didn't want the rebel leader to know of Ira's involvement in the death of so many warriors during the rescue of Erepu. He sought to find a distraction and avoid answering.

With deliberate slowness, Captain Von Tempsky removed his hand from the knife and eased himself upright from the chair. Immediately, the two warriors beside Te Whiti took a small step forward and raised their muskets in a fluid, practised motion, their fingers curling around the triggers.

"Enough!" cried Wiki, her eyes blazing in anger. She took a step towards Te Whiti, "I will not have any killing here. This is my home, not a battlefield!" She turned to Von Tempsky, "Captain, please sit." She pointed at the chair and waited for him to obey. With a look of pure astonishment, Von Tempsky meekly sat as instructed.

Wiki took another step and faced the two warriors. "*Hoatu koutou patu iho*!"

Uncertain, the warriors looked towards their leader. Te Whiti nodded. Immediately, both warriors lowered their muskets and relaxed.

Footsteps could be heard and Tami appeared, rounding the corner of the cottage. He moved as quickly as his aged legs could carry him, the urgency of the ringing bell highlighting his need to hurry. His sons, not far behind, were aiding Erepu, who was now walking cautiously with his staff. Tami stopped suddenly as he saw Te Whiti standing in front of his home. A look of recognition flashed across his face. He quickly looked around and took in the scene before him, his eyes darting from one man to another.

"I see Wiki has things in control," he said light-heartedly after regaining his composure and finished with a laugh.

Tami walked slowly towards Te Whiti and stopped directly in front of him. He raised both hands and placed them on Te Whiti's shoulders, leaned forward and looked up at the taller man who responded by lowering his head. They pressed noses together in the traditional *Māori* greeting called a *hongi*. Tami stepped back and then offered his hand in the *Pākeha* greeting. Te Whiti refused with a shake of his head.

Von Tempsky took the opportunity to slowly look around. He noticed more warriors partially concealed in the shadows of trees that bordered the farm. It finally dawned on him they were completely surrounded. Initiating any form of resistance was futile.

"Is good to see you, my friend, it has been too long," whispered Tami to Te Whiti.

Wiki looked surprised; she didn't know her father knew this man.

Te Whiti nodded and smiled.

"What can I do for ya?" asked Tami in a loud voice now that the formalities were over.

"Te Whiti!" yelled Erepu, who limped into view.

Seeing armed warriors, Charles, James and Henry paused in fear, ready to take flight.

Te Whiti smiled and walked towards his young friend.

"We have been worried about you, Erepu," said Te Whiti. "I'd heard reports you were killed. What has happened and why is it you ran to the *Pākeha* – you have much to tell?"

Wiki instructed Henry to bring out mats, and soon Erepu and Te Whiti sat in the shade and were sharing news. At one-point Te Whiti rose, looked to Wiki for permission and walked towards Ira; he studied him from a safe distance while she watched anxiously. Tami joined Captain Von Tempsky and both men chatted quietly while the captain kept a nervous eye on the warriors who still surrounded the cottage. Tami didn't appear outwardly concerned and wouldn't speak about how he came to be acquainted with Te Whiti. Wiki's brothers were sent out of harm's way back to the fields.

"Captain, would you join us, please?" asked Erepu.

Once seated on a mat, Von Tempsky looked curiously to Erepu in question.

It was Te Whiti who spoke. "Many of my people are against violence, Captain. We seek a peaceful solution to a difficult problem. We are guided by our faith and not by the actions of our enemies. I do not support the killing of men, women or children. But this is not to be seen as weakness, do you understand?"

Von Tempsky nodded, wondering where the conversation was headed. "You and your *Hauhau* warriors are hunted. You put yourself at great risk by being here."

Te Whiti responded in anger. "We are not *Hauhau*, what is this name? We follow *Pai Marire*!"

"Te Ua? Ha, you follow a madman," Von Tempsky's face showed disgust. "He has much to answer for."

"Te Ua is a good man. He's not an angry person; he is filled with love and compassion for his people and feels very strongly about what has been taken from *Māori*."

"Then why are so many acts of brutal aggression perpetrated in his name? How can you tell me about love and compassion when death follows Te Ua?" queried the captain.

Te Whiti's expression changed. "Because those acts of violence are not supported by him!"

Surprised at the revelation, Von Tempsky remained silent.

"There are some men, great men, who were once pious and moral; these men act unwisely and are driven by the torment of their souls."

"Who are these men?"

Te Whiti said nothing, reluctant to divulge names.

"Kaihoka Te Hua and Paora Rakahuru," said Erepu.

"And you believe these men are responsible for the horrific acts of brutality, and were not ordered to do so by Te Ua?"

Te Whiti nodded in affirmation.

Von Tempsky shook his head in disbelief, "What do you believe, Te Whiti?"

Te Whiti o Rongomai scratched his beard and gave the question some thought. "The *Pākeha* have some useful technology but not the kindness of heart to see that *Māori* possesses great knowledge, which, if adopted, would lead to stability, peace and a great new society."

"And of barbarism and violence?"

"If any man molests me, I will talk with my weapon, the tongue," answered Te Whiti without pause. "Just as I'm doing now. I am a man of peace and raised no weapon against *Pākeha* at Te Morere." The unspoken words suggested Te Whiti knew of the very real threat the Forest Rangers posed to him and his people.

Both men glared at each other.

"We have some information that we would pass to you," said Erepu, breaking the tension.

Intrigued, Von Tempsky turned to Erepu.

"Word has come that Kaihoka Te Hua will seek the death of a missionary, the Reverend Karl Menshen, in Opotiki. We feel Kaihoka must be prevented from committing more heinous acts," Erepu said.

"Another senseless barbaric decapitation?" The captain turned back to Te Whiti, who shrugged his shoulders.

"Listen to him, Captain," suggested Tami, who sat away from the group, listening.

Von Tempsky paused and looked towards Tami. In response, Tami nodded.

"If what you say is true, then the reverend should be warned."

"I have sent someone to warn him, but this does not mean that Kaihoka will stop. His hatred blinds him to our faith that once filled his heart, that saw joy and love."

"What happened to him?" asked the captain, although he suspected he already knew the answer.

"His wife and two beautiful daughters were slaughtered by *Pākeha* soldiers at Rangiaowhia, near Te Awamutu, as they sought shelter. Soldiers killed his sister the following day. Since then, Kaihoka has been consumed by hatred and revenge. His heart now beats without warmth," said Te Whiti sorrowfully.

"And what has the good reverend done to offend Kaihoka?"

"He believes that all missionaries are government vessels – that they spy and speak untruths to the government about *Māori*."

Captain Von Tempsky pondered what to do. "I cannot send men north to Opotiki at the moment; we are needed elsewhere. But once we have completed our task, I hope we can go in search of Kaihoka and Te Ua. General Cameron has already requested this. If the good reverend is clever, he will heed your warning and keep away from Kaihoka and his warriors. I can do little else."

"You can tell soldiers in Opotiki," suggested Te Whiti.

"Most soldiers aren't trained to track a man like Kaihoka; he will evade them forever, and I'm not even sure whether there are any soldiers in Opotiki at the moment. But if, as you say, Kaihoka is determined and unpredictable, the reverend should be very concerned."

There was a brief moment of quiet as each man reflected. Wiki was tending to Moana, who stirred and was restless. Te Whiti looked up and watched Wiki.

"The soldier who lies in the bed, Moana. He has killed many *Māori* warriors. My men talk of him– they say he is evil and gifted with powers bestowed by the devil. They call him the ghost."

Both Erepu and the captain listened.

"They say he flies through the bush and can hide like a spirit in the darkness. If you are touched by him, you die. They fear him." Te Whiti raised a finger and pointed to Moana. "I can have him killed now and become a great hero to my people."

Erepu looked shocked, his mouth dropped open, "No, no, you can't. He saved my life. Why do you say these things?"

Wiki turned her head. "Over my dead body! You will not kill him!" she replied, her voice edged with emotion. "Especially after all we've gone through."

Te Whiti wanted to make a point. He hid his smile and turned to look back at Von Tempsky. "What is the difference between a man like this and Kaihoka?" Te Whiti didn't wait for a response and continued. "I see this man in the bed. He is near death, but I know he is just a man, because if he were an evil spirit, he could never be this sick. Bullets would not harm him. If he lives, it will be because of her love and God's will." Te Whiti shifted his gaze again to Wiki.

"You won't have him killed," Von Tempsky shook his head for emphasis. "He is just like you, a young man of conviction and belief. The difference between Moana and Kaihoka is simple, and you know this. Kaihoka kills out of rage, whereas Moana kills not to satisfy a desire to see people die in horrific ways, but to protect people from men like Kaihoka."

Te Whiti looked thoughtful for a moment. "Do you sit here painting beside his bed because you are his commanding officer? No, I don't think so. Why do you watch over him?"

Now it was Captain Von Tempsky's turn to look thoughtful. "I am here because he is a unique young man. He is sensitive, brooding, and in need of a father figure, someone to slap his hand when he has done bad things, and to praise him when he has been good. Just as a father to a child."

"Like a son?" asked Te Whiti.

"Yes, like a son," replied the captain.

"I will not kill him. I am a pacifist, but many warriors do wish to see him dead. Perhaps when he recovers, he can find Kaihoka and protect good people from his evil ways?" Te Whiti added as he stood and stretched his cramped legs. He walked to the painting Von Tempsky begun and bent down to look at it more closely. "Who are these men, your soldiers?"

"Yes, the man lying down is Moana after he was shot; the other two men came to help, but it is not finished yet," added Von Tempsky defensively.

Turning from the unfinished painting, Te Whiti again looked to Captain Von Tempsky. "The killing and death … what does it bring?"

Von Tempsky stood and, like Te Whiti, eased the muscles in his back. "It brings an end to brutal acts of barbarism, so innocent people, both *Māori* and *Pākeha*, can live without fear of death. We don't seek death; we bring lawbreakers to justice, and, like the others, you will be brought to justice for your role."

"*Pākeha* justice!" Te Whiti laughed. "*Pākeha* did not seek permission to build their redoubt at Te Morere. They took land from *Māori* - and I'm to be punished…!" Te Whiti stepped towards the captain, then stopped. "Blessed are the peacemakers, for they shall be called the children of God."

"Amen," replied the captain.

Both men looked at each other, assessing and gauging.

Von Tempsky broke the silence, "Has Te Ua considered surrendering himself? The army is determined to apprehend him."

Te Whiti looked sad; he nodded, "I know this."

"Please talk to him about it. People are being killed in God's name, and both you and I know that is not what God wants for His children." Von Tempsky paused briefly as he recalled a Bible verse, "The righteous perish, and no one ponders it in his heart…"

"…Devout men are taken away, and no one understands that the righteous are taken away to be spared from evil," continued Te Whiti, completing the scripture and not allowing the captain to finish. "Yes, I agree with you, and I will talk to him."

Captain Von Tempsky nodded. "Do you promise?"

Te Whiti spun quickly and walked away, followed closely by his warriors.

CHAPTER TWENTY-TWO

God's will.

Mrs Emma Menshen was getting ready for bed when a loud knock on her door gave her a start. Wary of late-night visitors, she peered through the window and could just make out the outline of a woman standing in the doorway. Wrapping a shawl over her nightgown and clutching it tight to her throat, she nervously walked to the locked door and cleared her throat.

"Who is it?" she yelled.

"I must speak with you, it's urgent," replied the female voice.

Karl always told her never to open the door to strangers at night. She paused in indecision.

"Please," appealed the voice.

With a deep breath, Emma carefully opened the front door. A flickering lamp in the hallway cast a yellow glow over the plainly dressed *Māori* woman.

"Good evening," said the woman in a hurry. "I'm sorry to bother you this late, but I bring news."

From the open doorway, Emma Menshen leaned out to see whether the stranger was alone.

"I'm alone," assured the woman in perfect English.

"What news do you bring? Is this about my husband, Mr Menshen?" asked Emma, worry creeping into her voice.

"The Reverend Menshen is in grave danger. You must both leave here," the woman said.

"Why, what has happened?"

The woman anxiously looked over her shoulder to ensure she was unseen. "I must go," said the stranger, stepping back into the darkness.

"Wait! What do you know of this?" Emma asked.

"It's the *Pai Marire*, but I can say no more. You've been told." The woman disappeared into the evening, leaving Emma alone on the step.

For two days, she fretted over the stranger's late-night warning before they came.

Over the last few days, outsiders, mostly faithful followers of *Pai Marire*, had come to their peaceful community in Opotiki, and more continued to arrive by the hour. They came in ones and twos, in small groups, and then by the hundreds. She heard them as they brazenly entered the church without permission and then used it to poison their own congregation against them. Unable to accommodate them all, the devout and curious spilled out into the small street, filling the neighbourhood as they listened to the deranged, bombastic rant of a repulsive man who stood at the pulpit and incited hysteria, filling their heads with dissimulation - all in the name of God. It was astounding to Emma. She was incensed that they'd invaded their place of worship and violated it with a hate-filled tirade punctuated by the erratic tolling of the bell they rang with childish glee and without purpose. She knew Kaihoka was behind it; he'd been arousing discord since his arrival a few weeks ago - *the gall of the man!* She prayed for her husband to come home and put an end to it.

Mrs Emma Menshen again pulled her curtains apart to peer outside. As before, she observed two young *Māori* men standing guard a short distance away. When she attempted to leave her home, they physically barred her way. No amount of pleading or persuasion altered their minds. She'd threatened to tell her husband, the Reverend Menshen, she reminded them sternly. He would hear about their uncivilised, impious behaviour and be very displeased, perhaps even angered, she warned again, but her cautions fell on deaf ears– they just laughed at her.

Now things began to turn for the worse. Emma was frightened – not so much for herself. She knew that if they wanted to hurt her, they would have done so already, but she feared for her husband, the late-night visitor's warning still fresh on her mind. She knew with certainty that today was the day - the Reverend Karl Menshen was expected to arrive home.

On orders from her master, sailors scurried about the ship, easing lines and clearing the deck in preparation for docking. The sleek two-masted schooner *Eclipse* slowed dramatically, and to the relief of Reverend Thomas Grace, the canted deck returned to a more normal level as she approached the mouth of the Waioeka River at Opotiki.

Reverends Thomas Grace and Karl Menshen departed Auckland the following day after their dinner with the governor and General Cameron. As discussed, Thomas would travel to Opotiki with Karl, then journey into the interior to mediate between the Government and *Māori*. His mission, as defined by the governor, was to resolve any misunderstandings with local *Māori*. To Thomas's chagrin, Karl dismissed it as a waste of time and scoffed at the notion that *Māori* would respond positively to a sincere and honest discourse, especially from a preacher. As usual, both men agreed to disagree.

To Karl's immense delight, the voyage south was pleasant, the winds fair, and they arrived at their destination precisely on schedule. However, Thomas's view of ocean travel was considerably different. He felt that stepping aboard a ship was perilous and likely to end in some horrific misfortune. He attributed their safe arrival to the frequent prayers he offered, not to the expert navigation and ship handling of the *Eclipse*'s master, Captain Levy, and crew.

Captain Morris Levy ordered a slight change of course, and the helmsman swung the large wooden-spoked wheel, pointing the schooner's bow at a distant marker that would take them upstream past the jetty. In a wider part of the river, he would come about, lower the sails, and then drift down, making fast to the small dock he and his brother Samuel owned.

With a favourable wind and against the tide, the *Eclipse* slowly made her way up the river towards the small settlement of Opotiki.

Hearing an unfamiliar noise, Reverend Karl Menshen slowly closed the Bible he had been reading, looked up and across the short expanse of the Waioeka River, and saw a large horde of *Māori* impatiently gathered on the far bank, waiting for the *Eclipse* to arrive. Thomas also noticed the unusual sight and turned to Karl in question. Neither could offer an explanation and remained puzzled by the unexpected turn of events. Curious, both men rose from their deckchairs to observe more closely.

Approximately three hundred *Māori* men, women, and children stood at the water's edge. Some shouted; a few men carried coils of rope, others muskets, and some aggressively waved their fists in the air. It was not a friendly, welcoming party, and for the first time, Reverend Karl Menshen felt genuine concern.

Led by Kaihoka, the *Pai Marire* faithful were in a frenzy. All through the previous day and night, they chanted and danced around the recently erected *niu* pole. Women lay naked, prostrating themselves as Kaihoka predicted he would kill every minister and soldier he could find. Unbidden, he'd entered Karl's church and even preached from the pulpit, eventually soliciting an oath from the *Pai Marire* devotees to help him achieve his goal.

From the riverbank, Kaihoka could see the object of his hatred. Dressed entirely in black, the Reverend Karl Menshen stood arrogantly on the deck of the schooner like a demon, and beside him stood another reverend he knew and disliked.

Captain Morris Levy's brother, Samuel, who managed the store they owned in Opotiki, was pushing through the crowd and making his way along the riverbank, where he could hail the schooner after she turned and before she berthed. He nervously kept a wary eye on the frenetic *Māori* as he waited to issue his warning.

It was well known among *Māori* that the Reverend Karl Menshen held the governor's ear and was suspected of regularly apprising the authorities of *Māori* activities, even informing them of an audacious *Māori* plan to attack Auckland. Obstinate to a fault, the Reverend failed to heed warnings and falsely believed his exalted position in the community offered protection. Karl would be deeply disappointed to discover that Kaihoka's passionate and incontrovertible sermons not only won over *Māori* from neighbouring towns but also most of his own congregation. The Reverend Karl Menshen's parishioners would not offer support or come to his aid.

"Ahoy, *Eclipse*!" shouted Samuel once the schooner was within earshot.

Captain Levy walked to the starboard rail in view of his brother.

Samuel cupped both hands either side of his mouth. "Secure the hatches and deck. It's the gentlemen reverends they want!" he yelled.

With a wave, Captain Levy immediately sent the reverends below deck to safety and ensured all hatches were closed. Once secure, he watched his helmsman expertly manoeuvre the boat towards the approaching dock and the trouble. If Captain Levy had known what would transpire, he would have re-hoisted his sails and made off in haste.

Kaihoka issued instructions for the Reverend Karl Menshen and the Reverend Thomas Grace to be brought before him as soon as they came ashore. He left the riverbank and walked slowly back to his *whare*, where he would offer prayer and seek forgiveness for his sins.

Kaihoka's wife and two daughters were killed almost a year ago. The pain of their passing was raw and fresh, and his life would never be the same again. Government forces brutally murdered them when his family sought shelter in a house, an agreed-upon place of refuge near Te Awamutu. Adding to his misery, his sister was killed the following day in a similar manner. Convinced that local missionaries were acting in accord with the government, Kaihoka deemed them nothing more than spies who informed the authorities of the actions of local *Māori*. He firmly believed that it was a missionary who led government forces and directed them to attack his beautiful family.

The agony was overwhelming. The loss of his loved ones, innocent children and women, slaughtered by men who called themselves missionaries and hid behind righteousness and God, sickened him. Kaihoka would not allow the memory of his slain family to fade, and every subsequent missionary and soldier he saw was a stark reminder that they were just as responsible as those who pulled the trigger.

Te Ua Haumene came to Kaihoka and offered him hope. *Pai Marire* provided a spiritual and theological framework for the plight of *Māori*. It aligned *Māori* needs with Christian values, and Kaihoka embraced the new religion with a vehemence born of pure hatred.

Having concluded his prayers, Kaihoka made himself comfortable as he waited for the reverends to be brought to him. With the utmost care, he reached into his trousers pocket and extracted a folded, worn piece of paper. He had carried the paper for almost a year and looked at it virtually every day. With deliberate slowness, he unfolded it and held it to the light, not to read it, for he knew what it said and had memorised the note long ago, but as a visual reminder, a brutal affirmation of his task and intentions. He silently mouthed the faded words that now defined his life. *He that smiteth a man, so that he die, shall be surely put to death.* The line from Exodus in the Old Testament provided Kaihoka with the rationalisation that he was acting in harmony with Holy Scripture. He returned the note to his pocket.

Kaihoka's eyes blazed, his lips compressed into a thin line, and his face, once easily creased in jubilant laughter, was now a mask of loathing. He looked at his hands, tightly clenched into fists, the knuckles white, stark against his brown skin. Kaihoka spared no thought for the man he'd become or to the fire that raged deep in his belly. His pain and grief were balanced precariously between love for his lost family, God, and the inherent need for vengeance.

The *Eclipse* was safely moored to the small jetty, and Captain Levy quickly stepped ashore to speak with his anxious brother,

Samuel, leaving the schooner and her nervous passengers and crew in the care of his first mate. Together, they immediately set out to find Kaihoka Te Hua.

Voices alerted Kaihoka that men were approaching. He hoped the two reverends were being brought to him. He forced his hands to unclench, rose from the mat where he sat, and walked outside into the warmth and bright sunlight that failed to dispel the veil of darkness shrouding him in perdition. Blinking in the light, he saw the angry faces of the two Jewish Levy brothers approaching.

"What the dickens is going on here? Are you responsible for this?" shouted Captain Morris Levy at Kaihoka. "What business have you with my two passengers?"

Kaihoka studied the brothers standing before him. "They are government spies. They've been judged and will both be punished," said Kaihoka confidently

"Judged? Punished? How?" asked Captain Levy incredulously.

"For we will all stand before God's judgment seat, so each of us will give an account of himself to God," Kaihoka looked from one face to the next. "We seek retribution against Menshen here in Opotiki, and the other we will take back to Taranaki," said Kaihoka boldly.

"What type of retribution?" mocked the captain, not believing what he was hearing.

"They have already been judged by God. Their fate is equal to the crimes they have committed; they will be hanged."

The raised voices had drawn a small crowd, which began to surround them. Both brothers looked around in shock, their faces tense, as Kaihoka's words sank in.

"You need not be frightened; you are Jews and of the same religion as ours. You are not wanted by *Māori* and will come to no harm," offered Kaihoka.

Although somewhat appeased, Captain Levy was still genuinely concerned for the safety of the clergymen currently hiding aboard the Eclipse. He shook his head in disbelief.

"Hanged? Surely you can't be serious. These are men of God, peaceful men intent on helping their communities. How can you justify such unlawful actions?"

Angered, Kaihoka stepped forward. "What do you know of these men? Such sinful men! They hide behind the Bible they carry like a shield and preach empty words of godliness to the gullible who listen." Kaihoka's eyes narrowed to slits. Flecks of spittle gathered in his beard as he launched into a frenzied outburst. "In darkness, when no one can see them, they turn to their evil masters and seek the death of innocents. My people, helpless people, are killed and murdered by the hand of the *Pākeha* government … and those men," Kaihoka raised his arm again and pointed to the schooner. "Lead the way! And you say my actions are unlawful?" He laughed maniacally.

"Are you open to reason?" pleaded Captain Levy. "If it's money you want, take my stores, take my ship, but in the name of God, have some compassion. If the Reverends Menshen and Grace have done wrong, let them be judged by the law of the land."

"They've been judged by God – there is no higher authority!" Kaihoka shouldered past the brothers and headed towards the *niu* pole.

Samuel and Morris looked at each other in desperation.

"We can't allow this to happen," said Samuel quietly once Kaihoka was out of earshot.

"No, of course not. What can we do?"

The Levy brothers hurried back to their ship only to find the crew under guard by the *Hauhau*. Both reverends remained safe below deck, while Kaihoka was content to wait until they stepped ashore before making a move.

"Escape is the only option; I see no other recourse," said Captain Levy to the Reverends Menshen and Grace once the brothers were back aboard and below deck.

"Kaihoka isn't willing to see reason and is blind to common sense and rationality," added Samuel.

Reverend Karl Menshen sat morosely in the galley, looking down at his feet, unwilling to contribute to any plan that would keep them from Kaihoka's clutches.

"Perhaps if you were to talk to some of the chiefs who support him, they may be able to persuade him and prevent Kaihoka from continuing with this foolhardy action," suggested Reverend Grace with some hope.

Morris shrugged, "We have no other option available. I will try."

He quickly climbed on deck and disappeared to find a *Hauhau* chief.

Captain Levy sat in the shade of a solitary willow tree that stood like a single bastion of reason in the small township of Opotiki. Three chiefs from Taranaki sat with him. They greeted Morris like a long-lost brother, listened to his pleas not to harm either Reverend Menshen or Reverend Grace, and even asked the odd question or two, which gave Morris a glimmer of hope. They politely offered him food, consoled him on the predicament he was in, and even suggested that the good Reverend Menshen speak to Kaihoka directly in defence of the accusations made against him. The afternoon wore on, and Morris Levy thanked his new friends and returned to the *Eclipse*. As before, a handful of heavily armed *Hauhau* kept a close watch on the crew, preventing the *Eclipse* and the reverends from leaving. The large crowd that had previously waited near the jetty had long since dispersed.

"We have no other options," stated Captain Levy.

Reverend Menshen returned to his feisty self after hearing the news from the captain.

"I can make him see sense. If given the opportunity to speak to him as the chiefs suggest, I can convince him of the error of his ways," Karl said with optimism.

"I wouldn't advise him on the error of his ways, Karl," said Thomas Grace. "Perhaps you can just offer an alternative."

"Like being shot," retorted Karl.

"Diplomacy might be the best approach," offered Samuel

"Yes, perhaps you are right," Karl said quietly. "Let us all pray."

The Levy brothers looked at Reverend Menshen with bewilderment.

"Yes, both of you can join in. We share the same God, after all."

At the same time that Reverend Karl Menshen recited a prayer for their safety, Kaihoka Te Hua, only three hundred yards away, was also in prayer. Before him, eight hundred *Māori* listened passionately as he intoned.

Reverend Menshen rose from his seat, bent low, and headed towards the companion ladder. He stopped halfway and turned to Thomas Grace, who was a step behind. "I urge you to remain here, Thomas. I don't know with certainty how that heathen will react."

"Perhaps with both of us, our reasoning might be more persuasive."

"I disagree," said Captain Levy. "That fool of a man is unpredictable. It is best if you remain here, Reverend."

"Can't we use this opportunity to quietly hide Reverend Thomas somewhere?" suggested Samuel Levy to his brother.

The natural sounds of the creaking ship broke the silence as each man considered the options.

"It's dark now. We could lower the ship's boat over the port rail and take Reverend Grace to the other side of the river. They'd never see the boat," offered Captain Levy.

"The *Hauhau* on deck will see," replied Samuel.

"No, they'll all lead Reverend Menshen to Kaihoka as soon as he appears. They're farmers, not trained soldiers. Once they've gone, we could lower the boat."

"What do you say, Reverend?"

Before Thomas could reply, Karl spoke up, "I think it's a prudent decision."

"And you risk your life while I make good and escape?" said Thomas.

"We have no choice, Thomas," Karl smiled warmly. "Kaihoka will see sense. Go in peace, and may God be with you." Without waiting for a reply, Karl turned and climbed the companion ladder, leaving his friend behind. Both Samuel and his brother Morris watched as Karl was led away by the excited *Hauhau* warriors.

Reverend Menshen wasn't fearful or afraid. He believed that with a little bluster and some intimidation, he'd convince that savage Kaihoka to see the error of his ways. He'd instructed the rebels surrounding him of his wishes, and they immediately set out towards the *niu* pole where Kaihoka preached. He felt the utmost confidence in his ability to influence the man.

Karl stopped suddenly. He was shocked and disgusted by the sight before him. By the light of a large fire, he could see the naked forms of women kneeling. They were bent over in supplication, their arms reaching towards the pole as Kaihoka shouted and wildly waved his arms in fury. Karl didn't know the *Māori* language and understood not a word of Kaihoka's harangue. He'd always felt that, to become civilised and adapt to modern society, *Māori* should learn English, not the other way around.

Karl was roughly pushed in the back and forcefully thrown forward by his captors. Instead of heading towards Kaihoka, they took him to a nearby hut, where he was pushed inside. Despite his protests and demands, they ignored him. The reality and futility of his position were plain, and Karl was again in total despair.

Not far away, under cover of darkness and clouds, the *Eclipse*'s first-mate was releasing the lines attached to a boom as the small ship's boat was lowered into the river.

In the excitement of capturing Reverend Menshen, as Captain Levy had predicted, all the *Hauhau* guards forgot about Reverend Grace and left the *Eclipse* unguarded.

The small boat, securely held against the schooner's hull by two crewmen ready to take Thomas to the distant riverbank, waited for the reverend to climb aboard. Thomas handed down his satchel and travel bag, then carefully slid over the railing and somewhat unsteadily descended the short, shaky ladder into the waiting arms of the crewmen.

"Easy does it, Reverend."

Leaning over the handrail, Captain Levy waved goodbye. "Be safe, Reverend. We'll do our best to free Reverend Menshen."

"Thank you for all you've done, Captain."

The crewmen pushed off from the *Eclipse* and dipped their oars into the water, quietly pulling the small boat away. Within moments, the boat was swallowed by darkness.

Once the Reverend Grace was safely landed on the far bank, the two sailors quickly returned to the *Eclipse,* and the small ship's boat was hoisted and stowed on deck. Captain Levy and his brother Samuel were discussing Karl's plight in the galley when a crewman informed the captain that a messenger was waiting. Curious, both men returned to the deck, where a young *Māori* impatiently awaited them.

"The Reverend Menshen asks if you can attend to him?"

Captain Levy raised his cap and scratched his scalp, "What happened? Was he successful in persuading Kaihoka?"

The young messenger shook his head.

"Where is he?" asked Samuel.

"This way, I'm to take you to him."

The messenger showed Captain Levy to the hut where the reverend was held captive and then disappeared. The two guards at the door stepped aside and allowed Morris to enter.

A few small moths circled erratically around the small oil lamp, which sat on a wooden crate. A flax mat was unfurled, occupying most of the small floor space. The walls were stark and bare of any adornments, and Karl sat uncomfortably on a low stool. He rose wearily and greeted Captain Levy with a formal handshake.

"Reverend, what on earth is going on? How did Kaihoka respond?"

Reverend Menshen looked down at his Bible, the one he habitually carried. He gently rubbed his long, slender fingers over the leather cover, feeling the indentations and the raised gold lettering, then toyed with the silk ribbon bookmark that marked where he'd last read.

"Then I heard a voice from heaven saying to me, write. Blessed are the dead who die in the Lord from henceforth, yea, saith the spirit, they may rest from their labours, and their works do follow them."

"What are you saying?" asked the captain.

Reverend Menshen turned to his visitor, swallowed, and stepped forward. "God has decided my fate."

He placed his Bible in his jacket pocket and took out his fob watch. He looked fondly at the intricate engraving, then handed it to Captain Levy. With the other hand, the reverend reached into his trousers, took out several folded pound notes, and handed the money to the captain. "Please see that Mrs Menshen receives these items, Captain. The natives are particular about thievery."

Captain Levy was astonished.

"It appears that Kaihoka is intent on following through with his threat."

"To kill you?"

Karl raised his eyebrows in acknowledgement.

"But, Reverend, you can't give up hope. We will endeavour to persuade him to change his mind."

"Thank you, Captain, but I sincerely doubt it will have any effect; his heart is cold and empty. He intends to honour his pledge. In fact, members of my congregation have already come to visit me here to say goodbye, but none of them seems inclined to secure my release."

"And Mrs. Menshen?"

"She'll understand. She's been a good wife, and she knows I have the deepest affection for her."

Captain Levy looked at the watch and the twelve pounds he was handed. "I will do my best, Reverend … and shall return."

"Yes, of course you will. You have my gratitude, Captain. Go with God." Reverend Menshen solemnly pulled the Bible from his pocket, returned to his stool, and stared blankly at the far wall. His fingers listlessly stroked the Bible's cover.

Captain Levy ducked under the low doorway and returned to the *Eclipse*.

Less than two hundred yards away, Emma Menshen stood at the window of her home, totally unaware of the predicament her husband was in.

CHAPTER TWENTY-THREE

Ague

Wilbur Cok paused at the bottom of the path and looked up towards the cottage. Two days had passed since his last visit to the Henare home, and he feared the worst when he discovered what he would find. He had little hope for Moana's recovery; the infection had reached advanced stages, and few survived such an ordeal.

His arrival at the Henare farm was delayed. The wife of a Polish farmer was expecting the birth of their first child and encountered difficulties when, at the last minute, the baby turned in the womb. Unable to cope with the situation, the inexperienced midwife immediately called for Wilbur. Like the midwife, he couldn't turn the baby either; he'd been forced to perform an emergency Caesarean section to save a life, possibly two, and now he needed to accept that his patient here may have succumbed to the inevitable and passed away. Such are the verities of life, Wilbur reasoned.

His thoughts turned to Wikitoria, the woman who held a special place in his heart. She was strong, beautiful and intelligent, the kind of woman he'd always imagined would make a suitable and wonderful wife and mother.

Wilbur was also a realist and had no illusions that Wiki had any romantic inclinations towards him. He knew it wasn't to be, and never would be. He was destined to remain a bachelor, spending his evenings alone, in solitude, pondering life's injustices, as Cupid deemed him unworthy of attention. Bitterness and anger weren't part of Will's altruistic disposition, and he accepted his destiny with singular resolve, genuinely wanting nothing more than to see Wiki happy.

During his frequent visits to the farm, he observed Wiki's deepening affection for her patient. It became obvious to him that Wiki was captivated by Moana, perhaps, dare he say it, even in love, and would likely be very distraught and overcome by his death. It would sadden him to see her in such despair, and he hoped he could be there to offer support in her time of grief and need, and to willingly open his arms and do what little he could to ease her pain. He fully expected the worst.

Wilbur repositioned the errant lock of hair securely under his hat, hitched up his trousers, which always tended to slip down his narrow, lean frame, took a deep breath, and walked up the path, wearing a sombre expression befitting the occasion.

"Doctor Will!" exclaimed Wiki. She stepped out of the veranda's shadows, where she'd been beating rugs with a matten-klopper, and rushed towards him.

Surprised, Will stopped in his tracks as Wiki leapt onto him. She held him tightly.

This was not the welcome he expected.

"Thank you, thank you so much for all you've done. The fever has broken, and Ira is finally recovering!"

Will dropped his bag and pushed Wiki away, holding her by the shoulders.

"Take a breath, Wiki, and kindly explain what has happened."

"Not last night, but the night before, he woke without a fever and was hungry. After I fed him, I went to change his dressing and clean the wound. The swelling was almost gone, and there was hardly any redness."

"Wiki, that's truly miraculous," replied Will, shaking his head in amazement.

"Last evening, Ira slept undisturbed all night, and today he has more strength and a growing appetite. I can't believe it."

"Neither can I," Will said.

Wiki looked serious for a moment, "Will, I thought he would die, I really did."

"I never had any doubt," Will replied. "Let's go and see the patient, shall we?"

Ira was dozing. He lay with his eyes closed when Wiki and Will entered the room. Will was shocked. Although it had only been two days since he had last seen him, Ira's appearance had deteriorated considerably, leaving him a mere shell of his former robust self.

It truly is a miracle, thought Will. *How can someone survive such an ordeal after the body has taken such a drubbing?*

Ira opened red-rimmed eyes, blinked a couple of times, and licked his lips. Wiki picked up a glass and gently lifted Ira's head from the pillow so he could drink slowly.

He didn't fail to notice her tenderness and care as she helped Moana drink. He felt a brief pang of sadness, perhaps even envy.

"You are a remarkable man, Moana," said Wilbur with sincere admiration. "I've seen men with lesser wounds and ague succumb. You fought this and emerged victorious. I commend you."

Ira swallowed and closed his eyes. He wanted to sleep.

"However, we will need to change your dressings," informed Will.

Wiki and Will repositioned Ira on his side and began to remove the bandages. As Wiki had stated, the redness and swelling had noticeably decreased. Expertly, Will inspected both wounds and began to clean them.

"Where is the famous captain? Every time I've been here, he has been at Moana's bedside," inquired Will.

"Oh, Captain Von Tempsky has been temporarily recalled to Auckland," Wiki replied.

Ira's eyes flickered open.

"Will that be the last you'll see of him?"

"No, he should return in a week or so. It's been quiet here without him."

"Must have been important for him to leave. He seemed to be determined to spend as much time here as possible."

"The captain came almost every day. When he was here, I was able to sleep for a while," Wiki said. "He wasn't very happy about leaving for Auckland."

Will continued cleaning the wounds.

"You are going to have two remarkable scars, Moana. They'll be a good talking point and will certainly impress the ladies."

Wiki straightened and shot Will a scathing look.

From his position lying on his side, Ira could see from his peripheral vision the expression on Wiki's face. If he had the strength, he would have laughed.

"Ah, well, at least other soldiers will enjoy seeing such savage mementoes," countered Will, hoping to placate Wiki.

As before, Will spread Manuka honey over both wounds before finishing, then carefully eased Ira into a more comfortable position on his back. Ira's breathing indicated he was already fast asleep.

CHAPTER TWENTY-FOUR

Exposé

Karl Menshen didn't sleep. He spent a restless night pacing the small confines of the hut where he was held captive. Occasionally, he'd read from his Bible, quietly recite a prayer, and then resume his restricted wanderings. No one bothered him unless he appeared at the door, and a few harsh words from his guards encouraged the reverend to step back inside.

All night, the activity continued. *Didn't these people rest?* The chanting bothered him, and he felt the incantations confirmed his belief that the *Hauhau* embraced evil rituals and demonic worship - *they weren't Christian,* he lamented. They rang his church bell, not once, but all night. It was an insult to God, and Reverend Menshen was deeply offended and hurt.

As dawn approached, he began to receive visitors. At first, one or two members of his congregation came, just as they had when he was first confined here early last evening. Then more turned up. Eventually, they lined up outside the hut and patiently waited to greet him.

They politely entered the hut, wished him well, and sympathised with his predicament. At first, Karl tried to solicit their help, hoping to escape, but they refused to be drawn into any action that would upset their new spiritual leader, Kaihoka Te Hua. Many couldn't look Karl in the eye when they spoke, yet he still greeted everyone with the dignity befitting his position as pastor. One simple woman brazenly asked whether Mrs Menshen would still conduct Bible class, while another asked for his fishing pole.

And just as quickly, there were no more callers; they'd stopped coming. Being alone again gave Karl time to contemplate his fate. *What will become of me*? Would he die at Kaihoka's hands, or was this merely a ruse to frighten and harass?

He'd still not met with Kaihoka and fervently hoped his request to see him would be honoured. His pleas to the guards went unheeded; they all but ignored him, choosing instead, with great delight, to drink a fermented peach beverage that seemed to embolden them. He could hear the noise level rising as more succumbed to intoxication.

As before, Karl fingered his Bible as he sat again on the low stool. He caressed the leather cover, extolling its essence. It gave him hope and strength. Eventually, he found the silk bookmark and opened the Bible at the place he had last read. He paused in momentary reflection, then began to read aloud, his voice strong and resonant because he was determined not to show fear and cower, knowing God was listening, "I say unto you, He that believeth on me hath everlasting life. I am that bread of life–"

A voice at the door interrupted him, "Kaihoka will see you now. Come!"

With vigour, Karl quickly left the hut, his excitement causing him to leave his hat and Bible behind. He stepped outside into the fresh air and felt reassured. Finally, he could convince Kaihoka to change his mind. Surrounded by *Hauhau* warriors, he was led towards their leader.

"My hat, I forgot my hat! I must retrieve my hat," implored Karl once he realised he'd forgotten it.

Without waiting for permission, Karl hurriedly turned, pushed his way through the warriors, and headed back to the hut. He found his Bible, returned it to his pocket, set his hat squarely on his head, and hooked his fingers through the top buttons of his jacket as he walked cheerfully back to the warriors.

"They will kill you now," said a warrior.

Karl stopped suddenly and was immediately pushed roughly forward.

How could this be?

"What about my meeting with Kaihoka?"

"No meeting!" said the warrior; a few laughed.

He received another violent shove forward.

Karl stumbled, nearly falling. "Wait, wait, please! Allow me a few moments to pray. Let me go to my church and make peace with Almighty God."

The warriors stopped and conferred briefly.

"You may go," said an unknown warrior.

The procession changed direction and walked two hundred yards to the church. Karl entered cautiously, unsure of the extent of the damage the revellers had caused.

Not far away, Captain Morris Levy, his brother Samuel, and a local trader, Dr Agassiz, watched curiously as the reverend was roughly manhandled away. Captain Levy's crew were all released unharmed, although many of the stores and supplies aboard the *Eclipse* were pilfered. Even as he watched, Morris Levy could see a couple of warriors clambering over the rigging of his ship. They appeared to be untying a block and tackle and a good deal of his finest line.

"Bloody stuff is expensive; hope they don't take too much," said Morris to no one in particular.

The sound of barking drew the attention of the three men away from the ship as they watched a pack of dogs run haphazardly through the township.

"Think they'll go through with it?" asked Samuel.

"With what?" replied Morris.

"Killing the reverend."

"No, it's just bullying and bravado," replied Dr Agassiz.

Morris turned to look at his friend, "Care to risk your life on that?"

The community of Opotiki was small. A few Europeans lived harmoniously with local *Māori*, and the Levy brothers ran a successful small business. Generally, it was a quiet place. Kaihoka changed that. After visiting the Poverty Bay region, he was followed by hundreds of newly converted *Pai Marire* devotees from neighbouring areas. The Opotiki population swelled when an estimated eight hundred supporters arrived to pay homage to Kaihoka and listen to his sermons, a more militaristic version of the gospel Te Ua preached. For the last few days, he'd wound them up into a mania, plied them with alcoholic beverages, notably the potent peach drink, and made astounding claims against the government, *Pākeha* churches, missionaries, and, in particular, the Reverend Karl Menshen.

Local *Māori iwi* hadn't been particularly happy for some time. They were deciding whether to rebel against the British Colonial Government and join forces with *Māori* in the Waikato, so Kaihoka's arrival was perfect; it unified them.

The warriors aboard the *Eclipse* successfully removed the block and tackle from the rigging and now stood beneath the willow tree. One climbed into the branches and affixed the block to a thick branch, leaving the rope dangling freely. Seeing the activity, a crowd had begun to assemble. Kaihoka Te Hua walked from the *niu* pole, entered the growing throng, and waited.

Reverend Karl Menshen finally emerged from the church. Resigned to his fate, he walked with dignity and gravitas as he was led towards the tree. A few of his congregation reached out their hands, which he shook solemnly as he slowly made his way through the parting crowd.

Karl saw the rope and knew without a doubt that this was the moment; it was time. God called to him. Just as Jesus sacrificed his life for the sins of man, so would he. As a devout Christian, he would go to his death without fear and welcome judgment from his God. His faith gave him courage and strength. With resolve, Karl lifted his head.

A warrior immediately stood behind the reverend, removed his jacket, then his waistcoat. He handed both items to Kaihoka, who admired the fine cloth and, to the delight of the onlookers, immediately donned the vest and jacket.

Concerned for their own well-being and unsure whether they too would become the object of *Hauhau* attention, Captain Levy, Samuel and Dr Agassiz moved further away to a much safer distance. From their new position, they had an unobstructed view of the proceedings. They didn't speak; there was nothing they could say or do to help the poor man about to be brutally killed.

Emma could see unusual activity from the window of her small parlour. She'd spent hours at the window, watching and hoping her husband would be released. The rebel guards at the door told her that her husband had been found guilty of spying on *Māori* for the colonial government and would be punished - he'd been sentenced to death. She wept, her eyes puffy, dabbing her tears with a handkerchief. She couldn't see her husband, but could tell from the activity that he was near the tree she could only partly see.

Earlier, she'd rushed outside and tried to run past her guards, but they physically restrained her; they even hurt her, treating her roughly as they forcibly returned her to her home. She stood at the window, distraught and alone, already feeling a sense of loss. Tears ran freely down her cheeks, and she sobbed uncontrollably. Slowly, she slid down the wall and sat on the floor, her face buried in her hands; her back heaved. The handkerchief lay discarded on the floor beside her. Sensing something amiss, the cat rose from its slumber and walked towards her, easing its way through the tangle of her arms and lying down on her lap.

After being blindfolded, the rope was looped around his neck, then again for good measure, while his hands and feet remained untied. Karl kept his head upright and stood stoically, unmoving, as warriors fussed about him. Reverend Menshen was a proud man, and he would not give these heathens the satisfaction of seeing him beg for reprieve or break down in an emotional outburst of weakness. The strength he felt came from his faith. He spoke quietly, "Death is swallowed up in victory. O death, where is your victory? O death, where is your sting?"

With deliberate slowness, the rope was pulled taut, and the block and tackle creaked, then settled beneath the branch as it took the strain of Karl Menschen's weight. The unyielding rope tightened as warriors hoisted the reverend from the ground. Suspended by his neck, he swayed gently beneath the tree's outstretched branches.

Seeing the opportunity, a few devotees rushed to the swinging reverend, removed his shoes, and another removed his trousers, went through the pockets, and tried them on for size.

Unable to watch any longer and thoroughly disgusted, Morris and Samuel, along with Dr Agassiz, walked despondently away and returned to the *Eclipse*.

Reverend Karl Menshen was left to hang for an hour.

From the galley, a bottle of rum appeared, and liberal amounts of the golden liquid were poured into glasses, and a toast was offered to the brave reverend. The bite of the hard spirits that sailors favoured so much did little to remove the bitterness the three men tasted.

"What is it that provokes men's passions to such a degree and then persuades them to commit such heinous acts of barbarism?" asked Samuel as he peered into his glass.

"Is religion not a tool used to unify people?" replied Dr Agassiz. "All for a common good and a shared spiritual belief."

"Doesn't mean religion is bad," added Morris.

"No, of course not, but if religion bonds men together and then you politicise it … what do you have?" replied Samuel.

"Fanaticism," Dr Agassiz said wryly.

Morris laughed, but it lacked humour. "And remove the politics, and you have a compliant group of people. That places an incredible responsibility on the religious leader, does it not?"

"And that raises the question, should political leaders also be religious leaders? Should church and state be separate?" Samuel asked.

"Ah yes, now that's a suitable topic for debate," suggested Dr Agassiz.

The two brothers nodded in agreement and a philosophical silence filled the cabin.

"How many wars have been fought through the ages under a religious banner in an attempt to solve a political issue?" Samuel asked. "As an example, I urge you to look outside."

A reply wasn't forthcoming.

Morris uncorked the rum and poured another generous libation for them all. A few more followed.

The first mate quickly clambered down the hatch and along the companionway to the galley.

"Captain, you'd better come on deck and take a peek at what's going on."

"What now?" said Captain Levy as he rose from his seat. "Another hanging?"

The first mate led the three men up onto the deck and blinked in the bright sunshine. In the distance, a group of warriors were lowering Karl Menshen to the ground. Once untied from the rope, Karl was carried unceremoniously towards a small, fenced enclosure beside the church.

"I think we should have a closer look," said Morris, stepping off the *Eclipse* onto the dock.

The three men casually walked closer so they could watch without making their presence too obvious.

Karl was placed on the ground, his arms were spread and his legs were close together, his body took the position of a cross.

Morris couldn't believe what he was seeing. He turned to his brother in total astonishment.

"D-Did you see that!"

Samuel saw, and begun to retch, violently throwing up. Doctor Agassiz turned a deathly shade of pale and covered his mouth with his hand, his eyes wide in disbelief.

"He moved! The reverend is still alive!" Morris exclaimed, shaking his head in pity.

Again, all who watched saw the reverend's legs move. His hands unclenched, and he slowly moved his head. Reverend Karl Menshen was still alive, despite having been hanged by the neck for an entire hour.

Samuel wiped his mouth with the back of his hand and watched, morbidly spellbound. Kaihoka's followers began to chant, their incantations growing louder. An old axe was passed from hand to hand and made its way to the front, where a warrior received it and held the rusted tool skyward for all to see. The old axe had last been used to chop firewood – and it now had a new purpose. Morris stood transfixed as the chanting grew in intensity. He couldn't believe he was witnessing such a brutal and horrific act committed against another human being. It was inhumane.

The axe was raised high in the air, then, in a mighty downward arc, it descended, striking the exposed neck of Reverend Menshen. Samuel gasped and fell to his knees, his hands covering his eyes. Morris was immobile. *Surely Reverend Menshen's suffering had now come to an end.*

The old blade lacked a keen edge and failed to sever the head as intended. Again, the axe was raised as the chanting grew louder. A few followers turned away from the madness, the blood and gore proving too much. Some shouted in protest, only to be drowned out, their pleas going unnoticed. A few wept.

The blunt axe descended again, striking the body hard but failing to cut through flesh and bone. A large knife was produced, and without pause, a warrior began the grisly task of finishing what the axe couldn't. Unaffected by the carnage, Kaihoka watched, his eyes black liquid pools of unforgiving hate.

Dr Agassiz turned and walked back to the Eclipse, his shoulders slumped and his hands hanging limply at his sides. Samuel was sobbing. Morris stood appalled, his lips compressed, shaking his head in disbelief; he, too, was pale and transfixed, unable to move.

With elation, the head was finally severed, and the crowd mostly roared in appreciation, which only added to the blood-fuelled frenzy. With the decapitation finally accomplished and looking splendid in his new clothes, Kaihoka stepped forward and stood near the corpse. In his hand, he held a simple chalice stolen from the church and placed it near the body to collect the quickly draining blood. Many followers formed a line, and they waited noisily for their turn to drink. A few pushed others out of the way, hoping to move closer to the front in fear they'd miss out.

Kaihoka took the first drink and passed the chalice on. People took turns to drink from the vessel, then stooped to dip their hands in the blood that seeped onto the ground. They wiped it on their faces and arms, and on any exposed skin, and moved on. The chanting and orgy continued, but Kaihoka Te Hua wasn't finished yet.

In a vile display of theatrical showmanship, Kaihoka lifted the dripping head as a sign of victory, holding it high for all to see and witness. Those not gorging themselves on blood turned towards him, spellbound. With his free hand, Kaihoka gouged out an eye and held it, proudly displaying the dripping grizzly trophy for all to see.

"This is parliament!" he shouted and promptly placed the eye in his mouth and ate it.

His frenzied followers reacted in approval, their voices carrying far.

Paralysed with horror, Morris stood alone, taking in the grotesque scene. He wanted to run, to sail away in the *Eclipse* and never return – he couldn't move.

Without a qualm, Kaihoka quickly removed the second eye and held it aloft.

"And this is the Queen and British law!" The remaining eye quickly went the way of the first.

It was too much for Captain Morris Levy. Unable to bear witness to further atrocities, he returned to his ship.

Not content with providing the body of Reverend Karl Menshen with even a modicum of dignity through a Christian burial, the *Hauhau* abandoned the desecrated corpse and walked away. Adding to the carnage, the pack of hungry dogs running rampant through the community now had their turn.

CHAPTER TWENTY-FIVE

Opportunists

Colonel Henry Warren, Commander of British forces in Taranaki, crossed his legs and leaned casually against the armrest of his chair to find a more comfortable position. His haemorrhoids had recently flared up, and as was his habit, he looked at the small-framed portrait of Emperor Napoleon Bonaparte that sat at the corner of his desk, beside the pewter-framed picture of his wife. He reminded himself that if the infamous Corsican military genius was afflicted with such a disagreeable condition, then perhaps he too could still have his moment of glory. Although the discomfort eased a little, his mood remained dour. With an abundance of self-assurance, Colonel Warren took a deep breath and looked at the newly promoted major, who sat opposite, with some disdain.

"You'll be pleased to note, Major, that the 57th Regiment has largely restored peace to the immediate area around Taranaki. I do not believe your small, ineffectual force was even a contributing factor."

The major showed no reaction.

"But to the matter at hand. Lieutenant Roberts will provide the intelligence you require to deal with some problematic local *Māori*." Colonel Warren glanced at some paperwork on his desk. "It appears a minor chief, Te Kahuwai, is continuing to stir things up, and his antics contradict my assertion that things are well in control here. Some colonists are quite upset and have contacted Governor

Grey to complain. Against my better judgment, I've been ordered to provide you with assistance." Warren threw the paperwork back on his desk. "A total waste of my bloody time and resources!" The colonel used his arms to raise himself from the chair and carefully repositioned. *Damn haemorrhoids.*

Sensing there was more to come, the major remained silent and kept his expression blank.

"You may have had the past blessings and support of General Cameron, but that will no longer be a factor."

Surprised, the major did respond with a look of puzzlement.

"You didn't know, did you?" asked the colonel, savouring the moment. This time, he leaned back in his chair, re-crossed his legs, and smirked.

"Perhaps you could enlighten me, sir," asked the major.

"I think you'll find that the imperial forces will no longer merely tickle the native subversives and bend to the liberal policy of stroking cultural sensitivities, as General Cameron once advocated."

"Is General Cameron beginning a new campaign, Colonel?"

Colonel Warren laughed. "Yes, you could say that, but it won't be here in New Zealand. He's tendered his resignation to Governor Grey and will return to England."

The colonel uncrossed his legs and leaned forward, his elbows on his desk. "We're beginning a new campaign to rout native rebels, including that *Pai Marire* lot, from this entire region, and will remove any and all resistance once and for all. This will be a proactive engagement, not a reactive one."

The major chewed his bottom lip. *This unfortunate news would have a dramatic impact on all the armed forces, not to mention the small force he commanded. He'd liked Cameron and thought him a very capable officer. It was certainly a disappointment to see him leave.* "Who will be his replacement?"

"I understand Major-General Trevor Chute will be the new commander," Colonel Warren raised an arm and pointed a finger at the major. "I can tell you he won't pitter-patter around here, and he won't put up with your high-and-mighty ways."

The major ignored the slur, "I don't believe the *Pai Marire* are the real problem. It's the *Hauhau*– they're the fanatics, the violent ones who bear arms against the clergy and government."

"Naivety suits you, Major. As far as we're concerned, they're one and the same and will be dealt with harshly."

The major was tired of Warren's attitude towards him. Though outranked, he wouldn't sit back and allow this man to harangue him constantly for no good reason. "Then I hope Major-General Chute makes good use of his limited time in New Zealand. I believe the colonial office has every intention of recalling all its troops. I expect you'll look forward to returning home to England, Colonel." The major offered a pleasant smile. "I'm sure New Zealand's armed forces will clean up the mess after you leave."

Colonel Warren laughed. "And let me tell you something. It won't be your scurrilous lot. From what I hear, you'll soon be demobilised."

This conversation wasn't going anywhere. "Then I can only hope, sir, that Major-General Chute pays as much attention to his unavailing egocentric officers as he will in quelling any justifiable resistance."

"How dare you!" spat the colonel.

"I apologise, sir, did you make a personal inference?"

The red-faced colonel rose from his desk, spluttering.

The major remained seated. "If there is nothing else of importance you wish to discuss with me, I shall attempt to restore order among my scurrilous troops and thank you for your assistance." He slowly stood and fixed Colonel Warren with a steely look. "I have some real soldiering to do. Good day, Colonel Warren."

"Von Tempsky, you haven't heard the last of this!"

Major Gustavus Von Tempsky shut the office door a little harder than he meant to.

Major Von Tempsky and Lieutenant Roberts were quietly discussing the Forest Rangers' new mission in a dark corner of a local tavern in Te Awamutu. The tavern was mostly filled with rowdy soldiers and labourers, and the two officers were ignored.

"Unlike what Colonel Warren told you, I believe the real issue will arise further south, with a fellow called Riwha Titokowaru. I think he's a bit of a scoundrel," Roberts said, hefting the ale to his mouth. "He's been attracting a lot of attention from disaffected *Māori*." He wiped froth from his lips.

"Just another renegade or is he something special?" asked Von Tempsky.

Roberts smiled and took another large mouthful. "From what I can gather, this Titokowaru is another lay preacher and a devoted follower of Te Ua. He once promoted pacifism, like a few others, but has now changed his viewpoint and taken up arms to fight back. He's using clever tactics in minor skirmishes and meeting with some success."

"And what of pacifism?" asked Major Von Tempsky.

"He's come to learn that pacifism, while an admirable concept, isn't going to prevent land confiscations."

Both men laughed, causing a few heads to turn in their direction.

"If you have any dealings with him, be warned. Don't underestimate him; he's a clever one," suggested Roberts.

"And what of Te Kahuwai? Colonel Warren believes he represents a threat."

"Te Kahuwai is a minor chief of no consequence. He's a greedy opportunist, seeking wealth. More of a miscreant, really."

"If he is a nuisance, why would Te Kahuwai begin killing locals, as Colonel Warren claims, and what would he stand to gain?" queried Von Tempsky.

Roberts held his tankard with both hands, staring into the dark liquid as he considered his reply. With a resigned sigh, he looked to Von Tempsky. "Te Kahuwai is essentially a criminal. Many colonists have been scared into selling their land cheaply because of the fighting. My understanding is that Te Kahuwai is behind these isolated deaths. He kills a few people, and the Kingites or Te Ua and his *Pai Marire* followers are blamed. Colonists are frightened, and Te Kahuwai has someone offer them a low price for the land. He'll sell it for a much higher profit when things stabilise."

"Surely he should have been apprehended by now?" asked Von Tempsky.

"Actually, it's not as easy as you think. We believe he uses a sophisticated network of people and doesn't get his hands dirty himself. Because of that, we can't prove anything. Every time we think we are getting close, he seems to be a step ahead of us."

"Bit of a mess," said Von Tempsky, shaking his head. "And the Rangers have been tasked to put an end to his enterprise?"

"No, not quite," whispered Lieutenant Roberts. He swivelled his head to scan the room, ensuring he wasn't overheard. "Your mission is simply to find those responsible for the killings and violence and end it. His business activities will end as a result. No need to involve yourself in actual policing– let others deal with that.”

A scuffle broke out between a soldier and a labourer, and both Von Tempsky and Roberts watched with curiosity as the burly proprietor quickly settled the altercation. Once order had been restored, Roberts continued.

“The people actually doing the killing, whoever they are, appear to be hiding in the bush, then emerge and strike quickly before returning to the bush and disappearing.”

“So these killers, they are not part of the *Hauhau*?”

“We don’t know. While Te Kahuwai is from a local iwi that supports Te Ua, he may have some association with them or with people within the faction.”

Both men raised their tankards and emptied them.

“Do Te Kahuwai’s men pose a real threat to the colonists?” asked the major. “I’m curious about their tactics and training.”

“When they come out of hiding, they are a very real threat indeed. They’re a sadistic and very capable bunch of renegades. Come to my office tomorrow morning, and I’ll give you the intelligence report to read,” finished the lieutenant.

CHAPTER TWENTY-SIX

Departure.

The Henare farm was a hive of activity. Tami received a letter informing him that his ageing elder sister, Erepu's mother, had suffered a serious hip injury in a fall. Not in the best of health anyway, she was deemed too frail to travel, so Tami would take James, Henry, the youngest, and, of course, Erepu to visit her, leaving Wiki and Charles to look after the farm in their absence. They would depart the following day and make the thirty-mile journey south to Opunake by wagon.

In preparation for the journey, James, Charles and Henry were greasing the wagon's axles, while Tami and Erepu, now fully recovered, tended the fields. Wiki sat in her favourite chair under the veranda, darning her father's socks in the warmth and light of the late-morning sun. Beside her sat a basket containing an assortment of needles, buttons, cotton bobbins and small skeins of loosely coiled yarn in various colours. With remarkable ease, she threaded the large needle over the rent and pulled the fine-gauge yarn obediently behind it. She patiently repeated the process until an interlaced hand-woven patch covered the entire damaged area. No doubt her father would voice his ungrateful complaints, insisting that darned socks were painful on the feet. As Wiki so often reminded him, if he wore shoes and socks more often, his feet would become used to them. Reminding him to cut his toenails was a fruitless exercise.

She lifted her head again, as she'd done countless times in the last hour, and looked towards the other end of the veranda, studying Ira as he listened intently to Major Von Tempsky. She gave the two men some privacy as they discussed military matters and tactics. Although she heard snippets of their conversation, she wasn't paying them any attention, focusing instead on her own conflicting emotions.

At around the same time as her father, two brothers and Erepu would depart for Opunake, the handsome young man she had nursed back from the brink of death would also be leaving the Henare farm. He would travel by bullock wagon to Te Awamutu where army doctors would supervise his recovery and health.

The thought of Ira leaving the farm left her with an unexplained sense of loss and sadness. She was able to rationalise his departure and saw the wisdom in the decision to move him, but her feelings towards this man who had come into her life were new and perplexing.

It left her with an ache in her chest, shortness of breath, and a feeling of sorrow that made her want to cry, a sentiment she was totally unfamiliar with. He was part of her life, not just as a patient and someone to care for, but also as a man. He provided companionship and became a trusted friend. He was also attractive. No, she decided, he was beautiful and kind, and he intellectually challenged her; he made her self-aware and self-conscious. For the first time in her life, she felt more than just a daughter or a sister to demanding brothers; she felt like a woman, and that made her feel complete.

In the days since his fever broke, they'd talked, shared, and even laughed, though the exertion of laughing caused Ira considerable discomfort. She could see beyond his façade of detached coolness, and as they talked, she glimpsed a little of the violence and death he had experienced as a young man in the Crimea. With increasing understanding, she saw the vulnerability he tried so hard to hide and readily accepted the growing need to nurture and protect him. He infuriated her with his stubbornness and naivety, but then he'd look at her with his dark, liquid eyes and smile, and she'd feel herself wilt.

As she continued to observe the man sitting comfortably in a chair, a blanket draped around him, she felt despair. To Wiki, it was plain that Ira liked her; they were now friends, but she held no illusions that he had any romantic interest in her.

Wiki wasn't oblivious to the attentions of men. When they'd come calling and weren't driven away by her brothers, admonished by her protective father, or simply dissuaded from appearing at the farm again, she knew the signs and could see desire, even lust, in the faces of men who sought her affection. Ira displayed none of those tendencies. The exception, of course, was the first time they'd met, but then his behaviour was fuelled by alcohol and encouraged by her father, and since that evening, he had never deliberately said an untoward word that would cause offence. If the truth be known, admitted Wiki, there were times when he didn't seem interested in speaking to her at all and appeared incapable of stringing a coherent sentence together.

The feeling of loss returned, and with it came heartache. Wiki felt herself beginning to tear, and with her handkerchief she dabbed at her eyes.

Ira was surprised when the newly promoted Major Von Tempsky arrived that morning at the Henare farm, wearing his new insignia with pride. The promotion was well deserved, Ira told him. With a slight wince that was difficult to disguise, he reached out to offer his congratulations and gingerly shook the major's hand.

Von Tempsky wanted to share his news, including his orders that the Rangers would not pursue the radical Kaihoka and instead, begin an active search to engage rogue *Māori* in the Taranaki area who were burning farms and indiscriminately killing both *Māori* and Europeans. Armed with the intelligence report provided to him by Lieutenant Roberts, Von Tempsky sought his sergeant's advice and outlined his strategy.

As Von Tempsky detailed his plan, Ira, without moving his head, occasionally turned his gaze to Wiki. If she raised her head to look his way, then he'd quickly flick his eyes back to the major and the intelligence report he flourished.

Women were confounding - a sentiment shared by most men and discussed in great detail in the damp trenches of the Crimea, deep in the New Zealand bush, or standing with a glass of ale in a public house. He'd never heard of a solution that enabled him to understand and deal with women, and that could withstand the close scrutiny of those who judged common decency. Typically, men shook their heads in resignation and, with bravado, recounted a heroic incident in which they'd defeated female confoundedness against overwhelming odds. This frequently led to vigorous backslapping, with the aggrieved victor wholeheartedly agreeing that it was just another burden men had to bear, albeit a major one. Few men were brave enough to admit in public that there were repercussions and that women were seldom losers when it came to a duel of wit or unreasonableness. For reasons Ira didn't understand, Wiki held the high ground, and he felt outgunned, outmanoeuvred and outclassed in her presence.

One thing was clear. In the hours he'd spent lying in bed, suffering from his wound, he recalled dreams in which Wiki had held him tenderly and confessed her feelings to him. During one dream, he was convinced he saw and felt her tears. He put those thoughts down to delirium and a confused mind affected by ague - it couldn't be possible that it had actually happened.

Ira risked another quick glance. Wiki looked down and continued to darn her father's socks. She was concentrating on her task and did not notice him looking her way. As he watched, he felt his heartbeat quicken, his face flush, and he knew with certainty he would miss her when he left the farm the following morning. Wiki was special. She was unique, and, more surprisingly, she made him feel inadequate, almost helpless, in her presence. Without doubt, Ira knew that any tenderness or perceived affection she showed him was due to a woman's natural maternal instincts, not to any romantic inclinations towards him. He glanced up again and saw her wipe some dust from her eyes.

Tami walked around the side of the cottage and greeted everyone with his usual cheery remarks, though when he saw Wiki mending his socks, he scowled and muttered incomprehensibly under his breath.

"Mr Henare?" questioned Von Tempsky, who, out of respect, always addressed him formally.

"Captain, how can I help?"

"He's a Major now, father; address him properly," censored Wiki.

"He's a major what?" asked Tami, who couldn't restrain himself and burst out laughing.

Ira tried not to laugh and grimaced, the reaction causing some pain.

Wiki was trying to hide her own smile, but Ira's response caused her some anxiety as he grabbed at his side.

"I think you should reconsider and alter your travel plans," offered Major Von Tempsky. "At least until we have caught the renegades."

"Nonsense. We've made this trip hundreds of times and never had a problem, except for that one time we lost that rooster … never did catch the bugger, though. Do you remember that, Wiki? You chased that bird halfway round the mount," Tami laughed at the recollection, which ended in a fit of coughing. "I 'preciate your advice, Major, but we'll be fine."

"If Tami takes precautions, I don't see a problem," Ira offered, knowing Tami wouldn't change his mind. Ira looked to the major and shrugged. "Travel during daylight, and for added safety, try to find others and journey together as a group."

"Then at least take a musket with you," suggested Von Tempsky.

The conversation came to an abrupt end as all heads turned towards the sound of approaching footsteps. Labouring under the weight of a milk urn, Pippi pushed a small cart up the path towards them. His eyes flicked curiously from one person to another, paused briefly on Wiki as she rose from her chair, then quickly looked away towards Tami. Pippi licked his lips and said nothing as he finally arrived.

"You'll be wanting those veggies," stated Tami, forgoing his usual cheery greeting.

Pippi didn't respond, waiting anxiously as Tami disappeared around the house.

"We won't be needing milk for a while, no need to come by," Wiki said.

Pippi wouldn't look at her and kept shifting his gaze from his feet to Major Von Tempsky and Ira. "Oh … something wrong?" he finally asked.

"Mr Henare, James, Henry and Erepu are leaving for a while. They're going to Opunake, so while they're gone, we won't need any milk."

Wiki saw Pippi take a long hard look at Major Von Tempsky as he lifted the urn from the cart.

" … and Sergeant Rangitira will be departing for Te Awamutu tomorrow morning."

Pippi risked a quick look at Wiki, who was still standing with her arms folded defensively across her chest, and unconsciously licked his lips again. Both Ira and Von Tempsky watched.

In acknowledgement, Pippi quickly raised his head, then looked back at the ground. "What's happening then in Opunake?"

"Here ya go," said Tami, returning with a good-sized sack of vegetables. He placed them carefully on the cart.

No one replied to Pippi's question.

With one last look around, Pippi manoeuvred the small handcart and walked sullenly down the path to his wagon. "I'll be seein' ya soon nuff," he finally replied over his shoulder.

"He's a strange one is that lad," said Tami once Pippi was out of earshot.

Ira was still watching Wiki carefully and noticed her tension ease once Pippi had departed. Von Tempsky also noticed and made a mental note to find out more about the peculiar young man when he returned to Oakura.

In spite of a concerted effort, no amount of persuasion would alter Tami's decision to postpone his departure.

The following morning, not long after sunrise, a Forest Ranger's bullock and wagon appeared. Under terse instructions and a stream of precise orders from Wiki, the hapless Rangers loaded Ira onto the wagon. Convinced they were treating her patient with unnecessary roughness and showing no care for his comfort and fragile condition, the Rangers were subjected to a verbal barrage that any Sergeant-Major would have been proud of. At one point, unable to hide his mirth, Ira was caught grinning and was immediately set upon by Wiki, who subjected him to a tirade that rivalled what the troopers had just endured. Unsurprisingly, Tami, Erepu and her brothers said their goodbyes and had long since disappeared, wisely making themselves scarce, knowing what was in store.

Once Ira was positioned to Wiki's satisfaction and the Rangers were about to set off, she decided Ira's blanket needed another adjustment. She lithely climbed aboard the wagon and began to fiddle with its placement. She leaned over Ira and whispered in his ear, "You take care, Moana Rangitira. I want to see you healthy again real soon." The bullock, agitated by a fly, shifted restlessly and stamped a foot. The wagon rocked a little, causing Wiki's lips to brush Ira's. Ira looked into Wiki's eyes and opened his mouth to speak. He wanted to tell her how he felt about her. This was the time. His mouth remained open, but no words came to him. He couldn't think of the right thing to say or do. Wiki returned his gaze and waited.

He wanted to kiss her so badly… Ira finally closed his mouth and gulped. Frustrated at not being able to find the right words, he grimaced, angry at himself. Wiki misunderstood Ira's expression and again scolded the Rangers for having moved him roughly and causing him undue pain.

She climbed down safely and nodded to the driver. He snapped the reins, and with a loud "Hayaaa," the wagon rumbled away. Two forest rangers offered protection and support, leading the wagon, while two trailed in the rear.

It began with a wave, followed by a single tear and a trembling lip. Within seconds of the wagon disappearing around the bend, Wiki was weeping uncontrollably. Tears cascaded freely down her face, and her chest heaved as she buried her face in her hands.

For the second time that morning Wikitoria waved goodbye to those she loved.

CHAPTER TWENTY-SEVEN

Dressed in an assortment of European clothes and armed with their usual muskets and pistols, as well as many traditional *Māori* weapons, about two dozen warriors stood attentively on the cliff tops overlooking Wairoa's unusual black-sand beach far below.

Bathed in the soft pink glow of the setting sun, warriors were evenly spaced for almost half a mile and kept a watchful eye on their two charges on the beach and the immediate area around them. Some men fidgeted uneasily, nervous that government troops would launch a surprise attack and come hurtling from concealment in a cloud of blue smoke.

Pākeha soldiers were heading northwest from Wanganui, and Te Ua, reluctant to fight a battle he knew he couldn't win, decided to leave the Wereroa *pa* in Waitotara and head to safety in Opunake. Wairoa, only a handful of miles from his *pa*, was a natural place to rest.

The fear Te Ua's warriors felt was unfounded; there were no soldiers here yet. The only hunters in the area flew high above in lazy sweeping arcs, searching for prey amongst the low-growing vegetation and sparse coastal bush. The Bush Hawk, or Kārearea, was indifferent to the warriors who'd invaded its territory. The animals and small birds, disturbed by the uninvited intruders, were no match for its keen eyes, incredible speed, or sharp talons. A few warriors looked skyward as the silent hunter circled above.

Propelled by the gentle north-westerly breeze, a large puffy white cloud slowly drifted across the sun. Now backlit, brilliant rays of golden light fanned outwards like an open hand, with fingers extended, creating a kaleidoscope of vivid hues that painted the cloud deep orange near the centre and pink and magenta at its extreme edges. The colours were deep and rich, changing in intensity as the sun slowly sank. Free from the sun's grasp the cloud eventually floated past.

Te Ua paused to take in the splendour, revelling in the special moment of its incomparable beauty. The very same wind that moved the cloud caressed his face. It was the breath of God, and he felt the union, the unspoken spiritual coupling that reaffirmed his faith and devotion. His personal connection with God was unique; he knew this with absolute certainty, and with the breath of God on his skin, he understood its essence. Again, God spoke to him in the silence of nature's beauty, and Te Ua knew what he must do. It was another vision; although not what he expected, it was still a gift of clarity and purpose.

The roar of the surf brought him back to the present. Te Ua turned, looked up, and saw his men, alert sentinels guarding from the cliff tops. One man waved, and Te Ua waved back. With a smile, Te Ua looked to his companion.

"Why did you bring me down here?"

"Come," Te Whiti o Rongomai began to walk, his steps leaving deep imprints in the iron-rich black sand. Te Ua followed, eager for an answer.

"There, do you see it?" Te Whiti raised an arm and pointed to a large tree stump, awash in the golden light of the setting sun and partially buried in the sand.

Te Ua nodded and looked back to Te Whiti with curiosity.

"This is a Totara tree, or what is left of it. It has been here for many years, long before our ancestors came," said Te Whiti. "It is protected by this stone."

The two men approached the stump and Te Whiti knocked on the volcanic rock that protected the wood with his knuckle.

"From a single seed, this Totara tree once grew to be great, eventually to be destroyed, and then preserved."

Te Ua reached out and touched the stone. He turned and leaned back against the stump and folded his arms against his chest.

Te Whiti continued, "This is like *Pai Marire*, and we are about to be destroyed. What you began, what we created, will end, but we can preserve it and make *Pai Marire* last, just like the mighty Totara."

Te Ua looked deep into the eyes of Te Whiti as the setting sun's last rays of sunshine swept over him. Te Ua nodded in understanding and remained quiet.

"I want to show you something else," said Te Whiti as he gently tugged at Te Ua's elbow. Te Whiti led, and Te Ua followed as both men walked along the beach towards the cliff face.

"Have you seen this?" Te Whiti pulled from the base of the cliff a large oyster shell once buried by a millennium of sediment. Using his fingers, he swept away the sand and dirt, revealing a shiny, well-preserved shell. "This shell has been here even longer than the Totara … "

" … and the *Pākeha* soldiers cannot destroy this either, as they cannot destroy *Pai Marire*," added Te Ua, taking the shell from Te Whiti to study it more closely.

"No, my friend. *Pākeha* are not destroying *Pai Marire*. Our brothers like Kaihoka Te Hua are destroying it."

Te Ua looked up sharply, his eyes briefly flashed.

"We should go, it is almost dark," Te Whiti said gently, ignoring the expression.

Te Ua relaxed. "I'm sorry, and, of course, you are right. I know you speak of Kaihoka; he's become possessed by evil. Fire rages in his heart, once filled with love."

This time, Te Whiti remained silent.

"The *Pākeha* soldiers will kill him," added Te Ua matter-of-factly.

"And if you continue to evade the *Pākeha*, they will kill you when they find you," said his friend and confidant. "They march north, destroying crops and killing our people. They come for you, my friend."

Te Ua turned to face him, but Te Whiti's face was now shrouded in darkness. "I should have expected this, I should have known..."

On the cliff top, Te Ua's warriors began to follow the two men on the beach as they approached the sandy path leading upwards.

Te Ua stopped suddenly and clutched his head as if in sudden pain. "Yes, yes, yes! I see it now!" he shouted. "This is what God wants. We must hold fast to the faith, to love, and to law!" Te Ua removed his hands and grabbed Te Whiti by the shoulders. "Don't you see, my brother? God has told me twice that his people, forgetful, standing naked, on the island in two halves, will be restored, even to that which was given unto Abraham, for this is Israel."

"Hold fast to law?" questioned Te Whiti, "Which law do you speak of?"

"The Ten Commandments, of course. Can you not see?"

Te Whiti shook his head, puzzled at the sudden transformation in Te Ua.

Te Ua released Te Whiti and began stumbling up the path, mumbling. The abrupt change in Te Ua's demeanour was a cause for concern to his friend. Only moments ago, Te Ua had been rational and coherent, but now …

"Do you want the deaths of innocents on your conscience?" Te Whiti shouted after Te Ua. "God doesn't want death!"

Te Ua stopped, breathing heavily. He turned and looked back over his shoulder; the dark shadow of Te Whiti stood alone on the beach. "We don't bring death to innocents. *Pākeha* soldiers invade our land like the black hand of death."

"And we see God's smile of love even when others see nothing but the black hand of death smiting our beloved," answered Te Whiti, reflecting.

Te Ua's mouth opened as he was about to rebuke Te Whiti, but he stayed silent. With difficulty, he eased himself down and sat on the path—he felt a headache coming on. He shook his head in bewilderment, hoping to clear the fog. Moments later, Te Whiti climbed up and sat beside him, resting a comforting arm over his shoulder.

"Despair not, Te Ua. We are all God's children, and we seek the same thing - for our people to embrace *Pai Marire* and accept your teachings. I am not your enemy, but I fear for your safety. If you continue like this, you will die in a hail of musket fire. Your death will not be that of a martyr, and it will have been for nothing. My friend, you can do far more for our people while alive than dead."

"Yes, yes, you are right, Te Whiti," said Te Ua, appearing more focused. He swallowed once and collected his thoughts. "I have something I must tell you. Earlier on the beach, God spoke to me.

He sent me a message and told me that I must surrender to the *Pākeha*."

Te Whiti was surprised, and at a loss for words. This was what he'd hoped for.

"Does this shock you?"

"I don't know what to say."

"I do not trust the *Pākeha* soldiers. If I'm to go to them and surrender, will I be treated fairly, or will they just kill me? I am confused."

Both men pondered the dilemma.

"There is a man, a *Pākeha* soldier, whom I spoke with not so long ago," Te Whiti placed his hand reassuringly on Te Ua's arm. "He is one of their leaders, an officer. I looked into his eyes; his *mana* was strong. I could send word to him..."

"You trust an officer?" Te Ua laughed and shook his head again. "Who is he? Is he a good man?"

"Yes, he leads the Rangers."

"The Forest Rangers! The same Rangers where the devil walks! Oh yes, my friend, then they will kill me."

"No, I don't believe so. His name is Von Tempsky; he has honour."

"Where did you meet him?"

"I went to see our dear friend Erepu. He is with Tami, and Von Tempsky was there seeing to a wounded Ranger in the care of his uncle."

Te Ua smiled, "How is Tami, is he well?"

"He has spirit and is feisty; his daughter is just like him."

They both laughed.

"And Erepu?"

"He is better, and his injuries have healed."

"Yes, Kaihoka was very upset with Erepu, but I reminded him not to grow bitter. For it is given unto you to entreat your God to save his people. Erepu will find God again. He is a good young man, is this not so?"

"Yes," replied Te Whiti, "and a good friend."

"Would you trust this Von Tempsky with your life?" Te Ua asked.

Te Whiti fell silent for a few heartbeats as he recalled their meeting. "I think I did," he finally said.

"I have heard stories of a *rēwera*[8], Ranger walking the bush like an *atua*[9]. He can kill someone with a look and leave no mark. I do not trust this man of yours if he leads the Rangers, and I will not make a pact with the devil's friends."

Te Ua's word was final.

"Then I will find another, and I will also make you a promise, Te Ua. I will continue your work, and it will last hundreds of years, just like the oyster shell. It will be a new religion that will focus on discipline, faith, organisation and dedication."

"This makes me happy, but there is more … I saw a vision a while ago. It was of a great warrior who led *the Māori* to victory over the *Pākeha*. You will need this warrior to help you. Without him, our cause is lost."

"Who did you see?" Te Whiti asked.

Te Ua laughed, "I saw our friend Riwha Titokowaru."

"It is sad that a man's greatness is measured by the men he has killed. Perhaps it would be better to judge a man by the lives he has saved."

Te Ua smiled. He still held the ancient oyster shell, feeling the smoothness of the inside and the roughness at its edges. He wondered about his future and how the *Pākeha* would respond to

---

[8] *Devil*
[9] *Ghost*

his surrender. His disappointment was palpable. Many of his followers distorted his message, using *Pai Marire* as a call to action to commit horrendous acts of violence, to kill innocents, and even clergy, in barbaric ways.

While Te Ua did not approve of missionaries or their relationship with the government, the violent death of the missionary Menshen in Opotiki was unnecessary. Men like Kaihoka and Paora had gone too far. *Pai Marire* was now and forever tainted, and with sadness he realised that even if he did present himself to the government forces, *Pai Marire* would not be allowed to continue in its current form. Te Whiti spoke wisely; his new religion was a good idea.

Te Whiti's promise spoke of a bright future in which the interests of his people intersected with Christian values. Under the guidance of Te Whiti and his pacifist principles, righteousness could prevail. *But what of the men who sought and acted violently,* wondered Te Ua. *What would those men do who used Pai Marire to serve their own evil ends?* He turned the shell over in his hands and sighed. There was little he could do but condemn their actions.

"From this day forward we will call this moment in our lives *Te Tau Ariki*[10]." said Te Whiti quietly.

"And what will you call this religion?" Te Ua asked.

"*Parihaka.*"

With the onset of evening both men felt a chill. They stood, wiped the sand from their clothes and climbed the remainder of the way to the top of the cliffs where waiting warriors welcomed their return. In silence, the group walked back to their hidden camp.

---

[10] *A time of prominence*

CHAPTER TWENTY-EIGHT

Behind the barn owned by dairy farmer Mr Miller lay a squalid, single-roomed building. It wasn't considered a house or a cottage; it was simply a hovel. From a distance, it may once have been painted green, but up close, if anyone looked carefully, they probably wouldn't find any traces of paint. Moss, lichen and a medley of intriguing exotic flora lined the exterior walls, making the hut almost invisible to anyone on the track fifty yards away. Almost as an afterthought, and at a most peculiar angle, a steel pipe rose from the roof, smoke drifting from it, a good indication that someone had the misfortune of inhabiting the dilapidated structure.

Mr Miller considered himself a generous man and, having provided Pippi, his milk delivery driver, with employment, graciously allowed him to live in the building. Of course, Mr Miller charged nominal rent, which was deducted from Pippi's wages along with other charges for sundry items he deemed appropriate.

Pippi wasn't much of a homemaker and considered his dwelling a temporary abode, a place of refuge until he became wealthy and found something better. If living in such squalor wasn't bad enough, Pippi shared the comforts of his home with another.

Patricia was considerably older than Pippi, although no one had the inclination to calculate exactly how many years older she was. Her rather slovenly appearance aged her and only added to the mystery. Just in case he forgot, she frequently reminded Pippi that she was his woman. Needless to say, she was also many other local men's woman, and with Pippi's encouragement, she made herself available to anyone with a coin or two to spare.

Pippi and Patricia's relationship was curious and abusive. A bad day for Pippi was reflected in the bruises and marks he inflicted on her face. Today hadn't been a good day for Pippi, and as usual a few contusions now marked her appearance. She was lucky– a few more developing bruises were hidden and wouldn't have an adverse effect on her income-earning potential. After all, as Pippi reminded her, it wasn't her face that attracted clientele. Curiously, Patricia saw no reason to leave him and find a better man, and so this less-than-cosy arrangement seemed to work quite well for the romantic couple.

A devout Anglican, Mrs Miller encouraged Pippi and Patricia to attend regular church services, although neither felt inclined to do so. Pippi wasn't particularly spiritual, but Patricia was amenable to assuming a spiritual role if asked by her customers. She owned a threadbare Nuns' habit she'd liberated from the convent in New Plymouth a few years earlier. Despite their minor differences, they had one thing in common – they worshipped money. They had no qualms about what they did to achieve it, and little intelligence to keep it.

Patricia was curled up on their bed, trying to keep as much distance from Pippi as possible. This was extremely difficult in the small confines of the hut, but she had correctly assessed that the filthy table where Pippi now slumped was as far away as she could get from him. The soiled blanket was pulled to her chin, and the fire that sputtered in the hearth did little to keep out the evening chill or to prevent another beating if Pippi's evening didn't improve.

For the time being, she was relatively safe, as Pippi's head rested on his arms at the table, his steady snoring and the wind whistling through the walls providing the only comfort to the bedraggled and slightly inebriated woman.

A loud clatter at the door interrupted her reverie.

"Hey, Pippi, you there!" came a muffled voice.

Again, the door succumbed to a pounding fist. Patricia winced at the sound, recognising Big Pete's voice.

"Pippi, wake up, Big Pete's here for ya," she made no attempt to open the door. "Pippi!"

Pippi raised his head slowly and groaned loudly before he turned his head and, considerately, vomited on the floor.

"Aw, c'mon Pat, open the door!" yelled Big Pete on hearing her voice.

"Don't think you want to come in here. Pippi's been sick!" Patricia broke into a giggle.

"Pippi, open the bloody door!"

Pippi wiped his mouth on his sleeve, stood unsteadily, and groaned again. "Comin'!" He turned to Patricia. "Lazy bitch." He wobbled, took two steps, and fell against the wall, which threatened to collapse. Without moving, he unlatched the door, and it swung open, revealing the large form of Big Pete Maha.

Pippi took a moment's respite and leaned forward, his hands resting on his thighs. To Big Pete, it looked as if Pippi would be sick again. He spat instead.

"It stinks in here," said Big Pete, holding his hand to his nose.

Patricia found this amusing and began giggling again. "You come to play?" she asked hopefully.

"Nah, here to see Pippi, luv," he replied. "Maybe next week."

Pippi straightened and looked at Big Pete with watery eyes, "Whadya want?" He spat again.

"Wotcha got for me, Pippi?"

"I ain't got nuttin' for ya, Pete."

"You always got somthin' for me."

Pippi lurched back towards the table, and Big Pete wisely remained at the door where the air was cleaner.

"You don't want to upset me, Pippi."

Pippi rubbed his chin thoughtfully, trying to remember, his memory dulled by the ale he'd drunk. "You know the market gardener with the fat wife?"

"The Yugoslav?"

"Yeah, him. He's got family comin' over. There'll be a whole bunch of them."

"He's no good, no one cares 'bout him. Who else?"

"Um, oh, the army's gonna clean out all the *Hauhau* round here, all the way down south."

"We know that already, Pippi. C'mon, what else you got?"

"I heard the Mayor of Wanganui is going to Auckland, and will leave by boat from New Plymouth," Pippi smiled. He knew this piece of news was valuable.

"And how did ya find that out?" Big Pete asked.

"The cobbler, he's makin' him a new pair shoes, special like, for the mayor's trip."

"When is he goin'?"

Pippi shrugged. "I'll find out tomorrow when I brings the cobbler his milk."

"Good Pippi, that's good. Anythin' else?"

"That's it."

"You sure?"

"Yes, that's all."

"Tells him about that farmer, Pippi," Patricia offered from the safety of the bed.

Pippi turned and gave her a scathing look. He didn't want to tell Big Pete about the Henares. He was saving that for himself as he intended to pay that bitch Wikitoria a visit.

"What farmer?" Big Pete asked.

"It's nothin', Pete."

"Pippi, tell 'em." Patricia urged and began another fit of giggling.

Big Pete knew Pippi well enough to tell when he was holding out on him. He took a big stride towards the table; the menacing look on his face was enough for Pippi.

"Tell me, Pippi," Big Pete hissed.

Pippi sighed. "You know the farmer at Te Ahuahu, the one who lives on the small hill. The Henare farm grows veg. You know the place."

"Tami Henare," said Big Pete, his eyes wide in surprise.

"Well, he left for Opunake with his two boys and their cousin Erepu. Goin' to see his sick sister. He left his daughter Wikitoria and her oldest brother at home."

Big Pete thought carefully. He recalled that Kaihoka had wanted to find Erepu, and he knew that Erepu was out of favour with the *Pai Marire*, who were seeking him as well. But the *Pai Marire* wasn't the only one Big Pete sold information to. There were others, and they had specifically wanted Tami Henare. Tami had been on the list for a long time, and the reason for his death had to be carefully disguised. Yes, he thought, this was perfect. "But he's already gone to Opunake?"

"I'm not supposed to knows, but I heard he's comin' back on Sunday, two weeks from now."

Big Pete returned to the doorway for fresh air and scratched his head, "Comin' back from Opunake, you say?"

Pippi had a tankard of stale ale at his lips and nodded, spilling the liquid onto his coat and shirt.

Big Pete walked back into the room and set a shilling on the table. "For your effort, Pippi. Until next week." He strode from the hut, leaving the door ajar.

Pippi knocked the chair over as he rose from the table; he staggered to the open door and latched it. His fists were clenched as he turned to face Patricia.

Big Pete Maha didn't go straight home. He rode his horse to a small colonial cottage on the outskirts of Oakura. It was the home and workplace of Miles Southport, a surly Englishman and petty criminal. Dutifully, Big Pete shared his newfound information with Miles and was rewarded with some money, including a reimbursement for the two shillings he claimed to have given Pippi.

When not involved in criminal activities, Miles was also a blacksmith. Not considered tall at five-foot-eight, Miles had enormous shoulders and powerful arms, which he frequently used to emphasise his point of view. He rubbed his hairless scalp and considered what to do with this new information. Although not blessed with a quick mind, he was smart enough to understand its importance. Normally, Miles would travel alone to pass on his information, but tonight he decided to take Big Pete with him in case questions were asked that he couldn't answer.

Within fifteen minutes, both men were on horseback and heading away from Oakura with the unhappy screeching of Mrs Southport fresh in their ears. They rode for two miles in a northerly direction and approached a small cluster of well-maintained buildings surrounded by trees and some low bush - it was a *marae*[11] and also the home of Te Kahuwai. They didn't stay long but passed

---

[11] A communal or sacred place used for religious and social purposes.

on all the particulars of the Mayor of Wanganui's trip to Auckland and Tami Henare's visit to Opunake. The news was gratefully received, and by breakfast the following morning Te Kahuwai's lieutenants also had the information and their instructions.

After leaving the *marae*, Miles returned to his cottage a little richer, which managed to placate his adoring wife, while Big Pete decided to celebrate at the local Public House before it closed. He mingled with the regulars, talked to strangers, and sought useful information. One man he chose not to speak to was Lieutenant Roberts.

The lieutenant was on his way back to New Plymouth after an intelligence-gathering trip, in preparation for the new offensive against rebel *Māori*. He'd noticed the big man's demeanour as he flitted from table to table, and had overheard snippets of conversation suggesting the man was seeking information. Lieutenant Roberts's ears pricked up when he heard Tami Henare's name mentioned. As an intelligence specialist, Roberts was immediately suspicious.

"Who's the big fella?" Lieutenant Roberts casually asked the publican as he stood at the bar for a refill.

"That's Big Pete, sir," came the reply.

Roberts nodded, leaned against the bar, and feigned disinterest. "Yeah, he's a big boy, that one. I've never seen him 'round here before."

"He's a local lad, but not a real regular; he's always travelling."

"Oh, sounds like a great job to have," replied Roberts.

The publican obsessively wiped the bar top. "Don't know he has a job, but he always has money." He stopped wiping and looked at Roberts. "Not sure what interest you have in him, Lieutenant, but let me warn ya. Big Pete Maha is trouble. He'll smile at ya one minute, then whack you the next. I've seen it before, so be careful; he has some nasty mates and a worse temper."

The lieutenant thanked the Publican and returned to his table. He continued to observe Big Pete unobtrusively until he left the hotel about thirty minutes later.

The following morning, Lieutenant Roberts departed Oakura and headed north towards New Plymouth. There, he would meet Colonel Warren and Major Von Tempsky, then travel to Te Awamutu for an intelligence briefing. Big Pete was on his mind, and he was eager to share what he knew with Von Tempsky. As he expected, Von Tempsky knew nothing of the man. Lieutenant Roberts was well-connected and had built his own clandestine network of contacts who provided him with information. He quickly put the word out to everyone to find out all they could about Big Pete Maha. The Lieutenant felt uneasy and believed Big Pete was a dangerous player in the region. If his suspicions proved correct, the army would pay Big Pete more than a polite courtesy visit.

Big Pete was no fool; he'd seen the army officer watching him in the Public House. Although the reason for the Lieutenant's interest in him was unclear, he was determined to find out. The following morning, shortly before the Public House opened, Big Pete was outside, banging on the door.

"Who is it?" shouted a voice from inside.

"Sorry to bother you this early, but I left something here last night. I hope you found it?" Big Pete politely asked.

There was silence for a heartbeat or two, then the bolt was thrown back and the door was quickly unlocked. A young, fresh-faced youth stood at the door.

"I wasn't working last night, sir," the youth said, taking in Big Pete's immense size. "The publican will be downstairs in a moment. I can ask him if he's seen it."

"I'll wait inside, lad, if that's ok," said Big Pete with a warm smile and pushed his way past the youth to stand inside.

"It may be best to wait outside while I fetch Mr Connor," suggested the youth. He held the door ajar, but Big Pete wasn't going anywhere.

"Convey my warmest regards to Mr Connor and tell him his presence is required … if you please," said Big Pete condescendingly. "Now, if you'd hurry, I haven't all day!" He smiled to drive the point home.

The young bar-hand was already backing away. "If you'd wait right there, sir, I'll be right back with the publican."

The smile disappeared from Big Pete's face. It wasn't by good luck that he'd stayed out of jail all these years. He took precautions, and it was time to take another. Intimidation normally did the trick, and if the publican was smart, he'd be helpful and cooperative, and all would be well.

Within moments, the publican came down the stairs, the youth following tentatively behind.

"How can I helps you, sir?"

Big Pete looked down at Mr Connor and over his shoulder at the youth. "Might be a good idea if the lad found some work to do, wouldn't you say?"

"Run along, Tim, get those barrels up to the bar like I asked ya."

Big Pete watched the youth disappear into the bar. "Now then, I was here last night and saw the army fella asking questions about me. What was all that about?"

"Sorry, I have no idea what you be talkin' about, mister. If you've come here lookin' for trouble, you'll find it sure nuff. Now I'll ask yer once, real polite like, to leave the premises. I won't be askin' yer a second time," Mr. Connor smiled, the same expression he used to warn troublemakers at the bar. It normally worked quite well. Not this time.

The publican fancied himself a fairly dab hand at a fistfight. He'd bested many a tough man and rarely lost. His confidence was buoyed by his size. He wasn't a small man, and years of hoisting barrels of ale over his shoulder had given him remarkable upper-body strength. He looked Big Pete in the eye. "Get out!"

Big Pete stood over six feet five inches tall; he paused and nodded a couple of times. He slowly turned his back to the publican and took a step towards the door as if to leave. Mr Connor, pleased to see the brute leaving, encouraged him with a small push in the back. Big Pete reached for the door with his right hand and then whipped his elbow back, smashing into the publican's mouth. Teeth broke, and Mr Connor fell against the wall. With a painful moan, he slowly slid to the floor.

Big Pete turned, reached down, grabbed the publican by his shirt, and hauled him upright. Blood and saliva dripped from Mr Connor's cut lips onto his chin. He spat out broken fragments of teeth.

"What did the officer want to know 'bout me?" snarled Big Pete, all pretence of niceness forgotten. He shook the publican for good measure.

Mr. Conner groaned, "Nuffin, he wan'ed tuh know who you was, that's all."

"Why, what am I to the damn army?"

"Don' know, he did'n say."

"Likely bloody story … and what did you tell him?"

"Your name, is all. Is all I knows bout ya," Mr. Connor spat more blood onto the floor.

Big Pete's eyes narrowed as he considered the publican's response.

"If I find out different, you and me will have another nice chat. You hear me?"

The publican nodded.

"If anyone, anyone, is asking about me, then tell 'em nothing and let me know," Big Pete released him, and Mr. Conner slid back to the floor, blood flowing freely from his mouth.

Big Pete was angered and had a violent temper that was difficult to manage. He moved as if to leave and suddenly launched a brutal kick to the side of the publican. Mr. Connor passed out. Pleased the publican, understood his point of view, Big Pete stepped over the inert body and let himself out.

CHAPTER TWENTY-NINE

Realisation

No longer under the immediate care of doctors, Moana was permitted to do light exercises. Since his injury, he'd lost considerable weight and muscle tone and had lacked strength and endurance. In the three weeks he'd been at Te Awamutu, he'd regained some of the weight he'd lost and was working hard to restore his body to normal.

Tightly strapped to his back was a canvas bag containing several heavy rocks wrapped in cloth. He would jog for sixty seconds, then walk briskly for another sixty seconds, and repeat the process. He'd been doing this for two hours when he finally walked back to the barracks, sweat-stained and exhausted. Waiting for him was his commander, Major Gustavus Von Tempsky.

"What in God's name do you think you're doing?" bellowed Von Tempsky as Moana dragged himself up the steps to the barracks, where the major waited. "You're supposed to be doing light exercises, and may I repeat that, light exercises. Not gallivanting around the countryside like a carnival performer. You risk reopening your wounds!"

Moana was untying the rope that held the canvas bag securely to his back; he was out of breath, and his face was flushed.

"For heaven's sake, Ira, next you'll be traipsing through the bush and climbing hills."

Moana looked at Von Tempsky and raised an eyebrow.

Von Tempsky threw his hands into the air in frustration, "When?"

"Yesterday," panted Moana, "that's why I'm taking it easy today, sir."

Von Tempsky looked down at the ground and shook his head in disbelief. "Don't say another word. I do not wish to know what else you've been doing."

"Yes, sir, that's probably a good idea, sir," Moana smiled.

Unable to contain himself, Von Tempsky laughed and slapped Moana on the back. "It's great you are up and about but do be careful."

Moana sat down on the step and drank some water from his bottle, "I want to re-join the Company as quickly as possible. Once I'm fit, the sooner I can be with the men."

"It will be great to have you back, Ira. We all miss you. The doctors tell me they will release you to me in a week, but only for light duties."

"I'm almost ready for normal duties now, sir."

Von Tempsky shook his head in disbelief again.

"Are we going after Kaihoka?" Moana asked hopefully.

"Oh, he's a slippery creature, that one. He's completely disappeared. He evaded all the army patrols, and no one has seen hide nor hair of him."

"He's gone bush. I reckon he's gone into the Urewera's. That's where I would have gone. Finding him in there will be difficult," Moana took another sip of water. "There's a lot of bush and hills where a man can hide in that part of the country."

"I think you're probably right, Ira, but sadly the Rangers haven't been tasked with pursuing Kaihoka. Instead, we're still assigned to try to catch that group of rebels in the Taranaki region, led by Te Kahuwai, who've been randomly killing locals."

"The *Hauhau*?"

"Perhaps. We don't really know for sure. It seems to be more opportunistic than religious, though."

"This is the same lot you were after when I was at the Henare farm?"

"The very same."

"And no luck finding them?"

"No. Wherever we go, they're somewhere else. It's as if they're second-guessing us. They seem to know where we're going to be, so they go elsewhere."

"They've got spies and are watching us," said Moana earnestly. "We *Māori* can be very sneaky when we want to be."

"I know, I found that out from you," laughed Von Tempsky. "And, ah, have you heard from Wiki?"

Moana's face returned to a bright red colour. He looked at the ground and toyed with his bottle.

"Well?"

"Yes, she sent me a couple of letters; she says she misses me," Moana said, wanting to change the subject. "What brings you back to Te Awamutu?"

"The general wanted his staff to brief me on his new offensive. I can't say too much at the moment, but I'm hoping we aren't involved."

"You don't approve?"

"I'll obey my orders, Sergeant."

Moana smiled. "Of course, sir."

They remained silent for a few moments.

"Do you think once this business with Te Kahuwai is over they'll allow us to pursue Kaihoka? I know I can find him. What happened in Opotiki was horrible. Those responsible need to be punished."

Von Tempsky sat down on the step beside Moana. "Listen to me, Ira. Once this offensive in South Taranaki is over and the *Hauhau* have been reined in, they want to demobilise the Forest Rangers."

"They can't do that! What will the army do? They don't have the skill or ability to fight offensively in the bush."

"I agree with you. However, they want to form a new organisation called the Armed Constabulary; it's a cross between a police force and the military. It actually makes sense," replied Von Tempsky.

Moana looked sullen.

"Can I offer you some advice as a friend?" the major asked.

Moana nodded.

"Wikitoria is madly in love with you, and I know you feel the same way towards her."

Moana looked away, embarrassed and surprised. He opened his mouth to speak, but the major held up a hand.

"Pursue her, Ira, and marry the woman. When the Forest Rangers are disbanded, join the new Armed Constabulary. They'll need people like you, and it'll be much safer, especially for a married man. Promise me you'll do this, Ira."

Moana's mouth was open; he didn't know what to say or where to begin. "How do you know Wiki is in love with me?" he finally managed to say.

The major laughed. "Every time I came to visit, all those hours I spent at your bedside, she fussed and doted over you. The way she looked at you, touched you and cared for you. There is no doubt whatsoever that she is in love."

"I was just a patient, and she was doing a job you asked her to do."

"You are so young and naïve about women, Ira. For goodness' sake, man, open your eyes."

"Do you really think so? She's in love with me?" Moana asked.

Von Tempsky laughed again, "Oh yes."

Moana was smiling.

"But promise me you'll join the Armed Constabulary."

"Very well, I promise," Moana nodded.

Von Tempsky shifted his position. "Wiki is a wonderful woman. She has a great family, and Tami is a great man. You'll marry into a perfect family. They all love you, Ira, and think the world of you. Do not let Wiki slip through your fingers, or you'll regret it for the rest of your life."

Moana was positively beaming. He'd been completely blind to Wiki's attentions; those extra-soft touches and the care she'd shown him. He'd even seen the way she'd looked at him when she thought he wasn't watching. Perhaps the memories of when he was feverish and delirious were not dreams; they may have been real. Could the major's observations be accurate? Von Tempsky was an excellent judge of character and was seldom wrong, he thought. If what he says is true, then she does love me.

Von Tempsky was watching Moana closely. He saw the change in the young man as the realisation dawned. *Young men are clueless about love and romance.*

"I have another briefing to attend and must leave you now," Von Tempsky said, standing. "Do not over-exert yourself, do you hear me?"

"Yes, sir," beamed Ira. He couldn't stop smiling.

"If I hear you've been pushing yourself beyond reasonable limits, there will be trouble."

Later that evening, after he'd cleaned up and eaten, Moana decided to write a letter to Wiki. He lay on his bunk with pen and paper, thinking about what to write. He wanted to go to her, to visit, be with her, and profess his feelings, but he just didn't know where to begin or how to tell her. He fell into a deep, trouble-free sleep.

CHAPTER THIRTY

Discovery

Six sturdy wagons hauling logs were slowly making their way west towards Opunake. Two massive bullocks pulled each wagon as they laboured over the worn, well-used track to reach their destination. Progress was slow, but this was to be expected; the beasts weren't known for their speed, only their strength. Two men rode in the front of each wagon, including the seventh, which was smaller. It carried essential supplies such as food, camping equipment and other items to be used in the event of equipment failure or any unforeseen difficulties. The journey so far had taken four days, and the men expected to reach Opunake later that afternoon.

The weather had been favourable. The sun shone by day, and the evenings were cool but not unpleasant. Ahead, dark clouds threatened showers, but the locals assured the wagoners that any rain would pass to the north. The last thing these men wanted was for their cargo to be bogged down in mud.

One of the men in the rear supply wagon was not employed by the timber company and was merely hitching a ride. The Wesleyan minister, Reverend William Robertson, sat beside the driver and remained quiet, as he had for most of their journey. He wore black trousers, a white shirt buttoned to the neck, and a black jacket that he never removed, even when it was hot. For cover, he wore a wide-brimmed black hat that kept his face in the shade, and he clutched a

Bible possessively to his chest. He looked straight ahead and didn't engage the driver in any discussion or in any frivolous, unnecessary conversation. Had the driver been willing to discuss redemption or scripture, he might have found the reverend quite a lively companion.

The owner of the timber company was an elder in the reverend's church in Patea and a generous contributor to the Sunday collections. He suggested to the reverend that his wagons could provide transport from Patea to Opunake, and Reverend Robertson readily accepted.

Reverend Robertson had business to discuss with Opunake's new Wesleyan missionary resident and Hawera's Wesleyan Minister regarding a school they were proposing to build. This was close to William Robertson's heart, though this wasn't blatantly obvious; he was excited at the prospect that his dream would soon be realised.

Normally, the wagoners stopped for lunch around midday. Today, they delayed lunch until they reached a suitable stream near the outskirts of Opunake, where the bullocks would be unhitched, shackled, and allowed to drink and forage on the abundant Taranaki grass for an hour while the men ate.

The lead wagon swung off the track and stopped by a large tree that overhung the stream they sought. The other wagons followed. To everyone's relief, it was time to stretch their legs and ease the pain in their buttocks while they ate.

Reverend Robertson brought his own food and promptly sought a shady spot away from the others. He carefully unfolded a cloth and neatly laid out bread, cheese and a bottle of wine on it, near where his Bible lay. He removed his hat and quietly offered blessings. One of the wagoners walked off to find a solitary place to relieve himself just as the reverend was about to eat.

A loud, distant yell forestalled the reverend from enjoying his first mouthful. The wagoners all looked to one another in puzzlement. The reverend quickly rose, retrieved his hat, and walked to the group, curious as to the reason for the alarm.

"Oh my God!" cried the wagoner as he raced back towards the men. He was struggling to button his trousers. "There are bodies!" With one hand, he pointed back to where he'd come from, while the other held his trousers.

The wagoner foreman spoke up, "What did you see, Art? Show me."

Art stopped, and with a shaking hand, finally managed to button his trousers. He was visibly upset. "Other side of that rise, have a look. You can't miss 'em," he gasped. "I ain't goin' back."

Reverend Robertson trailed the group as they made their way over the small rise. The buzzing of flies gave away their position.

"Aw Christ, there's four of them. Dead they are," said one of the first men to arrive.

"Been here all day, I reckon," said another.

Everyone was in shock and remained quiet as they took in the grisly scene.

"They've all been shot," a voice broke the silence. "Why would anyone do this?"

"Anyone know who they are? Do you recognise them?" asked the foreman.

Reverend Robertson crested the rise and gazed at the four bodies. His face remained impassive as he stared. He swallowed once, and without taking his eyes off them, he replied, "The one on the right is Erepu Henare … I, I knew him," his voice faltered.

The wagoners all turned to the reverend in surprise.

"I'm not sure about the others, but I suspect the older one is his uncle, Tami Henare, and the two younger ones are his sons." A vein in the reverend's neck pulsed as he recalled his last conversation with Erepu. He removed his hat, took a breath, and closed his eyes. "May God be with them," he said quietly.

CHAPTER THIRTY-ONE

Southward

Moana was cleaning his Pattern Enfield rifle on his bunk. He'd spent the day target shooting and practising, something he hoped Major Von Tempsky wouldn't chastise him for, although the day before, he'd found a willing volunteer or two and spent a few hours polishing up his unarmed combat skills. As a result, he'd felt considerable pain afterwards, but nothing he couldn't work through. The physically demanding exercise felt good, and he didn't feel worse for it today. Although still not at his optimal best, Moana was reasonably happy with the progress he was making.

"S'cuse me, Sergeant."

Moana looked up in surprise; he didn't hear the trooper approach.

"Major Von Tempsky requests your immediate presence in the Company office."

Te Awamutu was a hive of activity– wagons loaded with stores were departing, Captain Martin's Royal Artillery Regiment was lined up and about to head out, and harried messengers on horseback were leaving camp while others returned. Under the watchful eye of barking sergeants, regulars were subjected to a barrage of orders and instructions as they cleared camp. Major-General Trevor Chute's offensive was about to begin; his army was mobilised.

Moana skirted the chaos and wove his way to the Company office, a short distance away. He was curious about the reason for his summons. He'd hoped his antics yesterday hadn't been reported to the major, or he would be in deep trouble.

He knocked once on the door and entered. Lieutenant Roberts rose from the chair he'd been sitting in and nodded to Moana.

"I'll be outside," he informed the major as he quietly left. His expression, as was Major Von Tempsky's, was a cause of immediate concern. Moana knew he was in trouble as he stood in front of Von Tempsky's desk.

The major's face was grim. He rose from his seat and motioned for Moana to sit. Von Tempsky strode from behind his desk and took the chair recently vacated by Lieutenant Roberts. He faced Moana and sighed.

"I see you took a beating yesterday," said Von Tempsky and pointed to a bruise on Moana's arm. He didn't smile.

He couldn't keep anything from his commander; how his commander found out was a mystery to him. Now Moana knew he was about to receive a serious tongue-lashing.

"One of the men you sparred with is in worse condition than you. He reported to the doctors last night with severe aches and pains. Two of the others are in no better shape and have been restricted to light duties. One has a severe wrist sprain and a suspected broken leg."

"That wasn't my fault, sir, he tried to kick me when I was down. I just defended myself."

"So, it was more of a brawl?"

Moana thought it best to remain silent.

"How are you feeling this morning?"

"I feel better each day, sir," Moana was surprised at the direction this conversation was going. His face conveyed his puzzlement.

"And your new injuries?" Von Tempsky again indicated the bruise on Moana's arm. "And the ones I can't see?"

"They're not a problem, sir. I forgot I had them until you brought it up," Moana kept his face straight.

"Are you ready to endure the rigours of full active duties?"

"Yes, sir."

Von Tempsky leaned back in his chair. His arms were folded, and he looked at Moana with an intensity Moana had never seen before. It was unsettling. Moana wasn't sure what to expect. Uncharacteristically, the major didn't smile. Something was amiss, and Moana tensed.

Major Von Tempsky unfolded his arms, leaned forward, and looked down at the floor at his feet; he was collecting himself. He sighed heavily and looked at his sergeant.

"Tami Henare is dead."

Moana's mouth opened in shock.

"As is Erepu, James and young Henry."

Then it closed just as quickly. He bit his bottom lip. He cleared his throat. "What happened?" he managed to say, his mouth suddenly dry.

"We don't know exactly. The report states that the bodies were discovered two days ago, just south of Opunake. They were shot–"

"Shot! No, who did it?" interrupted Moana. His eyes had narrowed to slits and his face was an expressionless, cold mask.

"Just wait a minute, Ira. Let me finish," Von Tempsky paused and waited for Moana to calm down. "The report states it was a robbery."

Moana shook his head in disbelief, "And Wiki?"

"She's been told and is … well, she's not doing well, Ira."

Moana stood and began pacing the room. He felt numb. He wanted to go to Wiki.

"There's something else you need to know,"

Moana stopped his pacing and faced his commander.

"Wiki believes that her family was killed because she and her family took care of you."

"What! Is that true?"

"She holds the Forest Rangers responsible for their deaths and wants nothing to do with us or you."

Moana rubbed his face. He looked at Major Von Tempsky with a muddle of unformed questions. He began to speak, then stopped as he tried to make sense of it all. "Is she correct? Is that why they were killed, because of me?" he finally managed to say.

Von Tempsky remained silent.

"What's been done about finding out who did it? What do we know?"

"Can I bring Lieutenant Roberts back? He is better equipped to answer your questions."

Moana nodded and walked to the window. He stared out but saw nothing except rage.

Von Tempsky walked to the door, said a few words that Moana couldn't hear, and within seconds the lieutenant re-entered. He offered his sympathies, patted Moana on the back, and waited awkwardly for the major.

"Sit," commanded Major Von Tempsky.

Reluctantly Moana returned to his chair.

"Tell Ira what we know, Lieutenant."

Lieutenant Roberts' expertise as an intelligence officer was widely recognised. No one was more skilled at disseminating information and then providing valuable assessments and theories that, more often than not, proved to be highly accurate.

"The initial report states that robbery was the motive for the killings. However, Mr Henare, Erepu and sons were taken to the eastern outskirts of Opunake, where they were shot. Mr Henare told his sister they were heading directly back to Te Ahuahu. This would have put them on a different route, not on the quieter, less-travelled eastern track where the bodies were discovered."

"So they were taken to a quieter place to be killed?" Moana asked.

"As it seems," Roberts nodded.

"Then the killing was planned?"

"That's what we believe, yes."

"By whom?"

Lieutenant Roberts turned to Von Tempsky, who gave an imperceptible nod. "About two weeks ago, a local man, known as Big Pete Maha, was overheard asking about Tami Henare in the Public House in Oakura. I was the one who overheard the conversation, and I then proceeded to find out what I could about this chap, Big Pete."

"I've heard of him, but never met the man," said Moana.

"It's probably a good thing; he's not a nice bloke. The publican at the hotel was severely beaten the following day and chose not to go to the authorities to lodge a complaint. All because I was seen with the publican asking questions. But the barman in the hotel's employ insists it was Big Pete who assaulted him. Further, Big Pete makes it his business to find out what is going on in and around the area by using informants. Through intimidation, and we also suspect financial incentives, he solicits information."

"For what purpose? That's what I'm puzzled about," asked Von Tempsky.

"I'll get to that in a moment, sir. Just over two weeks ago, a farmer attending to a colicky horse saw Big Pete visiting someone. He was walking his horse around his paddock in the evening when Big Pete appeared and went to visit a local."

"Who did he visit?" Moana asked, sensing this was crucial.

"Pippi!"

"What? The milk delivery man!" Moana cried.

"The very same," replied the lieutenant.

"Didn't he also deliver milk to the army while we were stationed in Oakura?" asked the major.

"Still does," replied Roberts.

"This could explain a lot about why we've been unable to make headway against the local rebels," Von Tempsky stated. "The damn toad is a spy!"

"That's what I believe too," agreed the lieutenant. "I suspect Big Pete collects information and passes it on to the rebels. Perhaps Pippi told Big Pete about the Henares' journey, and either Big Pete killed them or he passed that information on to someone else. I just don't know why," concluded Lieutenant Roberts. "That's where the trail goes cold."

"Could the *Pai Marire* be behind this? We know they wanted Erepu, and perhaps Tami and the boys just got in the way?"

"That's a possibility we can't discount either," replied the lieutenant. "Some have already accused the *Hauhau* of the killings."

"So this Big Pete fella is the key?" asked Moana.

"Yes, he is. Unless more information comes to light," stated the lieutenant.

"Do you believe the murders are in reprisal for the Henares' taking care of me?"

Lieutenant Roberts shook his head. "Honestly? No, I don't."

Moana rose from his chair and returned to the window. He stood deep in thought for a moment. "What is being done about it?" he turned to face both his commander and the lieutenant.

Major Von Tempsky looked at Lieutenant Roberts and shrugged.

"Colonel Warren has determined that the cause of death was a robbery gone awry. He is unwilling to devote any resources to investigating the incident unless, of course, new information becomes available. But on my urging, and as the 57th will be in the vicinity of Opunake, he has somewhat acquiesced and will allow a more detailed inquiry."

"Why am I not surprised?" Moana said. "Seems to me, while the murders were committed in Opunake, the investigation should be conducted around Oakura. Has anyone spoken to Big Pete?"

"He can't be found."

"And Pippi?"

"He was questioned briefly but typically he's not talking," said Roberts.

Moana shook his head and again faced the window. His mind raced.

This time, Von Tempsky looked to Roberts, who nodded.

"Ira, our orders have changed. We've been tasked to head south to Patea, where there have been increasing problems. The Rangers are leaving Te Awamutu, and you're coming with us and will be returning to full duties."

Moana turned to look at the major.

"We will pass through Te Ahuahu. Perhaps you could speak to Wiki. But truth be told, she will likely be in Opunake, where the funeral is being held." Von Tempsky paused, then resumed in a slower voice. "You may want to spend a day or two in Oakura to recover. The march will be gruelling for you," he suggested with a raised eyebrow.

Moana Rangitira was astute. He knew the ways of the military and felt he was a good judge of men. Although Major Von Tempsky was difficult to read, he understood the unspoken words quite clearly.

"And if I happen to run into Big Pete Maha, or Pippi?"

Von Tempsky stared blankly at him. Moana turned to Lieutenant Roberts – he too said nothing. He moved to face Von Tempsky again, who quizzically shrugged.

"Thank you, sir."

"I suggest you get organised and report to Sergeant-Major Bowers. We leave at five tomorrow morning."

Moana left the building bewildered. The deaths of Tami, Erepu, Henry and James stunned him. It was unfathomable, and in such a tragic circumstance. He thought of Wiki and hoped he could console her and help her with her grief. He imagined their reunion, with her rushing into his arms … In light of her reasoning about the deaths of her family, that joyous romantic meeting was now very unlikely. He was heartbroken. *Poor Wiki, how must she feel?*

"I hope we've done the right thing," Lieutenant Roberts said once Moana had left the office. "We're essentially allowing him to conduct his own independent investigation, and who knows what he'll do."

"And as you are totally aware, if we expressly forbade him, he would have gone anyway. You, me, and the army can't stop him," replied Von Tempsky.

"Then I hope he does the right thing," said Roberts.

"I have never encountered a man more suited to the task he is about to undertake. I pity those responsible when Ira finds them – and he will. Yes, he'll do the right thing; of that you can be sure."

The Imperial British Government was finding it increasingly difficult to justify the enormous expense of maintaining a large army in New Zealand. Von Tempsky was correct when he informed Colonel Warren that British troops would soon be withdrawn. The process had already begun, and, sadly for Major Von Tempsky, the 57th Regiment would remain for the time being. Colonel Warren's immediate responsibility and concern was to keep the military supply lines open from New Plymouth to Opunake in the south. To achieve this, the 57th built a series of redoubts and stationed soldiers to deal with any rebel activity. Other newly built redoubts between Opunake and Wanganui were another officer's concern.

One hundred miles south of New Plymouth, at Wanganui, military operations were handed to Major Thomas McDonnell, who'd been recalled from Opotiki. His attempts to locate Kaihoka Te Hua proved fruitless, although he'd met with success in suppressing the East Coast *Hauhau* movement. Major McDonnell was slowly working his way north from Wanganui to Opunake. His forces were enthusiastically laying siege to *Māori* villages – they destroyed crops, built redoubts and defeated any form of resistance en route.

Major Von Tempsky's Forest Rangers were assigned to assist Major McDonnell, would travel down the west side of Mount Taranaki, support Colonel Warren's forces when needed, and pass through Opunake on the way.

The first day of marching on the road, at the blistering pace set by Von Tempsky, was hell. Moana struggled. His feet and legs were sore, and his side ached. Driven by the task he'd set for himself and hoping Wiki would talk to him, he had all the motivation he needed to push beyond the agony and pain.

As requested by Von Tempsky, Sergeant-Major Bowers kept a close eye on Moana. There were times he thought Moana would collapse. He'd noticed Moana unconsciously holding his side and even stumbling once or twice. The pain must have been excruciating, thought Bowers. Most of the men saw him struggle, and a few approached the Sergeant-Major with concerns about his condition. There was little that could be done.

Bowers called a timely rest, under the pretext that the men were soft, poorly conditioned, and needed a break. Moana, he noticed, was relieved, although he never once complained or griped. He marched where he always did, near the centre of their strung-out column, and somehow, through sheer determination and guts, always managed to keep pace.

Some men offered to carry his pack or his Pattern Enfield, but Moana refused, insisting he was fine. He set a good example, yet, oddly enough, the number of complaints from the Rangers about sore feet and tiredness directed at the Sergeant-Major was much higher than normal.

Bowers attributed this to the men feeling sorry for Sergeant Rangitira and hoped their constant griping would encourage more rests. It worked.

The second day on the road brought improvement. Moana looked better and marched with more purpose. He never once looked as if he would pass out and maintained a strong stride. Von Tempsky was still worried and, without making it obvious, took every opportunity to enquire about his condition.

It was approximately one hundred and forty miles from Te Awamutu to Oakura, and the journey would take six days. By the sixth day, Moana was comfortable and showed no noticeable fatigue or unusual pain from his wounds. As the Forest Rangers marched over the undulating terrain towards Te Ahuahu, Moana thought constantly of Wiki. Was she correct? Did her family die because of him? He asked himself the question repeatedly but found no answers.

Finally, the moment arrived when the Rangers stopped at the bottom of the path to the Henares' cottage. Major Von Tempsky and Moana knew it was unlikely she would be at home, but they would check anyway. Moana and Von Tempsky walked up the path and knocked on the door, but it was quickly apparent that no one was there. Moana was still disappointed.

As previously arranged, Moana would remain behind while the Company continued. After saying farewell, Von Tempsky led his Company south. They camped on the south side of Oakura, away from the township. He didn't want his men sneaking off to the Public Hotel or other places of adult interest in the evening. Moana made himself comfortable on the veranda, where he'd spent so much time under Wiki's care, and planned his next move. After watering her plants, he was exhausted and soon fell asleep.

He was unsure how long he sat on the Henare veranda. It could have been minutes or hours. Eventually, he retrieved his possessions and, dejected, left the Henare farm – he didn't look back. He couldn't remember the walk into Oakura. His mind was reeling with a hundred thoughts. He was confused, angry, disappointed and felt guilt. When he finally arrived in Oakura, his mind was clear and focused; he had resolve and anger.

The briefing by Lieutenant Roberts was all he had. The information, although minimal, was still useful. Moana entered the Public House.

CHAPTER THIRTY-TWO

Reprisal

Moana stood at the door, casually surveying the room and its occupants. The barroom was about half full, mostly with locals. He was the only soldier, and because he carried his kit and gun, he attracted more than his fair share of attention.

One unknown voice called out, "You've missed 'em, lad. They passed through a few hours ago. If ya hurry, you'll still catch 'em." Others laughed in response, but the jibe wasn't mean-spirited, and Moana just smiled.

Within moments, they'd forgotten about him, and he finished looking about the room. He found an empty table near the far wall and dropped his equipment. He asked a man at a neighbouring table, someone he vaguely knew, to keep an eye on his belongings, then went in search of the publican. With a swollen, cut mouth, he wasn't difficult to find. He sauntered over, bellied up to the bar, and within moments the publican was pouring him an ale.

"Can you spare a moment to talk?" Moana asked in his friendliest voice.

The publican looked uncomfortable and glanced nervously around the room, but no one was paying them any attention. "I've got ta get another barrel, from the cellar. Follow me down."

Moana waited until he saw the publican disappear behind the bar, then followed. He saw the glow of a lantern lighting a ramp that headed down.

"Looks painful," said Moana.

"Bastard," came the venomous reply.

Moana nodded sympathetically.

"What do you want?" asked the publican once they were in the cellar.

"I'm looking for Big Pete. Do you know where he lives or where I can find him?"

"You a friend of his?"

"I am if it makes a difference. Otherwise, you wouldn't exactly call me a friend."

"Look, mate, I don't know what you want with him or where he is. Since he did this," the publican pointed to his mouth, "I ain't seen him." He gave Moana a careful look. "Why is it important for you to find him?"

"We have a difference of opinion."

"You be bloody careful. Have you seen the fella? He's a big, strong boy with a bad temper, that one."

"So I see. What about Pippi, the lad who delivers the milk?"

"That's easy. He lives behind the barn at the Millers' farm," the publican said, raising a meaty arm and pointing. "Almost a mile away."

The publican gave Moana the details and explained that if Big Pete found out he'd been giving out information, he'd be back to dish out more punishment. He expertly manoeuvred a large barrel onto a cart and wheeled it out of the cellar. Moana followed him up a minute later.

With the army out of town, it was easy to find a room. He left his kit and gun behind and gave the publican a wave as he headed out into the cool evening air.

The publican's directions were good, but it took him some time to find the dilapidated shed where Pippi lived. A few other abandoned structures littered the area, but it was the smell of smoke that finally gave the location away. Moana crept unseen towards the building. Once close, he circled it twice and listened. He heard voices, a male one, which he figured was Pippi, and a female. Judging from the whining tone of her voice, he thought she must be his wife. He approached the door and waited, listening intently. *No change. There must be only two people in the shed,* he surmised.

The quickest way in was always through the door, and few were sturdy enough to withstand a hefty kick. This one was flimsy at best. He gave it a good shove with his foot and ran in as the door fell off its hinges and landed on the edge of the bed, startling a woman lying there. She screamed. Pippi, whom he recognised, was slouched at a small table cluttered with debris and empty bottles. He looked up, surprised and annoyed. The stench was overpowering, and Moana wrinkled his nose in disgust.

Seeing the thin, reedy woman posed him no immediate threat, Moana strode to the table, hauled Pippi away and towards the door, closer to fresh air, and threw him on his back. He placed a knee firmly on his chest, then looked back to the woman.

"Don't you move," he warned.

He looked down at Pippi, whose face was familiar to him from the milk deliveries he made to the Henare farm. Moana bent low towards Pippi's face. "What did you tell Big Pete about the Henares?"

Pippi laughed, "I don't gots to tell you nuttin. You touch me and Big Pete'll have ya he will."

Reaching down, Moana grabbed Pippi's arm, holding it just above the elbow, and pushed it down and across his body. Pippi weakly tried to bat Moana's hand away, but Moana jammed it between his body and Pippi's and kept his weight on it. With his free hand, he firmly grabbed the wrist of the immobilised arm. With a surge of strength, Moana suddenly wrenched Pippi's arm up and away. The crack of a bone breaking broke the stillness of the night, and Pippi screamed in agony. The woman on the bed screamed again. It was unlikely anyone would respond to the noise. The barn and trees shielded the sound from Mr Miller's home, and the screams from Pippi's love nest were a common occurrence anyway. People were used to them.

Moana looked down at Pippi and asked again, "What did you say to Big Pete about the Henares?"

Sweat and tears streaked down Pippi's face. He was genuinely frightened and never thought of himself as a brave man. The pain was unbearable, and he passed out.

Pippi woke to water being splashed on his face. Moana stood over him.

"What did you say?"

Pippi coughed.

Moana bent down and grabbed Pippi's other arm.

"No, no, don't. I told him the Henares were going to Opunake, honest, that's what I said," gushed Pippi.

"Why were the Henares killed?"

"Killed? I don't know anything 'bout that," Pippi's pain couldn't mask the surprise at learning of their deaths.

"And what else did you tell Big Pete?"

"Uh, I told em what day they'd be comin' back. That's all, please believe me," he whimpered.

"Why did you tell him about the Henares?"

"Cause he pays me for information, but I don't know what he does with it."

"Did you tell him about me being at the farm?"

Pippi looked puzzled, "No, why would I do that?"

"You never mentioned me to Big Pete?"

"No, never. I've never said anything to him about you; I don't even know who you are."

"Have you ever told Big Pete information about the army, and what they're doing?"

Pippi didn't answer.

"Last time I'll ask nicely. Did you tell him about the army's movements?"

Pippi nodded guiltily.

"Who does Big Pete give the information to?"

"I don't know. I told ya, I don't know," Pippi pleaded, his voice rising an octave.

The woman on the bed was slowly gaining courage. She spoke for the first time, "Leave 'im alone, mister. He's done nothing to you. Piss off and leave us in peace."

Moana ignored her and continued to look down at Pippi who was whimpering, "Where can I find Big Pete?"

Pippi shook his head, which caused his bad arm to move. He cried out, "God, this hurts!"

"If you want to talk to Big Pete, 'cause you've information, how do you get hold of him?"

"He'll kill me."

Moana placed his foot on Pippi's arm. Pippi screamed again.

The woman slowly slid off the bed and ran at Moana with a rusty-looking paring knife. He easily blocked her panicked, uncoordinated slash and shoved her back. She fell against the far wall, dislodging a plank. She was half outside and remained there.

"How do you contact Big Pete?" Moana asked menacingly.

"I tell Sam the butcher at the Oakura market."

"And then what happens?"

"Big Pete comes here later, always at night."

"Are you sure?"

Pippi nodded, but not so vigorously this time.

"What you've done is treasonous. You will be hanged for this."

Pippi's eyes were wide open in disbelief. He began sobbing again.

If only Potter were here, thought Moana, it would make this so much easier. He couldn't leave Pippi and the woman here alone; they could warn someone when he left. In the morning, when Pippi didn't show for work, Mr Miller would come looking, and they didn't deserve to die because they were just stupid and greedy. His decision was easy. He pried the woman from the wall and ordered her to wrap a cloth around Pippi's neck to support the weight of his ruined arm. He would take them somewhere, tie them up and hide them until he came back. He scavenged about for some rope and found some discarded in the corner.

Pippi was reluctant to go, but with encouragement and help from his woman, he followed Moana away from their hovel. They were led to an old stable, long since abandoned, about half a mile back towards Oakura. Moana gave them water, gagged and tied them securely, and made sure they were comfortable. They couldn't escape and couldn't make a sound. Moana reassured them that he'd be back later.

Pleased to be away from the peculiar couple, Moana walked back to Oakura and thought about what he'd learned. Pippi was responsible for passing on information about the Henares' trip to Opunake, but he never told Big Pete about the wounded soldier under the Henares' care. Moana didn't think Pippi was lying, *so the killing of the Henares was not about him, as Wiki claimed.* He'd confirm that when he and Big Pete conversed.

Early the next morning, Moana returned with food. Amid complaints and constant whining, he allowed the couple to tend to their needs and stretch, even though Pippi was in severe pain and needed help. Once they had eaten and drunk, they were immediately retied. Moana headed back into town.

He positioned himself close to the butcher's stall at the market. He'd never met him, but he'd seen him at the Public Hotel many times. While he waited for Big Pete to appear, his mind drifted to Wikitoria and how she must be feeling. It made him sad. Perhaps they were never meant to be together, and she was never meant to be part of his life. Could Major Von Tempsky be wrong in believing she loved him?

Who would want to kill Tami – he was such a likeable and harmless man? Certainly, Erepu incurred the anger of the militant *Hauhau,* but would they go to such lengths to kill him and then three innocent people, two of whom were children? It didn't make sense. The hours passed slowly, and no one resembling the big man approached the butcher. By midday, the butcher packed away his stall and left. Moana returned to Pippi, frustrated.

He spent an uncomfortable night in the old stable, and in the morning he untied Pippi and told him to go to the butcher and leave a message, as he normally did. If Sam asked about his arm, "Tell him that's why you need to speak with Big Pete," Moana advised.

Assured that he would be close by, watching and listening, Pippi knew he would be killed if he disobeyed the instructions. Leaving Patricia behind, Moana followed Pippi the short distance to the market and then stood near him as he made his request of the butcher. Afterwards, they both returned to the old stable. Pippi was re-tied, and Moana waited until evening, hoping Big Pete would respond.

The hours of rest were beneficial to Moana. His body needed time to recover and heal after the gruelling march from Te Awamutu. Throughout the day, Moana dozed and ate when hungry.

He watched the road whenever he heard someone pass by, and by nightfall, he felt energised and ready. Pippi wasn't doing well and needed medical care. His woman had no desire to offer him any comfort or attention, so Moana ignored her. When Big Pete came, Pippi would be released.

Dusk fell at six o'clock, and about an hour after sunset, Moana heard the clip-clop of a horse coming up the track. The rising moon provided enough light to make out who was astride the horse, and the rider was clearly a very large man.

Escorted by close family friends, Wiki and Charles arrived in Opunake so she could attend the *Tangihanga*, the funeral, for her father, brothers and Erepu. The last few days had been extremely difficult for her. As if the tragic loss of her close family wasn't enough, her feelings about Moana lingered. Overwhelmed by grief, she found it easy to blame him and the army for the loss of her family. Her surviving brother, Charles, tried to convince her she was acting irrationally and that Moana was no more responsible for the deaths than he. As Wiki pointed out, there was no reason anyone would want to kill their father; he was a good man, loved by many. She agreed that Erepu angered the *Pai Marire*, but they wouldn't go to such savage lengths to kill him and then her father and brothers. The only possible explanation, she reasoned, was that unknown rebel fanatics had found out the Henares were nursing a soldier. She reminded Charles that Moana's exploits were well known and that his reputation as a Forest Ranger was almost mystical, and that the rebels saw an opportunity to exact revenge on the Henares for taking care of him. Surely it was a warning to others, she believed.

She couldn't forgive Moana, Von Tempsky, or the entire Forest Rangers. There was no room in her heart for them or their kind, but it didn't stop her from grieving. She'd lost her family and someone she thought she loved. For a short time, she'd believed she and Moana Rangitira were destined to be together, that he was special and affected her like no man ever had. How wrong she was. She couldn't see herself loving him. Each time she looked into his face, she'd be reminded of her lost family.

In the darkness, Moana was invisible. He crouched behind low-growing bushes and waited patiently as the horse and rider slowly approached. He wanted to avoid a brawl with the big man at all costs. He knew that, in his current physical condition, he would struggle in a fight and most likely re-injure himself. Speed and stealth would be his greatest weapons, and in that brief moment when the big man was surprised, he would act quickly to disable him.

Moana tensed—the horse was now beside him. He waited two heartbeats, then stepped silently out from behind the bush, coiled, and sprang up. Big Pete was completely unaware.

Thankfully, a musket was slung uselessly diagonally over his shoulders, a weapon the big man would never reach in time. Moana accurately gauged the big man's size astride his horse, and his leap was perfect. His arm snaked around Big Pete's neck and yanked backwards. Spooked, the horse lunged forward, and Big Pete was pulled from the saddle, sliding sideways off the horse's rump. One foot cleared the stirrup, the other did not. As the horse surged away, Moana lost his grip. The man fell backwards, landing heavily on his back on top of the musket, one foot still firmly held by the stirrup. Big Pete was dragged down the path as the powerful horse bolted. Knocked unconscious when his head hit the ground, Big Pete remained silent.

Moana jogged after the horse, which finally stopped about thirty yards away. Ignoring the still form of Big Pete on the ground, he cautiously approached the horse and spoke soothingly. Its nostrils were flared, breathing hard, and its eyes were wide with fright. Continuing to speak softly, Moana stroked its withers, moved up to its neck, and then let it sniff his hand before finally patting its head. With his gentle touch and calm tone, the animal began to relax as Moana flipped the reins over its head and held them firmly. He turned his attention to Big Pete.

He wasn't moving, and his breathing was ragged. *At least he isn't dead*, thought Moana. Removing Big Pete's foot from the stirrup was a little awkward, but the horse remained passive and didn't move, making the job easier for him. Once the foot was free, Moana tied the nervous animal to a fence alongside the track and bent down to assess the big man's injuries.

Even in the darkness, Moana could tell the injuries were going to be fatal. Big Pete lay in an unnatural position, his back clearly broken. He'd fallen on top of his musket, his weight driving hard into the wood and steel. It must have snapped instantly, he thought. Big Pete's eyes flickered open, and his breathing came in quick gasps, as if he were unable to take a deep breath. Tears had begun to form and ran, shimmering in the moonlight, down the side of his face. Moana leaned closer.

"You," grunted Big Pete quietly between breaths. "You are the ghost who walks in darkness."

"Who do you give your information to?" Moana asked, ignoring Big Pete's statement.

Big Pete closed his eyes.

"Pippi told you about the Henares. Who did you tell?"

The eyes opened and looked at the shadow leaning over him. Big Pete swallowed thickly. The ragged breathing continued.

"You are badly hurt and will die from your injuries. If you tell me what I need to know, I will end it quickly for you," offered Moana.

Big Pete blinked the tears away, he couldn't move, "Miles Southport … the blacksmith … down the path."

"Anyone else?"

Big Pete's breathing was laboured. He swallowed with difficulty. " Te Kahuwai … at *Marae* … two miles … down track."

"Did Pippi tell you about the wounded soldier at the Henare farm?"

"No," Big Pete grunted.

"One last question. Who killed the Henares?"

Big Pete made a guttural sound. He was having difficulty breathing. "Te Kahuwai's people," he whispered hoarsely.

Moana reached down and pressed his fingers into Big Pete's neck near his ear. He knew exactly where to press, how hard, and how to move his fingers … Big Pete died almost instantly.

Moana knew the *marae* was close by and began to formulate a plan. He would drag Big Pete to the side of the track and hide him, then take his horse and go to the marae. On the way back from the marae, he would drag Big Pete back onto the track and leave the horse untied. It would be apparent to whoever found the body that the cause of death was a fall. Big Pete's horse had shied at something, thrown the big man from the saddle, and he had fallen heavily, landing on his back and dying of his injuries.

The horse responded willingly to its new rider, the earlier unpleasantness now forgotten. Moana was a good horseman; he knew and loved horses and treated them well. Even skittish horses succumbed to Moana's soft voice and skilled hands. *If only women were as easy,* he thought.

The marae was small and situated about two miles from where Big Pete's body now lay. The main approach was a long, winding path that cut through tall trees and low-growing bush surrounding the compound. It consisted of a handful of buildings, three or four small *whare* and a larger meetinghouse, called a *wharenui.*

Through the trees, Moana could see the distant figures of people gathered around a fire in a sunken pit ringed by large boulders. He dismounted, tied the horse securely to a tree a few yards from the track, and gave it a reassuring pat. He knew there'd be dogs around, and they'd quickly give his presence away. He'd scout the area from a distance and then decide what to do.

He completed a near circuit of the marae, then backtracked, careful to avoid being directly upwind where the dogs could detect him. He saw about five men and a couple of women talking and laughing by the fire. *If there were others, they were probably children sleeping inside whare,* he thought. He waited and continued to observe them closely. They sang a few songs and joked a little, and judging from their conversation and behaviour, it seemed they'd been drinking for a while.

A sudden movement nearby made him slowly reach for his knife - he'd been seen. Before he could fully draw the long blade from his hip, a face appeared from the darkness, and a tail wagged frantically in a friendly, welcoming manner. A small, cream-coloured dog of mixed heritage stood before him and posed no immediate threat. However, the sudden appearance of its friend was a different matter. The new dog was older and wiser, and instinctively knew Moana was an intruder. It began to growl menacingly as the smaller, younger dog, now enlightened, stepped back. They did what dogs do best in these situations, and both began barking.

At first, the barking dogs were ignored. Moana tried to back away from the dogs, but for every yard he retreated, they followed and came forward. Eventually, someone at the fire grew tired of the incessant noise and threw a rock that narrowly missed Moana by a scant foot. He retreated further into the low trees and skirted around behind the marae, the dogs following close behind, and arrived back where he had left the horse. His plan to approach the *marae* stealthily, then find Te Kahuwai, was proving foolish. He stepped to the side of the horse, threw his arms over the saddle, and leaned against it. The horse's smell was pleasant. The dogs temporarily lost interest in him and returned to the fire. Moana considered his few options.

There was only one thing for it. Moana dusted himself off and walked casually down the path towards the marae, as if he hadn't a care in the world. As he drew near, the dogs ran towards him, barking incessantly to signal his approach. Within moments, he'd been seen. One man nudged another and pointed as Moana stepped out of the darkness into the light.

He greeted everyone warmly and stepped up to the large fire, rubbing his hands as if they were cold. Moana hefted a good-sized log from the woodpile and threw it on the fire, then, for good measure, tossed in another. The fire blazed, fiercely hot.

With undisguised mistrust and suspicion, they watched the soldier who strolled confidently into their midst, his Forest Ranger uniform adding to their unease and quiet fear.

"Which one of you is Te Kahuwai?" Moana asked casually. He kept the fire at his back so no one could creep up on him unseen. The heat was almost unbearable.

At least four of the heads turned reflexively towards a large, corpulent man with a short, bushy beard and an unruly mop of curls.

"Nice to meet ya finally," said Moana with a smile to the man with the bushy beard. "I take it you are Te Kahuwai?"

The man could hardly deny it. He nodded and spoke for the first time. "What do you want here?"

Moana took a casual step closer to him, "I've heard quite a bit about you recently."

"From who?"

"A friend of ours," Moana drifted closer, now about three yards from the man. "Big Pete." He took another small step.

"So what does Big Pete have to do with you being here? He wouldn't tell you anything about me." Te Kahuwai turned his head slightly and whispered to one of the men. The man nodded, stepped back and away from Te Kahuwai, and began to ease himself round the fire so he could approach Moana from the other side. Moana pretended not to notice.

"What I want to know is why you had the Henare family killed in Opunake?" He took another half step closer.

Te Kahuwai's eyes flicked from side to side. He was uncomfortable now. He couldn't believe this soldier had walked brazenly onto his *marae* and then openly accused him of the Henare killing. He stood, lifting his bulk from the large log he sat on. He appeared indignant at the accusation and raised both arms to emphasise his innocence.

The man creeping up from the far side was almost on him. Before anyone could react, Moana turned quickly, reached past the man's outstretched arms, and flicked him over his hip, where he landed heavily on the ground. The man was winded and gasped for breath. No one saw Moana wince in pain. He turned to face Te

Kahuwai and took another half step closer to him. He was almost within reach.

"Who do you think you are? Get the hell away from here!" shouted Te Kahuwai in a high-pitched voice.

Another man drew a wicked-looking knife from his waist and ran around Te Kahuwai, his intention obvious.

"You've no idea who I am and what I can do to you!" Te Kahuwai threatened.

Showing poor knife skills, the man didn't even slow and ran straight at Moana with a quick lunge. Stepping easily to the side, Moana lifted his arm and let the knife pass down his side. He then dropped his arm and squeezed, tightly trapping the arm with the knife against his uninjured side. With his other hand, he pinched the bundle of nerves at the inside of the elbow. The man yelled, thinking his arm would be broken, and the knife dropped onto the dirt. Moana spun quickly, came up behind and placed an arm around his neck, putting him in a chokehold; he still held the other arm with his spare hand. He increased pressure on the neck and felt the man begin to pass out. Within seconds, the man sagged. Moana held him tightly for a few more seconds and shifted his feet carefully in preparation for his next move. He lowered him to the ground.

One of the women screamed.

"Stop!" yelled Te Kahuwai.

Moana had no intention of stopping now. He'd positioned himself to spin and surprise Te Kahuwai, then come at him from behind. As he suspected, the large man was slow and unable to move quickly enough to counter his move. Moana spun, and before Te Kahuwai could react, he found himself gasping for air.

With his arm locked firmly around Te Kahuwai's fleshy neck, Moana began to squeeze and slowly lowered him towards the large rocks that ringed the fire. The heat was fierce.

Moana eased the pressure; he didn't want Te Kahuwai to pass out, not yet. Having recovered a little, both men on the ground crawled back. The remaining two men on the far side of the fire were immobile, either scared or unwilling to help; they didn't react.

"I'll ask you again. Why did you have the Henares killed?" He eased the tension on Te Kahuwai's neck a little so that he could talk. The heat from the fire was an added incentive.

"He was a traitor," squeaked Te Kahuwai.

"Keep going," encouraged Moana, surprised at the reply.

"He'd been working for the government and told them of *Māori* plans."

Moana shook his head in disbelief and looked around to ensure no one moved against him.

"All of you sit on the ground, on the far side of the fire. Now!"

No one moved. He lowered Te Kahuwai a little closer to the heat.

"Please, no!" he cried. "Do as he says."

Obediently, everyone moved away.

Erepu was young, caught up in the fervour and emotion of a new religion. Moana didn't see him as a government spy. It didn't fit with what he knew. "Erepu wasn't a spy; he couldn't be."

"No, no, not Erepu, the old man," said Te Kahuwai quickly.

"Tami?"

"He'd been informing the government about *Māori* actions during the First Taranaki War. We'd been wanting to kill him for a while," laboured the fat man. Breathing was proving difficult.

Again, Moana eased the pressure a little.

"When Erepu upset the *Pai Marire,* we knew it was our best chance, because everyone would blame them for the killing. We knew Kaihoka wanted Erepu dead. All we needed was an opportunity for Tami and Erepu to leave their farm together," Te Kahuwai rasped.

"Did Big Pete also tell you I was at the Henare farm?"

"You were? I wasn't told," he wheezed.

"But you also killed two innocent boys," angered at their deaths, Moana tightened the pressure.

"Arrgh," coughed Te Kahuwai. "You're a soldier … you know … er, casualties of war."

Moana was enraged. The pain and suffering this man had caused were beyond belief. Te Kahuwai placed such little value on human life, and even when challenged, he still felt no remorse. What did Erepu, James and little Henry do to justify being killed? They were innocents. He tightened his grip on Te Kahuwai's neck and thought of the pain and grief Wiki was enduring. As with the others before him, Te Kahuwai passed out quickly, and this time Moana held the pressure for considerably longer, struggling to keep the unconscious man upright. With the memories of Tami, Erepu, Henry and James vividly before him, Moana allowed Te Kahuwai's body to drop into the fire. A shower of sparks and hot embers flew skyward as the clothes immediately burst into flame. Both women screamed and turned away. In shock, the men remained unmoving. They stared at the burning body in horror.

"The Forest Rangers will be back here in a few days," he told them. Disgusted, he turned his back and walked away. The sound of yelling and screams filled the night.

He dragged Big Pete back onto the path and released the horse, ensuring the reins were draped over its neck. Big Pete's body and the horse would be found in the morning, and the cause of death would be listed as an accident.

Feeling sombre, Moana walked back towards Oakura and to the old stable where he'd tied up Pippi and his woman. They still lay exactly where he'd left them. Pippi wasn't in the best of shape. The woman didn't care a jot.

"Best if you go and see Doctor Will in the morning, Pippi. I personally recommend him. Once he's seen to you, you might want to make yourself scarce. The Rangers will be back, and they'll be looking for you," Moana advised. Without another word, he walked away. The revelation that Tami was a traitor echoed in his head. How could this be? It didn't seem right to him.

If what Te Kahuwai said was true, then Tami was spying for the government. Many *Māori* would hate him, yet powerful *Māori* like Te Whiti came to visit Tami and treated him like a long-lost brother. Within the Oakura community, Tami was treated with respect, and Moana never heard an unkind word or whisper suggesting people disliked the old farmer. Why weren't the Henares hurt when they were locked in the barn by the *Pai Marire* warriors – the rebels certainly had the opportunity? It was all a little perplexing. He wondered how Wiki would take this news and whether she would even believe him. All he could do was have the blacksmith confirm what Te Kahuwai had told him. He returned to the hotel, cleaned himself, and slept. He was looking forward to visiting Miles Southport.

Moana wandered downstairs to enjoy a big breakfast. He'd just finished his meal when the publican, Mr. Connor, sat down beside him.

"Did ya sleep well, Sergeant?"

Moana smiled, "Yes, thank you."

The publican nodded, "I just heard a few moments ago that Big Pete was found dead. Apparently, he fell from his horse, broke his back or something like that."

"That's tragic," replied Moana.

"S'pose you know nothing about that, do ya?" queried Mr Connor.

"Then you no longer need to worry about him coming in here and beating you up," Moana looked up at the publican with a smile. His eyes locked to the publican's.

"Thank you very much. I'm indebted to you, Mr Rangitira," he held out a massive paw.

Moana shook his hand, "My friends call me Ira."

The smithy of Miles Southport was easy to find. It took Moana only a few minutes to walk to the outskirts of Oakura, where he found a large, rusted sign leaning at a precarious angle, advertising the blacksmith's services. In faded letters, streaked with rust, the name *'iles outhpor , acksm t '* was barely legible. He walked into a good-sized courtyard and paused to look around. Wearing a leather apron, Miles was bending and shaping lengths of wrought iron into an intricate swirling design of twisted steel that looked like it could become an impressive, ornate gate.

Various wagons and carts littered the perimeters of the large yard. Like forgotten relics, some lay on their sides, succumbing to long grass and weeds that grew over and through them. All were in a state of disused neglect and obvious disrepair. Wagon wheels lay discarded, stacked untidily in a heap like a circular monument honouring the unwanted. A few others looked as if they were being worked on, with their rims being replaced. On the far left was a small colonial cottage. A woman appeared and began hanging washing on a clothesline attached to the house. She turned her head and observed Moana with an air of indifference before returning to her chore. Offering no acknowledgement or greeting, she picked up her empty basket, scowled at him, and returned wearily to the cottage. Moana turned his attention back to Miles, who was skilfully bending the iron using an upright pole anchored securely to a heavy workbench. A forge fumed benevolently behind him.

Miles Southport glanced up and saw Moana. He finished the bend, wiped his hands on a rag, leaned forward on his workbench and stared curiously at his visitor. A large dog lay nearby, it lazily opened one eye, saw nothing of interest and closed it, preferring to sleep.

"How can I help ya?" Miles asked, his unfriendly tone sharpened by a sneer. He looked past the soldier but saw no horse or wagon that needed his attention. He shifted his gaze back to the Forest Ranger, suspicious.

Moana took a few steps closer to the blacksmith and kept a wary eye on the dog. "Was hoping you could help me," Moana said casually.

"As I don't see an horse or wagon, and as you'd be a soldier like, then I doubts there's much I can do for you," Miles was within easy reach of a handful of tools and steel that could be used as effective weapons. "Might be good for ya to bugger off and leave me alone."

"Big Pete is dead," Moana offered.

Miles was visibly surprised.

"Broke his back when he fell off his horse."

The blacksmith recovered quickly. "That's a shame. He was a lovely man; he'll be sorely missed."

Moana met the blacksmith's hostile gaze with his own steely glare.

"Te Kahuwai also met with an accident last night."

"You've got me there, mate. Don't know him." Miles swallowed nervously, wiping his gleaming head with the dirty rag.

"I guess the heat got to him," Moana offered, taking another step closer to the blacksmith. "Accidents tend to come in threes."

Miles repositioned himself and placed a hand casually on an iron bar. He tensed, ready to launch an attack.

"What I want to know is, who do you give your information to?"

"Don't know what you talkin' 'bout,"

With exceptional speed, Miles lifted the iron bar and swung it powerfully at Moana. It whooshed past, missing by only inches. Had it hit, he knew the iron bar would have done serious damage. Moana swayed backwards, then took a big step towards Miles as he tried to control the swinging bar, its momentum carrying him a step closer to where Moana now stood. He stepped inside and landed a single hard jab to the middle of the blacksmith's chest. Miles dropped the bar and sagged to his knees, gasping, unable to breathe.

Unimpressed, the dog scratched at something and continued to doze.

Moana moved behind Miles, hauled him upright, and leaned him over the workbench; he kept his forearm pressed hard against Miles's back. "Who do you give your information to?"

"You bastard, I'll skin you for this," Miles was fighting for breath.

Moana picked up a hammer, leaned down and gently tapped Miles's knee with it. He yelled in pain.

"Do you want to walk with a limp and a cane?" asked Moana pleasantly.

Miles wisely changed his mind, "I gives me information to Te Kahuwai, no one else."

"What type of information?"

"Everything, troop movements, the lot."

"Are the rebels planning something against the government?"

Miles laughed, but it sounded like a cough, "Oh, just a little harassment at Warea."

"Why Warea?" Moana asked.

"Because of the inexperience of a commander at the redoubt. Easy pickings."

"And this doesn't bother you?"

"No."

"And you told Te Kahuwai about the Henares?"

Puzzled, Miles paused for a moment, "Yeah, them too. Why, what's it to ya?"

"Did you know that four of the Henare family are dead because of what you done?"

"So? Why should you or I care?"

Moana barely resisted the urge to end the life of Miles Southport.

"Why were they killed?"

"I got no bloody idea, mate. The ways I sees it, it's a *Māori* problem, and I don't give a toss either way," Miles said as he slowly regained control of his breathing.

"They're dead because of you."

The hammer impacted Miles's knee with considerable force. It was a hard and savage blow. Unable to support his weight, the knee failed. It twisted grotesquely, and Miles fell to the ground, writhing in agony.

"The army will be here to speak with you. I don't expect you to travel far."

"I won't forget you, you bastard!" yelled the blacksmith.

Disturbed by the noise, the dog rose, stretched and walked away.

Without another word, Moana headed back into Oakura, where he hoped he could buy a horse. He knew of one needing an owner.

CHAPTER THIRTY-THREE

The Tangihanga - Funeral

The Tangihanga was an elaborate ceremony. Despite the threat of war and violence nearby, friends of Tami and Erepu travelled long distances, risking their safety, to honour them. The *marae* was crowded, and as at all special events, people were united with friends and family they hadn't seen for some time. Laughter could be heard, children played, and above it all, the mournful *waiata* celebrating the lives of the deceased and their spiritual journey served as a sombre reminder of why they were here.

Respected elders were gathered near the cliffs overlooking Te Namu Bay, the site where the *Lord Worsley* met its demise and the birthplace of Te Ua's *Pai Marire* faith. This region of Taranaki had experienced much turmoil in recent years. Many died in rebellion against the imperial forces, and more were sure to fall, while even now military forces gathered not far away. With efficiency, the army systematically destroyed villages and crops, killing as they eliminated resistance from Taranaki *Māori*.

Not everyone supported killing and death. Men such as Te Whiti o Rongomai, Tohu Kakahi, Te Ua Haumene and Riwha Titokowaru were inspirational leaders who once preached peace and Christian values. When faced with armed soldiers, peace wasn't always a sensible option. How would *Māori* feed themselves, care for their children and elderly without land to grow crops? With the efficiency of a modern military machine, soldiers marched from the north and came from the south, dispensing *Pākeha* justice under the flag of the British Empire and Queen Victoria, who ruled supreme.

Aware of *Māori* feelings towards the military, Major Von Tempsky knew his appearance at the marae would cause unnecessary tension and perhaps even some hostility. He wanted to attend the funeral of Tami, Erepu, and the two boys because he considered himself a family friend. He'd spoken to Tami and Erepu for hours on various topics while Ira lay at death's door. He'd laughed with them, eaten with them, and consoled them. He even played with the boys. And now they were dead, killed needlessly for a reason that still escaped him. His superiors granted permission to attend the funeral on the condition that Lieutenant Roberts could also attend as his companion.

It hadn't been difficult to locate Tami's sister and her address in Opunake. He'd sent Tane Mahaia to her home with a letter offering his condolences and sympathies. He outlined the nature of their acquaintance and courteously asked permission to attend the Tangihanga and to bring a friend, not as military officers in the employ of Her Majesty's armed forces, but as unarmed grieving friends.

Tane waited while Tami's sister debated how to respond to the major's unusual request. She decided that if Tami and Erepu were still alive, they would both agree readily. Despite her misgivings and political views, if she was honouring Tami and Erepu at their *Tangihanga*, she must also respect the wishes of their genuine friends. Tane was handed a note along with two invitations to attend.

Wiki sat with other mourning women. She graciously accepted the condolences of those who came to the funeral as they passed by her and went on to view the bodies. She recognised a few faces, but many were strangers to her. She was surprised to see Te Whiti, the man who had come to the farm to see Erepu, and with him was another man who drew a lot of attention, though she didn't know who he was. She nudged the elderly woman beside her and pointed him out. "Who is he?"

"Surely you recognise him?"

Wiki shook her head; she had no idea.

The woman looked to Wiki incredulously, "That's Te Ua."

"Te Ua? He must be here because of Erepu," Wiki replied. She was surprised that a man of such influence and status was here at the *Tangihanga* for her cousin and father.

"No, m'dear, Te Ua is here because of your father, and of course because of Erepu too. But Te Ua, Te Whiti and Tami were once very close friends."

Wiki was puzzled, "He never spoke of them and certainly not their friendship."

The older woman said no more as she greeted a new arrival.

Wiki's thoughts returned to her father. How little she really knew about his earlier life. The people who had once been his friends, of whom she had only just become aware … She remembered when Te Whiti came to the farm and how warmly her father had greeted him. He'd never spoken of him, and he had remained tight-lipped when she'd asked him about Te Whiti later.

A slight commotion near the marae entrance drew her attention. Wiki looked up – she couldn't believe it. Her blood began to boil. *Of all the nerve.* Major Von Tempsky and his friend Lieutenant Roberts had just walked in. She looked quickly around, half expecting to see Ira.

Both officers paused, ignoring the stares and hushed whispers. They weren't familiar with *Māori* custom and protocol and uncertain what to do. Someone was kind enough to point them to Tami's sister and Wiki.

Von Tempsky looked around for people he recognised. Spotting Wiki, he raised his hand in greeting and walked over quickly. Lieutenant Roberts followed behind.

Wiki saw them walking towards her. She felt her cheeks redden with anger. She rose from where she sat and stormed towards them.

"Wiki, I'm so sorry–"

"How dare you invade the privacy of this family gathering?" interrupted Wiki, her voice raised. People stopped to stare and listen. "The death of my family rests squarely on your shoulders. You and your kind are responsible, and you have the audacity to visit here under the pretence of friendship!" She was almost yelling. "You dishonour them!"

Von Tempsky and Roberts were shocked. They noticed hostile glances coming their way. A crowd was gathering.

"In case you were wondering, Sergeant Rangitira isn't welcome either, so make sure you pass that on to him. I want you to leave. Go now!"

Te Whiti and Te Ua stood chatting with a group of people a short distance away. Te Ua always managed to attract attention and was swarmed whenever he was in public. Both men heard Wiki's raised voice and turned to each other. Te Ua nodded. They excused themselves from the group and walked to Wiki. Te Ua's warrior guards remained watchful in the background, and the presence of two *Pākeha* soldiers made them nervous.

"Why are you angry, Wikitoria?" Te Whiti asked gently as he arrived at her side. He nodded politely in greeting to Major Von Tempsky. If he was surprised to see the major, he didn't show it.

"It was their fault my father, brothers and Erepu died," Wiki broke into tears. "And yet they came…" she sobbed.

Von Tempsky and Roberts didn't know how to respond or what to say.

"Let us go somewhere to talk where we cannot be overheard," said Te Whiti kindly.

Te Ua looked surprised and warily eyed Von Tempsky.

Te Whiti led Wiki to a secluded spot behind a hut, where a few benches were strategically placed to overlook the cliffs and the sea beyond. With a nod, he indicated that the others should follow. Te Ua's vigilant bodyguards ensured they weren't disturbed and could talk privately. They weren't happy with two soldiers being so close to Te Ua.

Wiki sat on a bench Te Whiti had indicated, then dragged another over and sat opposite, facing her. The others sat where they could. Major Von Tempsky sat beside a man he had not been introduced to, while Lieutenant Roberts sat beside Te Whiti.

"This resentment cannot continue," began Te Whiti as Wiki dabbed away tears from her eyes. "You have much anger for these men– it is unjust, and you torment yourself. While I do have an issue with *Pākeha* soldiers and their government, the hate that grows in you for these men is evil and must stop. It is not the Christian way." Te Whiti paused and collected his thoughts. "There are some things you should know, Wiki."

All faces turned expectantly to Te Whiti, except Te Ua, who sat comfortably with a small smile on his face. He stared out across the ocean, preparing himself to listen to a story that amused him so.

In the background, above the murmur of conversation, children playing, and the gentle wind, the wailing of a *waiata* could be heard. It was fitting for Te Whiti, as his story was about the man they honoured and celebrated, and the song's words were sung so soulfully.

Von Tempsky and Roberts exchanged glances– their own interest was hard to disguise.

"Have you ever wondered how your family came to own the land you live on?" asked Te Whiti.

"Because father had worked hard and saved money? I don't really know. I never asked about it, and he never spoke of it," replied Wiki.

"You are right, Tami would never have talked about it. He purchased the land very cheaply; it was almost given to him."

"Given to him, by whom?"

"The government."

"The government, but why would they do that?" she asked.

"For the work he did for them."

Wiki opened her mouth to speak, but Te Whiti continued, "He spied on *Māori* for the government during the first Taranaki war."

"He was a traitor? No, this can't be!"

Von Tempsky's mouth fell open. "Is this true?" he asked.

"Very much so," Te Whiti confirmed.

Wiki shook her head in disbelief. "But you were still his friend. You said so yourself. If he was a traitor, you wouldn't be friends with him."

"Perhaps," Te Whiti turned to Te Ua, who remained silent and listened. He still wore a smile on his face.

"Tami Henare was a Kingite, just as I am and just as Te Ua is," said Te Whiti, pointing to Te Ua.

Von Tempsky almost fell off the bench; he was sitting beside the infamous leader of the *Pai Marire*. He turned to Lieutenant Roberts who looked like he'd been shot– he turned deathly pale.

Te Whiti ignored the surprised looks directed at his friend. He was enjoying this. He received a nod from Te Ua to continue. "It was decided that Tami wouldn't voice his thoughts and feelings publicly; he kept quiet. We even tried to keep our friendship secret. It was easy, because Tami was many years older, already had a family, and had begun his own life away from us. We gave him information that would benefit the Kingites, and Tami passed it on to the government. What hurt Tami most was seeing the land of his people confiscated and given to the colonists. He would often ask why. Why should the colonists receive *Māori* land? The deal Tami made was very simple. In exchange for giving the government information, Tami received land. The land your farm is on, Wiki, was his reward."

What Te Whiti told her explained a lot– it filled in the gaps she knew about her father. But it didn't tell her who had killed her father, her brothers and Erepu.

"Did the government ever suspect Tami was feeding them only select information?" Von Tempsky asked.

"No, never. It was all good information, and much of it concerned Te Kahuwai, the chief who sold land to the government that he didn't own. That land belonged to another chief, Wiremu Kingi Te Rangitake, whom we supported."

Lieutenant Roberts understood now. As an intelligence expert, he worked it out very quickly– he knew who had the motive for the killings. He spoke for the first time. "It was Te Kahuwai's people who killed Tami, Henry, James and Erepu, wasn't it, not the *Pai Marire*? Somehow they knew what Tami had done."

"Yes, we think so too," Te Whiti said sadly. "It was very easy for everyone," he looked at Wiki, "or nearly everyone, to believe that we, the *Pai Marire* killed your family because of Erepu. That isn't our way, Wiki."

"We believe that was their intention," All heads turned to Te Ua. His smile disappeared and was replaced with a look of sadness.

"And Ira has gone to seek revenge against Te Kahuwai's people," Von Tempsky said softly.

Te Ua looked puzzled, "Ira?" he said.

"The ghost who walks in darkness, the *atua*," Te Whiti answered.

Te Ua looked thoughtful.

"Oh dear God, what have I done?" cried Wiki. She stood, the realisation dawning that Ira wasn't part of the killings. "I must find him, go to him." Her hands went to her face. "What have I done?" she repeated. She looked around, looking uncertain.

"This man, the *atua*, is he a good man or is he the devil?" asked Te Ua.

"He might be the finest man I've ever met," said Major Von Tempsky.

"He is not the devil. He is a kind, sensitive man who is highly principled," said Wiki, regaining some of her spirit. "And I've hurt him terribly," her eyes welled with tears. "And now he's probably in danger."

"Where is he now?" Te Ua turned to Von Tempsky.

"Finding those responsible for the killings."

Te Ua looked thoughtful, "Then he is a friend, and God will watch over him."

Wiki looked down at Te Ua, her eyes red and puffy.

"Then we will find this man of yours," said Te Ua with a smile, "and you can make right the wrong."

Wiki sat back down.

Te Ua turned to Von Tempsky. "I have heard much about you. Te Whiti speaks well of you and believes you are a good man, even if you are a government soldier. He says you are someone I can trust, a man of honour."

"Yes, I hope so," said Von Tempsky.

"Then we need to talk. Come with me, please," Te Ua rose and began to walk away.

Von Tempsky turned to Te Whiti, who nodded. "Go with him."

Lieutenant Roberts couldn't believe what was happening as he watched Major Von Tempsky walk away with Te Ua.

"And Ira, where exactly is he now?" Te Whiti asked.

Lieutenant Roberts turned to Te Whiti. "We believe he was in pursuit of the people who murdered the Henare family somewhere in Oakura. But I honestly thought he would have come south by now. I can't imagine he'd be in any difficulty,"

"And who are these people Ira is pursuing?" asked Te Whiti.

"Two people we know of. We think the man who delivers the milk in Oakura, he is called Pippi, and another man called Big Pete Te Maha."

Te Whiti looked up sharply, "Big Pete! We know him well. He is a brother and follows Te Ua."

Wiki's mouth opened in surprise.

"I think you may find Big Pete follows many men, including Te Kahuwai," offered the lieutenant.

Te Whiti scratched his beard, "I think you are right. This explains much about him and his absences."

"I hope they both get what's deserved," said Wiki.

Te Whiti leaned forward and placed his hand softly on Wiki's shoulder, "If you forgive men when they sin against you, your heavenly Father will also forgive you, but if you do not forgive men their sins, your Father will not forgive your sins."

Wiki looked like she would burst into tears again, "Oh poor Ira. Did he know I did not want to see him, because I wrongly believed he was responsible?"

Lieutenant Roberts nodded.

"What have I done?"

"If you both have love in your hearts, then God will bring you together. Have faith, Wikitoria."

"Thank you, Te Whiti," she stood, leaned over and kissed him on the cheek. "Now I must go back. Charles will be looking for me."

Lieutenant Roberts stood, and Wiki leaned over and gave him a peck on the cheek. "Please accept my apologies." With a rustle of skirts, she spun and returned to the *Tangihanga*. Both men watched her walk away.

Te Ua and Major Von Tempsky were walking along the cliff tops overlooking Te Namu Bay, deep in discussion. At a discreet distance, his ever-present warriors followed. If need be, they would protect him with their lives.

Te Whiti looked towards Te Ua and Von Tempsky. This was what he had prayed for. He wanted to ensure Te Ua was not killed, and the only way to guarantee his safety was to find someone, a soldier he could trust to act on his behalf when he surrendered to the imperial forces. In Te Whiti's opinion, the *Pākeha* major was that man.

"When Ira returns we will learn what he discovered about Pippi and Big Pete," said Lieutenant Roberts.

Te Whiti turned from Te Ua to face the lieutenant. "Yes, I hope so. What will he do if he finds they were responsible for the killings? Will he kill them?"

"No, I don't believe he will, at least not intentionally, I hope."

Lieutenant Roberts was having an intelligence field day. His head was spinning from all he had heard. He couldn't help himself and thought he could ask one last question of Te Whiti, "Can you tell me about Riwha Titokowaru?"

Te Whiti laughed for the first time. Riwha probably had the best military mind of all *Māori* warriors, and the *Pākeha* soldiers were only now finding that out. "You wish to know about Riwha? Stand outside this marae for a day or two." Te Whiti clapped Lieutenant Roberts on the back, "Come, let's find some food and then decide how we can find that man of Wiki's." Te Whiti may be a pacifist but wasn't about to divulge any information about the man who would become the next thorn in the side of the government.

CHAPTER THIRTY-FOUR

Sequestered

Since the army departed Oakura, there was little demand for horses. Moana made a few enquiries and, without much effort, was now the owner of a very large bay mare. Once reunited with Big Pete's horse, he set off for Opunake as quickly as possible. The big horse, though certainly female, was unceremoniously named 'Pete' after her previous owner. As no one in Oakura knew what Big Pete actually called his horse, Moana doubted Pete would take offence at her new masculine name.

Moana was impatient to reach Wiki in Opunake, forty miles away, to explain to her what he'd discovered. The main road south was mostly flat and ran parallel to the coast. A few small undulating hills broke the monotony, and he would pass through some small villages and redoubts recently built and garrisoned by detachments from the 57th Regiment. On his left, snow-capped Mount Taranaki would watch over him all the way to his destination.

As he approached the tiny coastal village of Warea, Moana heard the distinctive crack of musket fire. Although sporadic, the sound immediately reminded him of Miles Southport's disclosure, and he felt a misguided urge to assist the soldiers. He slowed Pete to a walk and proceeded cautiously until he understood the nature of the shooting. Once he reached the outskirts of the village, he could see the redoubt and the garrisoned soldiers inside from a slightly elevated piece of ground. Two soldiers nervously guarded the village entrance, preventing anyone from passing through from the north, while he presumed two more were stationed at the southern entrance.

Recognising Moana's military insignia, the soldiers relaxed and waited for the sergeant on the big horse to approach.

"Having some trouble?" Moana indicated with his head to the redoubt.

"Some rebels crept up on us, but thankfully, we saw them, Sergeant. The problem is that the lieutenant doesn't know how many there are, and we've been trading shots with them all morning."

"Did he send any scouts out for a reconnaissance?"

The soldier nodded, "The first didn't come back, so then he sent two out. They haven't come back either."

Moana knew what Te Kahuwai's rebels were up to. They were trying to draw the troops out of the redoubt, hoping to pick them off one by one. It seemed their ploy was working. "Why hasn't he split his force and flanked them?"

"He thinks there are too many of them, Sergeant."

Pete stamped her foot, impatient to continue their journey. Moana gave her a reassuring pat on the neck.

He wanted to leave and get to Opunake, not play nursemaid to an inexperienced lieutenant. "Where's your lieutenant, at the redoubt?"

Both soldiers nodded.

Maybe this wouldn't take too long. He pointed to one of the soldiers, "You, take me to the lieutenant, but first find me a place where I can water and leave my horse."

They immediately set off into Warea.

"How can I help you, Sergeant?" asked the fresh-faced, youthful lieutenant inside the redoubt. A grizzled veteran sergeant stood at his side.

"Seems like you've got a bit of a problem," Moana replied.

"Nothing we aren't coping with. We'll send out another scouting party soon and find out how many there are."

"Did it work for you last time?"

"Excuse me?" asked the lieutenant in surprise.

The veteran sergeant's face remained impassive, but his eyes shone briefly. Moana thought he saw a hint of a smile.

The old sergeant turned his head quickly and shouted to his soldiers who were watching them, "What are you staring at, you worthless toads! Keep your eyes out there, not in here!" He shook his head in frustration. "So help me God, where do we find 'em, I do wonder."

Moana ignored the outburst. "You've already sent out your best scouts, and they haven't returned. Do you think sending out more will do what they couldn't?" Moana inclined his head in question. "How many scouts do you have?"

"Ah, presently all our scouts are in the field."

"Perhaps I can help, Lieutenant. Let me go out and assess the situation and I'll report back to you in no time at all?"

"Are you familiar with the complexities of scouting, Sergeant? I couldn't in good conscience allow you to go out to face the enemy ill-prepared and untrained now, could I?"

Agree with the officer and then leave. Wiki is waiting.

"Who are you with, Sergeant … and your commanding officer?"

Moana stared at the ground and hesitated. He looked up and sighed, "I'm with Company No. 2, Forest Rangers, sir. Major Von Tempsky is my commander."

The lieutenant took half a step backwards as if frightened, "Ah, yes, well, um, perhaps you could help us out a little, eh. How rude of me. I'm Harry Winslow-Smith."

"Moana Rangitira, pleased to meet you, sir," he offered his hand and the lieutenant shook it vigorously. "Now, how about getting your men to hold their fire while I'll pop out and see what we've got out there."

Moana smiled at the young officer and turned to walk out of the redoubt. The veteran sergeant gave Moana a nod, then turned to a soldier, giving him the evil eye for some perceived infraction or dereliction of duties.

"Sergeant Rangitira!" yelled the lieutenant.

He stopped and looked back.

"You forgot to take a musket!"

Behind the lieutenant, the veteran sergeant looked skyward.

Moana just waved and continued out of the redoubt.

From the safety of a barn, he looked out across the gentle, upward-sloping terrain. To the right, a few scattered trees and bushes offered the easiest and most obvious way to creep into the low hills. Choosing the left was much more difficult – only a few isolated bushes provided cover. If the rebels were any good, they'd cover the obvious approach from their left. The only sensible option was to take the harder route, go past them, then swing back and approach from their rear. Moana sighed. *This was not what he expected to do this morning when he woke.*

The sun was almost directly overhead, so he couldn't use shadows to his advantage. The darkness of his uniform wouldn't help him in the first stage as he crossed relatively open ground, though once he'd found bush and trees, that wouldn't be a problem. He spent a few minutes surveying each place of cover, the contours of the land, the depressions and shallows, and committed them all to memory. He knew the path he would take. He saw no movement - the rebels were carefully hidden. His sixth sense told him he was being observed. Turning to look over his shoulder, he saw the lieutenant watching him.

The first twenty yards would be the most challenging for Moana. He'd be exposed for a few brief moments on the open ground. Ahead were a couple more areas where he'd be vulnerable, and he'd need to be very careful. Musket fire suddenly erupted from the redoubt, clouds of blue smoke wafted up, and he could hear yelling and commotion coming from within. Moana froze momentarily. Then he smiled - it could only be the old sergeant creating a distraction. Good for him.

Crawling on his stomach was proving difficult. The hard earth and the occasional rock began to cause pain in his side near the wound. He had to rest and stop. After a minute or two, he continued, favouring his right side as best he could. The pain was tolerable, and soon he ignored it. He was totally focused on recalling the route he would take.

He lost track of time. The appearance of a single tree, then another, surprised him. He'd travelled further than expected and was finally at the bush line. He lay waiting, listening, tuning himself into nature and the life around him. He didn't move or make a sound; he breathed through his mouth, which helped him listen. There was no man-made sound to be heard, and even the musket fire had temporarily stopped. With infinite patience, he slowly rose and stood behind the trunk of a large tree. He was protected on either side by ferns and was all but invisible. He could finally look down towards the redoubt and saw a few tiny, unidentified figures within the compound. He carefully shifted his gaze and began a systematic search.

It didn't take him long to identify three rebel warriors. They were hidden in a trench and totally concealed from anyone looking up from the redoubt. None of them spared a glance behind to check their rear. But somewhere between him and the redoubt were also three scouts, either wounded or dead.

With the utmost care, Moana dropped and dissolved back into the bush - he disappeared. His pain and wound forgotten, he was now the hunter. If anyone looked, they would have seen his face briefly appear about forty yards from where he'd last been only minutes earlier. From the new vantage point, he searched for other places of rebel concealment. A slight flash of colour on his left drew his attention. It was the subtle movement of a branch. He scanned the immediate area and, slowly, he saw the outline of a soldier trying to drag himself away from the rebels. At least one is alive. *Where are the other two,* he wondered?

Two of the rebels moved. They crouched and walked quickly to a prepared firing point along a trench. First, one rebel fired. As he reloaded, the rebel furthest away fired, then the rebel who hadn't moved fired. The rebel who fired first ran back, quickly reloaded, and fired again. To all outward appearances, it looked as if many rebels were firing at will from dug-in positions along a thirty-yard line. Moana smiled. *Māori can be sneaky at times.* No wonder the lieutenant was confused about how many rebels there were. The rebels kept firing from different positions along their trench.

The rebels dug a trench about thirty yards long, curving along the contour of a low hill. They carefully heaped the dirt only on the side facing the redoubt and camouflaged it with branches, logs, and grass. The trench allowed them to move quickly from one end to the other without being seen. He thought they must have dug it in darkness over a few evenings.

To Moana, their intent was obvious; it was pure harassment, just as Miles the blacksmith said. The inexperienced lieutenant fell into their trap by continuing to send men out to investigate rather than sending a sizeable force to flank the rebels. An experienced officer would have observed the sporadic musket fire and deduced that they outnumbered the rebels by more than the three-to-one odds favoured by the army for a successful offensive engagement.

Moana knew the rebels would go through their routine again, and he had a plan.

Ten minutes later he arrived at a new well-concealed position behind the extreme left end of the trench where one of the rebels always fired from. This time, he was crouching and ready to spring forward. In his right hand, he held his knife, the long blade in a reverse grip, lying flat against his lower arm; he was ready.

His legs were beginning to cramp. He'd been in the same position for a while and was thinking about moving when he heard one of the rebels running down the trench. He stopped directly in front of Moana and fired, then began reloading. Another rebel fired from the other end and then ran quickly towards his friend near Moana. Another shot was fired from the rebel furthest away. The second rebel fired and ran away to his new position, leaving the first rebel with a loaded musket all by himself, only three feet away.

With the other rebel out of sight, Moana sprang forward. Using his right hand, he clamped the rebel's mouth and nose from behind while the left hand drove the knife between his ribs. The rebel's heart was still beating when Moana dragged him backward into the bush and lowered him quietly to the ground. He grabbed the loaded musket and smoothed the dirt in the trench with his foot before he disappeared.

He knew the remaining rebels would wonder why they hadn't heard a shot from this end of the trench, and he guessed that only one would come to investigate.

Moments later, Moana heard footsteps running. They stopped about five yards away, and he heard the rebel call his friend.

"Pakai? Pakai, where are you? You going for a piss?" The rebel began to walk slowly to the end of the trench, where Moana lay in wait.

A fern moved, and the curious rebel went to investigate. As he began to part the fern fronds, he leaned forward and, to his horror, discovered Moana. The knife streaked out and was driven firmly into the rebel's chest. Moana didn't allow him to fall. He quickly released the knife and grabbed the rebel, hauling him into the bush beside the warm body of his friend. He retrieved his knife and carefully wiped it on the rebel's clothes.

Stooped over, the rebel's loaded musket held to his shoulder, Moana edged along the trench. There was only one rebel left alive. Each step was placed carefully and silently. He neared the bend, stopped and listened, then took another step. The last remaining rebel must have sensed something was wrong. His face was turned to look down the trench, but his musket was pointing towards the redoubt. With a gasp, he saw Moana and swung the musket round, but he had to turn his body a full ninety degrees, which exposed his chest. Moana was ready, in position, and he fired.

Tearing a strip of cloth from the rebel's shirt, Moana tied the fabric to the musket and waved it in the air high above the parapet of the trench. He didn't fancy being shot as he stood and exposed himself to an eager sharpshooter in the redoubt.

Within moments, a dozen soldiers, led by the young lieutenant, were clambering up the slope towards him. It didn't take him long to find the other two scouts. Of the three, two were alive but wounded, and the other had died from a direct shot to the head.

"After we watched you leave, we never saw you again. We feared you'd been killed," said an out-of-breath Lieutenant Winslow-Smith. He stood panting, bent over with his hands on his thighs.

Moana watched the veteran and much wiser sergeant unhurriedly make his way up to the trench. He arrived without breathing hard.

"Who was it that ordered the troops to make all that noise and to begin firing in the beginning?"

"Ah, yes, I thought it sensible to authorise that distraction," Winslow-Smith replied.

The sergeant gave Moana a wink.

"If you hadn't done that, I'm sure they would've seen me. Thank you."

"You was gone for nearly three bloody hours, mate. Thought we'd lost ya. Nice job, although it beats me, it does, how you did it." The sergeant pulled out a worn clay pipe, checked there was tobacco in the bowl, clamped it firmly between his teeth, and began sucking furiously as he lit it. Satisfied it was well and truly alight, he pulled it from his mouth and pointed it at the trench. "C'mon, you lazy bastards, start fillin' it in!" The old sergeant stalked away after the malingerers.

"Can I make a suggestion, sir?" asked Moana.

"Only if it's a good one, sergeant," Lieutenant Winslow-Smith thought it funny and laughed.

"Cut back the bush another twenty yards further back, and also all the single bushes and trees between the bush line and the redoubt. Then every day send a patrol to walk the bush line perimeter to make sure this doesn't happen again."

"Yes, brilliant idea. We'll take care of that. Uh, but I would like to sincerely offer my grateful thanks to you for helping us out with that spot of bother, eh. You probably saved many lives today, Sergeant Rangitira."

"My friends call me Ira, sir, and I'm just doing my job," Moana realised he hadn't eaten in hours and was filthy. "Where can I clean up and grab something to eat? I'm starving."

"Of course, how rude. Come this way."

They walked down the gentle slope and back towards the redoubt. The sergeant at the trench watched them leave and noticed Moana's hand unconsciously go to his side.

"I think the lad's hurt, he is."

"Beggin' your pardon, sergeant," asked a nearby soldier.

"Mind your own bloody business, you, or I'll have ya fillin' this trench all by your lonesome sorry self!"

The four-hour delay in Warea had been costly. It was now mid-afternoon, and Moana knew he'd have to hurry to make it to Opunake by evening. He'd said his farewells to Lieutenant Winslow-Smith, his veteran sergeant, and then found Pete, who'd been rubbed down, watered and fed. Once saddled, he'd departed Warea and found himself thinking of Wiki again. He spared a moment for Major Von Tempsky, who must also be wondering where he was.

CHAPTER THIRTY-FIVE

Reunited

It was high tide, and a moderate swell pushed hungry waves onto and over the round boulders strewn beneath the cliffs of the small bay called Te Namu. A few birds flitted here and there, their antics and intentions known only to themselves as they darted around the sheer sides of the cliffs, then up and over to disappear into the expanse of the Taranaki countryside.

Ahead, a large bullock grazed contentedly on thick, lush grass. Disturbed by the intrusion of two men, it casually lifted its head to stare curiously, chewed thoughtfully for a moment or two, and then dipped its massive head to continue masticating. Its tail swished lazily as a fly's persistent harassment warranted some minor attention.

The breeze from the ocean was a little cool, so the late-afternoon sun felt good on the shoulders of Te Ua and Major Von Tempsky as they strolled along the cliff tops. Following at a respectful distance, a handful of very attentive and nervous *Pai Marire* warriors watched closely. They knew *Pākeha* soldiers were already camped at the outskirts of Opunake and were concerned for Te Ua's safety as well as their own.

Encouraged by Governor Grey, Major-General Chute's offensive was in full swing. The army was laying waste to *Māori* crops and villages and showed little sympathy for the affiliations of those they encountered. This was an all-out effort by Chute to quell once and for all, all *Māori* resistance, including *Pai Marire* and *Hauhau*, which he saw as one and the same. As far as the army was concerned, they were one and the same.

Te Ua stopped and raised an arm, pointing to the wreckage littering the bay below them. Major Von Tempsky looked in the direction Te Ua indicated.

"This is where it all began, right here. What you see is all that remains of *Lord Worsley*. That ship represented many things to me. It was here where God spoke to me through Gabriel," Te Ua closed his eyes and raised his arms. "There appeared to me the angel of God. He told me to fast for the sins of my people. And I passed one great day, when I subjected myself to suffering."

"Why were you chosen for this?" asked Von Tempsky.

Te Ua opened his eyes and lowered his arms. "Who could listen to the lowliness of the natural man who spoke? I was one small voice amongst many wise men."

"And has your voice caused the deaths of many?"

Te Ua turned his back on the major, took a few steps, then turned around to face him. "I said unto them, those who knelt before me, put an end to land disputes between you and your older brother or your father, for it belongs to you both. On the other hand, if it is a *Pākeha* - yes! And my words were used against me. How easy it is for men with evil in their hearts to hear only what they want. I did not, I do not, seek death. Rebelliousness is the cause of your destitution. This I said to them. You have altogether despised your God. You have said He is a false god. Let us not say that destitution comes from God. No, it comes from disobeying the words of God. Thus, we courted destitution." He looked closely into Von Tempsky's eyes. "Do you understand?"

"I am not a man of God; I cannot feel the strength of your spiritual love and connection as you do. But I know when a man speaks honestly from his heart and tells the truth. I also know when men do not listen and follow their own needs. This is where you find yourself with a problem," said Von Tempsky earnestly.

"You speak the truth, and yes, because of them I must act," said Te Ua. "I must surrender to the *Pākeha* soldiers to end needless killing. This is my role, and God gave me this task. He touched me with his breath, and I listened." Te Ua lifted his hand to his face. "Now it ends."

"This is a wise choice, Te Ua," affirmed Von Tempsky solemnly.

"Take me to your commander so I may surrender, but I ask only that my people, those who believe, be not molested. Can you do this?"

"Major-General Chute is at his headquarters on the outskirts of Opunake. We will go to him."

Te Ua turned his back on *Lord Worsley,* and they walked back towards the *Tangihanga together*.

"Congratulations, Major. The capture of Te Ua Haumene marks a fine victory for our armed forces."

Major Von Tempsky stood before the commander of the army, Major-General Chute, in the latter's temporary headquarters. "He did surrender, sir, and he has a condition, as you recall."

"I'm aware of that, and it would be inappropriate for me to accede to his demands. I certainly hope you did not make any promises that went beyond the scope of your authority, Major?"

"Of course not, sir. However, I feel I have an obligation to ensure his wishes are understood and respected."

"Yes, but I'm not making any promises to him. I have plans for our rebel leader and intend to capitalise on his capture. His captivity will be an effective tool to demoralise any rebel holdouts, not just here in Taranaki but also on the east coast and in the north. Altogether, a great moral victory, eh."

A staff lieutenant interrupted the general and whispered in his ear. Von Tempsky remained standing and waited. Having delivered his message, the lieutenant remained at the general's side.

"Your reappearance is most fortunate, Major. We urgently need your scouts and talents."

The lieutenant handed a document to the general, who glanced at it briefly.

"New resistance has arisen to the south. A chap called Riwha Titokowaru has challenged our authority and is making a blasted nuisance of himself. I want you to go at once to the aid of Major McDonnell, who is commanding the Native Contingent, and lend him a hand. This chap Titokowaru is making a stand and defending his *pa* at Te Ngutu o te Manu, just north of Hawera. How soon can you get there?"

"If we leave in the morning, we'll arrive in the early evening, sir."

"That's too late, damn it," the general drummed his fingers on his desk as he thought. "You'll need to leave tonight, I'm afraid, Major," he said, arriving at a decision. "McDonnell needs your help as soon as possible. I suggest you leave this evening and aim to arrive late morning."

"Very well, sir."

"Alright, you've got plenty to do so I shan't hold you up any further. Oh, and good work on capturing Te Ua. Splendid work, Von Tempsky."

"Thank you, sir."

Another of the general's staff lieutenants was waiting for Major Von Tempsky as he left the command tent. "Excuse me, sir!"

Von Tempsky looked at the serious face of the lieutenant.

"We have a sergeant, one of your men, I believe. He was trying to leave the camp and enter the marae. He didn't take it too kindly when he was told he couldn't go in there."

"Ira!"

"Excuse me, sir?"

"Where is he?"

"In the cookhouse, sir. He calmed down when he heard you were here and asked for you."

"Thank you, Lieutenant."

Major-General Chute's offensive was straightforward. He'd instructed Colonel Warren to press south along the western side of Mount Taranaki and ensure no rebels could escape in that direction.

The General sent other forces north from Wanganui - it was a classic pincer move. After clearing out the remnants of the *Pai Marire* at Wereroa *pa*, Waitotara, the army continued north. *Māori* forces under the brilliant leadership of Riwha Titokowaru numbered only about eighty experienced warriors; however, they were not easily overcome and held fast at Titokowaru's own *pa* at Te Ngutu o te Manu, a few miles north of Hawera.

On the other hand, Major McDonnell handpicked his best soldiers from the garrison at Patea, commanded the Native Volunteer contingent from Wanganui, and, together with Von Tempsky's fifty Forest Rangers, who were en route, brought his force to three hundred and sixty troops. The entire region between Wanganui and Opunake was extremely volatile and could erupt into outright war at any time. Major McDonnell believed dealing with Titokowaru would be simple and straightforward.

Pete was tethered to a bullock cart at the rear of the strung-out column, and Moana marched dejectedly in the column's centre. He was frustrated and disappointed, and he tried his hardest to arrive at Opunake before nightfall so he could find Wiki, but he was prevented from leaving Chute's camp to venture into Opunake and the marae. He didn't know where she was, and the likelihood of finding her now was non-existent. More than ever, he was concerned for her safety and hoped she would return to Oakura as soon as possible.

Von Tempsky and Roberts briefed Moana on the revelations about Tami Henare's past. It was a relief to Moana that Tami wasn't a traitor, but the old man had been a crafty so-and-so who fooled many people for quite some time. It still saddened him to think that Tami, his sons and Erepu had been slain in such a savage manner, and that circumstances had prevented him from attending the *Tangihanga*. He hoped Wiki would understand. When he asked Major Von Tempsky and Lieutenant Roberts where she was, no one knew; she'd disappeared.

Both the major and the lieutenant were keen to hear about Ira's exploits in Oakura, though they were disappointed that Big Pete and Te Kahuwai would not face the consequences of their actions and stand trial. Lieutenant Roberts arranged for a small detachment to return to Oakura and apprehend Te Kahuwai's network of informants and spies, or rather those who were still alive. The intelligence they would provide would be extremely useful.

The marching column made good progress. The track they marched along was well used, dry, and easy to navigate by moonlight. By midnight, Major Von Tempsky called a halt; by his estimate, they were halfway there. They would resume in the morning.

CHAPTER THIRTY-SIX

The energy of life

Major Thomas McDonnell cut an imposing figure as he gesticulated wildly towards the bush. He was impatient to press on and begin the much-anticipated assault on Titokowaru's *pa*, almost two miles away, and was piqued that he couldn't. Major Von Tempsky urged caution and suggested that, before attacking, they conduct a more thorough reconnaissance. The land here was relatively flat, and the bush dense. It would be easy to lose one's way, he warned. McDonnell was unimpressed by the late arrival of Von Tempsky's Company. However, he was quickly reminded that the Forest Rangers had received their orders late the previous afternoon and had marched half the night to arrive this morning.

On the advice of his NCOs, McDonnell finally acquiesced but stipulated that only three teams of two scouts were allowed to venture out. He feared Titokowaru would detect their presence if more scouting parties were dispatched. Moana told his commander that the *Māori* leader probably already knew; keeping hundreds of soldiers hidden so close to the *pa* was expecting a lot.

The Rangers selected their four best scouts while McDonnell selected two of his best.

Each scouting party was told to report back by one hour after daybreak the following morning and was given its mission instructions. Major McDonnell warned, "If you haven't returned on time, we're going in and I will give the order to attack."

Moana and Tane disappeared into the bush with their objectives clear. They would conduct reconnaissance of the left or west side of the pa, determine enemy strength, and identify any natural or man-made obstacles that would affect a quick ingress. They were also to map out the quickest and easiest route to the pa site.

The soldiers of the three contingents waited expectantly for the scouts to return, preparing for battle. Weapons were readied, knives sharpened, and muskets cleaned. Men went through their personal pre-battle routines. Some sat quietly, reading well-thumbed Bibles and reciting prayers, while others played games and a few wrote letters to loved ones.

Here, the Taranaki bush was like an impenetrable wall. Tall trees grew to amazing heights, forming an almost solid canopy through which filtered light seeped between leaves, spilling unevenly across the ground. Beneath the high canopy lay the second layer. Vines, creepers, shrubs and new growth added their own murky imprint, further trapping light and creating dark, eerie shadows. Lastly, ground cover camouflaged paths and obstacles alike. It was treacherous and challenging, even for the experienced.

The Taranaki lowlands around Te Ngutu o te Manu were flat. There were no vantage points or hills to climb where a scout could lie unobserved for days and safely observe the enemy from a distance. The bush rendered nearby Mount Taranaki useless as a landmark. The snow-capped peak and granite sides of the massive volcano were lost to those travelling on foot. Even climbing a tree to obtain a direction or bearing was impossible. Most trees had no branches at accessible heights, and those that did lacked higher branches that could be safely reached. Not only was moving swiftly and quietly through the dense bush challenging for the six scouts, but disorientation was a very real possibility.

The six scouts entered the bush together, then split into pairs, each heading to their own area of responsibility. As soon as they were alone, Moana stopped and sat with his back against a tree, motioning for Tane to do the same. He didn't speak and wouldn't unless absolutely necessary. He didn't need a rest, nor was he shirking his duty. He listened, attuning himself to the sounds and rhythm of the bush. He closed his eyes and felt the energy around him. The noises, the pattern of life among unseen creatures, seared into his mind.

It was dangerous here. He felt it, tasted it, but couldn't see it. Tane, more familiar with Ira as a scout than anyone else, could see the tension in his face. His eyes narrowed, intense, dark and forbidding. Now ready, Moana slowly stood – he made no sound, a ghost.

Time became irrelevant; hurrying meant death. This was the unspoken understanding between the master and his pupil. Together, Moana and Tane crept from shadow to shadow, bush to bush. Even the watchmen of the bush, the birds, never knew the two scouts were amongst them. They left no trail, no marks or tell-tale signs of their presence, yet slowly, step by step, they drew closer to Titokowaru's pa.

It mattered not to Moana when darkness fell. Their progress was so measured in daylight that when evening came, their advancement remained the same.

Twice, returning rebels passed them as they headed back to the *pa*, coming within feet of the two concealed Rangers. At no time was Moana surprised or caught in the open. As the rebel warriors drew close, the sound of the forest changed. It was like a warning bell, and both scouts paused, then continued when the danger had passed.

At one point, a single musket shot broke the rhythm of bush life. It was followed by panicked yells and a far-off scream that was abruptly cut off. Moana guessed that one, if not both, of the scouts in one of the other teams had been discovered. Titokowaru's warriors knew strangers were in the bush, and now they'd be extra vigilant and possibly waiting in cover for others they knew were nearby.

Tane was tasked with remembering their route, noting streams, misshapen or fallen trees, and their direction. Moana could tell from the moss and leaves which direction was north, and they'd been heading directly north for almost five hours.

A flicker of light caught their attention. The *pa* lay directly in front of them, across an open area cleared of bush. With infinite patience, they crept to where they could see the *pa* and its defences. They heard voices and saw movement. Once in position, they realised this *pa* was different– it was expertly fortified. Protected by earthworks and a wooden stockade, the *pa* was equipped to withstand a full assault. As ordered, they checked the western side and the front. All details were memorised.

With the full contingent of soldiers Major McDonnell brought, Moana didn't think it would be a significant challenge for experienced soldiers to attack the site. However, getting them here would be difficult. Both Forest Rangers observed and counted the number of warriors they could see, but it was almost impossible. Eventually, they slid back into the low-growing ground cover. They knew it was time to leave.

The return was much quicker. Moana knew that all the warrior scouts were now safely inside the *pa* and that there was little chance of discovery. They made a couple of wrong turns, their increased speed and the darkness testing their skills, but eventually they arrived, fatigued and dirty, safely back at camp in the small hours of the morning. One scouting team failed to appear, and Major Von Tempsky paced backwards and forwards like a worried parent concerned for their safety. Moana and Tane gave their report and all relevant details. Now it was up to Major McDonnell to decide how to proceed.

Ordered to clean up, eat and rest, Moana and Tane needed no further encouragement and were soon fast asleep. A few hours' rest was better than none, and both men were roused at daybreak.

Von Tempsky shook his head sadly when Moana asked about the two scouts who hadn't returned. It was unlikely they ever would.

"It will be a surprise attack," Major Thomas McDonnell informed his men. "We will split the force into two groups. I will lead one group along the route my scouts have recently mapped out. The other, commanded by Major Von Tempsky, will follow the path his scouts have established. Once both groups arrive unseen at the *pa*, we will, at a prearranged signal, unleash a hail of fire on the defenders and catch them unawares. With superior numbers and training, Titokowaru and his rebels stand no chance. Victory is assured."

McDonnell nodded to his chaplain, who stepped forward clutching a large Bible. A stern-looking man with a long, narrow face, the chaplain looked forlornly at the men. He cleared his throat, a reminder to remove all headgear. Three hundred and sixty soldiers shuffled nervously, removed their covers, and lowered their heads respectfully. "Almighty and most merciful Father, we humbly beseech Thee, of Thy great goodness, grant us fair weather for battle. Graciously hearken to us as soldiers who call upon Thee, that, armed with Thy power, we may advance from victory to victory, crush the oppression and wickedness of our enemies, and establish Thy justice among men and the good people of New Zealand." The chaplain looked up. "Amen." He stepped back, pleased that the major had allowed him to say a few words of importance.

Like Te Ua, Te Whiti, and many others, Riwha Titokowaru was Christian and educated by missionaries. He could read and write, quote scripture, and was trained as a *Tohunga*[12] by his people. He was intelligent and a quick learner. He didn't seek war and took positive steps to defuse tensions and avoid violence, but he was typically ignored. Like Te Ua and Te Whiti, Titokowaru expounded his pacifist views. Yet, this charismatic leader was prepared to fight for what he believed in. War was the last resort – and he took it. With Te Ua's absence as a cohesive leader, Titokowaru now assumed the vacant role. He'd fought at Te Morere and lost an eye; his face was now marked by a savage scar. He knew that *Pākeha* soldiers were coming to his pa, and he wouldn't just sit back and allow them to dictate how the battle would be won. Titokowaru would take measures to ensure victory.

In the early morning light, his people stood before him, uncertain and unsure. They knew armed soldiers were coming, and with calmness, Riwha Titokowaru offered a prayer.

"We are now one in Christ," he said. "The sea was deep between us, but He has made it shallow … Give over war … Do not say it is I who am laying down the law; it is Christ who is doing so. He makes us one." He looked over his people and dropped his head, "Hear our voice, dear Father, give us strength, as we give You our love, so we may overcome wrongs perpetrated against us. Give us the belief that we can triumph in Your holy presence, dear God.

---

[12] *Tohunga – An expert practitioner, chosen leader, or skilled specialist in traditional Māori society*

Spare us from darkness as we seek righteousness. In the name of Israel and those who have suffered, grant us peace … Amen."

Riwha Titokowaru and his warriors were ready.

Two columns of men snaked out in long lines as they entered the bush. For many, the darkness and closeness were oppressing–they became fearful. Moana and Tane retraced their path from the day before and, as quietly as possible, headed towards the *pa*. The Forest Rangers silently followed.

It was equally difficult for the other column. Muskets became caught in unforgiving vines, and soldiers stepped over hidden roots and half-buried rocks. It was proving difficult to remain quiet on unmarked paths. Major McDonnell urged his scouts to forgo stealth and move more quickly, but natural obstacles proved too much for many of the soldiers, unused to the confines of the almost impenetrable bush. They began to lag, and McDonnell was now fearful his column would fail to meet the timetable. Under unrelenting pressure to improve the pace, McDonnell's scouts inadvertently lost their way. McDonnell prayed that Von Tempsky encountered similar difficulty and that their progress slowed. The major feared Von Tempsky would arrive on time and be isolated and vulnerable to attack until McDonnell arrived.

Moana again urged caution as they approached Titokowaru's fortified *pa*. Something didn't feel right to him, and he suggested to Major Von Tempsky that the column halt so he could investigate. Apprehensive of arriving late, Von Tempsky compromised by sending Tane ahead, keeping Moana with him and leading the column at a slower pace for the remainder of the way.

The Forest Rangers and part of McDonnell's Native Contingent assigned to Major Von Tempsky were almost in sight of the *pa*. He ordered his troops to take offensive positions and to remain concealed until they received the signal to attack from McDonnell. As yet, there was no indication that McDonnell's group was in position. They appeared to be alone.

Tane was sent out to locate McDonnell's troops - he returned a short time later with the bad news. McDonnell still hadn't arrived.

Moana still felt uneasy, his sixth sense warning him of danger. Von Tempsky called for Sergeant-Major Bowers, and Moana explained his unease. Bowers, sporting a bad cut on his forehead from colliding with a low branch, dabbed at his head with a bloody rag and agreed with Moana; it didn't feel right. Moana asked Von Tempsky if he could circle around their position to check their rear, then suggested shifting from an offensive to a defensive position, allowing them to defend against all approachable angles. Trusting his best scout's advice, Von Tempsky agreed and asked Tane to remain their eyes and ears in a slightly forward position as Moana crept away.

By the time Lieutenants Small and Griggs began quietly issuing orders, Moana was already deep in the surrounding bush. He froze– before him lay the unmistakable fresh tracks of Titokowaru's warriors. The footprints suggested a large group of men had passed by a short time ago and had circled behind Von Tempsky's force. This could only mean they were surrounded. Without McDonnell's group to provide protection, they were highly exposed. Moana backed away as fast as he dared.

From a secure, elevated vantage point deep within the *pa*, Riwha Titokowaru, the Taranaki lay preacher, dressed smartly in a suit and wearing a bowler hat, nodded.

Moana had only just crawled back behind their defensive lines and was about to warn Von Tempsky when he heard the first shot fired.

Von Tempsky intended to survey the area just in front of the pa to evaluate the defences. He quietly moved towards Tane, but suddenly, the silence was broken by a gunshot. Tane jerked abruptly. "Tane!" he yelled. The single shot echoed through the bush. It was a horrific exclamation! Distant birds scattered.

Von Tempsky saw Tane's legs kicking and writhing. He'd been hit. His natural inclination was to go to his assistance, and he was about to leap forward to help when Moana yelled for him to return, "It's an ambuscade. Come back!"

The single shot came from near the pa, and it was a signal for the rebels who lay in concealment behind Von Tempsky's troops to rise and launch an intense barrage of musket fire into their positions.

Major Von Tempsky hesitated, freezing for a moment in indecision. Moana crouched, then suddenly sprang up and ran toward him.

Sergeant Bowers cry of alarm broke the spell.

A split second later, Von Tempsky launched himself towards Tane to drag him back to safety.

When Tane crawled forward to view the pa, he'd cleverly concealed himself so no one could see him from within the fortifications. Anticipating the tactic, Titokowaru wisely chose vantage points on either side of the pa to hide sharpshooters. Unknown to Tane, he'd been in full view of an elevated sharpshooter high in the bough of a tree. As Major Von Tempsky arrived at Tane's side, he also became visible.

After a quick reload, the rebel sharpshooter sighted his weapon squarely on his next target. He correctly accounted for the shot's tricky downward trajectory, patiently tracked his target's movement, and made micro-adjustments. He acknowledged to himself that there was no wind and squeezed the trigger just as Moana dove down near the major's legs.

The shot entered Von Tempsky's head, killing him instantly. More shots were fired, and Moana had to withdraw quickly or suffer the same fate. The sharpshooter's accuracy prevented him from dragging Von Tempsky's or Tane's body back with him.

McDonnell's force was a short distance away when they heard the first shot. Realising they had lost the element of surprise, the major ordered his troops to come to the immediate assistance of Von Tempsky's group, which was being attacked simultaneously from the front and rear. Needing no encouragement, McDonnell's men crashed through the bush to lend support.

Riwha Titokowaru placed his men carefully. In a sustained fusillade of accurate fire, they systematically cut down soldiers from both Von Tempsky's and McDonnell's groups. From their defensive position, Von Tempsky's men returned fire as best they could, but the concealed enemy were difficult to see. With only one prudent course of action left, Major Thomas McDonnell called for an immediate withdrawal. They were unable to retrieve their dead and left them where they fell.

Major Thomas McDonnell was called upon by his superiors to explain. Of the three hundred and sixty men who entered the bush, only three hundred and ten survived. Fifty soldiers were killed. Little did the major know that Titokowaru had defended his pa with only eighty men. Three were killed and seventy-seven survived. McDonnell lost his command and was replaced.

EPILOGUE

The chill wind swept down Mount Egmont, as the Europeans called the volcano, headed east, and passed through the Manaia Redoubt without pausing. Clouds obscured the mountain and followed the wind, gathering above the Taranaki lowlands, threatening rain. A large group of people, mostly men, stood near a hastily erected cross not far from the redoubt. A few wore uniforms; others did not. A handful of farmers stood respectfully to one side, listened attentively to the proceedings, and talked quietly amongst themselves when the opportunity arose. A woman stood near the cross and wept. Her two sons and daughter tugged at her arms, too young to understand the reason for her despair – they wanted to go to the nearby stream to play. An officer with his hands buried deep in the pockets of his coat stood at the rear of the assembled group.

Friends, family members and the curious gathered to hear the Reverend William Robertson memorialise the brave men who'd succumbed before their time to the ravages and brutality of war. Manaia lay about six miles southeast of Hawera and was a safe distance from the hostilities that recently plagued the region.

The reverend wore his usual black trousers, white shirt and black jacket, and looked commanding as he offered conciliatory words, read scripture, and ended the service with a prayer. This wasn't a funeral service, nor was this place a cemetery; the gallant men the reverend honoured had all been burned at a funeral pyre at the Te Ngutu o te Manu (The beak of the bird) *pa* by Riwha

Titokowaru. As the reverend closed his Bible, the men in uniform saluted.

Amongst others, Major Gustavus Von Tempsky was one of the brave men people came to honour and remember. *Māori* called him '*Manu Rau*', a hundred birds, for his ability to move quickly from one place to another.

One man stood slightly apart from the others. Unusually for a young man of his age, he wore civilian clothes. With his head lowered, it was plainly obvious to anyone observing that the man was fighting his emotions. Out of respect, he was left alone to mourn.

Overcome by sadness and despair, Moana grieved for his friend, confidant and commander. Gustavus Von Tempsky was more like a father, the father he'd never had, than a commanding officer. It was so difficult to imagine that Major Gustavus Von Tempsky had died.

The officer at the rear watched Moana with more than casual interest. His own expression and feelings mirrored those around him; he felt the loss too. Like many here at the service, he had lost a friend and felt the oppressive heaviness and loneliness of death. But in his own private way, he could still offer some comfort. There were distinct benefits to being an intelligence officer, and he'd used his skill to replace the chill of death with the warmth of friendship and love. With an unseen smile, Lieutenant Roberts turned and walked away. He knew Major Von Tempsky would approve.

Von Tempsky had always been larger than life. His personality, creativity and expertise were indelible. He was the type of man who would live forever, and in Moana's consciousness, he would. Grief was a new experience for him; it was an unfamiliar and unwelcome emotion. It was like his wound; it hurt beyond comprehension, the pain almost paralysing. Here, at the memorial service, the emptiness and sense of loss were overwhelming, almost too much to bear - he wiped his eyes. Not only had he lost someone he cared for and respected as a man, but the Forest Rangers were no more; they had been disbanded. Moana had never felt so alone.

He felt a presence; someone quietly walked to his side and stopped. Moana slowly lifted his head and blinked away the tears. As his eyes focused, he recognised the uniform of the newly formed Armed Constabulary and the impressive, unmistakable physique of his best friend, Rupert Potter. Not one for much talk, Potter stepped forward and embraced his friend. Words weren't needed; the closeness of shared experiences, friendship and understanding said it all. Potter released him, stepped back and smiled. Puzzled, Moana turned, and Wiki slid into his arms.

AUTHOR'S NOTES

This novel is a work of fiction. However, many of the characters in this story were real people, and most events in 'The Breath of God' actually took place. I altered some names out of respect for their descendants. Whenever possible, I sought to portray New Zealand's dramatic history faithfully and accurately, though I often found our historical records contradictory. When faced with the choice of which account was more accurate, I exercised my discretion as a novelist to select the version that best served the story. For those familiar with New Zealand's history, please forgive me for any timeline changes, omitted facts, or embellishments.

During my research, I often thought of the profound quote by literary critic and philosopher, Walter Benjamin, who said, "History is written by the victors." His words seem very appropriate.

I used published passenger recollections of the *Lord Worsley* shipwreck to begin this story. One thing that initially puzzled me was why the ship hit the rocks at Te Namu Bay. At first, I presumed the helmsman might have been drunk or inept, but no documented explanations existed. Through computer modelling and some quick calculations, the nautical experts I consulted proved that existing ocean currents, wind conditions, and a non-magnetically shielded compass probably caused *Lord Worsley* to drift from her charted course, exactly as I wrote.

The events surrounding Te Ua's realisations when the archangel Gabriel first spoke to him are somewhat unclear. Accounts differ on what he did to a young boy to prove he'd been gifted special powers by God. Some claims seem far-fetched, illogical and excessively brutal. I chose the least extreme version, in which it was alleged he mutilated a boy's leg and then miraculously healed it, leaving blood as the only evidence. I can't possibly begin to explain what really happened that day.

History has shown that religious fanaticism has led to horrific acts of brutality. The belief that 'faith' justifies 'violence' is no more evident today than it was one hundred and fifty, five hundred, or two thousand years ago. *Pai Marire* brought *Māori* together when they needed unity most, and through their faith and culture, *Māori* believers resisted the New Zealand Government's policy of land confiscations. However, some fanatical extremists used *Pai Marire* to serve their own ends, distorting Te Ua's message and committing appalling acts of barbaric savagery. I'm not qualified to comment on Te Ua's state of mind, but one thing is clear to me– as a sane man, it is doubtful he approved of such atrocities. Out of respect for the victims and their descendants, and to protect their privacy, I have altered some of their names.

History has recorded much of what Te Ua Haumene, Te Whiti o Rongomai and Riwha Titokowaru said. Many of the quotes of Te Ua that I used in *The Breath of God* were extracted in part, or in whole, from his book '*Ua Rongopai*' (the Gospel according to Ua).

When I first began writing 'The Breath of God', I knew very little about Te Whiti, and the more I researched, the more I came to respect and even admire him. Te Whiti remained committed to his pacifist beliefs even when those around him, his friends, took up arms to resist government forces. His impact on New Zealand culture has been lasting. The Parihaka Church, which he founded in Taranaki with his relative Tohu Kakahi, still thrives today. As a fitting tribute to his convictions, Te Whiti, many years after his death in 1907, even influenced Mohandas Gandhi's thinking. Again, where possible, I have used Te Whiti's recorded dialogue and his actual quotes to enhance the story. If I have misrepresented Te Whiti o Rongomai and his principles in this novel, I apologise. It was never my intention to cast him, or Parihaka, in anything other than a favourable light.

Moana Rangitira, Rupert Potter, the entire Henare family, and all the Forest Rangers, except Gustavus Von Tempsky, are fictional characters. Any resemblance to real people is purely coincidental and unintentional. Gustavus Von Tempsky was very real and, from all accounts, a colourful man with an interesting past. My portrayal of him is largely fictional, though, with a few exceptions, I have tried to remain faithful to his documented exploits and reputation. As I wrote, he was an accomplished painter, introduced the Bowie Knife to the Rangers, and was skilled in its use.

The Forest Rangers were disbanded when Von Tempsky attacked Titokowaru's pa. Historical records show that Major Gustavus Von Tempsky commanded the Armed Constabulary, Company No. 5, when he and Major McDonnell attacked Te Ngutu o te Manu. He wasn't commanding the Forest Rangers, as I wrote. However, my description of his death closely matches documented accounts. He was shot in the head and died while coming to the aid of a fallen soldier at Te Ngutu o te Manu after Major McDonnell's group became disoriented and lost the element of surprise. Von Tempsky's body was never recovered as Titokowaru cremated him at the pa.

The 'Travellers Rest' served as the temporary headquarters for the Forest Rangers in Papakura, and it was owned and operated by the American family Ben and Martha Smith and their six children. Major Jackson commanded the Forest Rangers for a short time before returning to his family and farming. It wasn't possible for me to detail all the exploits of the Forest Rangers; perhaps I will leave that for another book.

The battle at the Kaitake *pa* was very real. The *pa* site was shelled as I described, and a group of Taranaki militia volunteers crept through the night over treacherous territory to lay in wait and attack the rebel defensive positions the following morning. Various contradictory reports of this battle exist, and I hope my description reflects what really transpired.

The Te Ahuahu ambush was tragic. Sadly, a captain and a trooper were decapitated. Their heads were smoke-dried and displayed as trophies in various parts of Taranaki and the North Island's east coast, where they eventually ended up in Opotiki.

I can only imagine the puzzlement and consternation the garrison defending Sentry Hill Redoubt must have felt when the *Pai Marire* began walking en masse towards the redoubt with their right hands raised and chanting in full voice. Captain Shortt, along with seventy-five soldiers, successfully defended the redoubt against superior rebel numbers without the assistance of the Forest Rangers.

I don't know whether Governor Grey ate dinner with General Cameron and two clergymen. If he did, I can only hope their conversations followed the themes and viewpoints I outlined. I hope I was faithful to General Cameron's beliefs; he was vehemently opposed to the scorched-earth policy favoured by Governor Grey and was often criticised for the army's slow attacks on rebel forces, which he attributed to a lack of supplies and reliable supply lines. It is believed he resigned in protest and was replaced by Major-General Chute.

Based on my research, I made the presumption that Reverend Thomas Grace was a liberal. Therefore, it would make for interesting dinner-time conversation if his friend and fellow clergyman were conservative and held markedly different theological and political perspectives. I'd like to think that, if such a dinner ever took place, the conversation was true to each of their respective personalities and beliefs.

The tragic event in Opotiki was certainly a turning point for *Pai Marire*. Captain Morris Levy wrote to a newspaper, recounting in remarkable detail the events he witnessed. I used his graphic account as the basis for that part of the story. I believe my interpretation is similar to his description, though somewhat simplified. However, I did alter the method of Reverend Thomas's escape.

The death of the reverend in Opotiki was, without question, barbaric and tragic. No person deserves to die in such an inhumane way. Because of the subsequent legal issues surrounding his death, which came to prominence over a century later, I will avoid commenting on specifics. For clarity, I have changed his name to avoid any potential legal issues. I have no idea what happened to his wife, Emma.

Many have written that Riwha Titokowaru was a brilliant military strategist and engineer, perhaps the best *Māori* general ever. Baptised as a Methodist, he supported Te Ua and *Pai Marire*, and, like his friend Te Whiti, was initially firmly committed to peace. Later, he became a strong advocate for Parihaka. Despite his voluntary concessions to appease the government, imperial forces continued their punitive campaign in Taranaki. Frustrated, Titokowaru took up arms and eventually fought back. He lost an eye at Te Morere and his face was heavily scarred, but it didn't prevent him from looking dapper in European-style suits and a bowler hat. In subsequent battles he commanded, Titokowaru often fought against overwhelming odds and won, but his fighting wouldn't continue. He returned to his advocacy and practice of non-violence, assuming the role of peacemaker and earning the respect of many *Māori* and *Pākeha* community leaders.

In 1886, Riwha was involved in a peaceful protest in Manaia. He was captured and taken to Wellington, New Zealand's capital, where he was tried and sentenced to incarceration. He died a few months later.

It's difficult to assess if Titokowaru really did respect Major Von Tempsky. If he did, then to what extent? I think Riwha Titokowaru may have been somewhat relieved when Gustavus Von Tempsky was killed.

Some have written that Von Tempsky put his life recklessly in danger because he sought medals and recognition. Were Von Tempsky's actions at Titokowaru's pa, Te Ngutu o te Manu, the actions of an officer who sought distinction and fame, or was he genuinely concerned for the safety of one of his men when he came to assist? It is possible that jealousy promoted fanciful stories of Von

Tempsky as a glory hunter, but to me, he died a hero, coming to the aid of a fallen soldier.

When asked, the New Zealand Defence Force would not provide me with their assessment of Von Tempsky's capabilities. They declined, saying it would be inappropriate to comment. Unofficially, he is revered as an officer, and his irregular Forest Rangers Company may have been the inspiration behind New Zealand's present-day special forces. To this day, many Taranaki Māori still harbour resentment for Gustavus Von Tempsky.

As part of my research, I visited all the battle sites listed in this novel. In each case, including Te Namu Bay, the physical locations aren't clearly marked as places of historical significance and are often hard to find. The Sentry Hill redoubt (Te Morere), where so many men died, isn't signposted. Cows now graze peacefully over the eroded redoubt – visually, nothing remains. The Wereroa *pa* in Waitotora, once home to so many, is indistinguishable from the surrounding landscape. Locals wave an arm over a few farmhouses and pastures, pointing to the general area where the pa once stood, but there are no discernible features or signs. Small Te Namu Bay isn't listed on many maps. Many local Opunake residents I spoke to had never heard of it. By accident, I found a small blue sign in a residential cul-de-sac, nailed high on a lamppost, which led me down a narrow path between houses, across a stream, to an old, neglected pa on the cliff tops above the bay.

The Kaitake pa has been reclaimed by bush. Situated on a high peak, it is indistinguishable from the surrounding terrain, and typically no markers exist to indicate its location. Te Ahuahu, now absorbed into Oakura, is a peaceful village with no signage to indicate specific places of historical interest related to this story.

A permanent memorial is located at the 20-ha (50-acre) Te Ngutu o te Manu battle site and Historic Reserve on Ahipaipa Road, halfway between Kapuni and Matapu in South Taranaki. While it was refreshing to find a memorial, the pa and the battle site at Titokowaru's pa are not indicated.

It is disappointing that these historical sites have not been preserved. No doubt a lack of funds will be cited as a reason, but even a simple signpost or two is not expensive. While New Zealand's past is certainly controversial and *Māori* clearly suffered as a result of early imperial and colonial government policies, we should remember everyone, both *Māori* and non-*Māori*, who died as a result.

If you are interested in finding out whether 'The Great Taranaki Toe-Biter' lurks beneath the clean, fresh water of Taranaki rivers and streams, I urge you to visit the region. Carefully dip your feet and gently wiggle your toes.

I am grateful for all the assistance and help I received in writing 'The Breath of God'. Any mistakes and errors are entirely my own.

I welcome positive feedback.
Paul W. Feenstra.

For Want of a Shilling

"Feenstra excels at creating dynamic, engaging characters, and the cast of this tale is no different."

"When reading a Paul Feenstra book, I know that he is going to keep me engrossed in the story."

"Written with painstaking attention to details, background and historical accuracy, this historical military thriller will capture the hearts of those readers who love colonial fiction."

The mysterious Russian invasion hoax that shook colonial New Zealand.

What begins as a local murder investigation turns into a plot of global proportions. From the political agenda of England's Prime Minister to the Machiavellian son of Russia's Tsar to the famed exploits of America's Confederate ship *Alabama*. Intricately researched, this story draws on many recorded historical events and figures to weave a tale of intrigue, conspiracy and greed.

In January 1873, in a sparsely populated coastal community on Wellington's south coast, New Zealand, the peaceful lives of Owhiro Bay residents are shattered by the discovery of two brutal and senseless murders. Veteran soldier and local constable Sergeant

Moana (Ira) Rangitira of the Armed Constabulary investigates the murders, which leads him on a frantic pursuit of Russians.

Enraged by the Russians' actions, Governor Bowen, concerned that his superiors in England have little faith in New Zealand's ability to deal with foreign aggression, orders Ira and his best friend, Rupert Potter, to Auckland to rescue a hostage and prevent an escalating political crisis. They encounter smugglers, and Ira's violent past as a Forest Ranger resurfaces to haunt him when he is pursued through Taranaki's rugged bush and wilderness by a *Māori* war party intent on revenge.

Can Sergeant Moan Rangitira prevent the Russians from achieving their ultimate goal, and can he prevent Russia and England from going to war?

Other historical fiction books
by
Paul W. Feenstra
Published by Mellester Press

Boundary

The Breath of God (Book 1 in Moana Rangitira series)

For Want of a Shilling (Book 2 in Moana Rangitira series)

Gunpowder Green

Into the Shade

Falls Ende short story eBooks
1. The Oath
2. Courser
3. The King

Falls Ende full length novels.
Falls Ende – Primus (eBooks 1,2 & 3)
Falls Ende – Secundus
Falls Ende – Tertium
Falls Ende – Quartus
Falls Ende – Quintus
Falls Ende – Sextus
Falls Ende – Outlaw

Leonard Hardy's
A Sinister Consequence
A Questionable Virtue

A Gentleman at Heart